Liz Fielding wa[...] born [in...] Zambia before h[...] her own special hero and a couple of children on the way, lived in Botswana, Kenya and Bahrain. Seven of her titles have been nominated for RWA's RITA®; and she has won the Best Traditional Romance in 2000, the British Romance Prize in 2005 and the Best Short Contemporary Romance in 2006.

USA Today bestselling author **Katherine Garbera** is a two-time Maggie winner who has written 108 books. A Florida native who grew up to travel the globe, Katherine now makes her home in the Midlands of the UK with her husband, two children and a very spoiled miniature dachshund. Visit her on the web at http://www.katherinegarbera.com, connect with her on Facebook and follow her on Twitter @katheringarbera

New York Times and *USA Today* bestselling author **Kathleen Eagle** published her first Mills & Boon, an RWA Golden Heart winner, in 1984. Since then she has published more than forty books, including historical and contemporary, series and single title novels, earning her nearly every award in the industry including Romance Writers of America's RITA®. Kathleen lives in Minnesota with her husband, who is Lakota Sioux and forever a cowboy.

Mavericks

Mavericks: Taming the Bad Boy

LIZ FIELDING

KATHERINE GARBERA

KATHLEEN EAGLE

MILLS & BOON

First Published in Great Britain 2020
By Mills & Boon, an imprint of HarperCollins*Publishers*
1 London Bridge Street, London, SE1 9GF

MAVERICKS: TAMING THE BAD BOY © 2020 Harlequin Books S.A.

Tempted by Trouble © 2011 Liz Fielding
Ready for Her Close-Up © 2012 Katherine Garbera
The Prodigal Cowboy © 2012 Kathleen Eagle

ISBN: 978-0-263-28194-1

MIX
Paper from
responsible sources
FSC™ C007454

TEMPTED BY TROUBLE

LIZ FIELDING

CHAPTER ONE

Life is like ice cream: you have to take it one lick at a time.

—Rosie's Diary

'LOVAGE AMERY?'

If ever there had been a moment to follow Gran's example and check her reflection in the mirror before she opened the front door, Elle decided, this was it.

On her knees and up to her rubber gloves in soapy water when the doorbell rang, she hadn't bothered to stop and fix hair sliding out of its elastic band. And there wasn't much she could have done about a face pink and shiny from a day spent catching up with the housework while everyone was out, culminating in scrubbing the kitchen floor.

It was the complete Cinderella workout.

She couldn't afford a fancy gym membership and, as she was always telling her sisters, cleaning was a lot more productive than pounding a treadmill. Not that they'd ever been sufficiently impressed by the argument to join in.

Lucky them.

Even sweaty Lycra had to be a better look than an ancient shirt tied around the waist with an equally geriatric psychedelic tie. Sexier than the jeans bagging damply around her knees.

It wouldn't normally have bothered her and, to be fair, the man standing on the doorstep hadn't made much of an effort, either. His thick dark hair was sticking up in a just-got-out-of-bed look and his chin was darkened with what might be designer stubble but was more likely to be a disinclination to shave on Saturday, when he didn't have to go into the office.

Always assuming that he had an office to go to. Or a job.

Like her, he was wearing ancient jeans, in his case topped with a T-shirt that should have been banished to the duster box. The difference was that on him it looked mouth-wateringly good. So good that she barely noticed that he'd made free with a name she'd been trying to keep to herself since she'd started kindergarten.

Swiftly peeling off the yellow rubber gloves she'd kept on as a 'Sorry, can't stop' defence against one of the neighbours dropping by with some excuse to have a nose around, entertain the post office queue with insider gossip on just how bad things were at Gable End, she tossed them carelessly over her shoulder.

'Who wants to know?' she asked.

Her hormones might be ready to throw caution to the wind—they were Amery hormones, after all—but while they might have escaped into the yard for a little exercise, she wasn't about to let them go 'walkies'.

'Sean McElroy.'

His voice matched the looks. Low, sexy, soft as Irish mist. And her hormones flung themselves at the gate like a half-grown puppy in a let-me-at-him response as he offered his hand.

Cool, a little rough, reassuringly large, it swallowed hers up as she took it without thinking, said, 'How d'you do?' in a voice perilously close to the one her grandmother used when she met a good-looking man. With that hint of breathiness that spelled trouble.

'I'm doing just fine,' he replied, his slow smile obliterating all memory of the way she looked. Her hair, the lack of make-up and damp knees. It made crinkles around those mesmerisingly blue eyes and they fanned out comfortably in a way that suggested they felt right at home there.

Elle had begun to believe that she'd bypassed the gene that reduced all Amery women to putty in the presence of a good looking man.

Caught off guard, she discovered that she'd been fooling herself.

The only reason she'd escaped so far, it seemed, was because until this moment she hadn't met a man with eyes of that particularly intense shade of blue.

A man with shoulders wide enough to carry the troubles of the world and tall enough not to make her feel awkward about her height, which had been giving her a hard time since she'd hit a growth spurt somewhere around her twelfth birthday. With a voice that seemed to whisper right through her bones until it reached her toes.

Even now they were curling inside her old trainers in pure ecstasy.

He epitomised the casual, devil-may-care, bad-boy look of the travelling men who, for centuries, had arrived on the village common in the first week of June with the annual fair and departed a few days later, leaving a trail of broken hearts and the occasional fatherless baby in their wake.

Trouble.

But, riveted to the spot, her hand still in his, all it needed was for fairground waltzer music to start up in the background and she'd have been twirling away on a fluffy pink cloud without a thought in her head.

The realisation was enough to bring her crashing back to her senses and, finally letting go of his hand, she took half a step back.

'What do you want, Mr McElroy?'

His eyebrows lifted a fraction at the swift change from drooling welcome to defensive aggression.

'Not a what, a who. I have a delivery for Lovage Amery.'

Oh, no…

Back to earth with a bump.

She hadn't ordered anything—she couldn't afford anything that would require delivery—but she had a grandmother who lived in a fantasy world. And her name was Lovage, too.

But all the questions tumbling out of her brain—the what, the who, the 'how much?' stuff—hit a traffic jam as his smile widened, reaching the parts of her that ordinary smiles couldn't touch.

Her pulse, her knees, some point just below her midriff that was slowly dissolving to jelly.

'If you'll just take this…'

She looked down and discovered that this delectable, sinewy package that had those drooling hormones sitting up and begging for whatever trouble he had in mind was offering her a large brown envelope.

The last time one of those had come calling for 'Lovage Amery' she'd taken it without a concern in the world, smiling right back at the man offering it to her.

She'd been younger then. About to start college, embark on her future, unaware that life had yet one more sucker punch to throw at her.

'What is it?' she asked, regretting the abandonment of the rubber gloves. Regretting answering the door.

'Rosie,' he said. As if that explained everything. 'You are expecting her?'

She must have looked as blank as she felt because he half turned and with a careless wave of the envelope, gestured towards the side of the house.

She leaned forward just far enough to see the front of a large pink and white van that had been backed up towards the garage.

She stared at it, expecting to see some disreputable dog sticking its head out of the window. She'd banned her sister from bringing home any more strays from the rescue shelter. The last one had broken not only their hearts, but what remained of their bank balance. But Geli was not above getting someone else to do her dirty work.

'Where is she?' she asked. Then, realising this practically constituted an acceptance, 'No. Whatever Geli said, I can't possibly take another dog. The vet's bills for the last one—'

'Rosie isn't a dog,' he said, and now he was the one looking confused. 'That's Rosie.'

She frowned, stared at the picture of an ice cream sundae on the van door, little cones on the roof, and suddenly realised what she was looking at.

'Rosie is an ice cream van?'

'Congratulations.'

Elle frowned. Congratulations? Had she won it in one of the many competitions she'd entered in a fit of post-Christmas despair when the washing machine had sprung a leak on the same day as the electricity bill had arrived?

Surely not.

She hadn't had any warning of its arrival. No phone call. No letter informing her of her good fortune. Which was understandable.

This would have to be the booby prize because, desperate as she was, she wouldn't have entered a competition offering a second-hand ice cream van as first prize.

She wouldn't have entered one offering a *new* ice cream van, but at least she could have sold it and bought a new washing machine, one with a low energy programme—thus dealing with two problems at once—with the proceeds.

While unfamiliar with the latest trends in transport, even she could see that Rosie's lines were distinctly last century.

Already the sorry owner of an ancient car that had failed its annual MOT test with a list of faults a mile long, the last thing she needed was to be lumbered with more scrap.

'Congratulations?' she repeated.

'You appear to have twenty-twenty vision,' he teased.

'A very *old* ice cream van,' she pointed out, doing her best to ignore the gotcha grin, the faded black T-shirt clinging to those enticing shoulders and figure out what the heck was going on.

'Actually, she's a nineteen sixty-two Commer ice cream van in her original livery,' he said, without a hint of apology. On the contrary, he seemed to be under the impression that it was a good thing.

'Nineteen sixty-two!'

It beat the wreck in the garage, which had rolled off the assembly line when she was still in primary school, by thirty years. That was a stripling youth compared to Rosie, which had taken to the road when her grandmother was still in school.

'The old girl's vintage,' Sean confirmed. 'She's your Great-Uncle Basil's pride and joy, but right now she's in need of a good home.'

As he said this, he looked over her shoulder into the house, no doubt intending to emphasize the point.

He didn't visibly flinch but the hall, like the rest of the house, was desperately in need of a coat of paint. It was also piled up with discarded shoes, coats and all the other stuff that teenagers seemed to think belonged on the floor. And of course, her rubber gloves.

That was the bad news.

The good news was that he couldn't see where the carpet had been chewed by the dog that had caused them all so much grief.

'Vintage,' she repeated sharply, forcing him to look at her instead of the mess behind her. 'Well, it would certainly fit right in around here. There's just one small problem.'

More than one if she was being honest and honestly, despite the fact that the aged family car had failed its annual test and she was desperate for some transport, she wasn't prepared to take possession of a vehicle that was short on seats and heavy on fuel.

Walking, as she was always telling her sisters, was good for you. Shaped up the legs. Pumped blood around the body and made the brain work harder. And they all had a duty to the planet to walk more. Or use public transport.

She walked. They used public transport.

There was absolutely no chance that either of her sisters would consider using the bike when it meant wearing an unflattering helmet and looking, in their words, 'like a dork' when they arrived at school and college, respectively.

'Which is?' he prompted.

She didn't bother him with the financial downside of her situation, but kept it simple.

'I don't have a Great Uncle Basil.'

Finally a frown. It didn't lessen the attraction, just made him look thoughtful, studious. Even more hormone-twangingly desirable.

'You *are* Lovage Amery?' he asked, catching up with the fact that, while she hadn't denied it, she hadn't confirmed it either. 'And this *is* Gable End, The Common, Longbourne.'

She was slow to confirm it and, twigging to her reluctance to own up to the name, the address, he glanced back at the wide wooden gate propped wide open and immovable for as long as she could remember. The letters that spelled out the words 'Gable End' were faded almost to nothing, but denial was pointless.

'Obviously there has been some kind of mistake,' she said with all the conviction she could muster. Maybe. Her grandmother might well know someone named Basil who needed somewhere to park his ice cream van, but he wasn't her uncle, great or otherwise. And, even if she'd wanted to—and she didn't—she had no time to take on an ice cream round. End of, as Geli was so fond of saying. 'Please take it away.'

'I will.' Her relieved smile was a fraction too fast. 'If you'll just help me get to the bottom of this.'

'Some kind of muddle in the paperwork?' she offered. 'Take it up with Basil.'

'It's not a common name. Lovage,' he said, ignoring her excellent advice.

'There's a good reason for that,' she muttered.

One of his eyebrows kicked up and something in her midriff imitated the action. Without thinking, Elle found herself checking his left hand for a wedding band. It was bare, but that didn't mean a thing. No man that good-looking could possibly be unattached. And, even if he was, she reminded herself, she wasn't. Very firmly attached to a whole heap of responsibilities.

Two sisters still in full-time education, a grandmother who lived in her own make-believe world, and a house that sucked up every spare penny she earned working shifts in a dead-end job so that she could fit around them all.

'You don't like it?' he asked.

'No… Yes…' It wasn't that she didn't like her name. 'Sadly, it tends to rouse the infantile in the male, no matter how old they are.'

'Men can be their own worst enemies,' he admitted. Then said it again. 'Lovage…'

This time he lingered over the name, testing it, giving it a deliciously soft lilt, making it sound very grown-up. And she discovered he didn't need the smile to turn her bones to putty.

She reached for the door, needing something to hang on to.

'Are you okay?' he asked.

'Fine,' she snapped, telling herself to get a grip.

The man was trying to lumber her with a superannuated piece of junk. Or, worse, was a con artist distracting her while an accomplice—maybe Basil himself—slipped around the back of the house and made off with anything not nailed down. Well, good luck with that one. But, whatever he was up to, it was a cast-iron certainty that flirting was something that came to him as naturally as breathing. And she was being sucked in.

'If that's all?' she enquired.

'No, wait!'

She hesitated a second too long.

'Right name. Tick. Right address. Tick—'

'Annoying male, tick,' she flashed back at him, determined to put an end to this. Whatever *this* was.

'You may well be right,' he agreed, amused rather than annoyed. Which was annoying. 'But, while you might not know your Great-Uncle Basil, I think you're going to have to accept that he knows you.' He looked down at the envelope he was holding, then up at her. 'Tell me, are you all named after herbs in your family?'

She opened her mouth, then, deciding not to go there, said, 'Tell me, Mr McElroy, does she…it,' she corrected herself, refusing to fall into the trap of thinking of the van as anything other than an inanimate object 'does it go?'

'I drove her here,' he pointed out, the smile enticing, mouth-wateringly sexy. Confident that he'd got her. 'I'll take you for a spin in her so that I can talk you through her little eccentricities, if you like,' he went on before she could complete her punchline, tell him to start it up and drive it away. 'She's a lovely old girl, but she has her moods.'

'Oh, right. You're telling me she's a *cranky* old ice cream van.'

'That's a bit harsh.' He leaned his shoulder against the door frame, totally relaxed, oblivious of the fact that the rose scrambling over the porch had dropped pink petals over his thick dark hair and on one of those broad shoulders. 'Shall we say she's an old ice cream van with bags of character?'

'Let's not,' she replied, doing her best to get a grip of her tongue, her hormones, her senses, all of which were urging her to forget her problems, throw caution to the wind and, for once in her life, say yes instead of no. 'I'm sorry, Mr McElroy—'

'Sean—'

'I'm sorry, *Mr McElroy*,' she reiterated, refusing to be sidetracked, 'but my mother told me never to take a ride with a stranger.'

A classic case of do as I say rather than do as I do, obviously. In similar circumstances, her mother wouldn't have hesitated.

She'd have grabbed the adventure and, jingle blaring, driven around the village scandalising the neighbours.

But, gorgeous though Sean McElroy undoubtedly was, she wasn't about to make the same mistakes as her mother. And while he was still trying to get his head around the fact that she'd turned him down flat, she took a full step back and shut the door. Then she slipped the security chain into place, although whether it was to keep him out or herself in she couldn't have said.

He didn't move. His shadow was still clearly visible behind one of the stained glass panels that flanked the door and, realising that he might be able to see her pinned to the spot, her heart racing, she grabbed the rubber gloves and beat a hasty retreat to the safety of the kitchen.

Today was rapidly turning into a double scrub day and, back on her knees, she went at it with even more vigour, her pulse pounding in her ears as she waited for the bell to ring again.

It didn't.

Regret warred with relief. It was a gorgeous May day and the thought of a spin in an ice cream van with a good-looking man called to everything young and frivolous locked up inside her. Everything she had never been. Even the scent of the lilac, wafting in through the kitchen door, seemed hell-bent on enticing her to abandon her responsibilities for an hour and have some fun.

She shook her head. Dangerous stuff, fun, and she attacked the floor with the brush, scrubbing at the already spotless quarry tiles, taking her frustration out on something inanimate while she tried to forget Sean McElroy's blue eyes and concentrate on today's problem. How to conjure two hundred and fifty pounds out of thin air to pay for Geli's school trip to France.

There was nothing for it. She was going to have to bite the bullet and ask her boss for an extra shift.

Sean caught his breath.

He'd been having trouble with it ever since the door of Gable

End had been thrown open to reveal Lovage Amery, cheeks flushed, dark hair escaping the elastic band struggling—and failing—to hold it out of a pair of huge hazel eyes.

Being a step up, she'd been on a level with him, which meant that her full, soft lips, a luscious figure oozing sex appeal, had been right in his face.

That she was totally oblivious of the effect created by all that unrestrained womanhood made it all the more enticing. All the more dangerous.

Furious as he was with Basil, he'd enjoyed the unexpected encounter and, while he was not fool enough to imagine he was irresistible, he thought that she'd been enjoying it, too. She'd certainly been giving as good as she got.

It was a long time since a woman had hit all the right buttons with quite that force and she hadn't even been trying.

Maybe that was part of the attraction.

He'd caught her unawares and, unlike most women of his acquaintance, she hadn't been wearing a mask, showing him what she thought he'd want to see.

Part of the attraction, all of the danger.

He'd as good as forgotten why he was there and the suddenness of her move had taken him by surprise. He couldn't remember the last time he'd been despatched quite so summarily by a woman but the rattle of the security chain going up had a finality about it that suggested ringing the doorbell again would be a waste of time.

He looked at the envelope Basil Amery had pushed through his door while he was in London, along with a note asking him to deliver it and Rosie to Lovage Amery.

He'd been furious. As if he didn't have better things to do, but it was typical of the man to take advantage. Typical of him to disappear without explanation.

True, his irritation had evaporated when the door had opened but, while it was tempting to take advantage of the side gate, standing wide open, and follow up his encounter with the luscious Miss Amery, on this occasion he decided that discretion was the better part of valour.

It would take more than a pair of pretty eyes to draw him into the centre of someone else's family drama. He had enough of that in his own backyard.

A pity, but he'd delivered Rosie. Job done.

CHAPTER TWO

Take plenty of exercise. Always run after the ice cream van.

—Rosie's Diary

ELLE, hot, flustered and decidedly bothered from her encounter with Sean McElroy, found her concentration slipping, her ears straining to hear the van start up, the crunch of tyres on gravel as it drove away.

It was all nonsense, she told herself, mopping up the suds, sitting back on her heels. She'd never heard of anyone called Basil Amery. It had to be a mistake. But the silence bothered her. While she hadn't heard the van arrive, she hadn't been listening. She had, however, been listening for it to leave.

The sudden rattle of the letter box made her jump. That was the only reason her heart was pounding, she told herself as she leapt to her feet. She wasn't in the habit of racing to pick up the post—it rarely contained anything but bills and she could wait for those—but it was an excuse to check that he'd gone.

There were two things on the mat. The brown envelope Sean McElroy had been holding and a bunch of keys. He couldn't, she told herself. He wouldn't… But the key fob was an ice cream cornet and she flung open the door.

Rosie was still sitting on the drive, exactly where he'd parked her.

'Sean McElroy!' she called, half expecting him to be

sitting in the van, grinning at having tricked her into opening the door.

He wasn't and, in a sudden panic, she ran to the gate, looking up and down the lane. Unless he'd had someone follow him in a car, he'd have to walk, or catch a bus.

She spun around, desperately checking the somewhat wild shrubbery.

Nothing. She was, apparently, quite wrong.

He could.

He had.

Abandoned Rosie on her doorstep.

'If you're looking for the van driver, Elle, he rode off in that direction.'

Elle inwardly groaned. Mrs Fisher, her next door neighbour, was bright-eyed with excitement as she stepped up to take a closer look at Rosie.

'Rode?'

'He had one of those fold-up bikes. Are you taking on an ice cream round?' she asked.

The internal groan reached a crescendo. The village gossips considered the Amery family their own private soap opera and whatever she said would be chewed over at length in the village shop.

'Sorry, Mrs Fisher, I can hear my phone,' she said, legging it inside, pushing the door shut behind her. If she'd left it open the woman would have considered it an invitation to walk in.

She sat on the bottom of the stairs holding the envelope, staring at the name and address which was, without doubt, hers.

Then she tore it open and tipped out the contents. A dark pink notebook with 'Bookings' written on the cover. A bells and whistles cellphone, the kind that would have her sisters drooling. There were a couple of official-looking printed sheets of paper. One was the logbook for the van, which told her that it was registered to Basil Amery of Keeper's Cottage, Haughton Manor, the other was an insurance certificate.

There was also a cream envelope.

She turned it over. There was nothing written on it, no name or address, but that had been on the brown envelope. She put her thumb beneath the flap and took out the single sheet of matching paper inside. Unfolded it.

Dear Lally, it began, and her heart sank as she read her grandmother's pet name.

Remember how you found me, all those years ago? Sitting by the village pond, confused, afraid, ready to end it all?

You saved me that day, my life, my sanity, and what happened afterwards wasn't your fault. Not Bernard's either. My brother and I were chalk and cheese but we are as we're made and there's nothing that can change us. Maybe, if our mother had still been alive, things would have been different, but there's no point in dwelling on it. The past is past.

I've kept my promise and stayed away from the family. I caused enough heartache and you and Lavender's girls have had more than enough of that to bear, losing Bernard and Lavender, without me turning up to dredge up the past, old scandals. The truth, however, is that I'm getting old and home called. Last year I took a cottage on the Haughton Manor estate and I've been working up the courage to write to you, but courage was never my strong point and now I've left it too late.

I have met your lovely granddaughter, though. I had lunch at the Blue Boar a couple of months ago and she served me. She was so like you, Lally—all your charm, your pretty smile—that I asked someone who she was. She even has your name. And here, I'm afraid, comes the crunch. You knew there would be a crunch, didn't you?

Rosie, who by now you'll have met, is a little hobby of mine. I do the occasional party, public event, you know the kind of thing, just to cover the costs of keeping her.

The occasional charity do for my soul. Unfortunately, events have rather overtaken me and I have to go away for a while but there are people I've made promises to, people I can't let down and I thought perhaps you and your granddaughter might take it on for me. A chance for her to get out of that restaurant once in a while. For you to think of me, I hope. Sean, who brings this to you, will show you how everything works.

I've enclosed the bookings diary as well as the phone I use for the ice cream business and, in order to make things easier for you, I've posted the change of keeper slip to the licence people so that Rosie is now registered in your name.

God bless and keep you, Lally.

Yours always,

Basil

Elle put her hand to her mouth. Swallowed. Her great-uncle. Family. He'd been within touching distance and she'd had no idea. She tried to remember serving someone on his own, but the Blue Boar had a motel that catered for businessmen travelling on their own.

Haughton Manor was only six or seven miles away but she had to get ready for work and there was no time to drive over there this evening. Find out more. Neither could she leave it and she reached for the phone, dialled Directory Enquiries.

'Lower Haughton, Basil Amery,' she said, made a note of the number and then dialled it.

After half a dozen rings it switched to voicemail. Had he already left? What events? Scandal, he'd mentioned in his letter… She left a message, asking him to call her—he'd pick up his messages even if he was away—left her number as well, and replaced the receiver. She was rereading his letter, trying to make sense of it, when the phone rang. She grabbed for it, hoping that he'd picked up the message and called back.

'Elle?'

It was her boss. 'Oh, hello, Freddy.'

'Don't sound so disappointed!'

'Sorry, I was expecting someone else. What's up?' she asked quickly, before he asked who.

'We're going to be short-staffed this evening. I was wondering if you can you drop everything and come in early.'

'Twenty minutes?' she offered.

'You're an angel.' Then, 'Would your sister be interested in doing a shift? She's a smart girl; she'd pick it up quickly enough. I'm sure she could use the money.'

'I'm sorry, Sorrel isn't here, but I was hoping for some more hours myself,' she added, taking advantage of a moment when he was the one asking for something.

'You already do more than enough. I'll have a word next time she drops in to the use the Wi-Fi. It wouldn't hurt her to help out.'

'She needs to concentrate...' But Freddy had already hung up and she was talking to herself.

She read the letter again, then replaced it in the envelope and put everything in the hall drawer. She didn't want her grandmother seeing the letter until Elle knew what the heck was going on.

There was nothing she could do with Rosie, but she'd be at work before anyone came home. She had until tomorrow morning to think of some good reason why it was parked in the drive.

Sean told himself that it was none of his business. That Basil was just a tenant who'd asked if he could keep Rosie at the barn since there wasn't a garage at the cottage.

He'd only got dragged into the situation because he'd stayed overnight in London on the day Basil decided to do his disappearing act. And if Lovage Amery had been a plain middle-aged woman Sean wouldn't have given the matter a first thought, let alone a second one.

Why Basil hadn't just decided to leave Rosie with him was the real mystery. She was safe enough locked up in the barn.

Unless, of course, he didn't intend to come back.

Or hadn't actually gone anywhere.

He swore, grabbed a spare set of keys from the estate safe and drove across the park to Keeper's Cottage.

He knocked, called out, then, when there was no answer, let himself in. Nothing seemed out of place. There were no letters ominously propped up on the mantelpiece. Only a photograph of a young woman wearing an outrageously short mini dress, white knee-length boots, her hair cut in a sharp angular style that had once been the height of fashion. Her large eyes were framed with thick sooty lashes and heavily lined. The gloss and polish, the expensive high fashion were as far from Lovage Amery as it was possible to be, and yet those eyes left him in no doubt about the family connection. Shape, colour were a perfect match.

So that was all right, then.

Basil must have had some bookings for Rosie that he couldn't cancel and was lumbering his family with the responsibility. If they weren't keen, it wasn't his problem.

The light was flashing on the answering machine and after a moment's hesitation he hit 'play'.

Lovage Amery's liquid voice filled the room. 'Mr Amery? My name is Lovage Amery and I've just read your letter. I don't understand. Who are you? Will you ring me? Please.' And she left a number.

Genuinely had no idea who Basil was? On the point of reaching for the phone, the phone in his pocket rang.

He checked the caller ID. Olivia.

'Sean, I'm at the barn,' she said before he could say a word. 'Where are you?'

The leap-to-it tone of the Haughton family, so different from the soft voice still rippling through him, evoking the memory of hot eyes that you could drown in. A dangerously appealing mouth. It was the kind of complicated response that should have sent up warning flares—*here be dragons*—but only made him want to dive right in.

Bad idea.

'I'm on the far side of the estate,' he said.

'It's nearly six.' His half-sister's pout was almost audible.

'You know how it is, sis,' he said, knowing how much she hated to be called that. 'No rest for younger illegitimate sons. Why are you here?'

'It's my home?'

'Excuse me? The last time you were here was Christmas. You stayed for two days, then abandoned your children with their nanny for the rest of the holidays while you went skiing.'

'They had a lovely time,' she protested.

Of course they had. He'd made sure of it, sliding down the hill on old tea trays in the snow, building dens, running wild as he had, in ways that were impossible in their urban lives in London. But they would still have rather been with their parents.

'Look, I don't want to fight with you, Sean. I wanted to talk about the stables. I want to convert them into craft workshops. I know all kinds of people—weavers, candle-makers, turners, who would fall over themselves for space. Visitors to the estate would love to see demonstrations. Buy stuff.'

He laughed.

'What's so funny?' she demanded.

'The idea that you would know what a turner did, let alone be acquainted with one.'

'Wretch. Henry thinks it's a good idea.'

'That would be Henry who visits his estate twice a year. At Christmas…' also to abandon his children before jetting off, although in his case to the Caribbean '…and for the shooting.' And for the occasional extramarital weekend in the same cottage his father had used for the purpose. Like father, like son.

'It's his estate, not yours,' she pointed out.

'So it is. And he pays me to run it professionally. At a profit.

Not as occupational therapy for women whose marriages are falling apart.'

Clearly she had no answer to that because she cut the connection without another word. That was one of the drawbacks of a mobile phone. You couldn't slam it down to make your point.

He replaced the photograph, took a thorough look around the cottage to make sure he hadn't overlooked anything. He found nothing to raise alarm signals but he was still vaguely uneasy. Regretted not staying at the Amerys' house to check the contents of Basil's envelope.

He hadn't taken much notice when Lovage Amery had initially denied any knowledge of Basil. He had family he'd deny in a heartbeat but that message on Basil's answering machine certainly hadn't sounded like a family call—even to family you didn't like. He'd heard enough of those over the years to recognise one when he heard it. She had been polite, businesslike but there had been no emotion. And if he was sure of anything, he was sure that Miss Lovage Amery was packed to the brim with that.

He'd be going that way this evening. Maybe he should call in to see her again. Just to put his mind at rest. Basil was, after all, his tenant and there were implications for the estate if he didn't intend to come back.

And, just in case Lovage Amery was still denying any family connection, he used his phone to take a picture of the photograph on the mantelpiece.

'Freddy…'

'Elle! You must have flown!' It was a good start but, before she could press her advantage and put her case for another shift, he said, 'Not now. All hands on deck.'

Rosie was exactly where he'd left her, which wasn't promising. Sean had hoped that whatever was in the envelope would have made things clear and she'd be tucked up safely behind the doors of what must once have been a carriage house. Taken into the fold, as it were.

As it was, he braced himself before ringing the doorbell. And not just because of the effect Lovage Amery had on his breathing.

Whatever the situation, after his park and ride performance this afternoon he wasn't anticipating a particularly warm welcome.

The deep breath was unnecessary. The door was opened by a teenage girl who was a vision in black. Black hair, black dress, black painted fingernails.

'Yes?' she demanded, with manners to match the clothes. 'What do you want?'

'A word with Lovage Amery?'

'What about?'

'Tell her it's Sean McElroy,' he said. 'She'll know.'

She shrugged. 'Gran, it's for you!' she shouted, hanging onto the door, keeping him on the step with the kind of stare that would frighten a zombie.

Gran? 'No…'

She waited, expressionless.

'Tall, dark hair, hazel eyes? No one's grandmother,' he added.

The green eyes in her deadpan face narrowed suspiciously. 'You want Elle?'

'Do I?' Elle?

'She's at work. She won't be home until late.'

'In that case, I'll come back tomorrow,' he said.

'Make it before eleven. She starts work at twelve,' she said, making a move to close the door.

'What is it, Geli?'

Sean looked beyond the black-garbed teen to the source of the voice. Walking towards him was the girl in Basil's photograph, over forty years on. Her hair had faded to grey and these days she wore it up in a soft chignon, but the eyes, even without the heavy fridge of false eyelashes, were unmistakable.

'It's okay, Gran. He doesn't want you, he wants Elle.'

'I hadn't realised there was more than one Lovage Amery,' Sean said quickly, bypassing the teen in favour of her grandmother, who was undoubtedly the intended recipient of Basil's envelope. 'Did Elle explain to you about Rosie?'

'Rosie?' she asked, confused. Which answered that question. 'Who's Rosie?'

'Not who, what. The ice cream van?'

'Oh, that. I wondered where it had come from. Is it yours?'

'No...' This was even harder than talking to Elle. 'I left a letter for you,' he prompted. 'From Basil?'

'Basil?' She took a step back, the graceful poise crumpling along with her face. 'No,' she whispered. 'He wouldn't. He mustn't. Bernard will be so angry...'

'Gran...' The girl, a protective arm around her grandmother, gave him a furious look and, for the second time that day, the front door of Gable End was shut firmly in his face.

Freddy stopped her with a touch to her arm. Elle's instincts were to pull away, but she reminded herself that he'd known her and her family since she was eighteen. That it was avuncular rather than familiar. He was, after all, old enough to be her uncle if not her father.

'There's a big party at the corner table, Elle. They've got drinks and should have had enough time to sort out what they want to eat by now. Will you take care of them?'

Only one of the backup staff had turned in and it had been non-stop since she'd arrived before six. She was due a break, but that wasn't going to happen and she pasted on a smile, took her book from her pocket and said, 'Of course, Freddy.'

The large round table in the corner could take up to a dozen people and it was full, which might mean a decent tip. Or a lot of work for nothing much. You could never tell.

Smile, Elle, smile, she told herself as she approached the

table. 'Are you ready to order?' she asked. 'Or do you need a little more...'

The words died away as she looked around the table and found herself face to face with Sean McElroy and her knees, already feeling the pressure from nearly three hours of non-stop action, momentarily buckled.

Since yelling at a diner, demanding to know why he'd dumped Rosie and run, would not improve her chances of a decent tip, she braced her knees, cleared her throat, said to no one in particular, 'If you need a little more time I can come back.'

'No, we're ready,' the man nearest to her said, acknowledging her with a smile before going around the table, so that she could keep her eyes on her notepad. Everything went smoothly until they reached Sean McElroy. 'Sean?' he prompted.

'Sorry, I can't make up my mind. I'm rather tempted by the chicken in a herb crust. Can you tell me exactly what the herbs are? Elle,' he added, proving that his vision was twenty-twenty too, since he could obviously read her name badge across the table.

So much for hoping to avoid another encounter with those blue eyes.

She looked up to find them fixed on her, his expression suggesting that she had some explaining to do which, under the circumstances, was some nerve.

The woman beside him, slender, cool in a linen shift of such simplicity that it had to have cost a mint, straight blonde hair shining like something out of a shampoo advert, turned to look at him and, instantly sensing that there was more going on than just a discussion about food, frowned.

'I thought you were going to have the steak, darling. You always have the steak,' she added, declaring herself in possession.

'Do I? I hadn't realised I was so boring, darling,' he said, keeping his eyes fixed resolutely on Elle. The 'darling' had sounded like an afterthought. Maybe the woman noticed that too, because she followed his gaze to Elle and her frown deepened.

'The crust consists of fine wholemeal breadcrumbs,' Elle rattled off quickly, 'and a mixture of fresh herbs including parsley, lemon thyme, a touch of sage, seasoned and bound together with egg.'

'No *lovage*?' he asked.

Well, she'd seen that one coming. Was ready for it. 'No lovage, no basil.' She waited, pencil poised.

'A pity. I'll have the salmon.'

She made a note, moved on. It was just another table, she told herself as she brought a jug of water, went around the table with a basket of warm rolls.

'Roll, madam?' she asked the blonde.

She shook her head.

She moved on 'Roll, sir?'

Sean looked up, his face so close to hers that she could see a thin jagged scar just above his eyebrow. Had he fallen off his bike when he was little? Been cut by something? Been hand-bagged by some woman he'd seriously annoyed?

He took his time deciding, then, when she'd finally picked out his choice with the tongs and she was congratulating herself on keeping her cool when all she wanted to do was crown him with them, he murmured, 'Tell me, Lovage, who is Bernard?' At which point the roll shot out of the tongs, knocked over a glass of water and in the confusion most of the rolls landed in his lap.

'One would have been sufficient,' he said, rescuing the basket and picking warm bread out of his lap, while she scrambled on the floor for the rest.

'Fetch fresh rolls, Elle. Quickly as you can.' Oh, no, Freddy *would* have to be looking… 'And replace this glass,' he added, handing it to her. 'I'm so sorry, everyone. Can I offer you fresh drinks? On the house, of course.'

'How about a fresh waitress. Someone in control of her hands. And her eyes,' the girl in the linen dress suggested, pointedly brushing away a few drops of water. 'My dress is ruined.'

'There is nothing wrong with the waitress,' Sean said as Freddy mopped up the spill, straightened the table.

'We can all see what *you* think of her—'

'The accident was entirely my fault,' he continued, speaking to Freddy, ignoring the woman at his side. 'And there's no need for fresh drinks. We're fine.'

Sean watched Lovage—Elle—Amery walk away and discovered that he wanted to go with her. Take her hand and walk out into the dusk with her. Walk across the village, along the towpath by the Common. Walk her home and kiss her on the step, ask her out on a date, just like they did in the old days.

'What did you say to her?' Charlotte demanded, intensifying the feeling.

'I asked for the roll with pumpkin seeds,' he replied.

'And you certainly got it,' someone chimed in. Everyone laughed except Charlotte.

'I don't believe you. You were flirting with her from the moment she came to the table,' she accused.

Sean realised that the restaurant owner was still hovering. Listening. 'If I was, then I am one hundred per cent to blame, because she certainly wasn't flirting back.' He forced himself to smile at the man. 'We're okay, really. Thanks.'

It was a dismissal and he took the hint, leaving them to their meal. Another waitress brought a fresh glass, a new basket of rolls, and served their meal, but he only had eyes for Elle as she weaved with drinks and trays of food between smaller tables on the far side of the room.

Reassigned out of the danger zone by the restaurant manager and no doubt happy to go.

What on earth had got into him?

He'd just taken his seat at the table when he'd looked around the room and seen her, hair restrained in a French plait, luscious curves neatly encased in a black shirt and trousers, a long black pinafore tied with strings around her waist.

She'd been laughing over a friendly exchange with a family she was serving at another table and he'd experienced another of those breath-stopping moments, just like the one he'd had when she'd opened the door to him.

He should have guessed this was where she worked.

There were a fairly limited number of jobs where she'd be working at this time of night, or on a Sunday lunchtime. A late-night garage, a twenty-four hour supermarket or a restaurant. And the Blue Boar—a rambling restaurant with bed and breakfast facilities for businessmen—was within walking distance of Gable End.

As he'd watched her, he saw the guy who'd shown them to their table, the one who'd come to see what the fuss was about, stop her with a hand to her arm as she'd passed him.

It looked familiar. Possessive.

As did the way the man's eyes had followed her as she came towards their table.

It was none of his business, he told himself. None at all. But then she'd looked up, seen him, and he just hadn't been able to stop himself.

Elle walked into the kitchen the following morning, gritty-eyed, heavy-limbed, late after a restless night with a head full of pink ice cream vans and blue-eyed men, to find it blissfully silent.

Sorrel had presumably walked her grandmother to church before going on to take advantage of the free Wi-Fi at the Blue Boar. And Geli would be doing an early turn, dog walking at the animal sanctuary.

She dropped the envelope and van keys she'd retrieved from the hall drawer onto the kitchen table, then opened the back door.

The sun poured in, bringing with it the song of a blackbird, the scent of the lilac and she lifted her face to the sun, feeling the life seep back as she breathed in the day. Breathed out the unpleasantness of last night. That girl with Sean McElroy might have been beautiful, elegant and polished, but beauty is as beauty does, at least that was what her grandmother always said.

She suspected that beauty like that could, and did, do whatever it pleased and Sean McElroy was clearly happy to let her.

Freddy had moved her to another table after the incident with the rolls. He had been quick to reassure her that he didn't blame her for what happened but, after all, the customer was always right.

It should have been a relief. *Was* a relief, she told herself. Between Sean and his girlfriend, someone would undoubtedly have had their dinner in their lap.

She had enough on her plate sorting out Rosie, without that kind of trouble. But not before she'd had a cup of tea and got some solid carbs inside her, she decided, picking up an elastic band from the bowl on the dresser and fastening back her hair.

She opened the bread bin.

Nothing but crumbs. And a shake told her that the cereal box on the table was empty.

She was on her knees hunting through the cupboards for the packet she'd bought the day before when a shadow cut off the sunlight.

It was too soon for her grandmother or Sorrel and she looked up expecting to see Geli, ready for a second helping of breakfast before going into Maybridge with her friends. And out of luck because the empty box on the table *was* the one she'd bought the day before.

But it wasn't Geli.

The silhouette blocking out the light was that of Pink Van Man himself, but only momentarily, since he didn't wait for an invitation but walked right in before she could ask him what the heck he thought he was doing.

A fast learner.

CHAPTER THREE

Life is uncertain. Eat dessert first.

—Rosie's Diary

SEAN MCELROY looked so much bigger, so much more dangerous now that she was on her knees. Maybe he was aware of that because he bent to offer her a hand up, enveloping her in a waft of something masculine that completely obliterated the scent of the lilac.

Old leather, motor oil, the kind of scents unknown in an all female household, and she found herself sucking it in like a starving kitten.

Her eyes were level with a pair of narrow hips, powerful thighs encased in soft denim, closer to a man—at least one she wanted to be close to—than she'd been since she'd said goodbye to her dreams and taken a job working unsocial hours.

'How did you get in?' she demanded.

'The gate was open.'

Oh, great. She nagged about security but no one took her seriously. Except, of course, it wasn't about that.

Leaving the gate open was Geli's silent protest against Elle's flat refusal to take in any more four-footed friends, no matter how appealing. Why bother to shut the gate when there was no dog to keep off the road?

She shook him off, cross, hot and bothered. 'It's not an invitation for anyone to walk in,' she snapped, standing up without assistance.

'No? Just as well I closed it then,' he said. 'It could do with a new lock.'

'I could do with any number of new things, Mr McElroy. The one thing I *don't* need is an old van. Can I hope that your arrival means you've realised your mistake and have come to take her home?'

'Sorry,' he said.

'You don't look it.' He wasn't smiling exactly, but she was finding it hard to hold onto her irritation.

'Would it help if I said that I honestly believed you were expecting her?'

'Really?' she enquired. 'And what part of "Go away and take Rosie with you" didn't you understand?'

He ignored the sarcasm. 'I thought that once you'd opened the envelope it would make sense.'

'So why are you here now?'

He shrugged. 'I'm not sure. Just a feeling that something's not quite right. Did Basil leave a note?' he asked, nodding in the direction of the envelope. 'I'm a bit concerned about him.'

'But not about me, obviously. Your little stunt last night could have cost me my job. Did you enjoy your salmon?' she accused.

'I have to admit that the evening went downhill right after you dumped a basket of hot rolls in my lap,' he said.

'I hope you're not expecting an apology.'

'No. I take it you didn't get the message I left for you?'

He'd left a message? She shook her head. 'We were rushed off our feet last night. I didn't hang around to chat.'

'No?' There was something slightly off about the way he said that.

'Would you?' she asked. 'After six hours on your feet?'

'It depends what was on offer.'

She frowned and he shook his head. 'No, forget it. I'm sorry if you got into trouble but you have to admit that while you might not know Basil, the name Bernard certainly makes you all jump.'

'All?'

'Your grandmother nearly passed out when I asked her if she'd had Basil's letter,' he explained.

'Gran? Are you telling me that you came back here yesterday? After I'd gone to work?'

'I called in on my way to the Blue Boar. I did tell the skinny vampire that I'd come back this morning,' he said.

'Geli…' She smothered a grin. 'I haven't seen her this morning. I've only just got up. What did Gran say?'

'She wasn't exactly coherent, but I think the gist was that Bernard wouldn't allow her to receive a letter from Basil. She seemed panic-stricken at the thought.'

'Well, that's just ridiculous. Bernard was my grandfather but he's been dead for years,' she told him.

And yet there was obviously something. It was there in the letter.

'Tell me about him,' she said.

'Basil?' He shrugged. 'I don't know much. He's just an old guy with two passions in his life. Rosie and poker.'

'He's a gambler? Are you saying that he puts Rosie up as surety for his bets?'

'He'd never risk losing Rosie,' he assured her. Then added, 'Which is not to say that if he got into trouble some of his playing partners wouldn't take her in lieu if they could get their hands on her.'

'So, what are you saying? That you've been appointed getaway driver and I've been chosen to give her sanctuary?' *It… not she.* She was doing it now. But it explained why Basil had gone to the bother of registering her grandmother as Rosie's keeper.

'That's about the gist of it,' he admitted, stretching his neck, easing his shoulders.

'Don't do that!' she said as his navy polo shirt rippled, offering a tantalising promise of the power beneath the soft jersey. Talk about distraction…

Sean frowned. He didn't have a clue what she was talking about, thank goodness.

'Does he disappear regularly?' she asked before he had time to work it out.

'I wouldn't know. I'm his landlord, not his best buddy. But he garages Rosie with me and I was in London when he took off and he couldn't get in. It would seem that his need to disappear was too urgent to wait until morning.'

'So, what? He dropped a note through your letter box asking you to bring her here?'

'I'm sorry about that,' he said, looking slightly uncomfortable, no doubt thinking that she was taking a dig at him for doing the same. 'I assumed that once you'd read whatever was in the envelope you'd know what to do.'

What to do?

It got worse, she thought, suddenly realising exactly what this was all about.

'I'm sorry, Sean, but if you've come here expecting to be paid your rent, you're out of luck. I don't know Basil Amery and, even if I did, I couldn't help you. You're going to have to sell Rosie to recover your losses.'

'Sell Rosie? Are you kidding?'

'Obviously,' Elle said, back to sarcasm. 'Since she's Basil's pride and joy.'

'You don't sound convinced.'

'I can think of more important things to lavish your love on. I mean, how would you react to someone you've never heard of expecting you to run an ice cream round for him?'

Sean thought about it for a moment, then said, 'Why don't I put the kettle on? I make a mean cup of coffee.'

'I haven't got any coffee,' she said, tucking a wayward strand of hair behind her ear.

'Tea, then,' he said, picking up the kettle, filling it and turning it on. He took a couple of mugs off the dresser and since the tea bags were stored in a tin with 'TEA' on the front—life was complicated enough without adding to the confusion—he found them without making a mountain out of a molehill. So far, he was doing better than either of her sisters ever managed. 'Milk, sugar?' he asked, dropping a bag in each mug.

She wanted to tell him to go and take the van with him, but he was right. They needed to get to the bottom of this.

'Just a dash of milk.'

Was there any milk?

'How about sugar? You've obviously had a shock.'

'Of course I haven't,' she said, pulling herself together. 'This is some kind of weird mistake. It has to be.'

They weren't the most conventional family in the world, but they didn't have secrets. Quite the contrary. Anyone would give him chapter and verse...

He glanced back to her.

'What are you so scared of, Elle?'

'I'm not scared!'

'No?'

'No!' She'd faced the worst that the world could throw at her, but he was right, something about this put her on edge and, seizing on the fact that the kettle hadn't come on to divert his attention, she said, 'You have to give the plug a wiggle.'

He wasn't diverted, just confused, and she reached behind him.

'Don't!' Sean said as he realised what she was doing. He made a lunge in her direction, but not in time to stop her. There was a bit of a crackle and a tiny shock rippled up her arm, then the light came on and the kettle began to heat up noisily.

Her cheeks lit up to match but the rush of heat that invaded her body, starting at the spot where his hand was fastened over hers was, fortunately, silent.

Or maybe not.

Maybe the hammering of her pulse in her ears was so loud that Sean could hear it too, because he dropped her hand so fast that you'd have thought she was the one with dodgy wiring.

Without a word, he took a wooden spoon from the pot by the stove, used the handle to switch off the kettle and then removed the plug from the socket.

Whatever. Tea had been his idea.

But he wasn't done. Having disconnected the kettle, he began opening the dresser drawers.

'Excuse me!'

He held up a screwdriver he'd found in the drawer that contained bits of string, paper bags, the stuff that didn't have any other home.

'It's beyond help,' she told him. 'It's just…' worn out, past its use by date, just plain old '…vintage. Like Rosie.'

'It's nothing like Rosie,' he said, ignoring her protest as he set about taking the plug apart. 'Rosie is not an accident waiting to happen.'

'That's a matter of opinion,' she retorted.

'No. It's a matter of fact. She's completely roadworthy or I wouldn't be driving her.' He looked up. 'And I wouldn't have brought her to you.'

'No?' Then, realising just how rude she was being, she blushed. 'No, of course not. Sorry…'

'No problem.'

'I'm glad you think so,' she said, only too aware of the envelope that was lying on the kitchen table with all the appeal of an unexploded bomb.

The Amery family had lived at Gable End for generations. This was the house Grandpa had been born in and it was marked with traces of everyone who'd ever lived there.

Their names were written in the fly-leaves of books that filled shelves in almost every room. Were scratched into the handles of ancient tennis racquets, stencilled onto the lids of old school trunks in the attic.

Their faces as babies, children, brides and grooms, soldiers, parents, grandparents, filled photograph albums.

There was no Basil.

Okay, there were gaps. Photographs fell out, were borrowed, lost.

Or had some been removed?

Gran had recognised the name. According to Sean, she hadn't acted in the slightly silly, coy way she did when some man from the pensioners' club chatted her up, and they often did because she was still beautiful.

She'd nearly passed out, he'd said. Panicked. And then there was Basil's letter. He'd mentioned Bernard and referred to him as 'my brother'. The connection was definitely there. Maybe she just didn't want to believe it.

Taking a deep breath, she picked up the envelope—no one called her a scaredy-cat—and tipped the contents out onto the table so that he could see that she wasn't trying to hide anything.

'Here's Basil's letter,' she said, offering it to Sean, who was leaning against the dresser, still poking about in the plug with the screwdriver. 'You'd better read it,' she said, thrusting it at him before turning her attention to the notebook.

On the first page, where a printed note said *'In case of loss, please return to:'* the word 'ROSIE' had been written in block capitals, along with a mobile phone number. Presumably belonging to the phone on the table.

It was a page-a-day diary, she discovered, as she riffled through the pages, hoping for some clue. To the man. To his whereabouts.

There were appointments with names and telephone numbers by them. The occasional comment. Quotes by the famous, as well as Basil's own wry or funny comments on the joys of ice cream. There were only a couple of recent entries.

'He's written "RSG" on yesterday's date. Underlined. Do you know anyone with those initials?'

He thought about it for a moment, then shook his head.

'That's it, apart from "Service, Sean" written in the space for last Friday. Are you a mechanic? There's a collection of vintage cars at Haughton Manor, isn't there? Do you take care of them?'

'They come under my care,' he said. 'Basil asked if I'd change Rosie's oil, run a few basic checks to make sure everything was in good shape since he had some bookings. His back has been playing him up,' he added, almost defensively. Doing little jobs on the side that his boss didn't know about? Not her concern.

'How much does he pay you?' she asked. The last thing she needed was an elderly—vintage—vehicle that required high level, high cost maintenance, but she didn't appear to have much choice in the matter. The mystery remained, but the connection between Basil and her family appeared to be proved.

He shrugged and a smile teased at the corner of his mouth, creating a tiny ripple of excitement that swept through her, overriding her irritation, and it occurred to her that a man like Sean McElroy could be seriously good for her state of mind.

'Basil prefers to give payment in kind,' he said.

'Ice cream?' She looked at him. The narrow hips, ropey arms. Her state of mind and all points south. 'How much ice cream can one man eat?'

'Fortunately, I don't have to eat it all myself. He brought Rosie along to a family birthday party fully loaded with ice cream and toppings. The brownie points I earned for that were worth their weight in brake liners.'

'Family? You have children?'

'No. The party was for my niece. Half-niece.' He shrugged. 'I have a complicated family.'

'Don't we all,' she said wryly. 'But that's a lot of ice cream for one little girl's birthday.'

'It was a big party. My family don't do things by halves,' he said.

'No?' They had that in common, only in her case it tended to be dramas rather than celebrations. 'How do you know him?'

'Basil? He's a tenant on the Haughton Manor estate.'

'Keeper's Cottage. It's on the vehicle logbook,' she said. 'It's so near. I went there once on a school trip when we were doing the Tudors. It's beautiful.'

'So people keep telling me.'

'You live there too?' she asked.

'Live there, work there, for my sins. Or, rather, my mother's,' he said, before returning to the letter. 'Lally? Is that what people call your grandmother?'

'Yes.' She'd much rather hear about his mother's sins, but he'd changed the subject so emphatically that she didn't pursue it. 'I doubt many people know her real name.'

'Or yours?'

'Or mine,' she admitted.

'Well, Basil certainly does, and he's got a photograph of her on his mantelpiece to prove it.'

'You're kidding! A picture of my grandmother?'

He took a phone from his pocket, clicked through it and held it out to her. 'I took this yesterday when I let myself in. Just to be sure that he hadn't done anything…foolish.'

'Killed himself, you mean?' she said pointedly.

He didn't answer but that was what he'd meant. It was why he was here now. Why he'd wanted to see the letter.

'You have his keys?' she asked.

'Not personally. There are master keys in the estate safe. For emergencies.'

'Or when a tenant does a runner,' she said, taking the phone from him.

'It is her?' he asked about the woman in the photo.

She nodded. 'It was taken in the late sixties, before she married my grandfather.'

Her grandmother had been the height of fashion with her dark hair cut in a sharp chin-length bob by a top London stylist, her huge eyes heavily made-up, her lips pale. And the dress she was wearing was an iconic Courrèges original design.

She handed it back to him. 'How did you know this was gran?'

'I didn't until I saw her last night, but it was obvious she was related to you. The likeness is unmistakable.'

'But she was…'

She stopped. Her grandmother had been the pampered daughter of the younger son of the Earl of Melchester. A debutante. An acknowledged beauty.

One of the girls in pearls who'd featured in the pages of *Country Life*.

While the Amerys were a solid middle-class family, it hadn't been the marriage her father had planned for his daughter. No minor aristocracy to offer inherited wealth, park gates, maybe a title, so Elle's grandmother had been pretty much cut adrift from her family when she'd married Bernard Amery.

'I don't look a bit like her,' she said instead.

'Not superficially, maybe, but you have her mouth. Her eyes. Basil recognised you,' he pointed out. He looked again at the letter. 'Is your grandmother about?' he asked.

'No!' She shook her head. 'You can't bother her with this, Sean.'

'You haven't shown her the letter?'

'Not yet.' Once her grandmother had read it, Elle would be well and truly lumbered. And not just with an old crock that would cost a fortune to tax, insure, keep running. There were the obligations, too.

Oh, no, wait.

The connection had been made. He knew he'd brought Rosie to the right place and as far as Sean McElroy was concerned there was nothing more to be said.

She was already lumbered.

It was true, nothing good ever came out of a brown envelope. Well, this time it wasn't going to happen. She wasn't going to let it.

Whatever her grandmother had done for him in the past, Basil was going to have to sort out his own problems. They had quite enough of their own.

'They seem to have been very close,' he said, looking again at the letter. 'He says she saved his life.'

'He'd have had a job to end it all in the village pond,' she told him dryly. 'No matter what time of day or night, someone would be sure to spot you.'

'Your grandmother, in this case. No doubt it was just a cry for help, but she seems to have listened. Sorted him out.'

Her ditzy, scatterbrained grandmother?

'If that's the case, why haven't they seen one another for forty years? Unless…' She looked up. 'If she married his brother, maybe they fell out over her. She was very beautiful.'

'Yes…'

'Although why would Grandpa have removed every trace of his brother's presence from the family home? After all, he got the girl,' she mused.

'Of course he got the girl. Basil is gay, Elle.'

'Gay?' she repeated blankly.

'Could that be the reason his family disowned him?' Sean asked.

'No!' It was too horrible to imagine. 'They wouldn't.'

'People do. Even now.'

'They weren't like that,' she protested.

Were they?

Sean was right. Forty years was a lifetime ago. She had no idea how her great-grandparents would have reacted to the news that one of their sons was gay. Or maybe she did. Basil had mentioned his mother in the letter. If she'd still been alive, he'd said…

You could change the law but attitudes took longer, especially among the older generation.

As for her grandfather, Bernard, he'd been a slightly scary stranger, someone who'd arrived out of the blue every six months or so, who everyone had to tiptoe around. Breathing a collective sigh of relief when he disappeared overseas to do whatever he did in Africa and the Middle East.

'Whatever happened, Gran can't be bothered with this. She's not strong, Sean.'

As always, it was down to her. And the first thing she'd have to do was go through the diary and cancel whatever arrangements Basil had made. If she could work out what they were.

'What does this mean?' she asked, flicking through the notebook again.

Sean didn't answer and she looked up, then wished she hadn't because he was looking straight at her and those blue eyes made her a little giddy. She wanted to smile, grab him and dance. Climb aboard Rosie and ring her bell.

She took a deep breath to steady herself.

'It says "Sylvie. PRC" Next Saturday'?' she prompted, forcing herself to look away.

'PRC? That'll be the Pink Ribbon Club. It's a charity supporting cancer patients and—' He paused as he tightened the final screw in the plug.

'And their families,' she finished for him, the words catching in her throat. 'I know.'

'It's their annual garden party on Saturday. They're holding it at Tom and Sylvie MacFarlane's place this year.'

'Where's that?'

'Longbourne Court.'

'Oh, yes, of course. I'd heard it was occupied at last.'

'I saw the signs advertising the garden party when I passed the gates. Basil mentioned it when he asked me to change Rosie's oil. I got the feeling he'd volunteered to help because it meant something special to him.'

'He should have thought of that before he bet the farm on the turn of a card,' she said, suddenly angry with this man who appeared to have absolutely no sense of responsibility. Worse. Didn't have the courage to face them and ask for help, but left someone else to do his dirty work. 'But then, from his letter, he appears to have made a life's work of letting people down.'

'You're assuming that it's a gambling problem.'

'You were the one who mentioned it as a possibility,' she reminded him.

'Grasping at straws? Maybe that was the problem with his family,' he suggested. 'Maybe he'd flogged the family silver to pay his creditors.'

'Not guilty,' she said, earning herself a sharp look. 'And I thought you said it was a recent problem?'

'He's been living on the estate for less than a year, so what do I know? Maybe he only gambles when he's unhappy. A form of self-harming?'

No, no, no... She wasn't listening.

'I can't have Gran involved in anything like this, Sean.'

'All he's asking is that she—or, rather, you—keeps Rosie's business ticking over.'

'Is it?'

'That's what he put in the note he left me.' He looked again at the letter to her grandmother. 'This does make it sound rather more permanent, I have to admit.'

'Well, whatever he wants, it's impossible. I have a job that keeps me fully occupied and Gran doesn't have a driving licence,' she protested, clutching at straws. 'Besides, her concentration isn't that great. She'd think it was all a wonderful treat and give all the ice cream away. Or just wander off when she got bored.'

'Is it Alzheimer's?' he asked point-blank.

'No.' She shook her head. 'She always had a bit of a reputation for giddiness but she's had a lot to deal with over the years. She blamed herself for Grandpa's death, which is ridiculous,' she added, before he could start adding two and two and making five. 'He was killed in a road accident. In Nigeria. And then my mother died. She hasn't been quite focused since then. Her doctor thinks she simply blocks out what she can't cope with.'

'We all have days when we'd like to do that,' he murmured sympathetically.

'Yes...' Then, afraid that she was revealing more than

she should, 'You can see why I won't have her put under any stress.'

'Of course,' he said. 'But there's absolutely nothing wrong with your focus, Lovage. Maybe, since you've taken charge of the letter meant for her, you could at least stand in for your grandmother on Saturday.'

CHAPTER FOUR

There's nothing wrong with life that a little ice cream won't fix.

—Rosie's Diary

ELLE should have seen that coming.

'Didn't you hear me?' she said. 'I work on Saturdays.'

'Not until the evening and the garden party will be over by six. There's going to be a concert in the grounds in the evening,' he added, in case she needed convincing. 'I promise you it'll be more fun than waiting tables.'

'Really? On my feet all day dishing out ice cream to fractious children? Irritable adults. Nobody with the right change. Can you positively guarantee that?'

He grinned without warning. 'You're weakening, I can tell.'

It was hard not to grin right back at his cheek, but she made an effort.

'I'm not, but even if I was beginning to crack, we have another problem. I haven't a clue how to work one of those ice cream machines.'

'It's not rocket science. I'll show you.'

'You?'

Her heart gave a little flutter. She hadn't anticipated that he would stick around to help and she was almost tempted.

'Who do you think was filling the cones at my niece's party while Basil was chatting up all the yummy mummies?'

She rather suspected that the yummy mummies were lining up to flirt with Sean, and she was equally sure that he would have been flirting back.

'Well, there you are,' she said, trying not to care about the fact that she was simply one in a long, meaningless line of women who had been suckered by that smile. Reminding herself that he was already spoken for by the cool blonde from the restaurant. 'Problem solved.' He knew how the equipment worked and a smile, a body like that, would be very good for business. 'If you think it's such fun, then Rosie is all yours.' She offered him the diary and the keys. 'Have a lovely day.'

He grinned. 'There's no doubt about it. You and Basil are definitely kin.'

'Then you must know that you are stuffed. Nice meeting you, Sean. Don't forget to shut the gate on your way out.'

'Nice try, but I don't think so.' He folded his arms, leaned back. Going nowhere. 'If you won't do it, I'll just have to wait here until your grandmother comes home. Where is she?' He glanced at his watch. 'Church?'

'Sean!'

'Or I could run you through the basics now,' he said. 'Give you that spin around the village so that you can get a feel for her.'

So much for appealing to his better nature. Clearly, he didn't have one. 'This is blackmail,' she said severely.

'You do drive?'

She was tempted to tell a flat out lie and say no. Perhaps it was as well for her immortal soul that he didn't wait for her to answer.

'Only I couldn't help noticing that you have a rather lovely old car in the garage and if Grannie can't drive…?'

'I didn't say she couldn't drive. I said she didn't have a licence. The result of one too many speeding tickets. And it's not a lovely old car, it's a heap of junk beyond help according to the guy at the garage when it failed its MOT. I'm sorry, Sean, but the last thing I need is more useless transport.'

'Rosie isn't useless.'

'She is to me. Or maybe you're suggesting I start an ice cream round to cover the cost of a trip to the supermarket?'

'Why not?' he asked. 'I'd stop you and buy one any time.'

The words were out of Sean's mouth before he could stop them.

There were women in this world who, you knew at a glance, you should not just walk, but run away from. The ones who still blushed, who looked at you with everything they were thinking plain to read in their eyes, whose hearts had not yet built up a protective layer of scar tissue.

Old-fashioned women who believed in love and marriage and family. The kind of woman a man, if he believed in none of those things, flirted with at his peril.

He had just stepped over an invisible line and they both knew it.

Elle covered the moment, lifting her arms, removing the band from which her hair was slipping, refastening it in one smooth movement. His fingers itched to reach out and stop her, slide his fingers through it. Tell her she should leave it loose.

One step, two steps…

'Do you think Basil means to come back, Sean?' she asked, breaking the spell. 'You said you were concerned about him and that letter did sound very much like goodbye.'

He wanted to reassure her, but the fact that Basil had gone to the lengths of transferring ownership of his most treasured possession to a woman he hadn't seen in forty years had a certain finality about it.

'Your guess is as good as mine,' he said, meeting her gaze, acknowledging the unasked question. 'I'm simply following Basil's script.'

'And you're doing a fine job. Unfortunately, you appear to be in a one-man show.'

'I'd noticed.'

'Isn't there some kind of retirement home for old vehicles like Rosie?' she asked a touch desperately. 'Somewhere you could put her out to grass?'

And, just like that, the tension went out of him and he was struggling to hold back a smile. 'Like an old donkey?' he suggested.

'Yes… No! You know what I mean!'

'I know what you mean,' he confirmed, not bothering to hide his amusement as she dissolved into blushing confusion, 'but I think you'll find that in automotive circles they're known as scrapyards.'

'It's all just a joke to you, isn't it?' she demanded and just as swiftly the confusion was gone.

She was still pink, but it was anger driving her now. She was an emotional hotspot. Trouble. Delightful. Dangerous.

'You told me that she's vintage. Isn't that special?' she demanded. 'What about a transport museum?'

Elle knew she was clutching at straws but, between Grandpa's old crock in the garage and now the van, she was beginning to feel like a serial vehicle murderer.

'Somewhere boys—grown-up boys like Basil, and you—can go and drool over her?' she persisted.

'This is where Basil chose, Elle. He specifically wanted you and your grandmother to have her.'

'Why? If he thinks Gran is so great, why didn't he come and visit? Ask us for help if he needed it? We haven't got any money and the menu runs to chickpeas more often than chicken but we've got plenty of room. If he's family—' If? Was there any doubt? 'If he's family, we would have taken care of him.'

'Would you?'

'We're not exactly overburdened with relatives. He might not have needed us, but did it never occur to him that we might have needed him? When Grandpa died. When my mother died.' When the sky fell in. 'What was his *problem*?'

He shrugged again, drawing quite unnecessary attention once more to the kind of shoulders that any red-blooded woman would be happy rubbing against as she filled cones with cool, sweet ice cream. She could do with an ice right now to cool her off.

'Sorry,' he said. 'You'll have to ask the other Lovage to fill you in on the family secrets.'

'I can't do that.' Who knew what memories would be dredged up from Gran's confused brain if it was brought up now, when it could do no good? What harm it might do. 'You saw her, Sean. Something really bad happened here decades ago and I'm not going to be the one to bring it all back.'

'Which answers your question about why Basil hasn't come to you for help in forty years.' She swallowed. 'She saw Rosie last night,' he said, pushing her. 'She's going to want to know where she came from,' he warned.

'No, she's not, because you're going to take her back where she came from.'

Sean took another look at the letter. '"Lavender's girls"?' he queried, ignoring her desperate interjection. 'Lavender is your mother?'

'Was. She died.'

'So it's just you and the black moth?' he asked.

'Geli?' She stifled a laugh at his description. Kinder than 'skinny vampire', but not by much. 'Angelica,' she added by way of explanation. 'She's sixteen. There's Sorrel, too. She's just started at college.'

'Lovage, Lavender, Angelica, Sorrel… The horticultural theme continues. When did your mother die?'

'When I was the age Geli is now. It was cancer,' she said before he asked. 'The virulent kind that comes with the death sentence included in the diagnosis. And, before you ask, there is no on\e else. It's just the four of us.'

Suddenly her throat was achingly thick and her eyes were stinging. Why had he come here, raking up the past? Making her remember?

'Is there any danger of that cup of tea you promised me?' she asked.

'Just as soon as I've fixed this kettle. Why don't you go and sit in the garden?' he suggested with a touch to her shoulder. 'I'll bring it out.'

Elle would rather have stayed right where she was, moving into the comfort promised by that hand, rather than away from it. To be held, feel the warmth of an arm around her, rather than being given another cup of the eternally cheering tea. Maybe he recognised the need in her eyes because he turned abruptly away to plug in the kettle. Elle backed off, fled outside, pulling a heavy raceme of lilac down, burying her face in the sweetness of it, just as she'd seen her mother do. She'd never understood why she did that.

It wasn't an elusive scent that you had to seek out. It filled the garden and up close was almost overpowering but right now she needed it in her lungs, in her heart. Needed it to smother the painful memories that Sean's arrival had stirred up.

Despite what she'd said, she knew she was going to have to take Rosie. Not for Basil. He was no different from every other man who'd touched her life. Just one more man who'd messed up and then run away.

· Her grandfather had gone through the motions, done all the right things, but all at arm's length. He'd rarely been home and when he was there were no hugs, only a laughter-dampening gloom.

As for Basil, he hadn't cared enough about them to come and see if 'Lavender's girls' were all right. To pitch in and be a father figure—a grandfatherly figure—in their lives, when they'd needed one most.

Maybe that was why her mother had subconsciously sought out here-today-gone-next-week men, choosing relationships with built-in obsolescence. Choosing children whose love was unconditional, rather than some man whose presence cast a dark shadow.

Elle had welled up when she'd read that letter but it was phoney self-pitying sentiment. How could it be anything else when she didn't know Basil?

She did, however, know the Pink Ribbon Club and she owed them a lot more than a van full of ice cream.

One day out of her life was little enough in return for the kindness, the care they'd given her mother, easing her through her last days. And not just her mother. They'd been there for her grandmother, for three girls whose lives were falling apart, when there was no one else.

She'd always promised herself she would give something back when she had the time, the money to do so, and here she was, being offered the chance to do something positive to help raise funds so that other families could benefit as hers had done.

'Watch out!' Sean said as she stepped back, stumbled into him.

'Sorry.'

'No damage,' he said, sucking on his thumb where the tea had slopped over, drawing attention to his mouth. The crease bracketing one corner. 'Come on,' he said, looking up and catching her. 'I'll introduce you to Rosie.'

She knew what he was doing. It was no doubt what he'd planned from the moment he suggested she sit outside.

This was Geli's stray dog all over again.

'Just look at her, Elle...'

Her sister had known that once she'd seen the poor wretch she wouldn't be able to say no, and Sean was using the same tactics.

Look at this cute pink van. How can you resist?

He didn't wait, but headed for the gate, taking her tea with him. And the garden seemed emptier, flatter without him, as if he was somehow generating the buzzy atmosphere that raised her heart rate in a way that no amount of scrubbing could match.

At the gate he turned back. 'I'll give you the guided tour.'

Boom, boom, boom...

A buzz like an electric charge ran up her arm as he placed a hand at her elbow, supporting her over the worn path as if she didn't manage it all by herself at least twice a day. She should object. Tell him to keep his hands to himself. Except for that she'd have to be able to get her lips, tongue and teeth in a row to form the words. And then make her mouth say them.

Sean, on the other hand, was more likely keeping close contact in case she took the chance to shut and bolt the gate after him. Which was what she should have done. Would have done if she had any sense. But everyone knew that sense wasn't something Amery women were blessed with.

Despite the fact that she hadn't put a foot wrong in the seven years since she'd become the responsible one, she knew that the entire village was watching her. Waiting for the other shoe to drop.

For years they'd held their collective breath whenever the fair arrived in the village and dangerous young men flexed their muscles at the local girls.

They hadn't a clue...

Sean took the keys from his pocket, opened up the front door and reached in. A loud, slightly tinny rendition of 'Greensleeves' filled the air.

'No!' she exclaimed.

Too late. Before he could switch it off, a voice called out, 'You found him, I see.'

She swung around, her heart sinking as she saw Mrs Fisher peering over the fence, her attention fixed not on Rosie, but on the man at her side. The old witch had probably been keeping watch for him ever since yesterday afternoon. The ice cream chime, brief though it had been, had given her all the excuse she needed to dash out and take a second look.

'I asked Elle if she was starting an ice cream round,' she explained to Sean with a little laugh.

'Rosie is a bit too old for that kind of excitement,' he said. 'She's available for events, though. Parties. Weddings.'

Elle glared at him.

He handed her a mug of tea before taking a sip from his own.

'Parties? Well, that is interesting.' Mrs Fisher's eyes were wide as she took in every detail of Sean's appearance, storing it up to pass on, along with the news that he appeared to be very much at home in the Amery kitchen. 'You should put a notice up in the village shop, er...' She paused, waiting for Sean to fill in his name.

'I don't think that will be necessary,' Elle said before he could oblige her.

'You've got plenty of bookings, then?' she pressed.

'More than I can handle,' she assured her, keeping the polite distant smile on her face, the one that long experience had taught her was the only way to blank the busybodies.

'Well, that is good news!' She continued to look hopefully at Sean, but he'd taken the hint and, when it became obvious that neither of them were going to elaborate, the other woman said, 'Well, I must get on.'

'I'll bet you must,' Elle muttered as she watched her scurry up the road.

'Did I miss something?' Sean asked, putting his mug down on the windowsill.

'You might,' she told him, 'but she won't have. Why on earth did you tell her that Rosie was available for parties?'

'Because she is. Basil gave you free rein in his letter and, believe me, it's a lot more fun than being polite to the likes of me at the Blue Boar,' he said.

'No doubt,' she said with feeling, 'but not everyone is as much trouble as you. Or as rude as your girlfriend. And at least I'm guaranteed the minimum wage plus tips. How many bookings are there in Basil's diary?'

'I've no idea. Maybe you shouldn't have been so quick to rubbish the lady's advice about putting up a notice in the village store,' he jibed.

'That's no lady,' she muttered, 'that's Mrs Fisher. And when I said it wouldn't be necessary, it was because by tomorrow everyone within a five mile radius of Longbourne will know that I have an ice cream van parked in my drive and a man making free with my kettle.'

'That constitutes hot news in Longbourne?' he asked curiously.

'The hottest.' She lifted a shoulder, took a swig of the tea he'd brought her. He'd added sugar. She never used it, but maybe he was right about shock because it tasted wonderful. 'The jungle drums will be beating right now and within minutes the postmistress will be marking the date on the calendar. Starting the countdown.'

He frowned.

'Nine,' she prompted. 'Eight, seven…'

He muttered a word that wasn't quite six.

'To be fair,' she elaborated, 'we have history. My mother had a weakness for travelling men. The fact that all three of us have birthdays in late February is not a coincidence.'

He thought about it for a moment. 'You were all conceived in June?'

'He doesn't just make a mean cup of tea, he does mental arithmetic too.'

'No point in making a rubbish one. That was the last of the milk, by the way. I'll run you to the village shop in Rosie if you like. There's nothing like a live appearance to generate publicity.'

'That would give the old biddies a thrill.'

And not just the old biddies. Just the thought of being tucked up alongside him in Rosie sent a ripple of heat that had nothing to do with hot, sweet tea racing recklessly through her veins. And if you were going to get talked about anyway…

'I'm here to serve.'

Oh, yes!

'So what happens in June?' he asked.

She blinked. 'June?' For a moment her brain freewheeled before she managed to get A grip, engage the cogs, start thinking. 'The first week is the highlight of the Longbourne calendar. The only highlight,' she added wryly.

'The fair?'

'I never go myself. I just stand on the sidelines looking at the men putting up the rides, erecting the stalls.'

'Searching for a likeness?' he commented thoughtfully.

No doubt about it, he was good at mental arithmetic. Give him two and two and he came up with a neat four, no problem.

'I know it's stupid,' she said sadly. 'I mean, what would I say? You don't know me but I think you might have met my mother twenty-four years ago?'

'Actually,' he replied, 'I think it's far more likely that some man would look up, see you with the sun shining on your hair and remember a long ago summer interlude with a beautiful woman. Wish he was still young.'

She put the mug down on a low wall before she spilled her tea. Compliments were a rare commodity in her life and that one took her breath away. Then, aware that she was making a prize fool of herself and needing to get a grip, fast, she said, 'No awkward pregnancy or morning sickness to mar the memory for him.'

'What can I say?'

'You don't have to say anything. My mother was no poster woman for safe sex. Not much of an example to her daughters.'

In truth, she suspected that, as far as the village was concerned, Elle had been a real disappointment in terms of being gossip fodder but, with the house to take care of, Gran and two younger sisters to keep on the straight and narrow, as well as having to work to keep them all fed, she hadn't had a lot of time or cash to waste on the temptations of the Longbourne Fair. Temptations of any kind. Her life was on hold for the foreseeable future and the village biddies had shifted their attention to Sorrel once she'd hit puberty. No luck there, either. She was totally focused on her studies—she didn't want to end up like her big sister in a dead end job—to give them anything to gossip about.

But this year Angelica was looking promising. Sixteen was such a dangerous age and, obsessed with Dracula, she'd dyed her hair black, wore the palest make-up she could find and wore scarlet lipstick when she could get away with it.

Not that any age was safe for Amery women, as she'd found out when that Court Summons had arrived just after she'd started her first term at the local college.

Her hair was slipping from an elastic band that had lost its twang. Out of control, a bit like her. She gave it a sharp tug to restore order. Fat chance. Like her day, her week, her life it disintegrated in her hand.

'Drat,' she said as her hair collapsed untidily about her face and shoulders, digging around in her pocket to find another one, coming up empty-handed. 'It really needs cutting.'

'No.' Sean's smile faded as he lifted a handful, letting it run through his fingers. 'Believe me, it really doesn't. It's perfect just the way it is.'

CHAPTER FIVE

The perfect ice cream is like the perfect woman: cool, delicate, subtle, with a flavour that lingers on the tongue.
—Rosie's Diary

IT WAS a gesture of such intimacy that for a moment Elle couldn't think, couldn't breathe. Rooted to the spot, the only movement was the pulse beating in her neck, the rush of something irresistible sweeping through her veins. A weakness in her legs. The aching pull of desire for something that was unknown and yet as familiar as breathing.

As she swayed towards him, drawn like a magnet towards him, Sean let her hair fall. 'Come on,' he said, moving to the front of the van. 'I'll introduce you to Rosie.'

Elle remained where she was, her skin tingling where the back of his fingers had brushed her cheek. And not just on her cheek. Her entire body felt as if it had been switched on and was fizzing with energy.

'Elle,' Sean said with mock formality, 'may I present Rosie? Rosie, this is Elle. She's Basil's great-niece and your new keeper.'

'Sean,' she protested.

'It's you or Granny,' he reminded her.

'That's playing dirty.' She might have already made up her mind to do the Saturday gig at Longbourne Court, give something back to the Pink Ribbon Club, but that was going to be *the* extent of her involvement. Absolutely. Definitely.

'One of you is the registered keeper,' he pointed out. 'Your choice.'

She glared at him, but at least she was back in control of her legs and she was working on her breathing. 'I've got nowhere to keep her,' she pointed out.

'Won't she go in the garage?'

'The generations of junk only leave room for the car and I can't afford to have that towed to the scrapyard,' she told him.

'I'll do that for you,' he said.

'Oh…' She swallowed. Considering the money they'd spent at the garage over the years, they could have offered to do that for them, but she wouldn't ask. It took a stranger to finally offer his help.

A stranger with an agenda, she reminded herself.

'Any more objections?'

There had to be dozens, but right now she couldn't think of a single one and she turned to the van. 'Okay, Rosie,' she said, 'it seems that whether I like it or not I'm all you've got for now, so here's the way it is. Behave yourself or you'll join the rest of our transport. In the scrapyard.'

'A word of advice, Elle,' Sean said. 'Like most females, Rosie usually responds better to gentle handling.'

Something she was sure he knew from personal experience and she kicked one of the white-walled tyres.

He tutted. 'Asking for trouble,' he said with an annoying you-have-been-warned shake of the head that made her want to kick Rosie again.

'I don't need to ask; it comes calling.' Blue-eyed trouble wearing painted-on jeans and a melt-your-bones smile. 'This time driving a pink van,' she added pointedly.

'Trouble is my middle name,' he admitted. 'So? What do you think of her?'

'Honestly?'

'It's usually best, I find.'

'Yes.'

For a moment their eyes locked, her mouth dried and she turned abruptly to Rosie, staring at her with unseeing eyes while she counted her breath—in one-two-three, out one-two-three—until she was capable of rational thought.

'Honestly...' she repeated as she took in the gentle rounded lines. Honestly, she thought that Rosie looked like something out of a children's story book.

Pink and white with a chrome grille and little round head-lamps that gave the impression of a smiley face. The ice cream cones on either side of the roof, like a pair of rabbit ears, added to the illusion.

The Happy Little Ice Cream Van...

Here Comes the Ice Cream Van...

Jingle Goes the Ice Cream Van...

'I think she's very...shiny,' she said before she completely lost it. Rosie had been polished to a gleaming shine and, despite her advanced age, there was not a sign of rust to mar her im-maculate paintwork. Her hair swung over her face as she bent to take a closer look and she tucked it behind her ear. 'Tell me, did you buff her up specially before you came here?' she asked. 'To make her look particularly appealing?'

'I gave her a once-over with the hose and leather to remove the dust,' he admitted, 'but that's all. Basil wields the wax.'

'Something else he expects me to do, no doubt.'

'I think he'd excuse you the waxing, although no one wants an ice cream from a grubby van.'

'I think, whoever he is, he's got more neck than a giraffe,' she retaliated, taking another walk around her.

She wasn't particularly interested in the quality of Rosie's bodywork, but it was a lot easier to concentrate on the problem with Rosie between them. So that she couldn't see his shoulders, his muscular arms, be sandbagged by those blue eyes.

She paused, let her hand rest against the pink, sun-warmed metal of the door for a moment, trying to connect with this unknown great-uncle who had lavished such love on an inanimate object when he had a family living so close by.

Sean joined her. 'Honestly?' he prompted.

'Honestly, I have to admit that she is rather sweet.'

Okay. She was kidding herself. Her concentration was totally shot.

'Do you want to see inside?'

He didn't wait for an answer, but opened the door and stood back and, as Elle stepped up into the serving area, she was instantly assailed by the faint scent of vanilla, the ghost of untold numbers of ices served in Rosie's long lifetime. Echoes of the excited voices of children.

Her own memories of standing with a coin growing hot in her hand as she'd lined up with her mother to buy an ice at the fair. Not from Rosie… The van had been blue, like the sky, and she'd been happy.

Her heart picked up a beat and her mouth smiled all by itself, no effort involved. Fun. The word popped into her head unbidden. This could be fun.

Danger…

It was as if the word *fun* had clanged a warning in her brain. It couldn't be that simple. There was always a catch. Fun had to be paid for.

And with the thought came a brown envelope dose of reality.

On her hands and knees, scrubbing the kitchen floor, she might bear a passing resemblance to Cinderella but, while Basil fitted the role of Baron Hardup and Sean McElroy was undoubtedly a charmer, this was no fairy tale.

'Will you tell me one thing, Sean?' She looked back over her shoulder. 'Exactly how much rent does Basil owe the estate?'

She hadn't been conscious of him smiling until he stopped but at least he didn't pretend not to know what she was talking about.

'You really think I'd put you out to work to pay off Basil's debts?' he asked, his voice perfectly even.

'Man cannot live by ice cream alone and you seem very eager to drum up business,' she pointed out.

For a heartbeat, the blink of an eye, nothing happened. Then Sean's face emptied of expression.

'I'm convinced, Elle. You don't know Basil. And you certainly don't know me. Step down,' he said, moving back to give her room. She didn't move. 'Step down,' he repeated. 'Walk away and we'll forget this ever happened.'

'Just like that?' When he'd gone out of his way to persuade her that she was responsible? 'What happened to your determination to carry out Basil's wishes, even if it meant bothering a confused old lady?'

She wanted him to tell her that he would never have done that. Instead, he said, 'I'll tell Basil the truth. That you weren't interested.'

'And if he doesn't come back?'

'If he doesn't come back it won't matter one way or the other, will it?'

And, in a heartbeat, the connection between them—sizzling, flashing like that dodgy plug ever since she'd opened the front door and seen him standing on the doorstep—overloaded, snapped. Confused, disorientated, Elle felt as if some internal power switch had tripped out and she'd lost her bearings. Momentarily blind. Adrift. In the dark.

Sean McElroy hadn't raged at her for impugning Basil's character—if a gambler who ran away from his problems leaving someone else to pick up the pieces could be said to possess one. Or, worse, for impugning his own.

He hadn't lost his temper or raised his voice. He had simply switched off. Cut the connection.

She did it herself, using a polite mask to keep the Mrs Fishers of this world at bay, but this was something quite different. She had never dropped her guard with anyone before. Not even her immediate family. But her defences had crumbled beneath the spell of Sean's blue eyes.

She'd never understood why her mother had fallen for the

same line over and over. Now she knew how; lost in the grip of a response so powerful that it overrode sense, you could forget everything. To have that withdrawn was like having the rug pulled out from beneath you.

How could a man with such an expressive face, whose smile lit up a room, blank off his emotions so completely? More to the point, why had he needed to learn?

As always, there were more questions than answers. Only one thing was certain. She'd finally woken up sufficiently to question his motives and, having done so, she'd got exactly what she wanted.

Had wanted.

Life would be a whole lot simpler if she stepped away from Rosie, forgot she'd ever heard the name Basil and let Sean drive away, out of her life, so that she could go back to worrying about tedious stuff like paying the bills. Finding the money for Geli's school trip. Coping with her grandmother's total inability to deal with reality.

A lot safer if she could forget the way her pulse had quickened at the touch of his hand on her shoulder, her cheek, her hair. If she could tell him to walk away and leave Rosie to her. That she'd cope without him.

If only it were that simple. The Pink Ribbon Club was relying on Rosie to turn up next Saturday and she was determined to fulfil that obligation. Not just for the PRC but for herself. Stepping outside her small world and doing something positive, meaningful would give her a sense of accomplishment, self-worth.

Which left the small matter of the ice cream machine. While she might be able to work it out for herself, she could just as easily mess it up.

One look at his face, however, warned her that it was going to take a lot more than a simple, *I'm sorry, my mistake* to switch Sean McElroy back on. Soften eyes that were now the blue of case-hardened steel. Tease out the melt-your-bones smile that had been wiped from his face as cleanly as the incoming tide washed lines from the sand.

She took a deep breath. Okay. She'd been dealing with difficult situations since she was a teenager, confronting adults who thought they were dealing with a child. In a situation like that you learned fast not to show weakness, fear.

And, despite his annoyance, she had every right to question what he was getting out of this. He'd dumped and run yesterday, offloading Rosie without a second thought. So why had he come back?

Her hormones might be drowning in drool, but she doubted it was her sex appeal that was the draw. After all, he'd had the possessively glamorous blonde more than willing to keep him warm last night.

'You're right, Sean. I don't know Basil. By his choice,' she reminded him. 'And, right again, I don't know a thing about you either, but that's a two-way deal.' She didn't wait for his reaction, but took a step further into the van, ran her hand over the serving counter, slid back the window, making it her own before she glanced back at him. 'Neither of you knows a thing about me.'

She'd banked on him following her. He didn't fall for it. Didn't move, didn't speak. Simply waited for her to take a look around and then step out again so that he could drive away. And why wouldn't he? She was the one who'd been vehemently insisting that she didn't want to know.

It wasn't true, she discovered.

She wanted to know everything. Wanted to know about her mysterious great-uncle. Wanted to know what her grandmother had done for him. Why he'd been wiped from the family memory. Where he'd been all these years. Wanted to know what made Sean McElroy tick.

No. Scrub that last one.

She examined the stacked up cartons containing cones and the plastic shells used to serve ice cream sundaes.

'Did Basil usually leave all these inside the van?' she asked. Sean didn't answer. She turned to look at him.

'I have no idea,' he finally answered.

'His letter suggests he always intended to send Rosie here.' She shifted the boxes of cones to uncover pallets containing litre cartons of UHT ice cream mix. She poked a hole in the shrink-wrap and removed one to take a closer look. 'You did assume we were expecting her. A mistake anyone might make under the circumstances,' she added mildly, looking down at him through the open window. And prompted a slight frown to add to the tightened jaw.

Content that she'd re-established a connection, even if it was at the frowning end of the spectrum, Elle set the carton down on the serving shelf, leaving him to contemplate the fact that he wasn't infallible while she explored the storage cupboards.

'Generations of my family have lived in Gable End,' she said conversationally, filling the knowledge gap, then blinked at the powerful hit of chocolate as she lifted the lid on a box of flakes. 'Basil must have grown up here.'

She took one, bit into it. Used a finger to catch a crumb of chocolate on her lip, sucked it.

'My great-grandfather, Bernard's father and apparently Basil's too, was a stockbroker,' she went on, continuing to explore the contents of the cupboard. 'Did Basil tell you that?'

'We confined our conversation to the state of Rosie's working parts.'

Mini marshmallows, nuts…

Elle had a distant memory of an ice cream studded with marshmallows, her mother's laughter…

'He was a magistrate, too,' she said. 'And a parish councillor. A pillar of the community.'

'Stiff collar, stiff manners and a stiff upper lip,' he commented with perfect understanding.

Finally, a response to something other than a direct question.

'I couldn't say. I never knew him.' Then, frowning, she

looked up from a box of multicoloured sprinkles. 'Do you have a problem with respectability?'

His response was the slowest of shrugs. She waited and, finally, he said, 'It's nothing but a façade constructed to cover a multitude of sins.'

'You really think that?' she asked, jerked out of her carefully orchestrated build-up of family history to justify her trust issues. Not that they needed justifying, she reminded herself. She had a family to protect and had every right to be cautious.

'I wouldn't say it if I didn't know it to be true,' he said.

'Strange. While you lack the collar, you've got the stiffest lip, the stiffest neck I've ever encountered.'

That caught him off guard. Surprised him. His recovery was swift but she'd cracked the mask.

'Maybe I have a problem with narrow-minded people who see anyone who isn't like them as a threat,' he said. 'Who look the part but don't live it.'

Oh, now that was telling. Did he see himself as an outsider? Why?

'I can go along with that,' she said carefully, 'but certain rules are made for the common good. There are some things you can't take on trust.' She thumbed an imaginary smear off the hygiene certificate fixed to the interior of the van. 'Even Basil understood that.' Then, turning back to the carton of ice cream mix, 'I wonder if they do this in strawberry.'

She knew he was watching her, eyes narrowed, not sure what she was up to. That made two of them. Her common sense genes, the ones she'd inherited from the magistrate, and from Grandpa, were urging her to let it go. Let him go.

But suddenly she wasn't so sure about those respectable citizens any more. The ones she had worked so hard to emulate.

What kind of people cut off a member of their family? Wiped him out of existence?

'Sean?' she prompted, refusing to be ignored.

'Yes, strawberry and chocolate too,' he told her. Voice clipped, determined not to be drawn in.

'But not everyone likes strawberry ice cream, do they?' She raised an eyebrow, inviting his opinion, then, when he didn't offer one, 'Perhaps it would be safer to simply add a few drops of cochineal to the vanilla.'

'Cochineal?'

'It's a natural food colouring. Made from crushed beetles.'

'What are you talking about?'

She didn't rush to answer but put the carton down and turned her attention to the machine, lifting the lid to peer inside, letting her fingers play over the controls.

He said nothing.

She pulled on a lever.

'Lovage Amery,' he warned.

'La, la, la…' she sang, just like her grandmother when she was pretending not to hear. And laughed as, just like that, she discovered how her grandmother had got her nickname.

Sean swore under his breath as he stepped up, grabbed her wrist before she did any damage.

But that was the point of the exercise. To get him inside the van with her. Listening to her. Talking to her.

He'd watched her exploring the interior of the van, reeling him in with her mindless chatter and her come-and-stop-me-if-you-dare exploration of the machinery.

He'd been taken in by the blush, but while she might, impossibly for a grown woman, seem much too innocent for that luscious mouth and gorgeous body, she was nobody's fool.

It had finally occurred to her to challenge Basil's motives in asking for her help. Or, rather, her grandmother's help. Fair enough. He'd be asking questions if some stranger pitched up on his doorstep selling him a story about a long lost relative, burdening him with a high maintenance vehicle and a lot of hard work for little or no reward. Looking for the catch.

But he didn't care what she thought about Basil. Elle had changed *his* motives, *his* probity and, even after all these years, it was like being back in school, taunted with his background. Not one of *us*. Not in the local primary school where his father's title had been the barrier. Not at the expensive boarding school either, where his mother had been the problem. A cold draught on the exposed nerve of tooth.

'Crushed beetles?' he asked as she turned to him, her face all did-I-do-something-wrong? innocent.

Her eyes betrayed her. They glinted with something that matched the unconscious sex appeal. Threw out a reckless challenge that suggested there was someone else hidden inside her head, someone entirely different to the face she showed the world. Which of them, he wondered, would turn up if he did what he'd been thinking about ever since she'd opened the front door yesterday afternoon? If he put his arms around her and kissed her? The outraged innocent? Or the woman he'd glimpsed behind those eyes?

'It's pink food colouring,' she said. 'Completely natural. No E numbers. Pink ices for the Pink Ribbon Club?' she said. 'What do you think?'

He was thinking about her breath against his mouth, the softness of her skin, his fingers sliding through that silky mane of hair...

There were tiny florets of lilac caught up in it, he noticed. He'd watched her from the window as she'd buried her head in the bush and the scent of the flowers mingled with warm skin and the herby tang of shampoo. He wanted to lay his face against her neck and breathe it in.

'I think you'd have to label it unsuitable for vegetarians,' he said, keeping his eyes fixed on the food hygiene certificate. Rules... He had rules about sticking to women who understood that he didn't do emotional attachment. Commitment. Who just wanted to have fun.

'Good point. Pink sprinkles, then?' Her face relaxed into the smile she'd been fighting, lifting the corners of her mouth in careless enticement.

In his head he had rules, but his body was responding on instinct, urging him to make a move. Telling him that she wanted it as much as he did. That if he kissed her it wouldn't just make *his* day. It would make hers, too.

'Pink sprinkles it is,' he managed, hanging onto his concentration by his fingernails. Keeping his eyes level with the top of her head.

That was when he saw the ladybird taking a precipitous walk along a silky strand, the perfect distraction until it slipped and fell, tiny legs waving, no doubt wondering what the heck had just happened.

'Wouldn't it be perfect if you could buy pink chocolate flakes?' she said.

One minute you were minding your own business, quietly milking the greenfly and the next, wham, you were in the dark, your world turned upside down.

Pretty much the way Elle must be feeling right now. Although he was beginning to suspect that her world hadn't been that great to begin with.

'You can get white ones so pink shouldn't be such a stretch. Sean?' she prompted.

'Hold still,' he said, releasing her hand so that he could gently part her hair to set the ladybird free to fly away.

Her forehead puckered in a frown. 'What are you doing?'

'Extracting a real live beetle. If you will stick your head in a bush you must expect to attract the local wildlife.'

It was her cue to squeal. Fling herself into his arms. All she said was, 'Don't hurt it.'

'I'm doing my best, but it's all tangled up. You'll have to come closer.'

'Is it all right?' she asked anxiously, leaning into him.

'Give me a minute,' he muttered. More than a minute because, while she was showing no sign of girly nerves, both he and the ladybird were in a whole heap of trouble.

The bug, being a bug, didn't know it had to follow Elle's example of zen-like calm, keep still and co-operate. Instead, it panicked, getting into deeper trouble as it tried to right itself.

And Sean's hands were beginning to shake so badly that he was only making things worse.

'You were telling me your family history,' he said in an effort to distract himself from the warmth of her breath against his chest. Her breast nestling against his arm. 'Your grandfather,' he prompted. 'Bernard inherited the house?'

'As far as I know.' She looked up. 'The official version of family history is that he was an only child. Did he buy his brother out? I wonder. Or was Basil cut out of the will.' She was shaken by an involuntary shiver that telegraphed itself through his body. Elle was clearly a lot more upset at the discovery that her respectable elders weren't quite what they seemed than she was prepared to say. At least he'd had no illusions to shatter. 'How are you doing?' she asked.

'Can you move a little to the right?' he requested, his voice emerging through cobwebs that seemed to be blocking his throat.

'I barely knew him. My grandfather,' she added as she shifted a little, leaning closer so that more of her was in contact with more of him. 'He wasn't the kind of grandpa who sat you on his knee and read to you. Played Happy Families on a wet Sunday afternoon. I don't think he was a happy man.'

'Maybe he had a guilty conscience,' he suggested.

'Maybe. Would this be easier if we went outside?'

'Just keep still,' he said, putting his arm around her to keep her from moving away just as the ladybird finally got with the plot and crawled onto his finger. 'What happened when he died?'

'Nothing much. He left us all pretty well provided for and being a single mother wasn't that big a deal by then. Although three different fathers did tend to raise eyebrows.'

'Three?'

'I told you,' she said. 'History. We don't look a bit alike. Sorrel has red hair and under the black dye Geli is white blonde.'

While her hair was the colour and shine of the chocolate sauce Basil used on his ices.

'It must have been hard when she died,' he said. 'Your mother.'

'It knocked us all sideways for a long time, but then Gran met someone. Andrew. At least that's what he said his name was. He was charming, well-mannered and he made the world seem a brighter place for a while. It felt like we'd turned a corner. I'd scraped through my exams and had a place in the local college, a future, plans…'

She stopped, taking a moment to gather herself.

'It was all a con, of course.'

Of course.

'He parted Gran from her cash with the ease of a fishmonger filleting a trout, promising her the kind of interest rates that disappeared a decade ago. All very hush-hush, naturally. She was one of the lucky ones but she had to keep it to herself or everyone would pile in. Spoil it.'

'And once he had it all, he disappeared,' Sean finished for her.

At some point during the wind up of her story, the point she'd been trying to make about why she couldn't just trust him, his other arm had found its way around her so that he was holding her close.

'She must have realised pretty quickly, but the first I knew about the whole sorry mess was when I opened the door to a strange man who asked if I was Lovage Amery.' She pulled back her head, looked up into his face. 'I said yes, just as I did to you yesterday, and found myself holding a brown envelope.'

Sean remembered the way she'd avoided taking the one he'd been holding. Putting her hands behind her back.

'Was it a summons?'

'The first of many. Gran had been hiding the final demands from the utilities, the credit card companies, most for cards he'd applied for using her name…'

He muttered something under his breath as he realised what had happened.

'…and of course the letters from the bank. He did a pretty good job of forging her signature to clear out everything she hadn't already handed over. She'd been hoping against hope he'd come back before she had to face up to the truth.'

'At least you managed to hang onto the house,' he said helplessly.

'Only because Grandpa left it in trust for his grandchildren, so it wasn't hers to lose. Gran has the use of it for her lifetime but even if she died it can't be sold until the youngest of us is twenty-one. That's Geli. She's sixteen,' she added, almost as if she was warning him that there was no hope of money coming from that direction—and who could blame her? 'He never knew her, of course. Mum was still expecting Sorrel when he died. But maybe he understood Gran a lot better than we did.'

CHAPTER SIX

Everyone has a price. Mine is ice cream.

—Rosie's Diary

'You take after your grandfather.'

'Do I?' Elle pulled a face. 'I'm sure you mean that kindly, but if you'd known him you'd understand that's not a compliment.'

'I just meant that you're the responsible one. The one who worries about money. Takes care of everything. Everyone.'

Elle closed her eyes, remembering the embarrassment of the bailiff removing paintings, Great-Grandma's jewellery— Andrew had packed her grandmother's jewellery in his overnight case when he'd left 'for a business meeting'. The wedding china, family silver, antique furniture had all gone. Anything that would raise hard cash until all the debts had been paid.

They were fortunate there had been so much, but it hadn't felt like it at the time. When everyone stopped talking as she walked into the village shop each Monday morning to collect the child allowance from the post office after Gran had taken to her bed. Sticking her fingers in her ears, figuratively speaking, and la-la-ing until it had all gone away.

It had been the only cash coming in until she'd surrendered her place in college for a minimum wage job at the Blue Boar. Cleaning, working in the kitchen, before Freddy had moved her into the restaurant.

It had been the only job within walking distance from home. They hadn't been able to afford bus fares or petrol for the car and she had to be near enough to get home if her grandmother needed her.

She knew now that Social Services would have helped but at the time she'd been so afraid that, with her grandmother turning her face to the wall, they would have taken Sorrel and Geli into care if she'd asked for help.

'Responsibility wasn't a choice, Sean.'

'No.' Then, again, 'No. Look, don't bother your head about all this,' he said, holding her close. 'I'll keep Rosie until Basil turns up. And I'll take care of Saturday too.'

'So...what?' She leaned back to look him full in the face, her hands on his chest. 'Are you saying that you don't need me after all?'

Oh, no, he wasn't saying that. Holding her this way was stirring up the kind of basic need that had nothing to do with serving ice cream and if he didn't let her go, right now, she'd know it too.

The difference being that he understood that it was no more than a temporary, self-serving need. Nothing more than a passing attraction. He only did 'passing'; he had no understanding of any other kind of relationship.

Even while his body was demanding he go for it, his head knew that she wasn't kind of girl to indulge in a light-hearted, no-strings, bed-and-breakfast flirtation; the kind a man could walk away from with a clear conscience.

Elle had suffered enough hurt in her short life and while she would, inevitably, get her heart broken sooner or later, he would not be the one responsible for that.

'It's Basil who needs you,' he said, mentally distancing himself from her. 'But you're right, why should you put yourself out for a man you don't know, have never met? Who has never done a thing for you?'

'It's a mystery,' she said. 'As inexplicable as why he came to us for help after forty years of silence. Any ideas about that?'

'None whatever,' he said. 'But then family is not my specialist subject.'

'Mine either, it would seem. But I do know that what you have you should hold on to. Love them, keep them safe, whatever they do.'

And there it was. Right there. The reason he needed to step away. If he hadn't recognised her vulnerability within minutes of setting eyes on her, her belief in the importance of family, all the things he despised, would have sent up the kind of warning flares that a man who believed in nothing, no one, would do well to heed.

'Like your grandfather. Like you,' he said.

Take your hands off her now, McElroy.

'Maybe. How's the ladybird doing?' she asked.

'She gave up on me and rescued herself some time ago,' he admitted.

Step back…

'Did she?' She smiled. 'Well, good for her. She did a good job holding your attention while I explained why I have trust issues.'

'You had me at crushed beetles,' he admitted.

She smiled. 'I knew that would do it.'

Let her go…

'Actually,' he said, 'I think you're right about that. I'll stick with the pink sprinkles.'

'What makes you think you've got a say in the matter?' she asked. 'Rosie is mine, remember? It's my name on the logbook.'

'Are you telling me that you're going to keep her?'

'*You* had *me* at the Pink Ribbon Club, Sean. Just for Saturday. Lavender's girls have a debt to pay them. All I need from you is a quick tutorial.'

That wicked little come-and-get-me glint was back in her eyes now that she'd broken down the barrier he'd instinctively thrown up. It was the look of a woman who had won hands down and left him out for the count. But the bell hadn't rung yet.

His legs had ignored him, his hands were still resting just below her shoulder blades keeping her close, his thighs against her hips, and this time he'd didn't waste time asking himself which woman would show up if he kissed her.

He had to know.

Her eyes widened slightly as his mouth slowly descended, giving her all the time in the world to say no, do what he'd be unable to do and step back.

Her lips did part, as if she might say something, but all that emerged was a little quiver of breath, warm, faintly chocolatey, mingling with his own. Fizzing through his blood, intoxicating as vintage champagne, and he was within a hair's breadth of going to hell in a handcart when a crunch on the gravel, a loud, 'It's still here!' warned them that they were no longer alone.

'Geli…'

The blush was in full working order and he didn't need to send frantic instructions to his legs to move before he did something stupid. Elle did it for him, springing back as if she'd been caught with her hand in the till.

'I wasn't expecting you back so soon,' she said to her sister.

'Obviously.'

Sarcasm as only a teenager could do it.

Elle shut the serving window, not looking at Sean as she jumped down, her wobbly legs buckling as she hit the gravel in her eagerness to put some distance between herself and temptation.

As she put some stiffeners into her knees, she couldn't decide whether she was furious with her sister for turning up just as she was about to taste heaven, or grateful that she'd been saved from the biggest mistake in her life.

A quick tutorial…

What had she been thinking?

Thinking? That was joke.

For a moment back there it had been the gallopers, the waltzer, the big wheel, all the fun of the fair rolled into one and she'd been gone, with only one thought in her head. The one that confirmed she was her mother's daughter.

Wham, bang, thank you, ma'am.

'So are you going to tell me why we have an ice cream van parked in the drive?' Geli demanded.

Her youngest sister was definitely *not* going to be impressed by anything so defiantly pink and white invading her space. And, having glared at Rosie, she turned her attention to Sean.

'And who *is* he?'

Beneath the aggression, Elle recognised fear. Geli's body was maturing but, despite the emerging curves, she was still a child who'd never had a father and had lost her mother at a tragically early age.

Before she could reassure her, Sorrel walked through the gate, their grandmother at her side.

For a moment Elle held her breath, but her grandmother just smiled. 'Are we going to have ice cream?' she asked. 'How lovely. Can I have chocolate sauce?'

Sean glanced at her, clearly surprised that her grandmother hadn't recognised him, unfamiliar with Lally's ability to completely block out anything she didn't want to remember.

'Not just now, Gran. Sean is busy and I have to go to work.'

'Sean?'

'Sean McElroy,' he said, going with it and introducing himself before turning to her sisters. 'And you must be Sorrel?'

Sorrel threw Elle an amused look of approval. 'I'm Sorrel Amery, and this is Geli,' she said, hand outstretched. Despite being five years younger than Elle, Sorrel had the galling ability to appear the most adult of all of them. She was taking a degree in business studies and it was her stated intention to be a millionaire by the time she was twenty-five. She already acted and dressed the part.

Geli glared at Sorrel. 'My name is Angelica,' she said, which wasn't promising. She only ever used her full name when she was in the kind of mood that meant trouble. 'And we've already met.'

'How was church this morning?' Elle asked quickly before this conversation could develop into something her grandmother couldn't deal with.

'Oh, the sermon just went on and on so I left the vicar to it and went to find Sorrel,' Gran said.

'But she was supposed to be working!' Elle tried not to sound as exasperated as she felt. Freddy had given Sorrel permission to use the free Wi-Fi provided for the bed and breakfast businessmen but only at the weekend when they weren't busy. He certainly wouldn't appreciate her family turning up en masse.

'I didn't get in her way. I just sat and read all the lovely free newspapers in the lounge while she downloaded stuff from the Internet.'

Elle groaned. 'You'll get me the sack.'

'Oh, please.' Sorrel rolled her eyes. 'Freddy is never going to fire you; he's too desperate to get into your knickers.'

'No, no, no!' Geli declared, covering her ears with her hands. 'I'm too young to have that picture in my head.'

'Quite right, Geli. Don't be vulgar, Sorrel.' Gran patted her hair. 'Mr Frederickson was very kind. He brought us coffee and muffins and stayed to chat with me while Sorrel was busy. He's very fond of you, Elle.'

Geli snorted.

'He appreciates how hard you work, and wants to promote you to assistant manager,' Gran told her gleefully.

'I know, but I can't take the job.' A promotion would mean long hours with no chance to switch and swap shifts. And while the money would be more, she'd lose her tips. 'Now, if he offered me an extra fifty pence an hour,' she said, determined to turn the conversation away from any interest Freddy had in her knickers. Like Geli, the image was not something she wanted in her head. 'Well, that would be very welcome.'

'No such luck,' Sorrel said. 'He was just trying to make me feel guilty before he offered me a job.'

He certainly hadn't wasted any time. 'You don't need a job. I want you to stick to your college work so that you can keep me in my old age,' Elle said lightly.

'No nuts with the ice cream, young man,' her grandmother said, so quickly that if Elle didn't know better she might have imagined Gran was feeling guilty about Elle's lost opportunities. Then, taking Sorrel's arm, 'Let's go and have another cup of coffee. Elle never makes any these days. I'd forgotten how much I enjoyed it.'

Unfortunately, Geli didn't follow them.

'You know that Freddy was just plying Gran with coffee and cake so that he could pump her about what you do in your spare time?'

'Geli—'

'He wants to be sure you aren't spending it with some fit bloke. If he hears that you've been flirting with the ice cream man,' she said, giving Sean a flint-eyed stare, 'you can kiss your job goodbye.'

'Don't be silly,' Elle said uncomfortably, unwilling to get into any conversation that involved the word kissing—not when she could almost taste Sean on her lips. 'I thought you were meeting up with some friends from school and going into Maybridge this morning,' she said, dragging her mind back to reality.

'They decided to go to the multiplex in Melchester. Apparently, they've opened a new burger bar. Yuck, yuck, yuck.'

'Geli…Angelica…is a vegetarian.' Elle finally risked a glance at Sean.

'Really? It's a good thing you abandoned the crushed beetles option, then,' he said, his face perfectly straight.

Geli looked at him, looked at her, then said, 'Too weird. I'm going to get something to eat.'

'Geli—'

'What!'

'There's no milk,' Elle reminded her.

'Don't blame me!'

'Or bread.'

She sighed dramatically, then flounced off towards the village.

'Is it always like this?' Sean asked.

'Just an average day at Gable End.' Apart from Rosie. Long lost uncles. And a kiss that was no more than a breath on her lips.

'I'd better go,' Sean said. 'I've already got you into enough trouble without making you late for work.'

'Don't take any notice of Geli. I've worked for Freddy for seven years.'

'He's a patient man.'

'Patient?'

'Although you would have been rather young for him when you first started. What is he? Forty? Forty-five?'

Her cheeks heated up as she realised what he meant. 'No, Freddy's not interested in me in that way. It's just Sorrel's idea of a joke.'

His eyebrows barely moved. 'If you say so,' he said, looking not at her, but at Rosie. 'I never did get around to showing you how the ice cream machine works.'

Maybe not, but he'd come very close to showing her plenty of other things. With her whole-hearted co-operation.

Not that he seemed in any great hurry to resume the lesson where they'd left off—touching close, lips a murmur apart. And that was a Good Thing, she told herself.

She might not have entirely escaped her mother's live-now pay-later nature, but that didn't mean she had to follow her example and lose her head over the first man to make her heart, and just about everything else, go boom.

'There's no time now. Save it for Saturday,' she said.

'Saturday?'

'I'm sorry,' she said, arranging her face in a faintly puzzled frown, 'but didn't you volunteer to be in charge of the sprinkles?'

'Did I?' And there it was again. The barely-there smile that went straight to her knees.

'And afterwards you can take Rosie back to Haughton Manor and tuck her up in your barn until Basil turns up,' she added, making an effort to be sensible.

Something else he'd volunteered to do before they'd both forgotten about Rosie, ice cream, Basil...

'Oh, no! The letter!'

Sean should have been feeling only one emotion as he watched Elle race back down the path, long legs, long hair flying, to retrieve Basil's letter before her grandmother picked it up and read it.

Relief.

He'd come within a gnat's whisker of losing control, but Elle had just given him a get-out-of-jail-free card and it was long past time to remove himself from the temptation of those luscious lips, the danger of entanglement in a situation that should have a dedicated commitment-phobe running a mile.

'Saturday it is, then,' he said to no one in particular as he shut Rosie's door, locked up, gave her a little pat. 'I'll come over early and make sure you behave yourself.'

And he tried not to think about spending an afternoon in close confinement with Elle. The quick tutorial he'd promised her. Or the possessive way the guy who ran the Blue Boar had touched her arm.

Elle skidded to a stop in the doorway. Sorrel was standing by the table reading Basil's letter.

'Where's Gran?' Elle asked.

'Washing her hands. Tidying her hair. Getting ready for that "nice young man with the ice cream",' Sorrel added, patting her hair, mimicking her grandmother perfectly.

'There is no ice cream. At least not today.' She had half

expected Sean to follow her, but she was the one who'd said there was no time. 'Sean's gone.'

'Shame. I hoped you were getting serious attention from someone a little more appealing than Freddy,' her sister teased.

'I've locked up.'

Elle had sensed Sean's presence a fraction of a second before he spoke. A subtle change in the light, the widening in Sorrel's eyes, a charge in the air that had the fine hairs on her skin springing to attention...

Sean put Rosie's keys on the kitchen table. 'I'll come back later with the trailer and pick up the car.'

'Oh, yes. Of course.' She forgotten all about his promise to take their car to the scrapyard. 'I won't be here, but Sorrel...' her beautiful, elegant sister, the one in control of her hair, her figure, her life, if not her tongue '...will be here if you need a hand.'

'If you give me the keys, I won't have to bother anyone,' he said.

'Of course.' Elle took them from the key cupboard and dropped them into his palm, taking care not to touch him. 'I'll leave the garage door unlocked.'

'I'm not sure how much I can get for it,' he warned.

'Get for it? I was told I'd have to pay to have it towed to the scrapyard.'

'When you need towing you're in a buyer's market. I'll take a look at what needs doing, make a few calls. It's possible you'd do better advertising it on the Internet,' he told her.

'I didn't expect you to go to all that trouble,' Elle protested.

'Who'd buy it?' Sorrel asked at the same time.

He looked up. 'You'd be surprised,' he said, answering her sister. Then, in the slightly awkward silence that followed, 'I'll be here at about eleven on Saturday, if that's okay? It should give us plenty of time to run through everything before we go.'

'Thanks.'

'Tell your grandmother she can have all the ice cream she can eat then.'

'She'll enjoy that,' Elle said.

He nodded and was gone.

Elle turned on her sister, hands to her cheeks. 'Did he hear?'

'Does it matter?' she asked.

'"Getting serious attention?" Could you have made me sound more desperate?'

'Elle, you *are* desperate. If you're not careful, you'll succumb to Freddy out of sheer frustration.'

'Don't...' She took a deep breath. 'Just don't...'

'Only saying. You need to grab that one while he's available.'

'He's not,' she said shortly. He might have come close to kissing her just now but he'd been firmly attached to the linen-clad blonde last night. Or she'd been firmly attached to him. Which amounted to the same thing. She should be grateful to Geli for turning up when she had.

Give her a little time and she would be.

'But—'

'The subject is closed,' Elle announced firmly.

'Okay. But you could have cut the tension in here just now with a knife,' Sorrel remarked.

'C-L-O-S-'

'Okay, okay, okay.' Her sister held up the letter. 'Tell me about Basil.'

Grateful for the change of subject, Elle took the letter from her, giving her a quick rundown on the story so far as she folded it up and put it back in the brown envelope, along with the documents and diary.

'I'll do some digging on the 'net. See what I can find out,' Sorrel said, beating her to the top of the range cellphone and switching it on.

'I think you should stay away from the Blue Boar for a while. Freddy wasn't joking about offering you a job,' Elle warned.

'I know. He gave me the whole fitting-around-college-work, great-tips hard sell this morning. I told him I'd think about it. I could do with a new laptop,' she mused.

No…

'I'll see what I can do,' Elle said. Maybe there was something in the attic that had been overlooked. That she could sell. 'Just concentrate on college, get a good degree. When you're a millionaire you can run this family. Meanwhile, will you turn off that phone and give it to me?'

'I'm sorry?'

Not half as sorry as she was, Elle thought, holding out her hand. Sorrel did not hand over the phone. 'What?' Elle asked.

'I'm eighteen, Elle. An adult.'

'You're a student—'

'I'm old enough to vote, fight for my country, buy a bottle of wine and drink it if I want to. I don't want to "run this family", but I will run my own life,' Sorrel insisted.

'How?' Elle demanded. 'You don't even know how to use an iron!'

'It's not rocket science.'

For a moment the room silently vibrated with years of unspoken resentment. Elle's dreams and thwarted ambitions, pushed aside while she stepped up to keep them together. A family.

'No…' Elle took a deep, shuddering breath. 'You don't understand,' she said. 'I just don't want you to be…'

'What? Like you?'

'That would be a woman with no qualifications, no career.' No dream to inspire her. Just living from week to week, from hand to mouth, holding everything together. 'Point made, I think.'

'Elle…' Sorrel shook her head. 'I could never be you. You saved us from being put into care, saved Gran from completely losing her marbles. But maybe it's time to think about saving yourself now.'

'I don't need saving,' she insisted. Perhaps a little bit too fiercely, too defensively. 'But I'll think about it. If you'll forget about working at the Blue Boar.'

'Oh, please. If I want a job, I can do better than skivvying for Freddy.' Elle was still struggling to catch her breath when she added, 'In fact, with a phone like this, I'd never have to go near the place again. And you read Basil's letter. He's handed everything over to us. Asked us to take care of things'

'Sorrel…'

'He's got messages. Mostly people asking him to give them a ring,' she said, flicking through them. 'You can't ignore them.'

'Can't I?' Elle said dryly.

'Oh, no, this is different. "Change in schedule."' she read. '"Need van on Tuesday. Upper Haughton location. Eight a.m. Confirm. KS."' She looked up. 'What do you think that means?'

'I've no idea.'

'I could call him and find out?' she offered.

'If you want to be useful, Sorrel,' Elle snapped, taking the phone out of her hand and switching it off, 'prove how adult you are, you can start by organising some lunch for Geli and Gran.'

Sean wasted no time going back with the trailer to pick up Elle's old crock while she was at work.

Geli came out, standing pointedly, arms crossed, keeping an eye on him. A couple of neighbours walked slowly past, lingering by the gate. He kept his head down, his mouth shut and wished he'd waited until later. When Elle was home.

What better way to spend a Sunday afternoon than making ice cream? Maybe he could have persuaded her to take a walk by the river. They could have had a drink at the pub down by the lock. They might even have finished that kiss…

'Do you want me to drive Rosie into the garage?' he asked Geli.

'Did Elle ask you to?'

'No.'

She shrugged, walked away.

He took a deep breath and told himself that Saturday was quite soon enough.

CHAPTER SEVEN

If your ice cream melts, you're eating it too slowly.
—Rosie's Diary

ELLE found Monday a mixed sort of day. It was her day off, which meant she didn't have to be on her feet for hours, a smile on her face no matter what.

On the downside, it was the day she tackled the business end of life. Paid bills. Dealt with 'stuff'. She didn't enjoy it but, having lived with the results of her grandmother sticking her head in the sand and not dealing with it, she never put it off.

First thing every Monday morning, she holed up in the little office she'd made for herself in a bedroom which, back in the days when the Amery name was respected, had been the quarters of a live-in maid. At her desk, she could pretend that she was running her own business. Nothing huge. She'd never had her sister's ambition. But doing the accounts, balancing the books, planning menus, shopping lists, she could, for an hour a week, lose herself.

Today, thanks to Great-Uncle Basil, there was more 'stuff' than usual. Messages to deal with. Appointments to cancel. No time for dreaming.

Having balanced the weekly accounts, checking every detail to make sure that nothing had been overlooked, she picked up the bells-and-whistles phone that had caught Sorrel's eye, turned it on and started with the most urgent of the messages.

'Basil?' a hard male voice snapped before she could speak. 'Where have you been?'

'Actually, I'm not Basil,' Elle said. 'My name is Lovage Amery...' it had to be the first time she'd voluntarily used the name but it had a rather more authoritative ring to it than Elle '...and I'm responding to a message left on his phone. Who am I speaking to?'

Always get a name. Make a note of any phone call. Confirm the relevant points in writing. Hard-learned lessons.

'Sutherland. Sutherland Productions,' he said impatiently. She wrote it down. 'Tell Basil I need the van in Upper Haughton at eight o'clock on Tuesday morning. We've got to shoot these outdoor scenes while the weather holds.'

Scenes?

'I'm sorry, Mr Sutherland. Basil has been called away and he won't be available—'

'What do you mean, called away? Who are you?'

'Lovage Amery,' she repeated.

'You're what? His wife, daughter?'

'Niece.' Allegedly.

'Well, Lovage, here's the bottom line. Your uncle signed a contract with my production company. What's more, he took a deposit.'

Her heart missed a beat. 'But he's not here,' she said, doing her best to keep calm. 'He's away on business.'

'Did he take the van with him?'

'Well, no—'

'Then what's the problem? The contract's for the van, a driver and a full load of ice cream. Just make sure it's in Upper Haughton at eight o'clock tomorrow morning.'

'But you don't understand—'

'No, love, *you* don't understand. If the van's not there, on time, ready to go on Tuesday morning, he's going to be responsible for all costs involved in finding a replacement.'

Elle felt the bottom fall out of her stomach. 'Costs?'

'The film crew, the actors on standby and if I lose the weather—'

Actors? What on earth had Basil got her into?

'That won't be necessary,' she said quickly. 'I'll be there.'

'Don't be late.'

'Can you tell me how long it's likely to take?' she said quickly before he hung up.

'I've booked the van for the whole day, but an hour should do it, love,' he said, and then she was listening to the dialling tone.

Elle put down the phone and said, '*Lovage*. It's *Lovage*.' Then she tucked her hands beneath her arms to stop them shaking.

Her first call and already she was being threatened with the law by some bully of a man Basil had signed a contract with. Taken money from. Who called her 'love'.

And there were dozens of messages…

She made it to the bathroom before she threw up, sank down onto the floor, head on her knees, arms around her legs, shivering.

'Elle…?'

She gathered herself, looked up, saw the fear in her grand-mother's eyes.

'It's okay, Gran. Nothing to worry about.'

'Really?'

'Really,' she said, pushing herself to her feet. Her legs still felt wobbly hollow, but she managed a smile. 'Just something I ate. I'm feeling much better now.'

Angry was better than sick. And she was very angry.

Angry with Sean, who'd mesmerised her with those blue eyes. Even when she doubted him, doubted Basil, she'd fallen under his spell.

Angry with herself for bothering to explain her trust issues as if she was in the wrong for doubting him, instead of sticking with her instincts, questioning his motives.

Angry that she'd allowed sentiment to override her natural

caution. Or was it simply lust turning her brain to mush? A genetic flaw...

It took her nearly an hour to return calls, check the diary for the next couple of months. Follow up bookings. And when she was done she had a list of dates, places, names and phone numbers of more than a dozen people who Basil had taken money from. Who expected Rosie to turn up and do her stuff. Seven birthday parties, not all of them for children, a silver wedding anniversary, a hen night, a wedding, a company party, a retirement and the film company.

So much *'fun'*.

Not.

Just a logistical nightmare to fit in around her working schedule.

As if that hadn't been enough, the post had brought Rosie's new logbook, proving that this hadn't been a spur of the moment thing.

It would have taken the licensing authority a minimum of a week to turn that around.

Basil had planned this. He'd taken deposits to fund his flight and now either she, or her grandmother, was Rosie's registered keeper. It made no difference. Elle, as always, was the one who'd have to deal with the fallout.

'Thanks! Thanks a bunch!'

Sean was looking at proposals for the new treetop walk laid out on the map table when Elle burst into his office.

Her cheeks were flushed, her hair looked as if she'd been combing it with a pencil—or maybe a pen since she appeared to have a streak of ink at her temple—and her hazel eyes were blazing with golden sparks that lit up his office like the sun coming out on a dull day.

'Lovage...' The name suited her so much better than the bland 'Elle'. Felt so right on his tongue.

A seething little noise escaped her lips. 'Don't you dare "Lovage" me. I am Elle. Elle for livid.'

'I'm sorry, Sean.' Jess, the estate secretary, hurried in after her but he shook his head, waved her off. She shrugged and left the room.

The surveyor, avoiding his eyes, rolled up his drawings. 'I'll take a look at this and get back to you later in the week, Sean,' he said, visibly smirking as he shut the door on his way out.

Not surprising. She looked like a brown hen he'd kept as a boy, her feathers ruffled up when the cockerel had taken liberties.

He fought the smile. She was mad enough already.

'Problem?' he asked.

'You could say that. I've got a television producer threatening to sue me if I don't turn up tomorrow on set with a full load of ice cream. Apparently, Basil not only signed a contract, he took a deposit,' she threw at him.

Any desire to laugh left him. He'd stood bail for the man's character and he'd let them both down.

'It's not the only one.' She leaned against the map table, as if standing up was suddenly too much effort, and he turned a chair, took her arm and eased her into it. 'I've spent half the morning going through his messages, his diary,' she said, looking up at him. 'He's taken deposits for at least a dozen other events and while no one else, apart from the bride, is threatening to sue, they do all want Rosie, or their money back.'

He could have said a dozen things but while most of them would have made him feel better, none of them would have been of any use to Lovage.

'Well, that explains why he didn't leave her with me,' he said grimly.

'Does it? What difference would it have made?' she asked wanly.

'I'd have told them to sue.'

She swallowed, even paler now. 'I can't do that.'

No. He'd got the message. Loud and clear. Basil was family and, while he might be a liability, he was *her* liability. Family was something to be cherished, protected.

It wasn't something he'd ever encountered on a personal level—he'd just been a problem. One that he'd had to solve in his own way.

'You didn't sign the contracts,' he pointed out.

'Maybe not and, to be honest, I'm not quite sure how I stand legally with everyone else but the film company contracted for Rosie. And she's now officially registered to me.'

'Would you like me to speak to them?'

She shook her head. 'The film producer isn't going to make my Christmas card list but where else is he going to get another Rosie at such short notice? It's just an hour of my time.'

'If you say so. What about the rest of the bookings?'

'I don't have the money to pay back the deposits,' she said. 'And the bride cried.'

'I'll bet she did,' he muttered.

'No... When her husband-to-be bought ice creams on their first date he gave her his chocolate flake. She knew right then and there that he was the one and only,' she explained.

'He probably doesn't like chocolate.'

'Sean!'

'Sorry.'

'Anyway, she wants to give him hers. It's to be a surprise. At their wedding,' she said.

'And I'll bet you cried when she told you that,' he said knowingly, folding himself up in front of her so that she didn't have to look up.

'No... Yes... Stupid.' She blinked, close to tears now, and he took her hands in his. They felt ridiculously small and they were shaking. And why wouldn't they? She'd been dumped on, threatened and been made responsible for fulfilling Basil's promises. Or paying back the deposits he'd taken.

And Sean had been an unwitting accessory.

Grasping her hands tightly to hold them steady, to reassure her that he wasn't going to abandon her to deal with this on her own, he said, 'Not stupid.' It wouldn't have done it for him, but he appeared to be in a minority of one when it came to the prospect of happy ever after. 'It's her big day and if she wants an ice cream van to make it perfect then she must have it. Just tell me what I can do.'

'Find Basil?' She raised long dark lashes. They were clumped together with the tears she hadn't been able to hold back and he lifted a thumb to wipe away one that had escaped, his hand lingering to cradle her cheek.

'I'll do my best,' he promised, 'but he could be anywhere.'

'Probably not in a duck pond, though,' she said, her mouth tucking up at the corners, a precursor to a smile.

'Probably not,' he agreed wryly. 'Did you have any luck with finding out what RSG means?'

She shook her head. 'I did wonder if it might be short for some casino where they were holding a high stakes game?'

'We seem to be thinking along the same lines,' he said. 'I'm beginning to have some sympathy with your grandfather cutting Basil out of his life.'

'He doesn't need your sympathy and neither do I,' she said. 'What I *do* need is a lesson in how to run the ice cream machine. It won't wait until Saturday.'

'That's why you're here?' Sean asked. Not to yell at him for getting her involved. Just to ask for his help?

'I'm sorry but your number isn't listed so I had to come and find you. And you're right, Rosie is cranky, at least until I got the hang of her.'

'I said she had her moods, but you're right, cranky probably is nearer. But I don't understand. I put my number on the message I left at the Blue Boar.'

Elle shrugged. 'I asked this morning, but no one could find it.'

'But I gave it to…' He shook his head.

'Who?' she demanded.

'Your boss.' He'd written a brief apology, along with his phone number, on one of the pile of paper napkins brought to mop up the spillage. 'He probably thought I was trying to pick you up.'

'Probably,' she agreed. 'I've worked there since I was eighteen. He still thinks of me as a kid needing to be protected.'

'Does he? I'd have said Sorrel was nearer the mark.'

'No,' she denied, much too quickly, a hot blush searing her cheeks.

'Well, you know best,' he said shortly, rising to his feet. 'Come on. Let's get out of here.'

As she got to her feet, he ushered her through the door. 'I'll be out of the office for an hour or two, Jess,' he said as he passed her door.

Elle stopped. 'I'm so sorry. I don't know what you must think of me,' she said to his secretary.

'Don't worry about it.' His secretary gave her a knowing look. 'I'm sure you had good cause.'

Elle turned to him. 'I barged into a meeting, didn't I? I didn't think. I was just so angry.'

'Jess is right. You had good cause,' he said, but she was frowning.

'I thought you were a mechanic?'

'I'm a bit of a jack of all trades,' he said evasively.

Jess's eyebrows rose slightly, but all she said was, 'Don't forget that you've got a meeting with Sir Henry at one.'

He checked his watch and turned to Elle. 'Did you come in Rosie?'

'It seemed like a good idea. Since I don't have an ice cream machine on my bike,' she replied, making a brave stab at sarcasm, which was a relief. Reproach he could cope with. Tears were something else. It also meant that he didn't have to go to Longbourne.

'It shouldn't be a problem,' he told Jess, 'but if he turns up before I get back—'

'I'll tell him that you were called away on a matter of urgency on the far side of the estate.'

'The truth, the whole truth and nothing but the truth,' he assured her, before pushing open the door to the courtyard where the staff vehicles—and Rosie—were parked. 'Actually, Basil has got one of those.'

Elle frowned. 'What?'

'A bike with an ice cream cabinet fixed to the front. The precursor of the ice cream van. He's been cleaning it up, getting it back into working order.' He risked a smile. 'He's still got some way to go.'

She leaned against Rosie's door. 'You know what, Sean?' she said, trying to match his smile but having a little trouble controlling her bottom lip. It took all his willpower not to take possession of it, still it with his tongue, make her forget all about her terrible morning. Forget everything. 'That's the first piece of good news I've had today.'

'Well, let's build on that,' he said briskly. She hadn't come here to pick up where they'd left off in the vanilla-scented interior of Basil's van. She wasn't looking for comfort either. Not the only kind he was capable of. She'd come for practical help.

Time, he could give her.

He'd have offered her the cash to pay back the deposits that Basil had taken if he'd thought for a minute that she'd take it. But he had seen enough of Lovage Amery to know that wasn't the way she did things. He wasn't going to assuage his guilt for getting her into this mess that easily.

She was going to honour Basil's commitments come hell or high water and if Basil Amery had walked into the yard at that moment Sean would have been hard pressed not to flatten him.

'Shall I drive?' he offered.

'Where are we going?'

'Somewhere we won't have an audience lining up for handouts the minute we start up the machine.'

Elle would normally have insisted she was capable of driving anything, anywhere, but she was still shaking. Not with rage, this time. This was far worse.

She couldn't shout at Basil, and kicking Rosie didn't help.

Sean had been the only person for her to yell at but, infuriatingly, he didn't have a listed number and she hadn't been able to pick up the phone and demand that he come to Gable End.

Instead, she'd struggled for ten minutes to start a very reluctant Rosie—who was undoubtedly bearing a grudge for that kick—and then driven the big van with unfamiliar gears through the narrow, winding lanes with impatient drivers hooting and gesturing furiously as she'd held them up. And there'd been no seat belt.

She didn't know where Sean lived on the estate, or how to find him. She'd had to stop at the main entrance and ask at the gate, where they'd directed her to the main office. More time wasted.

By the time she'd parked behind the wing that housed the main office, caught a glimpse of him through a window looking oh, so relaxed, she'd been about ready to explode. She'd waved off the woman who'd tried to stop her, storming into the office, but then he'd turned, looked up, a smile lighting up his eyes as if he was truly pleased to see her. Said her name with that whisper-soft drawl.

Not Elle, but *Lovage*.

He was the only person who'd ever called her that and for a moment, no more than a heartbeat, she hadn't been able to think.

She'd gathered herself again, almost immediately, but she hadn't been able to sustain her righteous anger. Not when he'd folded himself up before her, taken her hands so tightly in his, asked her what he could do to help. She'd just spilled it all out. She'd very nearly made a total fool of herself when she was telling him about the young bride. The girl had been so sweet, so in love. Of course Elle had cried…

And just now, when he'd stopped beside her, all she wanted to do was lean into his strength, for once let someone else take the burden.

But it wasn't Sean's problem. He'd simply delivered Rosie

as requested. She would rearrange her shifts as necessary. Get it done. Move on.

'Is it okay for you to just leave like this?' she asked.

'Don't worry, I won't get the sack if the boss hears I'm hanging out with the ice cream girl in office hours,' he assured her, unlocking the door, following her up into the cab. 'Knowing Henry, he'd just want to come and check you out for himself.'

Rosie started for Sean first time. No surprise there; Elle was pretty sure everything he touched started first time, including her.

They sped through the narrow, winding private lanes of the estate that visitors never saw before pulling into the parking area in front of a big old barn surrounded by a wild flower meadow. But not the workaday barn she'd imagined when he'd told her where Basil garaged Rosie.

One end had a pair of high double doors, sure enough, but two-thirds of it had been converted into a stunning home, with high windows looking out across the river. The kind of home that was often featured in upmarket homes and gardens magazines.

'Okay. First things first,' Sean said, wasting no time in heading for the business end of the van. 'The generator. It powers the lights, the freezer for the lollies and the ice cream machine.'

She watched while he switched it on, then took *Rosie's Diary* from her bag, carefully listing each stage of the procedure in the notes section at the back.

'I haven't got any lollies.'

'I imagine Basil picks up a supply from the cash and carry before each gig. You have to take them out when you've finished and keep them in a freezer, so you don't want to buy more than you need for immediate use.'

'Right.'

She started a second list. Lollies. She needed to count the stock she had. Would she have enough for all the bookings Basil had made?

Sean switched off the generator. 'Okay, now you try.'

She started it, following her notes to make sure she hadn't missed anything. It wasn't difficult, but he wasn't going to be around when she did this for real tomorrow.

'Got it. Now what?'

He showed her where to pour in the mixture, watched while she opened a carton and filled the tank.

'That seems simple enough.'

'It'll take fifteen minutes before you can deliver an ice cream. Just time for a sandwich and a cup of coffee,' he told her.

He didn't wait, but jumped down, unlocked the door to the barn and disappeared inside.

Elle found him in the kitchen. There were no units, just solid wooden furniture and shelves, rather like the old-fashioned kitchen at Gable End that had, thankfully, escaped a nineteen-fifties make-over and was now back in fashion. The only difference was that Sean's did not bear the evidence of generations of use. And his big American fridge wasn't decorated with fridge magnets holding photographs, messages, the shopping list.

Sean put the kettle on the Aga, took a loaf from a wooden bread bin. 'Cheese and pickle?'

Her stomach rumbled loudly at the prompt and without warning he grinned. 'I'll take that as a yes.'

It had been hours since the breakfast she'd thrown up and she suddenly felt hollow. Which no doubt accounted for all the wobbly leg stuff, the tendency to tears. She was just plain hungry.

'Can I help?' she offered.

'You'll find butter and cheese in the pantry,' he said, slicing the bread.

She fetched them, washed her hands, then buttered the bread while Sean sliced the cheese. He looked sideways at her. 'You've done that before.'

'I've made a few sandwiches in my time,' she admitted. 'Pulled a few pints.'

'Tossed a few rolls into diners' laps?'

'Jill of all trades, that's me,' she said, suddenly remembering the message he'd left for her. That Freddy hadn't given her and had denied ever seeing. 'Only particularly annoying customers get food thrown at them, though.'

'I'll bear that in mind.' Then, as he spooned coffee into a cafetière, 'What were you going to study at college? Before everything went pear-shaped?'

'Cooking.' She pulled a face. 'Somewhat ironic under the circumstances.'

'Tragic, I'd have said. So, what was the dream?'

'Dream?' she repeated, as if she'd never heard the word, never sat there, pretending, at the table she used as a desk...

'You must have had one. Your own restaurant? A Michelin star by the time you were twenty-five? Television chef?'

'Good grief, nothing that grand.'

He looked at her. 'No,' he said with a smile. 'That's not you at all.'

'Oh, thanks.'

'You would have dreamed of something warm, cosy—'

'If you must know,' she cut in before he could make things any worse, 'I had my heart set on an elegant little restaurant for ladies who lunch. Cloths on the table. Morning coffee. Simple lunches. Afternoon tea with freshly made sandwiches, scones, exquisite cakes. Good service.'

'Nostalgia squared.'

'Be careful what you wish for,' she said, layering on the cheese while Sean opened the pickle jar. 'Right now, I've got all the nostalgia I can handle.'

'Don't knock it. The estate shop makes a tidy profit from people who want jars of pickle, conserves that look as if their great-grandmother made them,' he said.

She glanced at the one he had opened, which bore a supermarket's own label. 'Not you, obviously.'

'I didn't have that kind of great-grandmother,' he said, slathering it onto the cheese. 'But plenty of people seem to go for it despite the high price tag.'

He fetched a couple of plates and mugs while she sliced the sandwiches neatly in half, then cleared up and wiped down on automatic.

'Do you want to take those outside?' he asked, pouring water on the coffee. 'I'll bring the mugs.'

'Don't trust me with anything that hot, hmm?'

'Am I that transparent?'

'Oh, yes,' she said, laughing. Then, unable to stop herself, 'At least on the surface.' She wished she'd kept quiet, but he was looking at her, waiting. 'You're quick to empathise, Sean, but you keep yourself hidden. I haven't a clue what you're thinking right now.'

For a second he was shocked into silence, then he said, 'Of course you have. I'm thinking that it's lunchtime and I'm hungry.'

'Point proved, I think,' she said, picking up plates and leaving him to follow with the coffee.

She walked through a room that rose high above her to the exposed beams of the barn. The floor was polished oak, the furniture was large, comfortable, old. The walls were pale to provide a simple backdrop for a dark Impressionist painting of a distant hill that was a prominent local landmark.

It had a clean, spare beauty that was in total contrast to the clutter of Gable End. A simplicity that gave away absolutely nothing about the man who lived there. No photographs. No treasures picked up on life's journey. No memories, no family. Except that wasn't right.

He'd told her that Basil had taken Rosie to his niece's birthday party. And a niece meant he had a brother or sister.

She opened high French windows that led out onto a paved terrace overlooking the river. The midday sun was sparkling on the water and, ignoring a couple of ancient Adirondack chairs that were placed side by side close enough for two people to reach out and hold hands, she followed a stepped path that curved away down to the river and a small dock.

CHAPTER EIGHT

Forget love. I'd rather fall in ice cream.

—Rosie's Diary

SEAN took his time over the coffee. The lesson, he reflected, was never to ask a question to which you didn't want to hear the answer. He was practised at that. Good at keeping things light. People at a distance. Never digging beneath the surface to find out what made them tick. Taking care never to expose his own inner thoughts or feelings.

Elle challenged that in him. She told him stuff that he didn't want to know. Intimate, private stuff that seeped into his psyche, settled in the small dark spaces of his mind that had been left unoccupied. Stirring up the dust, disturbing the cobwebs.

He'd walked away from her yesterday, determined to stay away until Saturday morning. At the garden party, he rationalised, they'd be too busy to do more than pass out ice creams, take the money. And she'd be off to work as soon as he'd dropped her off and brought Rosie back to the barn.

Except Rosie wasn't coming back with him. And Elle was here right now.

He'd walked away, determined to put time and distance between them, but she'd come with him, lodged in his mind, stirring his body in ways that refused to be ignored. Driving him from his bed in the early hours to sit on the dock, his feet in the cold water of the river.

She'd been there when he woke.

His first thought had been of Elle, wondering what she was doing. How it would feel to turn and see her lying beside him. Hair tumbled over her pillow, lips soft, her lashes lying against her cheek. Every part of her totally relaxed in the total trust of complete surrender that letting go of consciousness in the presence of another person involved. It was why he never stayed overnight with any woman but always slept alone in his own bed. Refusing to give up that control to anyone.

It was why he'd fled the back of the van the minute they'd set the ice cream in action, leaving her to follow or not as she chose.

The memory of their last encounter in that small space was too vivid. The desire too intense.

He picked up the mugs. It would pass.

It always passed. His father, his half-brothers and -sisters demonstrated the fact on a regular basis. They were not a family with any emotional staying power.

And Elle was an emotional minefield. Best avoided but, if that was impossible, to be handled at long distance with the utmost caution.

He followed her through the living room, expecting to find her stretched out on one of the chairs on the terrace. But no. Typically, she'd ignored the obvious option and was down on the dock, leaning back, propped up on her hands, face to the sun, shoes off and legs dangling over the edge. Invading his space and filling his head with images that he wouldn't be able to get out of his mind. That would stay with him, haunt him, torment him.

She turned as the boards moved under his feet. 'This is lovely,' she said. 'Not what I expected.'

He didn't ask her what she'd expected.

'Do you fish?' she asked.

He shook his head. 'I leave that to the kingfishers. That's why the grass is left to grow over the bank so that there are shady places for the fish to hide.' Keep to the practical. He could handle that.

'I've never seen a kingfisher.'

'You have to be quiet. Still. Lie up in the grass further along the bank…' Instantly, his mind filled in the picture of the two of them lying in the long grass, touching close, waiting. And afterwards… After the vivid flash of blue, the kiss that would follow. And everything else.

No! The answer to her question was just… No. Keep it simple. Keep your distance.

'So why the dock?' she asked. 'The rowing boat?' And, gratefully, he seized on that.

'The dock was built to ship grain and wood down the river to Melchester. This is a tributary to the River May,' he added. 'As for the boat, I use it to keep an eye on what's happening with the wildlife, particularly the water voles and otters.'

'You've got otters here?' Her eyes lit up, sparking a dangerously hot response.

'They're making a comeback,' he said, sitting on the far side of the plates she'd set down beside her, using them as a safety barrier between them.

Better.

He bit into the sandwich they'd made together. Filling his mouth with food to keep himself from saying something stupid. Like inviting her to spend the afternoon with him. Offering to show her where the kingfishers were raising a family in a muddy hole in the riverbank.

Elle groaned as she took the hint and took a bite of her own sandwich, keeping nothing back. She said what was on her mind, her expression betrayed her every thought, drawing him in. Raising questions.

'Good?' he asked.

'Blissful. Wonderful cheese.'

'It's made in our dairy,' he said. 'We do good business in the farm shop.'

'We?'

'Developing income streams so that the house is self-sustaining is part of my job. We supply our home farm dairy products direct to the big London stores as well as local outlets,' he elaborated.

'So where do the vintage motors come in?'

'Nowhere. There were all sorts in barns and outbuildings all over the estate. Classic cars, farm machinery, old tractors. I was going to sell them off, but then realised that they could be a useful attraction. You've seen one Tudor beam, you've seen them all,' he said with a grin.

'I suppose.'

'Sorry if I misled you. I did find an old Morris that I got working one summer when I was about fourteen,' he offered. 'I taught myself to drive on the back roads of the estate.'

'Taught yourself?'

'No one knew I had the car. I hid it here. The barn was a wreck back then. Abandoned.'

A mallard with a flotilla of fluffy ducklings spotted them and came scurrying over.

'Oh, aren't they gorgeous!' Elle said, looking down as they gathered beneath his feet. 'They seem to know you.'

He shrugged, broke off a corner of his sandwich and dropped it to the mother duck, welcoming the distraction from old memories. Old hurts.

'I found a duckling that had been caught up in a plastic bag when I was a boy. It's so unnecessary, so annoyingly careless. I couldn't get anyone else bothered, so I began taking the boat out to clean up the rubbish that had been washed down from further upstream or blown in from the estate. I still do it myself when I have time.'

'No wonder Mrs Duck thinks you're a pal.'

'She only loves me for my bread and cheese. Try it.' She tossed in a few pieces of bread and found herself surrounded.

'Cupboard love,' she agreed, laughing.

'Is there any other kind?' he said.

'Don't you know?' she asked softly.

'Do you want to go for a walk along the bank?' he offered, needing to move, do something physical to get away from all this emotion spilling out. He didn't wait for an answer, but got to his feet, held out a hand. 'I can't promise an otter or a kingfisher, but if you keep very quiet...'

She grasped it, pushed her feet into her shoes, and he kept it fast in his as they walked along the bank, knee-deep in grass, late spring flowers. He pointed out a swan's nest on the far bank. Holes where water voles lived. A grebe and her family bobbing about beneath a weeping willow. Keeping it neutral.

'You clearly love it here. How long have you lived on the estate?' she queried.

That was the trouble with talking. It was like tossing a stone in the millpond. It hardly disturbed the surface and yet the tiny ripples it caused were unstoppable.

'I was born here,' he admitted.

'How wonderful to grow up with so much freedom.'

'I suppose.' No one had cared what he got up to as long as he didn't cause any damage. Or disturb the pheasants. It should have been an idyllic childhood. 'All of the fun, with none of the responsibility.'

So much for not saying any more.

'The late Baronet had a little midlife crisis fling with a secretary in his London office,' he explained. Better he told her himself than she learned it from someone else. 'He installed her in a weekend love-nest in one of the cottages on the edge of the estate.'

'Oh. I see.' She hadn't needed the connection spelling out. Nor had she responded with prurient interest or exclaimed over the fact that his father was a Baronet, even if he had been born on the wrong side of the blanket. 'Didn't his wife object?'

'She stayed in London and waited for him to get over it, which is probably why my mother played the pregnancy gambit. Bad decision.'

'Oh, come on, Sean. You don't know that's what she did.'

'It's a fair guess.'

'It was a love affair. Babies happen. Believe me, I know. And she chose to have you. Keep you.'

'Of course she did. I was her bargaining chip.'

'You are such a cynic.'

'And you are such a romantic. Sir Henry was never going to leave the daughter of an earl for a typist,' he said caustically.

She didn't say anything, just held his hand a little more tightly.

Her wordless empathy sparked a warmth that shimmered through him and it took him a moment to gather his thoughts, return to the expressionless recital of his history.

'He let my mother keep the cottage on a grace and favour basis, gave her a settlement to keep her sweet. It was in the days before an abandoned mistress's first action was to sell her story to the tabloids.'

'Does she still live here?'

'No. She was killed in a road accident when I was ten.'

'Oh, Sean… That's so tragic.' And this time she leaned against him so that it was the most natural thing in the world to let go of her hand and slip his arm around her. 'Tell me about her.'

'I…' He found himself floundering. No one ever asked him to talk about his mother. The cottage had been cleared when his mother died. Her clothes sent to a charity shop. Her personal belongings put in a box, stored away in the back of a cupboard somewhere. Her life brushed out of existence. 'She wasn't a happy woman.'

'I'm not surprised. It must have been horrible for her. Why didn't she go home to her family?'

'Not all families are like yours, Elle. They disowned her. Me. Sins of the flesh and all that,' he said gruffly.

'My family doesn't seem quite so great right now,' she said. 'What about your father?'

'Having got away with it once, he thought he had carte blanche but Her Ladyship did not prove so amenable the second time he strayed, rather more publicly, with a high profile fashion model, and he found himself free to remarry. He had three more children with wives number two and three before he broke his neck in a hunting accident.'

'That's a lot of family.' She sounded almost envious.

'Hardly family. I spent my early school years at the local primary being beaten up by the village kids for being "posh". Then, after my mother was killed, I was sent away to boarding school, where everyone took their lead from my half-brothers by treating me as if I was invisible,' he told her evenly.

'Kids can be so cruel. Where did you live?' she asked. 'When you weren't at school? Not with the family, I take it.'

'The adults only came for the shooting and Christmas. The kids were dumped here with their nannies for the holidays but I lived with the estate manager. His wife didn't like it but she wasn't about to say no to Sir Henry. The old man was okay. He kept me busy, encouraged my interest in wildlife, suggested I take a degree in estate management.'

'Definitely an outsider,' she said, but more to herself than to him. As if he'd answered some question that had been bothering her.

'Maybe,' he said, plucking a daisy, 'but this was my home in a way that it could never be theirs.'

'And now? What? You run the estate?'

'It never lets you down, never hurts you. It just is.'

'So you cherish it, keep it safe for a family who never gave you the love you deserved,' she said, as if pointing out the oddity in staying.

'They don't own it, Elle, any more than I do. It's entailed. Held in trust for the next generation. But, while they spend a few weeks a year here, I have it all the time. I control it, make the decisions, instigate the projects to keep it solvent for Henry, my half-brother and the present Baronet, to rubber-stamp.'

'Is that why he's coming today? To rubber-stamp one of your ideas? All the fun *and* all the responsibility.'

She was so wrong about not knowing what was beneath the surface, he thought. She saw right through him to the heart.

He grinned. 'All the fun and I'm paid for it too,' he replied as they reached the edge of the meadow and turned back.

'And with a fabulous old barn as your play house.'

He looked up at the barn. 'This doesn't go with the job. It's mine.'

'I thought the estate was entailed?'

'One of the advantages of living with the estate manager was access to the maps, the deeds. This stretch of land was bought much later, in the late eighteenth century. An add-on. Not part of the entail. I marked it out in my head as mine when I was fifteen years old.'

'They gave it to you?' she gasped.

'A gift to the dispossessed? I don't think so. I had some of the money the old man had given my mother, enough for a deposit, and I made an offer when Henry was being taken to the cleaners in the divorce courts. He could have sold the barn to a developer—a point he used to drive up the price—but he stuck with the devil he knew in the end.'

'Someone he trusted.'

'Yes. He knows where his best interests lie. But it's my footprint, my mark on the estate. More than any of his full brothers will get.'

'Are they resentful?'

'Not noticeably. They're all too busy running investment banks, or the country, and playing marital musical chairs to have time to spare for Haughton Manor.'

'That's a shame. A place like this needs people to bring it to life.'

'I suspect Henry would sell up to a sheikh or a pop star like a shot if he could, but he's stuck with it. It's my job to ensure that it doesn't cost them anything.'

'And the marital merry-go-round?' she probed gently.

'Not for me, Elle. I've seen enough marriage break-ups and confused, hurting kids to put me off the institution for good. I'm not about to join the party and add to the mayhem,' he warned her.

'Does your girlfriend know how you feel?'

'Girlfriend? Do you mean Charlotte?'

'If she's the dim one who believes that water will ruin linen, then yes.'

He laughed, enjoying the fact that she could be as catty as the next woman. 'Charlotte isn't my girlfriend. She's just a friend I sleep with occasionally. After her performance on Saturday, she's not even that.'

'A friend?' she asked. 'Or a sleeping partner?'

He looked at her. Her eyebrow was quirked up, but he suspected the question was more than casual interest. The thought warmed him.

'I don't do the second without the first,' he said, holding her gaze. 'And my friends don't usually take out their temper on someone who can't fight back.'

'Who?' She frowned, then, as the penny dropped, 'Do you mean me?'

'Who else?' And, without warning, it was suddenly too intense, too important. He pulled a face, managed a grin. 'Who knew that Freddy isn't ever going to sack you?'

'Oh, very funny,' she said, pulling away from his arm to gather up the plates and mugs. 'Come on. It's time to show me how to make the perfect ice cream cone.'

Sean, a cold space where a moment before there had been a warm woman, found himself wishing his half-brother and her ice cream to the devil. Wishing that he had the afternoon to show her the river.

There was no need to talk when you were drifting along with the current, letting it push you into the bank in some quiet place where you could forget about everything but the girl in your arms.

'All you have to do is press this button and the machine dispenses exactly the right amount of ice cream.' Sean was standing behind her, one hand over hers as she held a cone poised beneath the nozzle. With his other hand, he pressed the button and moved the cone beneath it as the ice cream descended.

It was hard enough to concentrate with his arms around her but then, as he leaned over her shoulder and took a mouthful of the result, his chin grazed her temple and she turned to look at him.

'Your turn,' he said.

'My turn?'

A smear of ice cream decorated his top lip. Without thinking, her reflex was to lick her own lip as she imagined how it would feel to lick it off. How it would taste. How *he* would taste…

For a moment she thought he was going to bend lower so that she could, but instead he dropped his free hand so that his arms were tight around her, took possession of the ice he'd made and replaced it with an empty cone.

'You try,' he urged, his hand still around hers, holding it steady.

Right. Ice cream.

He'd made it look deceptively easy but, with that image in her head, with him pressed against her back, she couldn't concentrate.

Her first attempt was more splodge than swirl, most of which would have fallen off if she hadn't caught it in the palm of her hand as it tilted sideways. He turned and reached for a bowl he'd had the foresight to bring with him and she dropped in the mess, took the damp cloth, ditto, and wiped her hands.

'You've done this before,' she said.

'I remember the mess I made of the first few, but practice makes perfect. The secret, as with most things, is not to rush it.'

'Absolutely.' She could pipe cream on a dessert and this couldn't be any harder than that. But when she'd piped cream in the Blue Boar kitchen she hadn't had Sean standing so close that she could feel his breath stirring her hair.

'Maybe if I try it myself,' she suggested, then instantly

regretted it as he stepped back, leaning against the counter, regarding her with eyes that seemed darker today.

She forced herself to turn away from the sight of his tongue curling slowly, sensuously around the ice cream, although, even with her back turned, the image remained, burned bright against her retinas. That was probably why it took her four more attempts before she produced a perfect cone.

'You're a fast learner,' he said as she finally indulged herself, letting the cool ice slide down her throat. Rosie had been standing in the shade, but it was still hot inside, even with the service window slid back. 'After your first effort I thought it would take most of the tank before you got it.'

'How many ices is that?'

'About twenty to a carton, I think.'

'Thanks for the vote of confidence,' she said wryly.

'I should warn you that when you take Rosie to kids' parties you'll need plenty of hand wipes because they'll all want to have a go.'

'You're quite the expert,' she commented.

'Hardly that, but my niece and all her friends did. Yet another reason why Basil left me to it. I was plastered in ice cream, chocolate sauce and just about everything else in that cupboard by the time they'd finished.'

'How old is she?'

'Daisy? Six.' He glanced at her. 'Why are you smiling?'

She shook her head. 'I was just imagining you swarmed with little girls all wanting you to show them how to make their own ices.'

'It was no laughing matter,' he said. But his mouth was calling him a liar. 'Believe me, I needed a very large Scotch afterwards to settle my nerves.'

'I don't think so.'

She was beginning to get the measure of Sean McElroy and she'd bet he'd been brilliant with them. Any boy who'd get mad enough about one dead duckling to take on the task of keeping the river safe for wildlife would surely grow up to be an ace uncle. A great dad, too, if only he dared to take the risk. Trust himself and come in from the cold.

Although definitely not with Charlotte. He was well rid of her.

She mentally slapped herself. The woman had been fighting for what was hers. It was what any woman would do. Not that it made any difference. The blonde was totally wrong for him. Or was that the point? If he was avoiding commitment, there was safety in being with someone so wrong.

'Why are you smiling?' he asked.

'Just thinking about you. And girls.'

'Don't say you haven't been warned,' he said, assuming she was talking about little ones. Probably just as well.

'You can come along and say I told you so, if you like.'

'You've got me for Saturday. Be content with that.'

'Saturday? But…'

'But?'

'Nothing.'

Everything.

The whole point of him coming along on Saturday was to show her how to operate the machinery and then take Rosie away afterwards. But he'd already shown her how to produce the perfect ice. And Rosie wasn't going anywhere until Elle had fulfilled Basil's promises.

He was still waiting and she pulled her shoulders together in what she hoped was a careless shrug.

'You don't have to come on Saturday now. Not unless you want to,' she added. Which was ridiculous. Why would a grown man want to spend Saturday afternoon dishing out ice cream?

He finished the cone, straightened. 'You really hate taking help, don't you?'

'Me? No…'

'You do everything. Run the house, cook, work all hours to keep everyone. You don't even want your sister to take a part-time job.'

'She's in her first year at college,' she protested.

'Most students have no choice, Elle. They have to get part-time work to support themselves. It looks good on their CV when they start looking for a job.'

'Not working as a waitress at the Blue Boar.' Although, according to Sorrel, she could do a lot better than that. 'It's important for her to concentrate on her studies. Make something of her life.'

'Because you missed out?' She didn't answer. 'Maybe you should be thinking about that, too. What are you going to do when they've left home?' He tucked a finger beneath her chin, tilting her face up so that she couldn't avoid his searching gaze. 'What about *your* dreams, Elle?'

She swallowed. Right now, with him standing this close, there was only one dream in her head and it had nothing to do with cupcakes.

'I'll think about that when they're both through college.'

He shrugged, let go, stood back. 'Fine. Be a martyr if that's what you want.' She'd scarcely had time to draw breath and object before he added, 'They won't thank you for it and you're not going to be much use to them if you break down trying to do everything.'

'I'm not being a martyr,' she declared. She was just doing what had to be done. 'I'm all they've got.'

'Geli is as old as you were when you took on responsibility for the family.'

'Are you saying that I've done my bit and now I should of-fload it onto her?' she demanded.

'No.' Then, 'Ignore me. I don't know what I'm talking about. Just accept that, like it or lump it, you've got me on Saturday. It'll be a long afternoon,' he said before she could object—and she really should object. 'Anything could go wrong.'

'Thanks. That really fills me with confidence.'

'You'll be fine. You just need a little practice on some real customers. Come on. You can give away some ice cream. Make a few people happy.'

'But…'

'The alternative is throwing it away so that I can show you how to dismantle the machinery for cleaning,' he warned.

'Haven't you got to get back to your meeting?' she asked, close to caving in.

'I'll meet, you serve and then we'll come back here and finish the lesson.'

He didn't give her time to argue, or consider what lesson he had in mind, but climbed behind the wheel and headed back in the direction of the Manor. As they got nearer, he said, 'Time to drum up some custom.'

'Does that mean I get to play the jingle?'

'You'll have to learn how, first.'

'Okay,' she said, looking over the dashboard. 'What do I push?'

'Push?'

'I assumed there'd be a button or something. To start the disk?'

'Disk? Please! This is a vintage vehicle, madam. Built before the age of seat belts and the Internet,' he said.

'Oh, right. The Dark Ages. So, what do you do?'

'This,' he said, taking hold of a handle beside him in the driver's door. 'You wind it up here, then switch it on and off here.' He demonstrated and a ripple of 'Greensleeves' filled the air. 'Your turn.'

Elle regarded the far door. To reach the chime she'd have to lean right across Sean. Get dangerously close to those firm thighs and what was undoubtedly a six-pack beneath the soft linen shirt he was wearing.

'I can't reach,' she said cravenly.

He leaned back in his seat. 'How's that?'

'It would be far too dangerous while we're moving,' she said primly. Miss Sensible.

His response was to slow down, pull over. 'We're not moving now.'

'It's still—'

She broke off as he put his arm around her waist and slid her across the worn, shiny seat so that she was nearer the door. Nearer to him.

'How's that?' he asked, looking down at her. 'Or would you like to be a little closer?'

'Any closer and I'd be in your lap!' she said, laughing, then let out a shriek as he slid his hand beneath her knees.

'No! I can manage,' she exclaimed. Possibly. If she didn't think about the fact that her cheek was on his shoulder, her breast mashed against his ribs, her shaky leg tight up against his rock-hard thigh.

She swallowed. Tried not to think about the warmth of his body against hers. The way his hand fitted into her waist and just how good it felt there. About the fact that she could hear the slow, steady beat of his heart. It had to be his, because hers was racketing away like a runaway train.

'Are you sure you can reach?'

'Mmm...' She could reach but, for some reason, she'd forgotten how to speak. 'Do you want to give it a go, then?'

'What?'

'Oh, the jingle!' She would have blushed, but her entire body was already flushed from head to toe. 'Absolutely!'

At least she'd regained control of her tongue. Whether she could keep her hand steady as she eased it through the small space between the steering wheel and an even more dangerous intimacy remained to be seen.

It felt like that party game where you threaded a loop over a wire that would buzz if you touched it. Would a buzzer go off if her wrist brushed against the denim stretched tight across his hips?

'Got it,' she said with a little gasp as she reached safety, winding up the mechanism the way he'd shown her. Not moving, but remaining tucked up against him as the tinny notes of 'Greensleeves' once more floated out across the parkland.

It was over too soon.

'Again?' he asked and she laughed, looked up and her eager

yes died on her lips as she realised that his mouth was mere inches from her own.

This close, in this light, she could see a deep crease at the corner of his mouth that must once have been a dimple, tiny flecks of green in the blue, giving his eyes the colour of the sea on a perfect day. The scar above his left brow.

The potent scent of his warm skin overlaid with vanilla was making her light-headed and she reached out, traced the jagged line of it with the tip of her finger.

'How did you get this?'

'I can't remember. Maybe it was when I fell out of a tree.'

'Ouch.'

'Or when I crashed my bike.'

She caught her lip.

'Or in one of those playground fights. It still hurts a bit,' he added. 'If you felt like you wanted to kiss it better.'

She didn't hesitate. She lifted her head an inch and her lips found his. Or maybe he'd come to meet her halfway. She didn't know, didn't care, only that as he pulled back to look down at her she wanted more. More kisses. More of him.

Was that how it had been for her mother? That rush of desire flooding through her veins? Making her breasts tingle, her lips burn for a man's touch? Making her feel powerful, in control…

'I remember now,' he said, his voice so low that it seemed to vibrate through her, setting off a chain reaction that spread out to every part of her body. 'It was definitely the tree. I also broke my collarbone.'

'Here?' He caught his breath as she slid her hand beneath the open neck of his shirt, feeling the shape of the bone, pushing it back so that she could lay her lips against the warm skin.

'I cracked a couple of ribs too and there was a terrible bruise…'

CHAPTER NINE

*A world without strawberry ice cream? That's a world
without summer.*

—Rosie's Diary

A SHARP rap on the window jerked Elle back to reality. She
banged her elbow on the steering wheel as she disentangled
herself, then she was back in her seat, pink, dishevelled, flustered, while Sean slid back the window.

'Henry?' Sean said, calmly acknowledging the man who'd
rapped on the window.

'Sorry to interrupt when you're so obviously busy, Sean, but
I haven't got a lot of time.'

'Hang on, we'll be right with you.'

Sean, apparently not the least embarrassed or flustered,
drove into the staff car park, angling the van across three
spaces so that the serving window was facing the centre of the
courtyard.

A silver Range Rover pulled into a space next to them and
Henry, who looked so much like Sean that he couldn't be anything other than his brother, climbed out.

'So, what's going on here?' he asked as Sean slid back the
serving hatch, giving her a chance to catch her breath, fan the
heat from her cheeks.

'Charity, Henry. The way it works is that Elle will give you an ice, while I relieve you of a donation for the Pink Ribbon Club.'

'Oh, right!' he said, laughing. 'Walked right into that one, didn't I?' He offered her his hand. 'Henry Haughton.'

'Elle...' She cleared her throat. 'Elle Amery. How d'you do?'

'Amery?' He glanced at Sean.

'Basil's great-niece,' he explained. 'She's standing in for him.'

'I'm not complaining.'

'You may not say that when you see the mess I make of your ice cream,' Elle said, taking a starched white coat from a laundry bag, several sizes too big, she'd found in one of the cupboards. Perching a cap on her head.

'What can we get you?' Sean said. 'A vanilla cornet with all the extras?'

'I think you're the one getting the extras,' Henry said, grinning, as he took a wallet from his back pocket. 'I'll pass on the ice, thank you, Elle. But put this in the kitty for your good cause.'

He handed her a note and she stared at it. Fifty pounds?

'Thank you, Sir Henry. That's incredibly generous.'

'Henry will do. Any girlfriend of Sean's—'

'Is a girlfriend of Sean's,' Sean cut in sharply.

Henry shrugged unrepentantly. 'No harm putting in a bid, is there? I rather like that milkmaid look.'

'You'll be okay?' Sean asked her as his brother headed into the office.

'Fine,' she assured him.

'Any problems just—wind up the jingle.'

Before she could answer, he'd jumped down, heading for the office.

Girlfriend...

'No...' He'd got that wrong. Sean didn't have girlfriends; he just slept with girls who were his friends.

And the problem with that was...?

As if her hot, vivid thoughts had reached out and touched him, he turned in the doorway, looked back. One corner of his mouth tilted up in a smile as if he knew exactly what she was thinking, as if he was thinking much the same thing. Her heart jolted as if it had been hit by one of those cardiac paddles that were the mainstay of hospital dramas. And not just her heart.

Desperate, Sorrel had said and maybe she was right. But Freddy was never going to generate anything like that reaction inside her body.

Not if he—or she—lived to be a hundred.

'Pretty girl,' Henry said as they walked towards the office. 'Deliciously…buxom.'

'And all mine,' Sean said without thinking.

His brother raised an eyebrow. 'That's unusually possessive of you.'

'Just warning you off before you get any ideas. How are your domestic arrangements these days?' he asked pointedly.

Henry smiled. 'Not a lot of fun. Hattie is pregnant.'

Pregnant? It took him a moment before he gathered himself sufficiently to respond. 'Well, congratulations. I had no idea you were contemplating adding to your brood.'

'Hattie's idea. Second wives,' he added, as if that said it all. But he was smiling nevertheless. His potency confirmed.

'She's well?'

'Morning sickness morning, noon and night. I thought I'd seen the last of that. But she's through the first three months, the scan is good and I'm allowed to share the news.'

'She must be so happy.'

'Ecstatic. When she's not being sick. But it's going to mean a few changes. I'm going to be easing back on work in the City, spending more time here.'

'Oh? Problems?'

'No.' He shrugged. 'Yes… Banking isn't what it was but there'll be a nice golden handshake and I'm going to sell the London house, buy a flat instead.'

'Well, you seem to have everything worked out. And it will be good to have a family living in the house. I've noticed how the public respond to that lived-in warmth when I've been to look at other historic houses,' Sean said.

'Hattie suggested we might do weddings.'

'Definitely problems.'

'That would be intrusive,' he pointed out. 'If you're going to be living here. The Manor isn't that big.'

'In the Orangery, she thought. I said she'd have to talk to you. And Olivia had some scheme she's mad keen on, too,' Henry said.

'We did exchange a few words on the subject.'

'I heard.'

'She's split up with that idiot she's married to, Sean. She didn't want me to tell you. You're so judgemental, but if you could give her a little slack?'

Judgemental? Was that him? Walking around with a holier than thou attitude? Sean wondered in dismay.

'Just find her something to keep her mind off things. She'll soon lose interest,' Henry said.

'Occupational therapy.'

'Exactly. I can leave that to you, then?'

Sean glanced out of the window to where people were gathering around the ice cream van. He could see Elle laughing as she handed the estate surveyor an ice, completely at ease, but then she spent her life dealing with the public.

She looked across, as if aware that he was watching her, and he knew exactly what she'd say to him if she was standing beside him.

Half-sisters are family, too. To be cherished, kept close.

It was what she'd done. Taking responsibility for them all, giving up her own dreams, her own chance of a family, because there weren't many men who'd take on that kind of baggage. Troublesome teens, an ageing grandmother losing her grip on reality.

He, on the other hand, had spent his entire life keeping his family at arm's length, watching as their marriages fell apart and feeling smugly superior.

But while they'd got it wrong more times than not, they hadn't been afraid to take the risk. Or pick themselves up and try again.

Was he, after all, the loser?

'I don't suppose there's any chance that you'll settle down soon?' Henry asked, leaving the question unanswered. 'You seemed to be pretty close to the girl in the ice cream van just now,' he said, looking out into the courtyard. 'That is a smile that would be a pleasure to come home to. Very welcoming. On the other hand, there's nothing wrong with a romp in the hay.' He shrugged. 'After all, you do live in a barn. Where is Amery, by the way? Not done a bunk, has he?'

'His rent is paid for the quarter. He's gone away for a while, leaving Elle to hold the fort. I've been showing her how everything works.'

'And doing a very thorough job, I noticed.'

'Watch your mouth, Henry.'

His brother smiled, clearly satisfied with the response he'd provoked. And Sean's prickly reaction was proof that his brother was right on target. Henry's broad grin suggested that he knew it too, but he didn't push his luck, just said, 'Remind her that Basil always put in an appearance at the Steam Fair at the end of the month.'

'I don't think…' he began, then let it go. It was probably one of the bookings in Basil's diary. 'Tell me,' he asked instead, 'do the initials RSG mean anything to you?'

Henry considered for a moment. 'Royal something or other? Society, maybe.'

'Unlikely, I'd have thought.'

He shrugged. 'Try the Internet.'

'Well? How did you do?'

Elle's smile was as wide as the Cheshire cat's.

'Fourteen more or less perfectly turned out ices, all with

chocolate flakes or sprinkles. Fourteen happy customers. And, along with your brother's contribution, a total of a hundred and twenty pounds for the Pink Ribbon Club.'

Sean whistled. 'Did I say you were a fast learner?'

'The Haughton Manor staff are incredibly generous. Obviously they were prepared to pay for the ices, but when I told them that the ices were free and all I wanted was a small donation for a very worthwhile cause…'

Her smile, impossibly, widened and she lifted her shoulders, practically to her ears, so totally delighted that he wanted to pick her up and hug her. She was just so thrilled. Nothing held back. His brother was right. She had a smile you'd want to come home to.

'Don't forget to take out your costs,' he warned, fighting off the impulse to go for it, make it his. He'd been telling himself that it was Elle he was protecting by keeping his distance, but it wasn't anything that noble.

He was the one who'd be left hurting if it didn't work out. Abandoned. Even as he yearned for her touch. The natural, eager, open-hearted warmth that had got her mother into so much trouble.

He needed to keep it practical. Feet on the ground.

'Diesel, supplies,' he added.

'Oh, but I couldn't—'

'You must. You'll have to replace the ice cream mixture, buy fuel,' he reminded her as he turned away to settle into the driving seat. Start her up. Keep his mind, his hands busy. 'You're giving your time, Elle. No one expects you to subsidise the charity. Or Basil. You can't afford it.'

'I suppose,' she said, slightly deflated, as she settled beside him.

'Just keep clear records, receipts, so that you can prove what you spent to the taxman.'

'No problem. I'm used to accounting for every penny,' she said, even more dispiritedly. Then, making an effort, 'I liked your brother.'

'Women always do, but then he always reacts generously to a sexy smile. It's why his first wife divorced him.' Then, instantly regretting his cynical response to what had been a genuine reaction to Henry's generosity, 'You caught him on a good day. Wife number two is expecting a baby.'

She frowned. 'You don't approve?'

'Not my business.' He was clearly going to have to work harder at being a warm human being if he was going to pass Elle's empathy antenna. 'He said it was Hattie's idea, but he seemed pleased with himself.'

It wasn't the reaction his own birth had evoked and a shadow crossed Elle's face, too. No doubt she was thinking about the unknown father she had sought out year after year at the Longbourne Fair.

His own father had been a very distant figure, but at least he had taken responsibility for him.

Elle, however, shook off whatever dark thought she was harbouring and laughed. 'I know what your problem is. You've just realised you're going to have one more little niece or nephew to plaster you with ice cream.'

'A nephew, I hope. They're more likely to grab an ice and run. Not like little girls, who want to decorate them.' Decorate him. He glanced at her. 'On the downside, Olivia, one of my numerous half-siblings, has split up from her husband.'

'I'm sorry.'

'It was her second marriage. My family seems to feel single-handedly obliged to keep the statistics dynamic.'

'With you as ballast.'

He glanced at her. 'That's pretty much what Henry said.' Then, afraid that he'd said too much, 'He also reminded me that Basil is expected to bring Rosie to the Steam Fair we hold in the park over the long holiday weekend at the end of May. Is it in the diary?'

'The weekend was blocked out, but Basil hadn't written anything in.'

'I suppose he thought I'd tell you.'

She turned to look at him, then, 'Why? He's taken a lot for granted, Sean,' Elle said. 'We're family, but why would you bother?'

Sean had asked himself the same thing. Why had Basil got him involved with all of this? They were acquaintances with a shared interest in old vehicles. Basil allowed him to buy him a pint now and then at the Haughton Arms. But this went way beyond that.

'Maybe,' he said, struggling for an answer, 'maybe he thought it was time I did.'

'Bother?'

Bother. Get involved. Get a life. Not end up like Basil, old and living on his own.

'You did explain the situation?' she asked. 'To your brother.'

'You'll make a mint of money,' he pointed out, avoiding a direct answer. Because he hadn't explained. He wanted her in the park for three whole days. Wanted her close enough so that he could look up and see her in the place he called home. Look up and smile when she saw him.

'*Basil* will make a mint of money,' she retaliated. 'If the sun shines. All I'd get out of it is three days when I couldn't go to work. When I wouldn't be paid.'

'Read the letter again, Elle. Basil transferred ownership of the van and all that went with it to you. He made it clear enough that whatever you earn is yours. And the Steam Fair is for enthusiasts who come from all over the country. A drop of rain won't put them off.'

'But…'

'What kind of deposit did Basil take for his bookings?'

'I don't know about the film company, the man wasn't exactly chatty, but the bride told me she'd given him a non-refundable twenty-five per cent deposit. Twenty-five per cent of what, I have no idea,' she added.

'Enough to cover the cost of buying supplies,' he suggested thoughtfully. 'Presumably he did that for every booking. He has left you well stocked. Ready to go without any outlay.'

'You're saying that he's used the money to start me—well, Gran—up in business?'

'He didn't normally do more than one or two events a month. He wouldn't have needed that much.'

She frowned. 'But…'

'It was a hobby for him, not a business and he turned away a lot more bookings that he accepted. With all the bookings he's lined up for the next couple of months… Well, it suggests he might have been thinking along those lines.'

'I thought he'd taken the money and run,' she said dazedly.

'Apparently not.'

'But if that's the case, why didn't he give us the paperwork on his clients?' she demanded. 'Explain what he was doing more clearly? Why did he just disappear?'

'I've no idea, but I suspect he knows a lot more about you than you realise. Maybe he thinks it's time you got out of the Blue Boar and chased your dream?'

'I promise you,' she said frankly, 'I never dreamed I'd be driving an ice cream van for a living.'

'But that's not what you'll be doing,' he pointed out. 'You've got bookings from a film company, for a wedding, and didn't you say there was some kind of business do as well as the more usual kids parties?'

'A business do and a retirement party,' she admitted.

'Then you haven't got an ice cream round, Elle. What you have is an events business.'

She opened her mouth to protest, closed it again. Then she looked at him. 'Where is he, Sean? What is RSG? I'm getting really worried about him.'

Sean took her hand for a moment, an instinctive gesture of comfort. But, even as he did that, he began to suspect that what Basil was doing was playing games. The old man wanted to be back in the comfort of his family home, the centre of attention, but he'd made some promise he couldn't break.

* * *

Upper Haughton was the kind of picturesque village that decorated biscuit tin lids. No intrusive modern street lighting or yellow lines painted on the road and, since there was only one way into the village from the main road, there was no through traffic to cause problems.

All it needed to become the fictitious village in a nineteen-sixties drama series was for the modern cars and signs to be removed before the cameras could roll. Since it had already been used in a picturesquely rural detective drama, and the parish council had been handsomely rewarded for the inconvenience, the villagers knew the ropes and were, on the whole, happy to co-operate.

Elle had become intimately acquainted with every part of it throughout a very long morning.

'An hour should do it', Kevin Sutherland had said. Ha!

She'd turned up in good time but it had been two hours before anyone took any notice of her. She'd then spent an age trying to teach the idiot actor how to produce an ice cream that anyone would want to eat, trying not to think about Sean, his arm around her as he'd taught her to do the same thing.

Finally, she'd driven around the green dressed in a white coat and peaked cap so that from a distance it would look as if it was the actor driving the van while the director filmed 'establishing' shots. Playing the jingle and trying really, really hard, not to think about how she'd kissed Sean. Bold as brass. A proper little hussy...

It would have been fun but for the fact that she was supposed to be at work at twelve and it was already half past. She couldn't even phone and let Freddy know she'd be late. The production assistant had locked her cellphone away before she was allowed on the set. The last thing they needed, apparently, was for one to start ringing in the middle of a 'take'.

And now, just when she could escape, she'd been grabbed by a reporter from the *Country Chronicle*, the monthly county magazine. She assumed it was because everyone else was too busy, but apparently not.

'We're doing a major feature on the filming and we're particularly interested in any local businesses that are involved,' she said. 'It'll be good publicity for the county. Bring in visitors.'

She doubted whether a picture of her and Rosie would do much for the local economy but, irretrievably late for work, she answered questions and posed for pictures with Rosie, ice cream in hand.

Then, before she could escape, the local television news team took her place. She smiled and went through the same routine with them. This time with the ice cream dripping over her fingers.

She binned the ice cream, licked her fingers and took the sheet of paper that the production assistant handed her, along with her phone.

'Thanks, Elle. Sorry it took so long, but you were great.'

'No problem.' She looked at the paper. 'What's this?'

'The shooting schedule for the rest of series one. I've marked the days we'll need Rosie.'

'Series *one*?' Elle looked at the list, saw half a dozen days highlighted. 'I thought this was a one-off?'

'Good grief, no. The ice cream guy is having an affair with the wife of the landlord of the pub. Lots of tension.' She smiled. 'It's edgier than the usual nostalgia stuff for this period—mostly sex and horses combined with crooked local politics and murder. The networks are salivating.'

Elle wasn't quite sure what to say, other than *help*.

'Rosie is part of the cast,' the woman continued, as if this was something she should be glad about. 'And, heaven forbid, even if the show does fold after series one, it'll still be great publicity for you.'

Publicity!

'Here's your payment pro forma. I've attached my card. Send your invoice direct to me and I'll make sure it goes through quickly.'

On the point of telling the woman that the last thing she needed was publicity, Elle saw the amount on the pro forma.

Three hundred pounds, less the seventy-five that Basil had already been paid as a deposit. For one day. And not even a whole day.

She swallowed. Hard. Managed a strangulated, 'Thanks.' Cleared her throat. Three hundred pounds. An events business. 'I'll get right on to it.'

CHAPTER TEN

Put 'eat ice cream' at the top of your list of things to do today and you'll get at least one thing done.
—Rosie's Diary

SEAN couldn't concentrate. All he could think about was Elle. How she'd looked as, relaxed, her bare feet dangling over the edge of his dock, she'd lifted her face to the sun. Her concentration as she'd tried to fill her first ice cream cone. The pink flush to her cheeks as she'd leaned across him to reach the chime, looked up, kissed him. When he'd kissed her.

He should be grateful to his brother for coming along when he had or the heat they'd been generating would have melted the ice cream.

Fortunately, there was nothing like a meeting with Henry to remind Sean why he never got involved with anyone. And Elle didn't have time, even if he'd wanted to. She'd needed to get back to Longbourne to be there when her sisters got in from school. Another good reason not to get carried away.

She was not his kind of girl. Not free to flirt, free to stay or go as she chose. And yet this morning, when he should have been focusing on building plans for an extension to the dairy, all he could think about was whether she was managing Rosie on her own and how the filming was going. The softness of her lips. Her fingertips walking along his collarbone…

It was as if she'd taken up residence in his head, distracting him, filling his thoughts in ways that no other woman had ever managed.

He picked up the phone to call Olivia, suggest she come down to Haughton Manor so that they could discuss her ideas for the stable block. Anything to take his mind off Elle. And he found himself dialling Elle's number instead.

His call went straight to voicemail.

Instead of hanging up, he listened to her voice, seeing her face, her eyes as she invited him to leave a message. Remembering the way she'd licked her upper lip, seeking out a crumb of chocolate, and how he'd hardened in immediate response.

'Elle…' He hadn't intended to leave a message, but her name escaped him before he could stop it. 'Just checking that every-thing went okay this morning. I'm doing my best to chase down Basil.' And still he didn't hang up. 'See you Saturday.'

He tossed the phone on the desk.

Pathetic. A fifteen-year-old boy could have done better.

'What's for tea?' Geli asked as she walked through the back door.

Elle looked up. 'Good grief, is that the time!' She usually heard the Maybridge bus pulling into the village, had the kettle on before her sisters had crossed the road, but the afternoon had flown by.

She hadn't taken Sean's suggestion that she had an embryo events business seriously but when she'd got home yesterday afternoon she'd unloaded most of the boxes from Rosie's inte-rior, ready for the film set this morning. Tucked away behind them, out of sight, she'd found a box file containing Basil's paperwork.

There wasn't much. Simple accounts, his invoices, receipts from suppliers, an account card for the local cash and carry. She hadn't had time to look at it then. She'd barely had time to put together supper before she'd left for work, but as soon as she'd got away from the film set she'd called Freddy and, claiming a family crisis—Basil *was* family and he'd disappeared; that surely had to count as a crisis—apologised for missing her lunchtime shift.

He'd been so concerned, insisting that she take the evening off as well, that she knew she should be feeling a lot guiltier than she did. But today she had other things on her mind.

Sean, for one…

He'd asked for her number in case he heard from Basil, but she hadn't expected him to call her just to ask how things had gone this morning.

She'd longed to call back, tell him about it, that it wasn't a one-off contract, that it was more important than ever that Basil was found so that she could be sure what he'd meant when he'd transferred Rosie to her. His casual 'See you Saturday' suggested he didn't expect—or want—that and she pushed away the memory of standing beside him, working together as they made a sandwich for lunch.

Refused to dwell on the small joy of sitting beside him on the dock as he'd told her about his family. Shared his pain. Tried to forget how he'd wrapped his arms around her to demonstrate how to produce the perfect ice cream…

It was the possibility of starting her own business that was the big one.

Her mind might keep wandering off, wondering what Sean was doing right now, counting off the days until Saturday, but she'd yanked it back into line. Done what she'd always been good at and concentrated on reality.

'What's all this?' Sorrel asked, picking up the sheet of paper on which she'd been brainstorming names for her embryo company.

If she was going to have a business, it wasn't going to be a hobby.

'Scoop? What's that?'

'Not Scoop, but *Scoop!* In italics, with an exclamation mark.'

'I'm starving,' Geli said, dumping her bag. 'What's for tea.'

'Open a tin of beans,' Elle said distractedly, waiting for Sorrel's reaction to the name.

'*Scoop!*' Her sister lifted an elegant brow. 'This is for Rosie, I take it?'

'You're not going to start an ice cream round?' Geli demanded, horrified.

'No, an events business. I've got some bookings.'

Geli rolled her eyes but Sorrel put her laptop on the table, pulled out a chair and sat down. 'You know there's a big market for this kind of thing. A lecturer at college hired an ice cream van for her little girl's birthday party last month.' She thought about it. 'It could have been Rosie.'

'Where's the tin opener?' Geli asked.

'For heaven's sake, it's in the same place it's been for the last fifteen years.'

She got a 'huff' and a noisy opening of drawers in response.

Maybe Sean was right. She did do too much for them. She hadn't expected anyone to open a tin for her at that age. On the contrary. She'd been the one coming in from school and getting tea for everyone else.

'What kind of bookings?' Sorrel asked.

'A surprisingly wide range.' She ran through them, determinedly ignoring the bad-tempered clatter from Geli. 'And the icing on the cake is that Rosie is now a member of the cast on the television drama series they're filming at Upper Haughton.'

'What?' Geli's scorn dissolved in an instant. Beneath the bored exterior, the pale face and black charity shop clothes, there apparently lurked an ordinary teenager who was just as impressed with fame as the next girl.

'That's what I was doing all morning. The *Country Chronicle* took photographs.'

'Excellent,' Sorrel said. 'We can use that on flyers and the website.'

'Website?' Whoa…

'I think we should have a blog, too. *Rosie's Diary*?' She

looked up. 'Time to put your IT skills to good use, Gel. You *can* spare us some of your precious time to design something and get us online?'

'Will I get paid?' she demanded, quickly recovering her disdain.

'Of course you'll get paid,' Sorrel replied before Elle could stop her. 'You'll be tax deductible. Make a note of the time you spend. We'll work out an appropriate hourly rate later. We'll need letterheads and invoices, too. Something simple, neat…'

'Okay, but I can't work on an empty stomach,' Geli said pointedly.

'You'll have to be registered for VAT,' Sorrel said, ignoring her. 'I can probably do that online.' She lifted her laptop onto the table and began to makes notes. 'This is so great. Exactly what I need for a project. *Setting Up a Small Business.*' Then the cool mask slipped and she grinned. 'You do realise that we are going to need a broadband connection?'

'What?' Elle looked at the pair of them. 'Let me get this right. You'll help me, but only as and when it suits *you*? For money, or because it will make a neat college project and it means you'll get broadband? Well, thanks. Thanks a bunch.' She stood up. 'You know what? This is *my* business and if I'm going to have to pay someone "an appropriate hourly rate"…' she did that really irritating quote mark thing with her fingers because she wanted everyone else to be as hacked off as she was '…I'll get a professional. Someone who knows how to open a can of beans.'

The room fell silent and, without warning, she could hear Sean saying, 'You really hate taking help, don't you?' She'd denied it, but it was true. She just didn't trust anyone else. It wasn't only about money, it was everything. Shopping, cooking, cleaning. If she didn't do it herself, it wouldn't be right…

For years she'd done it all. Been not only sister, granddaughter, but mother to all three of them. They took and took and took and it was her own fault for letting them. For not making them do their own washing, get their own food. Because she wanted to make it up to them. Losing their mother, the stuff that they took for granted. Be…perfect.

But Lavender had been *her* mother, too. Adorable, funny, warm, but not perfect. Far from perfect. And she wouldn't have done all this. Wrapped them in cotton wool. Spoon-fed them.

'It's…um…done,' Geli said tentatively. 'Shall I open another tin? Make beans on toast for everyone?'

'That would be great,' Sorrel said. 'And put the kettle on. I think we could all do with a cup of tea.'

Elle, torn between the need to curl up in a corner and bawl her eyes out or burst out laughing, sucked her cheeks in.

'You think you can buy me off with baked beans and tea?' she asked, trying to be tough.

'It's a start,' Sorrel said. 'Now, tell us about *Scoop!*, which is a totally brilliant name, by the way. We'll listen and then you can tell us how we can help.'

'Actually, you were just about there,' she admitted. 'I realised I'd need a website, but the blog is a great idea, especially with the filming.'

'What are you going to wear?' Sorrel asked.

'Well, Rosie is early nineteen-sixties vintage and I thought… Do you remember the trunk full of our great-grandma's clothes we used to dress up in? They are the right era. Late fifties, early sixties.'

'Oh. My. Goodness. You're right. They would be just perfect. They'll need a good wash. Shall I see to that?' Sorrel offered.

'Maybe you should start with something a little less challenging laundrywise,' Ellie suggested. 'But I'd welcome a hand with the formalities.'

'I'll make a list.' Then, 'Are you going to give in your notice at the Blue Boar?'

'Not immediately. Let's see how it goes. Is something burning?' Elle asked.

Before either of them could answer, the door opened and

her grandmother appeared from the morning room where she'd been dozing away the afternoon in front of an old movie.

'Elle,' she said, looking surprised. 'You're here.'

'I've been here all afternoon, Gran.'

'But…' she looked back into the morning room '…you're in there. On the television. Talking to a reporter on the local news.'

They all rushed into the morning room, but the news had already moved on to another item.

'You *were* on the television,' she insisted. Elle was about to explain when the telephone rang.

Sorrel picked it up. 'Oh, hello, Mrs Gilbert. Did she?… Did you?… For your granddaughter's birthday? I'm afraid Elle isn't here at the moment,' she said, cool as a cucumber, holding Elle off. 'I'll ask her to check the diary and call you back first thing in the morning. No problem.' She turned to Elle. 'That was Mrs Gilbert. The woman who owns the garden centre? Mrs Fisher was talking about Rosie in the post office—'

'I'll bet she was,' Geli interjected dryly.

'—and then she saw you on the television. I would have taken the booking but I had no idea when Rosie's free, or what to charge.'

'How old is her granddaughter?' Elle asked.

'Good point. And I should have asked how many children they've invited. That's going to affect the cost. We're going to need a see-at-a-glance wall chart for bookings. And a price list,' Sorrel said.

'I can work that out now I have Basil's paperwork.'

'Who's Basil?' Geli asked.

'Basil…' Her grandmother grabbed for the back of an armchair but, as Elle and Sorrel exchanged a desperate look, she seemed to gather herself, straighten her back. 'Basil,' she said, 'is Grandpa's brother. Your great-uncle.' Only then did she let Elle ease her back into the armchair.

'But…Grandpa didn't have any brothers,' Geli said.

'Just one. They were chalk and cheese. Bernard was an

engineer, captain of the local rugby team. Big, strong, sports mad. The kind of man every girl wanted to be seen with. Basil was a couple of years younger, artistic, a bit of a clown, but all the girls adored him, too. He was so easy to be with.' She shook her head. 'It was all an act, of course. The clowning. I found him one day by the village pond trying to work up the nerve to end it all. Silly boy.'

'Why?' Sorrel asked. 'Why would he do that?'

Elle threw her a warning look, but her grandmother was oblivious. In a world of her own as she remembered the past.

'He'd been going out with a girl from Lower Haughton, but only so that he could be near her twin brother. He knew he was gay and it terrified him.'

'But that's awful,' Sorrel gasped.

'The law had changed by then, but attitudes hadn't. He couldn't bear the shame of his parents knowing. Bernard... He was his hero.'

'So what happened? Where has he been all these years?' Geli asked.

'I let out his secret. The girl he'd been going out with was my best friend. She adored him and I didn't want her to get hurt,' their grandmother revealed.

'*You* told her?'

'We were at a party and she was all over him. I couldn't bear it. I told Basil he had to tell her or I would. Bernard overheard us. He thought I was playing fast and loose with the two of them and he'd followed us to find out what was going on. I sometimes think he only married me to keep the secret in the family.'

'Secret?'

'Basil went home and faced his father. The old man told him that he had to leave. Disappear. Never come back, never contact the family ever again.'

'Just like that?' Elle asked.

'He gave him money, a lot of money, but it wasn't right. If his mother had still been alive, I'm sure things would have been different. I don't think Bernard ever forgave himself for what happened. Or me.'

'Oh, Gran,' Elle said sadly.

She looked up. 'I was just trying to help.'

'Of course you were.'

It explained so much, Elle thought, as she hugged her. And made it even more imperative that she find Basil. Bring him home.

'The beans!' Geli yelled.

Later, when they'd got rid of the smell of burning beans and the ruined saucepan, Elle retired to the privacy of her own room to call Sean.

'Elle? Is there a problem?'

'No,' she said. Nothing could be wrong when she was lying on her bed with his voice rippling through her, soft and warm as melted chocolate. 'Not wrong, exactly. Just different.'

'How different?'

'Are you sitting comfortably? It's a long story.'

He listened while she filled him in on the family secrets.

'How do you feel about that?' he asked when she'd finished.

'Sad for them all. But it explains a lot about why Grandpa was the way he was.'

'Life is endlessly complicated.'

'I suppose.' She settled lower against the pillows. 'But the odd thing is that since she's told us Gran seems…I don't know… more…here.'

'She's been living with that guilt for a long time. Telling you must have felt like a weight being lifted from her. You did say that the doctor told you she was blocking out what she couldn't deal with.'

He'd remembered?

'Mmm… We're all feeling a bit giddy at the moment, I think, but it's more urgent than ever that we find Basil and bring him home.'

'Of course. Do you want me to search the cottage? I only glanced through the place before, just to make sure he hadn't taken an overdose and was lying… Well, you know.'

'I know,' she said.

'You could come over tomorrow and we could do it together, if you like? We could reprise the cheese sandwiches. Feed the ducks again. Maybe take the boat out.'

'That is so tempting.'

'Haven't you heard? You should always give in to temptation,' he teased.

'I really wish I could.' Then, realising that she might have been a little too eager, added quickly, 'You've done so much already.'

'And you've already missed an entire day's work.' He sounded a touch off. 'Freddy will be missing you.'

'Rosie isn't going to replace my job, Sean. Not yet, anyway. I have bills to pay.'

'I know. Leave it to me. I'll see what I can find.' Changing the subject, he said, 'So, tell me about today. How does it feel to be a television star?'

'Rosie made the evening news, I'll have you know,' she said. 'And she's going to be featured in the *Country Chronicle*.'

'Hot stuff.'

'You'd think so, but it isn't like that.' And at his prompting she told him all about the filming. The endless waiting around. Had him laughing at her description of the good-looking but thick actor who couldn't make a ice cream cone to save his life. Doing things over and over again.

'It doesn't sound as much fun as you'd think.'

'Mostly it was just mind-numbingly boring,' she admitted, 'although it did get a lot more exciting when I discovered how much they were paying me.'

'That will do it every time. So are you beginning to take me seriously?' he asked.

'Absolutely,' she said without hesitation. He was so easy to talk to, share things with that, before she knew it, she'd told him about her plans for Rosie. The name she'd thought up.

'Scoop?'

'With an exclamation mark. What do you think?'

'I like it. Short, snappy, memorable. Make sure you have some flyers with you on Saturday and we'll spread the word.'

'The girls are working on them now.' Then, reluctantly, 'I suppose I'd better go and see how far they've got.'

'Let me know if you need anything printed,' he offered.

'That's really kind of you, Sean, but if we're going to be a serious business we need to get ourselves properly organised.' Then, when the silence went on a moment too long, 'This is not me being unable to accept help. I am making an effort to let go a little. Trust my sisters. Other people.'

'Me?' he asked. 'Do you trust me?'

The question was so unexpected that for a moment she floundered.

'You're wise to hesitate.'

'Am I?' she asked. 'What exactly are we talking about here?'

'We've already covered the question of money,' he reminded her.

Elle opened her mouth, closed it and, heart beating just a little faster as she ran her tongue over dry lips, said, 'What else is there?'

He didn't answer. Her call?

She swallowed. Her heart was pounding in her ears now. 'I'm sure that a man so determined to avoid commitment must practise safe sex.'

'Sex is never safe. Not if the emotions are engaged.'

Was he warning her that while men could be uncommitted, emotionally disengaged—that *he* would be uncommitted— women were always going to be hurt?

'Life is not safe, Sean. My mother died young, but she filled every moment of her life with…life. By the time she was my age, she'd had lovers, children.' Heartbreak, maybe, risk, but joy, too.

'You're not like her, Elle.'

'How do you know that?'

'You need a forever man who'll make you the centre of his life.'

'Her father, my grandfather, was a forever man,' she told him. 'And I wouldn't want the life my grandmother lived with him either. Meantime,' she said, moving on quickly because he'd made it more than clear that he couldn't handle 'forever' and assumed she couldn't handle anything else, 'if I'm going to run *'Scoop!'* as a serious business I have to do this properly. Not rely on favours from friends.'

'I thought you were learning to take help? Yours wouldn't be the first local business who'd used our copier in an emergency,' he argued.

'If there's an emergency, I promise I'll call you. And I would still like you to look after Rosie since you know her so well. But not in return for ice cream.'

'And if I insist on being paid that way?' he asked, his voice teasing, evoking the memory of his tongue curling around creamy ice. 'Rosie and all the works as a birthday treat.'

'For your many nieces and nephews?'

'I was thinking of something a little more...personal.'

'Oh...' As she lay there, her skin was so sensitive that every inch of clothing was a torment, her lips burned for the cooling touch of his ice-chilled mouth. Her breasts felt heavy and the ache between her thighs, the hot poke of desire, made her reckless. He might not be interested in commitment, but then she wasn't free to give it and, without stopping to think, she said, 'Well, if those are your terms, I'd have to do my best to fulfil them,' she said, so softly that she might have been talking to herself.

'You see how easy it is?' Sean said, and even though she couldn't see him she knew he was smiling.

'But I get to choose how it's served,' she went on, as if he hadn't spoken. 'Exactly where to pipe the ice cream…'

'*Elle*…' He wasn't laughing now.

'Where to drizzle the chocolate fudge sauce.' He uttered one word that assured her that she had his full attention. 'A special one made with coffee liqueur. I love coffee liqueur…'

'Excuse me, Miss Amery, but are we having phone sex?' he asked, his own voice pure Irish cream.

'Elle!' Geli yelled from the bottom of the stairs. 'I need you to look at what I've done.'

She sighed. 'With my family, it's the only kind we're ever likely to have.'

'You're forgetting my birthday.'

Geli was thundering up the stairs. 'Elle! Where are you?'

'No.' She wasn't about to forget this telephone conversation. Ever. 'When is that? I need to make a note to keep the evening free.'

'I'll leave that up to you,' he said. 'Whenever you have a spare afternoon or evening just…call me.'

'Elle!' Geli burst in, then stopped. 'Oh. Were you asleep?'

'Maybe,' she said, rolling over, pushing the phone out of sight beneath her pillow as she swung her legs to the floor. 'Just give me a minute. I'll be right down.'

She splashed her face with cold water. It wasn't enough. Her body felt aroused, as if Sean had been there in the room with her, lying beside her, touching her, undressing her. It was going to take a cold shower to bring her back to earth.

CHAPTER ELEVEN

Six or sixty, it still hurts when your ice cream falls from its cone.

—Rosie's Diary

Sean tore off his T-shirt, shucked off his jeans and plunged naked into the river.

The cold hit him like a blow, but the fire Elle had stoked up in him refused to die down and he swam upstream until it felt as if he were warming the water, rather than the other way around.

His brother was right. Lovage Amery had a smile to come home to. A voice that warmed him through, touching something buried so deep inside him that he hadn't known it was there. Even now was afraid to examine too closely for fear that it was an illusion.

She was a woman who had taken everything that life could throw at her and still took on emotional complications without reservations. No caveats or conditions. No ifs or buts...

No fear.

She had that from her mother, he suspected. It was the whole-hearted grasp on life that had somehow eluded him.

They were complete opposites in that. He'd taken a step back, determined not to break her heart, but he'd completely misunderstood her.

Elle might cling obsessively to physical security, but she

gave love as if it came from a bottomless well. Would risk her heart without a second thought. While he was prepared to risk anything but. Hoarding his feelings like a miser, protecting them from danger, keeping them locked away until they were stunted, miserable things without value.

She was ready to come to his bed if he wanted her, and there was no doubt that he wanted her.

But forever?

How could you know, be sure? Or was that what she was telling him? That you couldn't ever be certain, but it was worth the risk anyway.

He stopped fighting the river and let it carry him home, but as he reached the dock he discovered he was not alone.

'Wild night-time swimming isn't going to do your cold any good,' Charlotte said, stepping in front of him so that he could enjoy a close-up of her stunning ankles. 'Just as well I came bearing honey and lemon.'

'I never saw you in the Florence Nightingale role,' he said, pulling himself out of the water, forcing her to step back or be showered. Using his T-shirt to dry himself.

'You have me,' she admitted. 'I was lying about the honey. But then we both know that your sudden cold on Saturday night was of the diplomatic variety.'

'The chill was real enough,' he assured her and she sighed.

'I know. I came to apologise for being such a catty witch, Sean.'

'In that case you're in the wrong place. It was Elle who could have lost her job.'

'Elle…' For a moment she hesitated as if there had been something in the way he said the name that betrayed him. Then, as if dismissing the thought, she arched her brow and said, 'Oh, please. Her boss had his hands all over her.' She'd noticed it, too? 'Very possessive. If she's in trouble it's your fault for flirting with her.'

'Pots and kettles, sweetheart,' he said, reaching for his jeans, pulling them on. 'You always make a point of flirting with good-looking waiters.'

'Maybe I do, but I never look at them the way you were looking at her.'

He didn't argue. Charlotte flirted in the same way she breathed. Without thinking about it. He only flirted when his interest was engaged. And Lovage Amery had grabbed his total interest from the moment she'd opened her front door to him.

When he didn't respond to her needling she let it go. 'Oliver Franklin was at the party on Saturday. I let him take me home.'

'Did he give satisfaction?' he asked idly.

'I didn't…'

'No, of course not. He's on the list of men you might eventually marry. You need to keep him eager.'

'He asked me to have dinner with him one day this week,' she said, offering him one last chance to change his mind. 'I said I'd call him.'

'Do that. You've kept the poor sap at arm's length for long enough.' Her face betrayed her. 'You'd never settle for me, Charlotte. I don't have an estate of my own, a title, money. I'm just someone you're filling in time with while you scope out the market.'

'And the waitress will, I suppose.' She sounded forlorn, but she didn't deny it. 'It's time to grow up. Take the next step.'

She sighed. 'Is that what's happened to you?'

He didn't know what had happened to him, only that the type of relationship he'd enjoyed with Charlotte wasn't enough for him any more. As he leaned close enough to kiss her cheek, he said, 'Be sure to send me an invitation to the wedding.'

She gave a little shiver. 'I don't think so.' Then, 'It's hard, isn't it?'

'Growing up?'

'Falling in love. But you're right. You're fabulous in bed, but you're not husband material.'

She didn't wait for an answer but turned and walked away, her heels beating out a sharp staccato on the dock.

She was wrong, he thought, as he stretched out on the dock, staring up at the stars, the sound of her little roadster racing through the estate roads growing fainter and fainter until the night was reclaimed by small insects, a nightjar, the occasional splash of a small river mammal. So wrong.

Falling in love wasn't hard. Compared to not falling in love it was a piece of cake. That required concentration. Lose it for a moment and love slipped unnoticed under your defences as sweetly, as effortlessly as an ice cream sliding down a parched throat on a summer's day. No drama or noise. Just a smile, a touch, a kiss was all it took to bring down even the most powerful fortifications, so that without warning you were falling, with nothing to grasp hold of.

He'd still been hot and horny when he'd emerged from the river and a repentant Charlotte, eager to make up, should have been a gift. A week ago he wouldn't have thought twice. A week ago his life had been simple.

Today there was only one woman he wanted in his bed. Not just for an hour or two, but to wake up with. He wanted to open his eyes and see Elle's hair spread over the pillow. Her lashes lying against her cheeks. See her open her eyes and smile.

But forever?

It was clear that, like his brother, he'd reached some kind of turning point. He just wasn't sure where this new turn was taking him.

A tap on the dining room door on Saturday sent Elle's heart swooping up into her mouth, her hand flying, scattering the leaflets she was piling up across the table.

'Sorry. I didn't mean to startle you. Your grandmother said I'd find you in here,' Sean said.

'You didn't startle me. I saw you pull in.' Saw him jump down from the Land Rover he was driving today.

She was in the old dining room, empty since the bailiffs

had carried away the Regency dining room suite, the china, the silverware that had once graced it. Now it was the *Scoop!* Office-cum-store room with cartons of cones, pallets of ice cream mix piled up at one end.

Leaflets, boxes of stationery that had been quickly run off on the printer at the Small Business Unit set up in the college were on an old bookshelf they'd moved down from one of the bedrooms.

A large planner was pinned to the wall so that they could see all their bookings at a glance but the pièce de résistance was the rail of clothes that they'd brought down from the attic. Glamorous Madmen dresses from the early sixties.

For the Pink Ribbon Club, she'd picked out a dark pink dress with a sweetheart neckline, nipped in waist and a full skirt that was exactly Rosie's era. She'd pinned up her hair in a classic chignon. Painted her lips and nails bright pink to match her dress.

Sean had played his part. He was wearing a black T-shirt with the word '*Scoop!*' written in pink sparkle across his chest. The fact that it exactly matched the fonts Geli had chosen for the flyers and their letterheads could not be coincidence.

'You've been cross-referencing our designs,' she said, weirdly shy after the intimacy of their phone call. The kiss they'd shared. She was never tongue-tied, but it was as if she didn't know what to say. As if he didn't know what to say.

They hadn't spoken since then. He'd only sent a text telling her that he hadn't found anything useful in Basil's cottage. She'd sent one back saying thanks for looking. It was as if they'd almost stepped over some precipice and were wobbling on a dangerous edge and it could still go either way. One wrong word and it would all be over.

'You look absolutely amazing, Elle.'

'A bit different to the usual get-up,' she agreed, self-conscious in such unaccustomed finery, so much make-up. Maybe that was it. All starched up, she didn't feel like herself.

'You've been busy.'

'Yes. Panicking mostly.'

That raised a smile from him. Better. She began to relax.

'I saw the website. And the blog. *Rosie's Diary*? I thought Rosie sounded very like you,' Sean said.

'Did she?'

She wanted to ask him what she sounded like. Whether he liked it. Wanted him to put his hand on her cinched-in waist, pull her closer, kiss her neck. Maybe if they lost themselves in desire everything would be all right, but the mind-reading thing didn't seem to be working today.

'I'm not sure that's a compliment,' she said finally.

'Aren't you?' The smile lines deepened imperceptibly. 'Jess enjoyed it. And my sister, Olivia, loved the stuff about the filming.'

'Your sister? The one whose marriage broke up?'

'She's got an idea for craft workshops in the old stable block and needs something to keep her occupied.'

'And you're letting her play with your estate?' she asked incredulously.

'She'll soon get bored, but I thought, what would Elle do in this situation?'

'Now that is a compliment.'

He shrugged. 'What harm can she do?'

She let her hand linger briefly on his shoulder. 'None at all, Sean.'

He took her hand, kissed her fingers, kept hold of them. 'You did a great job of selling the PRC Garden Party. On the blog. It was both funny and touching...'

She swallowed. It had been hard writing that.

'I've ordered some Rosie badges,' she said, eager to change the subject before a tear that had been threatening all day ruined the sixties eyeliner that Sorrel had applied so carefully. 'To give away at children's parties.'

'Turning them into walking advertisements for your business? Nice one,' he approved.

'And of course we have the retro clothes.'

'They're fabulous,' he said, flicking one-handedly through the rail, stopping at a glamorous full-skirted halter neck black lace dress. 'Where did they come from?'

'The attic. We used to dress up in them when we were kids. Mum used to do our hair, make us up. I thought I'd wear that one for the evening events,' she added. 'With very high heels and bright red lipstick. What do you think?'

'I think that the businessmen will believe they've died and gone to heaven,' he said. 'And the old guy at the retirement party will probably have a heart attack.' He turned to look at her. 'I'm in danger of having one just thinking about it.' Then, as if he'd said more than he meant to, 'Hadn't we better go?'

She gave a little yelp as she checked her watch. 'Can you bring those leaflets?'

She didn't wait for a reply, but practically fled the room.

Sean gave himself a moment, gave her a moment, but as he gathered up a pile of leaflets advertising *Scoop!*, he saw the smear of pink on his thumb where it had rested close to her mouth and, unable to help himself, he rubbed it against his lower lip, tasting it. Tasting her.

Forget about some old guy having a heart attack when he saw her in the black lace. He'd come close when he'd seen her in the pink dress and there was a lot less of her on show in that one.

There had been a moment, no more than a heartbeat, when Elle had turned and her entire body had appeared to lift in welcome. Or maybe it had been his own instinctive response to the sight of her. An urge to reach out and touch her. Just a hand to her arm. The kind of small, intimate gesture exchanged by lovers.

They weren't even close. They'd shared just one kiss. So why did he feel more like her lover than he ever had with any woman he'd known?

What was this intimacy that had nothing to do with sex, lust? This belief that he knew her? That somehow her thoughts, her feelings mattered more than his own? The powerful draw that brought him back to her even when she'd told him to go.

All week, wasting precious time hoping to find some small clue, he'd cursed Basil up hill and down dale. But Basil was the one excuse he had to keep coming back to her. Even when the risk of it scared him witless. Even when he needed no excuse.

It was Elle who'd led the way on the phone, boldly teasing him, making promises.

She was such a curious mixture. Capable in ways that the Charlotte Pickerings of this world could never imagine. A woman who'd learned very early in life to deal with loss, officialdom at its worst, hardship, she would hold the world at bay to protect her family.

'Sean!'

He smiled at the imperious summons in her voice.

Not a curious mixture, a glorious one.   She deserved to be wooed, courted, made to feel valued. He might not be able to give her the kind of commitment she deserved, but he could at least give her that.

'Sean!'

'Right with you,' he said, following her into the kitchen where she was standing holding up the retro pink kettle he'd bought her.

'What,' she demanded, 'is this?'

'A kettle?' he offered.

For a moment their eyes met and he dared her to turn it down.

'Thank you.' She turned quickly away. 'Sorrel is coming along with us to learn the ropes.'

Her sister glanced at her. Clearly it was the first she'd heard of it but she was quick on the uptake. 'Can't wait.'

'Just Sorrel?' Sean asked, not entirely sorry to have a little chaperone to keep things from boiling over. They needed time. They needed space. 'What about you, Angelica? Aren't you desperate to learn the trick of producing the perfect ice cream?'

'I'm too busy tweaking the website and blog,' she said, flicking her mouse and leaning sideways so that he could see. 'I'm putting some of those cute things Basil wrote about ice cream in Rosie's speech bubbles at the head of each page.'

'Neat idea. And that's a great cartoon of Rosie. Who did that?'

'Me,' Geli said, doing her best to look cool, but failing miserably. 'I'm going to take arts and design at college.'

Elle, helpless to stop herself, drank in his profile, the straight nose, firm chin, long fingers as he leaned forward, raking back the dark hair sliding over his forehead with long, slender fingers. Trying not to think about what they could do to her.

Instead, he took the mouse, clicking through the pages until he paused on one and looked up, catching her before she could look away.

'Everyone has a price—mine is ice cream…?' His right brow kicked up. 'Basil wrote that?'

'He must have been thinking of you,' she said and was finally rewarded with one of his killer smiles. The kind that sent heat surging through her veins, leaving her shaky, helpless.

But the mention of price reminded Sean that he had something for Elle and, taking out his wallet, he produced a cheque. 'I sold your car.'

'Did you advertise it on the Internet?'

'No. I emailed a description to some enthusiasts I know. It's not a lot, but this way you don't have to pay commission.'

Elle took the cheque, looked at it, then up at him, eyes narrowed in suspicion. 'Not a lot?'

'She's an old classic and while she had a few internal problems, her bodywork was in amazingly good condition. I'd have made more if I'd had time to do some work on her, but I thought you might need it now,' he told her.

'Thank you again.' Then, turning to Geli, she said, 'Take care of this. It's your trip to France paid for and enough for a driving school car to take Sorrel through her test next week.'

And, having handed the cheque to Geli, she took Sean's hand, wordlessly, in her own for the briefest moment.

'Okay. Time to go.'

At the garden party, Sean watched Elle add a frilly white apron to her outfit.

'One of your delicious ices, please, Miss Amery. Something very pink if I'm going to be a walking advertisement for your wares.' He stretched out his arms to display the sparkly logo emblazoned on his chest. 'No one I pass will be able to resist the temptation.'

He saw her swallow down whatever she was going to say. 'Would you prefer a shell or a cone?' she asked.

'Give the man a cone,' Sorrel said, then, when Elle glared at her, she rolled her eyes. 'It would do it for me.'

Elle decorated the ice lavishly with pink mini marshmallows and sprinkles, then wrapped the cone in a pink paper napkin. 'Is that pink enough for you?' she asked as she handed it to him.

'I'd have liked to have seen a few crushed beetles,' he teased as he put down his money.

He could see that she was dying to tell him that he didn't have to pay, but she pressed her lips together to stop the words and, by then, a queue was forming.

He licked a groove up the side of the ice, sucked the top into his mouth. 'If you have any problems, get the announcer to…' he met her eye '…call me.'

For the first hour Elle didn't have time to think, which was just as well. If she'd had time to think, Sean's provocative 'call me' would have had her melting faster than her ices.

Not that he'd rushed back.

From her high viewpoint, she'd caught glimpses of him from time to time, working his way through the crowd, always talking to someone or other. He seemed to know an awful lot of people. Most of them women. One of them was the blonde with the linen dress from that evening in the Blue Boar.

She tried not to look, but couldn't help herself. Not that they talked for long. The blonde turned and headed for the car park. And finally Sean headed for her.

'Everything okay?' he asked. 'No problems?'

'None,' she admitted.

'You can cope if I shoot off? Bit of a panic back at the estate.'

The mind-reading thing worked two ways, she discovered. The fact that he was lying was coming off him in waves.

'Another baby duck in distress?' she asked sweetly, calling herself all kinds of a fool for all the angsty thoughts she'd had just an hour or so earlier. She didn't wait for his lying answer, but waved him away. 'Don't get your feet wet.'

He frowned and she thought he was going to say more, but he let it go, raised a hand to Sorrel, turned and walked away.

'What is it with you two?' Sorrel asked.

'I don't know what you mean,' Elle denied.

'You look at one another as if you want to tear each other's clothes off and yet you're keeping each other at arm's length.'

If only.

'Sean doesn't do commitment, Sorrel.'

'So?'

Pretty much what she'd been thinking until he'd looked her in the face and lied.

'Just leave it,' Elle said, turning to serve someone.

The Royal St George Golf Club was on the far side of the country on the south-east coast. Charlotte had got his round robin email asking if anyone knew what RSG might stand for. Apparently Oliver played golf and had been to the Open the last time it had been played there.

And Sean had seen some golf trophies in Basil's cottage. He'd tried phoning, but they'd refused to give any information about members or guests, which meant that he had to go there.

He hadn't told Elle where he was going because he hadn't wanted to get her hopes up. Just as well. He'd been clutching at straws and now he was stuck in a motel with a toothbrush and cheap razor from a slot machine instead of sending out for a takeaway and spending the evening with Elle and her family, sitting out beneath the lilac tree, with the blackbird serenading them.

And, with luck, getting a kiss goodnight for his trouble.

He checked his watch. Picked up his mobile phone and called her. Listened to her phone ringing until it was picked up by voicemail. Listened to her asking him to leave a message, but then cut the connection. There was no message. He had nothing to tell her. He just wanted to talk to her, hear about her day. Hear her laugh.

Tomorrow. He'd call her in the morning, tell her where he was, what he'd done. What an idiot he was.

Elle had looked at her phone when it rang, seen the caller ID and left it to be picked up by voicemail.

It had been a good day and a bad day.

Until Sean had left Longbourne Court to follow the blonde home it had been a pretty good day.

They had made a lot of money for the PRC. Exactly how much she'd work out in the morning. More than enough not to feel guilty about having to deduct costs.

All the leaflets had gone, thanks to Sean, although how many were now trampled into the grass for the Longbourne gardeners to pick up remained to be seen.

But it had gone downhill from there. Sean hadn't returned and when they'd packed up just before six, Rosie decided to sulk. By the time Elle had managed to get the trick of coaxing her into life, her day had hit rock-bottom. And when they did get home, only she knew how to dismantle the ice cream maker, how to clean and disinfect it. Only she had a precious hygiene certificate—now stuck up beside Basil's inside Rosie—thanks to her stint working in the Blue Boar kitchens.

Then she had gone to work. Late again.

How could he?

She didn't expect a forever commitment from a man she'd met only a week ago, who had given her fair warning that the word wasn't in his vocabulary but, no matter how short it was to be, it had to be total commitment while it lasted.

It seemed he couldn't even manage that.

She ignored the phone for as long as she could before, unable to help herself, she picked it up. Called up her messages.

Nothing.

Sean hadn't bothered to leave one. Not even a simple good-night and, despite the warm night she shivered, rolled off the bed and closed the window to shut out the heavy scent of the lilac.

CHAPTER TWELVE

Don't drown your sorrows. Suffocate them with ice cream.

—Rosie's Diary

ELLE got up early when she heard Geli making a move. Made her breakfast before she went to do her dog-walking stuff, then shut herself away in her office to rationalise the accounts for the PRC charity.

She checked stock, making a note of what they needed to reorder, and kept herself busy making a cake as a treat for everyone. They deserved it.

Doing her best not to think about the previous Sunday when she'd slept in, got up when everyone else had gone out. When Sean McElroy had walked into her kitchen and turned her world upside down.

Difficult with that pink kettle gleaming across the kitchen at her. With her pink dress hanging in the scullery waiting to be washed in the morning. With Sean leaning against the frame of the open door.

Geli had left it open when she'd rushed off to walk her waifs and strays and after a night shut up in her bedroom Elle had been glad of the fresh air. She really was going to have to start locking it.

'Hi,' he said. 'Something smells good.'

'I made a cake.'

'You are a domestic goddess. Any chance of a cup of tea to go with it?' he asked.

'It's too hot to eat, but help yourself to tea,' she said, waving in the direction of the kettle. 'You know where everything is.' Proud of the fact that she'd managed to control the wobble in her voice. 'You look as if you've had a hard night.'

He rubbed a hand over his unshaven chin. 'You could say that,' he said, pushing himself away from the door. He checked that there was water in the kettle and switched it on. Pulled out a chair and collapsed onto it.

Now he was closer, she could see that he looked exhausted. 'Duck give you a hard time, did she?'

'Duck?' He managed a grin. 'Not a duck. It was a wild goose. I didn't have a problem at the estate, Elle, but then you already knew that, didn't you?'

'I knew you were lying to me, if that's what you're asking.'

'Yes, well… The truth is that I drove to Kent yesterday afternoon.'

'*Kent?*' That was on the other side of the country and if he'd driven there and back since yesterday afternoon it was hardly surprising that he looked exhausted. 'Why?'

'I send out an email to everyone I know asking if they knew what RSG might be. Someone suggested Royal St George. It's a golf club.'

He'd driven all that way just to find Basil?

'Let me guess. The someone would have been Charlotte?' He looked up. 'I saw you talking to her. Just before you left.'

'Someone she knows suggested it. She gave me a lift home so that I could pick up my car.' He smiled wryly. 'She didn't know it was for you or I doubt she would have bothered.'

'Probably not,' she said dryly. 'Does Basil play golf?'

'There were some trophies in his cottage.'

'Recent?'

'Nothing since nineteen seventy-five.'

'And for that you drove what, four hundred miles, on the off chance that he might still be playing?' she exclaimed.

'He might have been there. Then I'd have been a hero instead of an idiot.'

'Stay with the idiot,' she advised. 'RSG could mean anything.'

'I know. I spent most of the night surfing the 'net and discovering just how many anythings it might have been.'

'Such as?'

'The Red Star Garage?'

'Basil comes to you for spanner work,' she reminded him.

'Ridge Side Gardens. Rodney, Simmons and Garth. Roundabout Servicing Guide…'

'It's a Rumpelstiltskin puzzle, Sean.'

He looked confused.

'Like the name in the fairy tale,' she said. 'Off the wall. Unguessable. Reorder Sparkly Gravel. Ring Supermarket for Gravy. Retrieve Second Gargoyle.'

'Reverse, Stop, Go?' he suggested, grinning as he caught on.

'Far too sensible. Ribbons—Silver and Gold…' She stopped. 'Actually, that makes some kind of sense. I've got those on my own shopping list. For the wedding. And the hen night. Why didn't you tell me?' she asked. 'Where you were going. I would have come with you.'

'Would you? What about Freddy? You'd have missed work.' He shook his head. 'I didn't want to get your hopes up.'

'My hopes can handle the occasional disappointment.' She wasn't sure she could take another evening, night, believing that he'd abandoned her for another woman. 'But thank you.' She leaned forward and kissed his forehead. 'Do you want some breakfast?'

'Actually, all I want right at this moment is to hold you, kiss you, then lie down and go to sleep for ten hours. But breakfast would be good to be going on with.'

'Breakfast can wait.'

She stood up, held out her hand and, as he took it and stood up, she turned and walked through the house, up the staircase, into her bedroom. She closed the door, then, her heart pounding like the entire timpani section of the London Philharmonic Orchestra, she said, 'Hold me.'

'Elle…'

She lifted her arms, put them around his neck.

'What are you doing?' he asked, putting his hands around her waist.

'Shh,' she whispered, relaxing against him. 'No questions. You're holding me.'

'And now I kiss you?'

'Tick,' she murmured.

'Close your eyes.'

She obeyed and he kissed each lid with a butterfly touch of his mouth. She waited, breath held, but when she finally opened her eyes, he was just looking at her. And so she kissed him. A brush of her lips against his.

That was all it was meant to be, but the touch of his day-old beard against her cheek stirred a darker need that shivered through them both and, with a groan, he gathered her, holding her so that his body was touching hers, warm, hard, as the kiss deepened into something fierce, desperate.

The need to breathe drove them apart but they clung together for what seemed like an age. Until Elle wished she'd told him to lie down first so that she could have held him, watched him while he slept. So that she could have been the first thing he saw when he woke.

Instead, she lifted her head. 'Lie down, Sean. Sleep for as long as you need.'

'Elle…'

'Mmm?'

'Remind me, next time I list my heart's desires, to be a little more ambitious.'

'The bathroom's through there,' she said, but she was smiling.

* * *

Sean slowly surfaced from a dream so vivid that he could still smell the scent of Elle's shampoo. Opened his eyes and for a moment had no idea where he was. He rolled onto his back. Somewhere a door banged. A dog barked and Geli's voice protested unintelligibly from somewhere below him.

Not a dream, then.

He was lying in Elle's bed, the scent was in her pillow, her sheets. He had been honest with her and she had responded. No games, no nonsense. And, clearly, if his body had berated his lack of ambition, his brain had known his limits.

Holding her, kissing her, had been beyond special, but the moment his head had hit the pillow he'd been asleep. And maybe his heart had known something else. Elle was right. They barely knew one another; they needed time to build something that would last.

It was a new concept for him, but one which, as he'd driven through the dawn, had drawn him to Elle rather than the estate, lending wings to his wheels.

He checked the time. Just gone three. Not ten hours, but long enough. Long enough without Elle beside him. He rolled off the bed and saw that she'd left him a message:

'Rocky Road, Sasparilla and Ginger Beer.'

He laughed. 'We'll get you, Rumpelstiltskin,' he said, then looked out across the garden. He was right above the lilac tree, he discovered, and tied to it there was a dog, a scruffy terrier with a battered ear, drinking from a bowl.

Geli, tearful, was looking at someone out of sight. 'There was no room at the rescue centre. I'll find her a home. I *will*!'

'Better do it before Elle gets home.' That was Sorrel. The practical one. 'She can't take on any more right now, Geli.'

He leaned out of the window. Since his car was parked in the drive, his presence could hardly be a secret.

'Is she house-trained?' Geli looked up, startled, her eyes wide to see him emerging from her sister's bedroom window. Okaaay, so he'd got that one wrong. 'The dog.'

'Absolutely!' Well, she would say that. 'It's just that her owner died and there was no one to take her in.'

'So no one would worry if I took her home with me?' he said.

'Would you?'

'I might. For a cup of tea.'

'Well… I'm *supposed* to do a home check first, to make sure you've got enough room for her. And proper fences,' she said.

'Will the Haughton Manor estate do?'

She blinked. 'All of it?'

'She'd have a couple of acres to herself, give or take the odd fox passing through.'

She shrugged. 'I suppose that would be okay, but who'll look after her during the day? When you're at work. I'm assuming you don't have a wife or a live-in partner?' she added pointedly.

'You assume right. And I'll take her with me to the office.'

'They'd let you do that?'

'I'm the boss.'

'Oh.'

He thought she'd be pleased, but instead she looked disappointed, as if she was hoping that there really was no one to take the dog. So that she could keep her.

'Of course I will need someone to take care of her in the evenings when I help Elle with Rosie. Or if I have to go away for a day or two.'

'It would have to be someone responsible,' Geli said.

'Absolutely, and I'm prepared to pay the top rate for a reliable dog-sitter. If you can recommend anyone, Angelica?'

'Well, I suppose you could bring her here,' she said casually. 'I could look after her. Elle couldn't object to that, since she wouldn't be costing us anything.'

'On the contrary,' he said. 'So? Will I do?'

He heard himself making a commitment. Open-ended. He should be panicking but he wasn't.

'I'll give you a trial period of a month. Just to make sure you take to one another.' She sighed. 'And if you're going to sleep here on a regular basis, you'd better call me Geli.'

Sorrel stepped into view, looked up. She didn't say anything. Just smiled and raised both thumbs in approval behind her sister's back.

'Where is Elle?' he asked when he joined them in the garden, folded himself up to make the acquaintance of his new best friend. She practically threw herself at him.

'She left a note to say she'd gone to fetch Gran.' Geli lifted her shoulders in an awkward little shrug. 'She wanders off sometimes, gets on a bus, then phones Elle in a panic when she doesn't know where she is.'

'I'll go and fetch them,' he said, taking out his phone, digging in his pocket for his car keys. And coming up empty-handed. Which explained why Geli hadn't seen his car. Elle had taken his vintage Jaguar coupé on a granny hunt…

In his ear, Elle's phone went to voicemail, which probably meant that she was still behind the wheel. Hopefully on her way home.

'Lovage…' he went inside '…thanks for the respite care. I hope Lally's okay. Give me a call if I can do anything. You'll find my fuel charge card in the glove compartment if you need it,' he added, giving her the pin number. Something else he'd never done. 'I'm going home now to change into something that doesn't sparkle but I'll be back later for a slice of that cake.' Then he called for a taxi.

'Can I get you some toast or something?' Geli asked when he rejoined them in the garden, clearly eager to show her gratitude.

'Thanks,' he said, 'but right now…' He looked at the dog. 'What's her name?'

'Mabel.'

'Mabel. Right… Well, Mabel and I have to go shopping for dog stuff. Food. Bowls. A basket.' The dog, he discovered, was listening. Following his every move with desperate, anxious eyes.

He took a breath, said, 'Tell your sister that I'll pick up some pizza.' If she'd been out all day hunting her grandmother, the last thing she needed to do was cook.

'No worries. I'm making a spag bol.' Sorrel smiled at him. 'You could pick up some Parmesan cheese, if you like.'

His car was pulled up neatly in the drive when he returned bearing a block of Parmesan soon after six. He resisted the twitchy need to check its immaculate bodywork and instead walked through the rear, Mabel hard on his heels.

There was no one in the kitchen. 'Hello?'

He put the cheese on the table, peered into the morning room. Lally, dozing in front of the television, opened her eyes.

'Where's Elle?' he asked.

'Oh…er…I think she went upstairs…'

Elle lay back amongst the crumpled sheets, exhausted from driving on pins in Sean's beautiful car. From tension. She was always afraid of what she'd find when her grandmother wandered but she'd been sitting in a pub being chatted up by some old guy who'd bought her a drink.

This was perfect. The pillow smelled of Sean and she nestled her cheek where his had been, breathing in the spicy scent of his shampoo, or his aftershave, listening to her messages. Sorrel asking if she was okay. Her phone company trying to sell her a more up to date package. Sean… Oh, help! Oh, bless…

She hit call back, waited impatiently. Somewhere in the house a phone began to ring and she sighed, recognising the ring of Rosie's BlackBerry.

Geli was out. Sorrel had gone to the village shop to fetch cream to fill the cake.

No… It had stopped now. Sorrel must be back.

Sean answered his phone. 'Elle?'

'Sean…'

'You sound surprised. You did call me?'

'Sorry, I just…' She stopped. 'Yes. I called you. I've just got home and picked up your message. I'm sorry about taking your car.'

'It's okay. I'm glad it was there for you. All well?'

'Yes. Gran decided to go off and look for Basil. She caught the bus to Melchester, but got off when she recognised a pub they all used to go to. It was all changed inside and when he wasn't there she panicked.'

'Have you asked her what RSG means?'

'On the way home. No joy.'

'Just a thought. What are you doing?' he asked.

'Right now?'

'Right now.'

'I'm lying with my head in the dent you made in my pillow.'

'I wish I was still there,' he murmured.

'Me too.' Wished he was lying beside her instead of just being a disembodied voice in her ear. 'I wish you were here, lying beside me, holding me. Kissing me.'

'You'll have to move over,' he said.

'Get here and I will,' she said, then, as there was a tap on her door, she realised that the sound in her ear was the dialling tone.

'Come in…'

The door swung open.

'Sean…'

'Your wish is my command.'

She didn't speak, just moved over and he came and sat beside her, kicked off one of his shoes.

'Sean! Mabel has just eaten half a pound of Parmesan cheese!' Sorrel called up the stairs.

'Mabel?' Elle queried.

'A dog.' He pushed his foot back into the shoe, took her hand, pulled her to her feet, held her for a moment. Kissed her. 'It's a long story. Maybe we should go for a walk while I tell you. I suspect, right now, she's a walking time bomb.'

'Where on earth did she come from?' Elle asked as they headed across the Common towards the riverbank. 'If I'd imagined you with a dog it would have been some glossy pedigree, not that sorry excuse for a mutt.'

'Her owner died. She had nowhere to go.'

'So you took her in?' The commitment-phobic male who didn't have as much as a goldfish in his spare and beautifully furnished home? Why wasn't she buying that? 'Between waking up this afternoon and now?'

'It was an emergency.'

'So would that be permanently? Or until you can find a good home for her?' she asked.

'A dog isn't just for Christmas, Elle.'

'A pity more people didn't realise that. I suppose you could change her name,' she said.

'Wouldn't that confuse her?'

'Actually, I don't think dogs care what you call them. As long as you call them.'

'And what about you? Are you Elle this evening? Or Lovage?' he said.

'Is there a difference?' she asked carelessly. As if she didn't know.

'There is a touch of split personality about you. This morning you were most definitely Lovage. Warm, loving, with passion simmering just beneath the surface. You were Lovage when I arrived just now, but you seem to have morphed into the practical, down-to-earth Elle.'

'Is that a problem?'

'No. I like you both,' he said.

They walked beside the river, with Mabel eagerly sniffing every tree. Called at the pub for a drink. Had something to eat sitting outside. Were home by nine.

Sean shut Mabel in the Land Rover, then walked Elle as far

as the side gate. 'What have we got this week with Rosie?' he asked.

'We?'

'I feel bad about abandoning you to Rosie's moods yesterday.'

'I coped. I will cope. It's my business, Sean, and I'm taking it seriously.'

'Does that mean you'll be giving in your notice at the Blue Boar?' he asked casually.

'Not yet. Not until I know Rosie is capable of supporting us. I need to know that I have some money coming in.'

'Scared?'

'Witless. So thank you. I would be grateful for your help at the company reception on Wednesday,' she said.

'That would be a black lace dress affair?'

'Absolutely.'

'Then nothing will keep me away. Anything else?'

Oh, yes. What she wanted, had wanted all evening with a scratchy kind of longing, was for him to kiss her witless. Be the man she'd left in her bed that morning. But he was right. She was being practical, careful Elle and he was taking his cue from her. Being a friend.

'Don't worry about Wednesday. You're a busy man and Sorrel is going to help me,' she assured him.

He put a hand against the wall behind her, leaning in, backing her up so that she could feel the warm brick catching at her hair, pulling it free from the restraining plait. 'That would be the Sorrel who's been working all week to get *Scoop!* up and running. The same Sorrel who isn't supposed to be deflected by anything until she's got a first class degree?'

She could feel his breath against her temple. Her own breath seemed stuck somewhere between in and out and going nowhere.

A hot, sexy friend who was turning her insides to mush and tossing sense out of the window.

'Good point,' she gasped. 'But if you take her place, who'll look after Mabel?'

Elle being practical. Showing him how commitment worked.

'Geli said she'd dog-sit any time.'

'Geli? When?' Then, catching on, 'Is this one of her waifs and strays?'

'Not now. I'm on a month's trial, but I'm not giving her back.'

'Wednesday, then. Six o'clock.'

'I'll be here.'

She swallowed. 'Great. Can Mabel wait while you have a cup of…tea?'

Sean smiled at the way she'd carefully avoided the 'coffee' euphemism.

'I'm sorry.'

Truly sorry. He'd had time to think this afternoon. About Elle. About himself. About the two of them. He didn't want this to be some casual relationship that they fell into and then out of as quickly. He wanted to get to know her. Wanted her to get to know him. It was too important to rush, but right now this slow courting was scrambling his brain.

He loved the fact that they had talked this evening, shared the small stuff, laughed a lot. But it was a good thing that it was Elle in residence tonight because otherwise he wouldn't have been responsible for his actions.

'I'm afraid Mabel is not quite as house-trained as I was led to believe. She'll chew the seat to shreds if I leave her in the car. You might get Sorrel to run the Trades Descriptions Act by Geli.'

'What can I say?'

'Kiss me?' he suggested.

She swallowed. 'Kiss me,' she whispered.

And he cradled Elle's head in his hands and kissed her. A

long, lingering kiss that left him wanting more. Hopefully left her wanting more too. And then he walked away while he still could.

Mabel chewed Sean's boots, chased the ducks, stole his breakfast while he had his back turned and rolled in anything disgusting that she could find.

But then she lay on his feet beneath his desk in the office, sneaked onto the sofa at night and pressed against him to have her ears rubbed, woke him with a wet nose under his chin. And she was quick. She'd learned that while he'd tolerate the loss of his breakfast and was prepared to hose her down no matter how bad she smelled, the ducks were off limits.

And he learned, too. Learned that, like the land, people responded more readily to warmth than prickly reserve. Olivia was relaxed and was coming up with ideas for the stable block that had him eating his words. And she and Hattie were ganging up to promote the Orangery as a wedding venue. He should have hated it, but found himself enjoying the tussle. And Elle had been part of that, punting for wedding business for Rosie when they'd all had supper together at the barn with Henry and the children, down for the long weekend, after the Steam Fair.

And he'd retrieved the box that contained his mother's possessions, found a photograph of his mother.

'Your father took this,' Elle said, when he showed it to her.

'How do you know that?'

'Look at her eyes. They're shining. Anyone can see that she's looking at the man she loves. She was lovely.'

'Yes, she was. I hadn't realised.'

'Put it in a frame. Remember her, Sean.'

Elle loved having Sean at her side at evening functions. Excluding the hen night. Those girls might be wearing angel wings but when they were out for fun any man was game and she was beginning to think of him as hers.

It was dangerous, risking-the-heart territory, but that was what a heart was for. To give. And she'd already given hers. It was his. All he had to do was take it.

Sean… Well, he seemed to feel that he needed to prove something to her. Or maybe to himself. That he wasn't like her father. Or his.

That he didn't just want one thing. That he was fine with her family. Maybe getting that way with his own. Healing…

No problem. Some things were worth waiting for. Meanwhile, she had him for walks, for supper occasionally, and for kisses that made it increasingly hard to say goodnight.

And she still had the 'call me' option. His birthday, as she'd discovered from Olivia, wasn't that far off.

Sean felt his heart expand under Elle's warmth. She filled his evenings with fun, his heart with love. Shared quiet days with him with only Mabel at their heels while they explored the river, lay in the meadow, hidden from the world as the wild flowers reached full height. While he tested a strength, a certainty growing in him that he was more than he believed. While she learned to trust that he would be there for her. Always.

CHAPTER THIRTEEN

The most blissful words in any language. Vanilla ice cream with hot fudge sauce.

—Rosie's Diary

'I'M REALLY sorry, Freddy, but I can't work tomorrow. In fact, I need to talk to you about my hours.'

She'd switched shifts with the girl who owed her from the previous week but Freddy had found out and had called her in early, apparently furious. As if it made any difference to him as long as he had staff cover.

'Saturday is a big day and you are my top waitress but clearly you have more interesting things to do these days,' he said, tossing the *Country Chronicle* on his desk, open at the article featuring the television shoot in Upper Haughton. 'You appear to be running your own business around mine.'

She hadn't seen the new edition of the magazine but, as there was a large photograph of her standing in front of Rosie, describing her as 'local events entrepreneur, Elle Amery' there was no point in denying it.

'This was on the sixth?' he said. 'The same day as the "family crisis" that kept you from work?'

'It was a family crisis. My great-uncle has disappeared and I had to stand in for him. He'd signed a contract with the film company and they were going to sue if someone didn't turn up.'

Freddy didn't look impressed. Well, she wasn't sure she'd have believed her, either. ...*I had to spend the morning filming a television programme; I didn't want to do it, honest, but I didn't have any choice*... Not the world's most convincing excuse.

'I suppose this is why you've been swapping your shifts, letting other women take them when you're too busy for the day job? Did you think I wouldn't notice?'

'I never left you without cover,' she said, wondering why on earth she was feeling so guilty. It wasn't as if he'd paid her for the day she'd missed. 'It's why I can't work on Saturday. Rosie, that's the ice cream van,' she explained, 'is booked for a wedding.'

'I see. And yet I seem to remember that not long ago you were asking me for extra hours because of yet another financial crisis at Chez Amery.'

'It was all very sudden, Freddy—'

'And then, of course, there's the small matter of the dress you ruined.'

'Excuse me?'

'The Honourable Miss Pickering, the young lady whose dress you drenched while you were flirting with her boyfriend, brought in the receipt. She expects compensation.'

'A few drops of water wouldn't ruin a linen dress,' she protested.

'She said it was wild silk.'

'Not in a million years. She's trying it on.'

Freddy reached out, touched her cheek with the tips of his fingers. 'No, my dear. I think that would be you.'

She took a step back. 'Me?'

'Little innocent, Elle Amery. Leading me on with those big eyes. Promising me. Soon, soon... But always making me wait a little longer. All lies.'

'Freddy,' she said sharply, hoping to make him snap out of it, get a grip. She backed away, stumbling against a chair. He was on her before she could move, trapped against the edge of his desk, the wall to one side, Freddy the other.

'I've been good to you, Elle. So good to you. And so patient.' She tried not to flinch as he stroked her jaw, but almost fainted as his thumb brushed over her lips. He caught her with his other hand, his fingers biting into her arm as he held her up, pushing her back against the desk with his body. 'Very good and very patient and it's time to stop playing the innocent little girl with me.'

'Freddy...' This time the word was squeezed through her throat as he leaned closer.

'But you're not a little girl any more, are you?'

Oh, no. No, no, no...The words were filling her head but they couldn't make it through the fear blocking her throat, a great hard lump...

'I saw the way you looked at that man. He left a note and his telephone number, but I won't have you picking up men right under my nose.'

This was her fault.

Freddy had always been protective of her. She'd been so young when she'd started working for him and he knew her history, the trouble she and her family were in. She'd been grateful for his help, even though she'd always known, on some subconscious level, that it was more than a fatherly interest. That she needed to take care.

But the job had been too important and she'd ignored the warning voices, pushing them to the back of her mind. And everything had been fine, under control. Until this moment, she had never felt threatened by him.

'I've seen you with him. Walking across the Common when you should have been here, with me...'

Noooo...

If she didn't do something, scream, use her knee, fight him, he was going to touch her, kiss her. Do something much worse.

Cleaners. Where were the cleaners?

But it was as if her vocal cords were set in concrete and, like a rabbit caught in the headlights of a car, nothing was getting through from her brain to her limbs.

His breath was on her cheek, his mouth inches from her own and the further back she leaned to escape him the more vulnerable she became.

She was close to blacking out, gasping for breath, when a sharp rap on the door had Freddy spinning round, leaving her slumped against the wall, struggling for breath.

'Who let you in?' Freddy gasped. 'We're not open.'

'A cleaner was just leaving but I'm not here to eat.' Sean stepped from the shadow of the lobby and into the office, his face set in the expressionless mask that she'd seen once before.

'I'm sorry to disturb you at work, Elle, but when I went to the house your grandmother told me that Mr Frederickson had called and asked you to come in early.'

'This is a private staff meeting—'

'I can see exactly what this is...' Sean's voice was so cold that Elle shivered '...but your quickie over the desk is going to have to wait until I've passed on a message.'

What? Then, bypassing the 'quickie' remark, 'What message? Have you found Basil? Where? Where is he?' It came out as little more than a croak.

He didn't answer, simply handed her a postcard with a picture of Brighton Pavilion on one side. On the other was a brief message:

Thought I was a goner, but it turned out to be a gallstone. Spending a few days by the sea. Keep an eye on Rosie for Lovage. I'll be home at the weekend. Basil.

'He's okay,' she said.

'Apparently. RSG *is* the Royal St George. But it's a hospital.'

Sean turned away from her flushed cheeks, tousled hair, the

unfastened top button on her shirt, calling himself every kind of fool.

He'd seen it on that Saturday night, when Freddy had pawed her and she'd smiled right back at him.

He'd seen the way she'd blushed when Sorrel had teased her about the man, changed the subject when Geli had been rather more forthright. The way she'd brushed aside his warning that Freddy's interest was more than fatherly.

Idiot that he was, it had never occurred to him that she would go to such lengths to keep her job. Keep her family. Even when she'd told him that she would do anything for them.

Damn Basil. Damn Rosie. Damn his own foolishness for falling for the blushing innocence. No one that innocent could have played him so sweetly, drawing him in despite his determination to run, not walk away. Left him weak with frustrated longing with phone teasing innuendo.

That she was her mother's daughter there could be no doubt. While he'd been daydreaming about days on the river, walking her through the wild flower meadow that he'd regenerated, his head in the clouds, she'd have had him over Rosie's counter that first Sunday if her sisters hadn't come home unexpectedly.

He didn't have a problem with that. She was free to do what she wanted, with whom she wanted. It was her dishonesty that curdled in his gullet.

At least with Charlotte there had been no pretence.

But Elle had made him believe in the possibility of forever, made him want it. Him. Sean McElroy. The man who'd seen it all and had known it was all hogwash, pie in the sky, a cloud cuckoo land fantasy from the day he was born. Who always kept relationships casual, never got emotionally involved. Who wasn't going to mess up his life grabbing for something as ephemeral as love, fall into the trap of caring enough to get hurt. Fall in love.

That he couldn't forgive.

But it finally explained why she was adamant that Sorrel should not take a job at the Blue Boar. Elle was the sacrifice, although not much of one if the way she'd been panting for it was any indication.

He stopped, turned.

Stupid, foolish girl. Why hadn't she gone to someone, asked for help?

Elle watched Sean walk away. He was going to leave her? He really believed she'd been a willing participant?

While fear had paralysed her, anger sent a shot of adrenaline surging through her and as Freddy made another grab for her she handed him off, jamming the heel of her hand beneath his nose then walked away.

Sean, far enough away to confirm that he'd been about to walk away and leave her, had apparently changed his mind and was coming back. Too late. She walked past him without a word.

'Elle…'

She didn't look round, didn't stop.

Behind her, the door of the Blue Boar was flung open. 'If you go now, Elle,' Freddy called after her, 'you won't have a job to come back to.'

'Constructive dismissal. Sexual harassment. Assault. You'll be hearing from my solicitor,' she said, not bothering to turn around, not missing a stride, the adrenaline still pumping hard. She'd been listening when her sister had been talking about employment law.

About to add that the Honourable Miss Pickering could go whistle for her dress, she didn't bother. Freddy had been lying about that. She'd known it the minute he'd said the dress was silk.

Behind her, she heard a car door close, the throaty purr of its engine and Sean pulled alongside her in the Jaguar she'd once borrowed with such a light heart.

'Get in, Elle,' he said, leaning across, pushing the passenger door open.

One glance confirmed that he looked as grim as she felt but

she didn't slow down from the headlong charge that was taking her home. She had to keep moving. The minute she stopped, the adrenaline would run out and she'd collapse in a shivering heap. She simply told him, in the fewest syllables possible, to leave her alone.

He cruised along the kerb, keeping pace with her. 'At least let me take you home.'

'You left me.' She kept walking. While her legs kept moving she was in control. 'I can't believe you thought I was lying back and taking one just to keep my job.' He didn't deny it. 'Well, I did tell you I'd do anything for my family. I guess you believed me.'

'If you'd seen it from where I was standing…'

'I am *not* my mother,' she declared. 'I am not *your* mother either!'

Realising that she was attracting attention from the bus queue, she crossed the road and walked across the Common. Sean abandoned his car and came after her.

'Shall I take you to the police?' he asked.

'And say what? It's his word against mine. He'll say I was willing and you'd back him up, wouldn't you?' she snarled.

She took out her phone as she walked, leaving messages for both Sorrel and Geli on their voicemail not to go near the Blue Boar on any account.

Sean kept pace with her but did not speak again, made no attempt to touch her, hold her, comfort her. He simply walked with her until she reached her gate and then watched her go inside.

Elle went straight upstairs, stood under the shower, letting the water mingle with the stupid tears that were stupidly pouring down her stupid cheeks. All tears did was make your eyes red. It was only when the water ran cold and she began to shiver that she made an effort to pull herself together, try an old trick her mother had taught her. Look for something positive in everything bad.

Freddy's attack had shaken her. It had been vile. But it had forced her to face up to something that deep down she knew, had been doing her best to ignore as she clung to her safety net.

Sean… Well, he had, whether he believed it or not, rescued her. And he had warned her about Freddy. Which made her a fool if nothing worse, she acknowledged as she plugged in the hairdryer. He'd also brought her good news of Basil who'd apparently been afraid he was dying and was now living it up in Brighton.

She picked up the postcard that she'd been clutching as she walked home. Winced. Realised that her hand was swollen. Just how hard had she hit Freddy?

No. She refused to waste another second of her life thinking about him. From now on she would devote herself to making *Scoop!* a success.

Not just something to fit in around the 'day' job but something to build on, make her own. Her dream. And as she dried her hair she crowded out the horror of what had just happened by making lists in her head of the stuff she still had to do.

That was scary too but, the minute she stopped, Sean McElroy filled the vacuum. His blue eyes. The way his hair fell across his forehead, his jeans clung to his backside. His expressionless face as he'd stood in the doorway of Freddy's office seeing yet another woman who had no moral core.

Sean, who had no concept of permanency in relationships. Who assumed the worst because he never looked for the best.

She wanted to weep again. Not for herself, or for the possibility of something special that they'd lost, but for his impoverished life.

She sighed. Time to put the bad stuff behind her, go and find Gran and tell her that Basil was okay. That he'd be home soon. Home. Not some rented cottage on the Haughton Manor estate, but here, where he belonged.

Looking on the bright side, she now had all the time in the world to get stuff ready for the wedding.

She folded up the Blue Boar's black uniform, not sure what to do with it—returning it was not an option—and pulled on a pair of the brightest shorts she could find, with a tank top, and went, barefoot, into the kitchen.

The pink kettle was still hot and she found her grandmother, straw gardening hat tilted at a saucy angle, in the morning room, enjoying a cup of tea.

She wasn't alone.

'Oh, there you are, Elle,' her grandmother said. 'Sean tells me that he's heard from Basil.'

'Yes. He sent a postcard.'

'Really? Where from?'

'Brighton,' she said shortly, picking up the teapot. Sean rescued it before she dropped it and poured tea into a waiting cup.

'You're harder to get rid of than a bad penny,' she said ungratefully.

'You're not the first person to say that. Let me see your hand,' he said calmly.

'It's nothing,' she said, not wanting him to touch her, but, as she jerked away, she knocked it on the table, cried out. 'Owww... That hurt.'

'Not as much as Freddy's broken nose, if that helps,' he said wryly.

'No...' Okay, she'd hit him and maybe there had been a bit of a crunch, but... She shook her head. 'No.'

'You didn't see the blood. Come on, let's get some ice on this.' Sean kept hold of her wrist as he walked through to the kitchen, then rummaged around in the freezer until he found a tray of ice cubes. 'Rolling pin?'

Her hand was throbbing now and she didn't argue. 'First drawer.'

He tipped the ice on a tea towel and battered it until it was crushed, then, supporting her hand from beneath, he pressed the ice pack against the swelling.

'I can hold it,' she said dully, focusing on his neatly knotted tie, the perfectly ironed shirt. Not his usual working clothes. He'd been going somewhere, she thought, and had stopped by to give her the good news. Then, when he didn't let her go, 'If I broke Freddy's nose, he'll be the one coming after me for assault,'

'Nonsense. He'll tell everyone he tripped over the step.'

'He won't let me off that easily.'

'He'd be wise to consider it, or it might become a reality.'

'Don't! Please,' she said tightly.

'You're protecting him?' he bit out.

'No.' She shook her head, then forced herself to look up. Be bold, honest, true. 'I'm protecting *you*.'

His head went back as if she'd slapped him, knocked the breath out of him and for a moment neither of them spoke.

'Don't you have an estate to run?' she asked him.

He nodded, clearly relieved to be offered an escape. 'I should have been in Melchester an hour ago.'

'Then go.' Still he hesitated. 'I'll be fine.'

'You have my number…' He stopped as if realising that the offer to ride to her rescue was a hollow thing. 'I'll see you tomorrow.'

'There's no need, Sean. Sorrel and I can manage the wedding.'

'You won't be able to load up, or drive Rosie with that hand,' he pointed out. 'What time are you leaving?'

'Twelve. I have to pick up the freezer stuff from the cash and carry.'

Sean made it to the gate before the pain hit him, brought him to a halt. The realisation of what he'd lost. No, what he'd thrown away.

What kind of man was he?

He could empathise with a dead duckling suffocating in a plastic bag, but people… His mother, his ever increasing family. To them he was judgemental, harsh, cold as January charity.

All the while he'd been congratulating himself that he'd

opened up to his family, made big strides in being a man who Elle could trust, rely on, he'd been fooling himself.

When it mattered, when he'd seen Elle locked in Frederickson's arms, even though he knew her, knew what kind of woman she was, he'd instantly leapt to the wrong conclusion. Seeing only what he'd expected to see.

'Love them, keep them safe. Whatever they do.'

Her words mocked him.

He'd moved nowhere. He was still thinking of himself, of how *he* was being hurt. And yet, even when he'd let her down in the worst way, Elle was still more concerned for him than herself. Concerned that, in an attempt to redeem himself, he would be the one charged with assault.

'I'm protecting you...'

Three little words shattering the barrier layered on over the years with each loss. A barrier against feeling anything. It came at him now like a whirlwind being sucked into a vacuum. Battering him, tearing at him, cutting him.

'You have my number...'

Hollow words indeed.

He took a deep breath and began to walk back across the village to where he'd left his car. Time to put that right.

Elle tried to work, concentrate on *Scoop!* Updated *Rosie's Diary*, picking at the keys one-handed, trying not to let herself think.

She'd been forced to tell her sisters and her grandmother what had happened with Freddy, so that they understood they had to stay away from the pub. In case the police did turn up to question her. She told them as little as possible about Sean's part in the events, but he'd walked her home, told her grandmother that there had been a bit of a unpleasantness. They knew he'd been there, had drawn their own conclusions.

She knew she should contact the police herself. Make a complaint, if only to protect some other girl. Except Freddy wasn't like that with anyone else. Not even the sixth-form girls who worked at the weekend.

It was just her. Looking back, analysing it, it was all there. The obsession. She was his little virgin. His... But then Sean had turned up and suddenly she'd been snatched away from him. Spoiled...

Just thinking about it made her feel sick. Talk about sticking your head in the sand.

Sean arrived dead on time the following morning, wearing his *Scoop!* T-shirt, looking good enough to eat. The slightly haggard look just made him appear all the more dangerous.

He knocked on the back door and, unlike Mabel, who rushed in, he waited politely on the step.

'Here he is,' Geli cried as Mabel ran around her feet, hoovering up the crumbs she'd made getting herself some lunch. 'The hero of the hour.'

'What? No...'

Geli took one look at them, said, 'Walkies!' and, grabbing a sandwich, raced after Mabel.

'Some hero,' Sean said bitterly. 'What did you tell them?'

'As little as possible. Shall we go?'

This was as bad as she'd thought it would be. Worse. If there had been anyone else available to help her, she'd have called to tell him that she didn't need him. Should have called him anyway. But her hand was stiff and the pain went right up to her shoulder; also, she hadn't been able to quite give up on the hope that somehow, when she saw him, it would be all right.

Wrong.

In those few minutes when he'd thought she was Freddy's willing victim, when she had seen just how fragile a relationship could be, something had broken inside her.

Trust. There had to be trust. But she'd leapt to the wrong conclusion when she'd seen him following Charlotte from the Pink Ribbon Club Garden Party. How could she blame him for disbelieving the evidence of his own eyes?

'How's your hand?' he asked as she reached up to take Rosie's key from the hook.

'Fine.' She flexed it without thinking, then wished she hadn't. 'Thanks to your first aid.'

He beat her to the key, took her hand and looked for himself. The swelling had gone down, but there was a painful black bruise where a blood vessel had broken.

He covered it with his own hand. 'I'm sorry, Elle. I should have been the one with the sore knuckles.'

The hand covering her own bore no sign of damage and she reached for the other to reassure herself. 'So what *did* you do to him?' she asked. 'Freddy.'

'Do?'

'You must have done something. His receptionist brought me a large cheque and an apology less than an hour after you left.'

'Maybe he realised just how much trouble he was in,' he said.

'Maybe he had some help,' she said knowingly.

He shrugged. 'I just had a little chat with him. Laid out his options. Reminded him just how bad a sexual harassment case would be for business. Brought up some of the finer points of employment law.'

'But…'

'I employ seventy-odd people, Elle. I do know what I'm talking about.'

'That's it? Only Jenny, the receptionist who brought the cheque, said he'd been taken to the local A&E.'

And she'd lain awake all night imagining Sean under lock and key.

'All I did was talk to him, Elle. He blustered for a bit, but he soon saw reason, wrote a cheque to cover the salary you were owed and the compensation that would have been awarded by an employment tribunal for constructive dismissal. He wrote the apology I dictated, leaving no one in any doubt what he was apologising for.'

'That must have been more painful than his nose,' she remarked.

'You didn't see it.'

'And you don't know Freddy,' she declared, then blushed.

He laid a palm against her hot cheek. 'Neither did you.' Then, 'Once he'd despatched his receptionist, I ran him down to A&E to be patched up. And what do you know? I was right. He told the nurse that he tripped over a step.'

'Sean…'

'And, just so that you don't have to avoid that end of the village, you'll be glad to know that he's left his deputy manager in charge. The Blue Boar is going on the market from today and in the meantime he'll be taking a long vacation. For his health.'

She swallowed. 'I don't know what to say.'

'Nothing. Don't say a thing…'

A shadow crossed his face and she wanted to reach up, put her arms around him, tell him not to beat himself up. Turn her face, press her lips against the cooling hand. Before she could succumb to the temptation, he let go. Just as well.

Nothing she could say or do would change the way he was feeling right now. There was only one person who could forgive Sean for the mistake he'd made. Himself.

It made her heart ache for him. Not with pain, but with love. For a man who'd made such a big journey, found his family, opened himself up to risk. The pain would come, though, because in that instant she understood that without him there would be a cold, hollow place inside her. One that she would feel all her days.

'Come on. Let's go and stock up with lollies. Make this a wedding that no one will ever forget,' she said.

Unlikely, Sean thought later. Her hand might be sore but it hadn't stopped her giving the bride everything she wanted.

She was wearing a full-skirted calf-length dress in silvery-grey and white stripes with a black velvet belt to emphasize her waist, with little white lace gloves and a tiny black hat. Crisp, gorgeous, no one would have known from her big smile what she'd gone through in the last twenty-four hours.

After the ceremony, in the little Greek temple at Melchester Castle, she'd presented the bride with an ice cream wrapped in some frilly silver thing so that it looked like a bouquet, decorated with silver sprinkles and with a white chocolate flake that had been sprayed with edible silver food paint.

The bride removed the flake, gave it to her new husband with the words, 'On our first date, Steve, you gave me your chocolate flake. Now I'm giving you mine. Life is for sharing and this is my pledge that I'm going to share all of mine with you. All the better, all the worse. All the chocolate.'

'Is that all it takes?' Sean asked as Elle rejoined him inside Rosie. 'A chocolate flake?'

As they watched, there wasn't a dry eye in the place as he broke it in half and handed one piece back to his bride before sucking the ice cream off the half he was holding.

Just as well there was a rush from the guests to get their own ices and he had his hands full or he might have shed one himself.

How could he have ever doubted her when he'd recognised that rare innocence…? No. That was wrong. Not innocence. What made her different was a lack of guile. There was no calculation in what she did. She felt; she responded. More like her child-of-nature mother than she would want to believe.

'You did an absolutely fabulous job,' he said afterwards, as they headed back to Longbourne, silver ribbons fluttering from Rosie's extremities. 'I'll tell Hattie she has to include you and Rosie in her wedding brochure.'

'I couldn't have done it without you.'

About to say *any time, anywhere*, he realised just how hollow those words would sound to her.

'You could do anything you wanted. You're a natural, Elle.'

'You pushed me, Sean. Made me go for it. I was scared witless. And angry.' She shook her head. 'I hadn't realised how angry I was. With everyone. Basil was just one more person wanting to steal my life, but you…' She touched his arm. It was the first time she'd reached out to him since he'd let her down and it went through him like an electric shock. 'You gave it back to me.' Then, as if afraid that she'd said too much, 'Let's hope Basil hasn't changed his mind about Rosie now that he doesn't think he's about to die.'

'Elle…' He pulled over, brought Rosie to a halt in a small layby in a country lane. 'I have to say something.'

She waited. 'I'm listening,' she prompted over the ticking of Rosie's engine. The sound of the generator.

'That's my problem. I don't have the words to tell you how I bad I feel. When I think what might have happened with Freddy…'

'You stopped that. I wasn't doing well there for a minute, but you gave me time—'

'Not enough.'

'You gave me time,' she repeated, 'to save myself. And you were coming back.'

'What?'

'When I came out of the Blue Boar, you'd stopped walking away. You were facing me. Coming back for me. Why?'

'Because…' He stopped. It would be so easy to lie. So easy to say that he'd realised he was wrong and was coming back to save her. But only the truth would do. Everything that was in his heart. 'I stopped because I was so angry with you.'

'With *me*?'

'Oh, yes. I wanted to tear Frederickson apart with my bare hands, but it was you I was really angry with.' Once the flood-gates were unlocked it all came pouring out of him. 'Angry with you for letting any man do that to you. For not valuing yourself. For not punching him in the eye the first time he'd come on to you.'

'That *was* the first…'

'For not punching him in the eye the first time he touched you, held onto your arm a little too long. I wanted to shake you, Elle, tell you that you were a fool. Tell you that you are worth so much more than that. I wanted to shake you because you had made me believe and suddenly it was all falling apart. Shake you and hold you so that you'd know you never had to do that again. Hold you and tell you that I love you…' And he stopped. That was it. Those were the words. 'I love you.'

'Enough to give me your flake?' she teased shakily.

'Enough to give you my life. Will you take it?' he asked simply.

Elle looked at him. How could you resist a man who'd lay himself bare like that? Mess up and admit it. Be so painfully honest that it hurt to watch. He'd come so far in the time she'd known him. He was always a big man, challenging life, making it back down. But he'd learnt to be kind to himself. Let people close enough to hurt and, when it had hurt, he'd still come back for more.

She'd fallen in lust with him at first sight. Thought she'd grown to love him. But this feeling was bigger than that. They'd been good for each other. Each challenging the other's fear and bringing out something shining and new in a few short weeks. What could they achieve in a lifetime?

'Final answer?' she asked.

'That depends. Because I'll go on asking until I get the right one.'

There was a rap on the serving hatch. 'Excuse me, but are you open? Only we'd like an ice,' a voice said.

Elle gave a little gasp and then burst out laughing.

'We really are going to have to stop meeting like this,' Sean said, hauling himself out of his seat. 'Can I get you something?'

'Yes,' she said, grinning. 'But it will wait.'

Rosie came to the wedding all gussied up in pink and white ribbons. Basil was in charge, decked out in a striped blazer and straw boater.

Geli rode the ice cream bicycle in matching gear, handing out ice lollies to visitors to the estate as well as wedding guests.

All Sean's nieces, under the control of Sorrel, gorgeous in pale mint silk, were dressed in ice cream coloured tulle.

In the Orangery Basil walked Elle through their friends and family as a harpist played 'Greensleeves', and delivered her to Sean.

The ceremony was brief but moving and afterwards the word for the reception was definitely *fun*. Hattie had created a marquee that looked like a seaside show tent, flags flying. Olivia had found a Punch and Judy man to entertain the children. And there was candyfloss, bouncy castles, roundabouts and a ride-on train. There were donkey rides, too. And even a mini beach with buckets and spades.

Sean, caught by Elle's grandmother, looked around for Elle. She seemed to have disappeared and he wanted to slip away to the barn where they were spending the night before leaving for their honeymoon in the morning.

He'd shared her with everyone for long enough.

A mobile phone began to ring and Lally pulled it out of her pocket. 'Hello? Oh, it's for you,' she said.

'Me?' He took the phone. 'Sean McElroy?'

'Remember you said when I had a free evening to call you?'

'Vividly.'

'Well, if you can find me, it's your birthday.'

He found her waiting for him in one of the Adirondack chairs overlooking the river, a cold box at her feet.

He leaned over and kissed her. 'Is that ice cream you've got in the cool box?'

'I've decided that today is your birthday, Sean,' she said, lifting her arms and sliding them around his neck. 'It's time to unwrap your present.'

He lifted her to her feet, held her. 'Since I found you, my Elle, my Lovage, I've been reborn. Every day has been a gift.' And his kiss was a promise that he would make it his life's work to return the treasure a hundredfold.

READY FOR HER CLOSE-UP

KATHERINE GARBERA

This one is for my family for always believing in me and making me feel special even though I know I'm not.

One

What had she been thinking?

Gail Little took a deep breath and walked into the makeshift hair and makeup area for the set of the reality-TV dating show *Sexy and Single*. She had never in her entire life thought of herself as sexy, but single…now, that was something she had buttoned up. She'd always thought she'd hook up with a guy in college, and they'd fall into a relationship as they both started their careers. Then, after three years of dating, they'd get married, but now she was staring down thirty and still alone.

"I'm Kat Humphries, the PA for *Sexy and Single*. I'll also be your handler for all of your segments."

Gail shook Kat's hand. She'd expected to see Willow Stead—the producer of the show and one of her best friends—instead of a PA. Willow had gotten the idea to do the show when Gail had signed up with Matchmakers Inc. Though Gail had only told her friends she wanted to find a husband and didn't meet the right kind of men at work, the truth was she wanted a family of her own and her biological clock was ticking. So she'd signed on with the dating service, never expecting her experiences would become the focus of a TV show.

Kat looked to be in her mid-twenties and wore a pair of slim-fitting jeans and a T-shirt from a bar in Mexico. Her long brown hair was pulled back in a ponytail, and she had an earpiece attached to the radio at her belt.

"Follow me," Kat said.

Gail nodded and went with her to a bank of lighted mirrors set up against the wall. This was behind-the-scenes television that few viewers ever saw. Not very glamorous, but as the owner of a very successful PR firm, it was a world Gail knew well. Funny that she never pictured herself as the one going onstage.

"Have a seat here. The hair and makeup people are on their way. You're a few minutes early."

"Sorry about that. I didn't want to be late," Gail said. Kat nodded, but held up one finger as she listened to something on her headset.

"Please stay in here until I come back to get you," Kat said. "We want to capture that first moment when you and your match see each other."

Gail wanted to groan. But she knew deep down that if she stayed in her rut any longer, her life would be nothing but work, and her dreams of a family and all that went with it would never be realized.

She stared at herself in the mirror as she waited for the hair and makeup person to arrive. Her thick, curly hair with its wild, out-of-control style framed her face. She reached up and pulled her hair back…that was how she usually wore it for work. Because let's face it, she thought, her unruly hair didn't scream sexy and single.

A man and woman approached her. "Hello, Gail. I'm Mona, and this is Pete. We're going to be doing your hair and makeup. Just sit back and relax."

Gail did just that, wondering what she'd gotten herself into. She'd wanted a man to spend her holidays with instead of being home alone, which might have been fun for Kevin in the *Home Alone* movies, but for her, a grown woman, it had been…lonely. She craved the perfect Christmas, for example, and images of it played in her mind like home movies. She was in the business of image and reality, so why couldn't she create the perfect image and reality for herself?

She'd developed a PR plan to take herself from a business success to a personal success. She was very good at enacting her plans, so she had no doubt this one would work. Of course, she hadn't expected Willow to love the idea so much that she'd turn it into a reality TV show.

"Okay, we're done," Mona said.

They turned her back to face the mirrors. Her thick, unruly hair had been straightened and styled to brush her shoulders. Her eyes were bigger than she'd ever seen them before. Her lips were so large and perfect. She'd had no idea a little lipstick and eye shadow could make her look like this. She didn't recognize herself.

"What do you think?" Pete asked.

"I don't look like me," she said.

"Sure you do, honey. Just not the you that is usually in the mirror," Mona said.

And that had been exactly what she'd wanted. "What do I do now?"

"Wardrobe," Pete said. "Your dressing room is over there."

She walked over to the tiny dressing room in the corner. There was a woman sitting there reading a paperback book—one that Gail had just finished. This was the life she was used to, and Gail felt as though she could just sit here for a few minutes. The woman put the book down and smiled at her. "Looking good."

"Thanks."

Gail had the feeling that Alice must have experienced when she fell down the rabbit hole, because twenty minutes later she stood in front of a full-length mirror in a couture gown by Jil Sander. The well-fitting top came to a V, revealing her cleavage, while the peplum skirt gave her hips a flattering fullness, hitting her midthigh. She looked sexy and glamorous, two things she'd never felt before.

Kat came back and signaled that it was time to go. Gail realized her hands were sweating and started to wipe them on her skirt but stopped—this gown cost more than her entire wardrobe. She was going to mess this up. No matter how much magic these stylists had done to her outside, inside she was still the woman who'd spent all of her time working. She had no idea how to make real small talk. This was a mistake.

"Two minutes until you will go into the 'confessional,' then it's down to the ballroom, where you will meet your date, Ms. Little," Kat said.

Gail was nervous. And that wasn't like her. She wasn't the type of woman who let anything stand in her way once she'd made up her mind.

A tech guy in black pants and a polo shirt came over and attached a microphone to her collar. She should approach this the same way she approached a client at her PR firm who needed more exposure. She'd smile and pretend the glam woman staring back at her in the mirror was who she really was.

She stood up and walked over to the entrance to the small room that had been made out of moveable walls and pipe and drapes. No privacy at all. But then, that was reality television.

"Just push the button and start talking. Don't worry—if you mess up, just start over. We're going to edit it," Kat said.

"What am I supposed to say?"

"Tell us what you are thinking before you meet your match."

She stepped into the room and walked over to the camera. She sat down in front of it and pushed the record button. There was a small monitor where she could see herself, which just made her uncomfortable, so instead she stared into the lens of the camera.

"Let's see.... I'm Gail Little and I own a public relations firm. I am beyond nervous.

"That's it. I signed up with Matchmakers Inc., because I didn't want to let another year go by without meeting someone. I work all the time and don't meet many single men in my job," she said. Then she took a deep breath. She was rambling.

"I'm anxious to find out more about the man that has been picked for me." She pushed the stop button and got up and walked out of the room.

She'd done the best she could. She turned resolutely to walk back to the makeup area. "All done?" Kat asked.

"Yes."

"This way, then. Your date is waiting for you."

They stepped into the hallway and the soundman checked her microphone. "Bob is the cameraman who will be shooting you. He will be in front of you as we enter the ballroom. Don't look at Bob. Instead, look toward the table where your match is waiting."

"Okay," she said. Bob waved at her from the end of the hallway.

"Walk toward Bob and then enter the ballroom. It's been set up for an intimate dinner for two. As soon as we are out of the shot, I will signal you. Just start walking."

Kat and the soundman joined Bob at the end of the hall, and it felt like an eternity before she was given the signal to go. She walked down the hallway, feeling silly that they were taping her walking. But she forgot about that when she stepped into the ballroom.

There were a few production people in the room as well as a man who stood with his back toward her. But she was distracted when Jack Crown stepped in front of her.

"Hello, Gail," he said.

Jack Crown was gunning to beat out Ryan Seacrest for hosting the most shows on TV and was obviously the host of this one. He'd been an all-state athlete in high school and then went on to win the Heisman Trophy in college. He'd been a first-round draft pick and then suffered an agonizing injury in his very first professional football game. But he'd smiled up at the cameras and just shrugged his massive shoulders saying that America hadn't seen the last of him, and he'd been right. He started showing up on television regularly hosting reality shows for the Discovery Channel.

"Hello, Jack," she said. "What are you doing here?"

"I'm the host of the show. I'll be chatting with both of you at the end of your dates."

"Okay," she said. "Now?"

"No, we want to see how you both react to meeting each other," he said, stepping away. Her date had large, strong shoulders that tapered down to a lean waist, which she could see because he wore a well-fitted jacket.

"Stop," Willow, the producer, said, her voice loud in the quiet of the room. It was funny because Gail had never been at work with Willow before, and the booming voice didn't sound like her friend's. "You are going to see each other for the first time in just a moment. I want you both to look at each other and not the cameras. Kat, move her into position."

Kat directed Gail to a spot that was marked on the floor with tape. Gail stood so close to her match that she could smell the woodsy scent of his cologne. And she noticed his thick hair was a brown color with shots of golden-blond in it.

"We're ready to shoot now. Please turn and face your match," Willow said.

The man turned and Gail's breath caught. Then her heart sank. It was billionaire New Zealand hotelier and nightclub owner Russell Holloway. She recognized him from his constant exposure on TV and in magazines. He couldn't be her match. Surely this was a joke. He was a playboy with a reputation as a love-'em-and-leave-'em guy. Why would he go to a matchmaker?

Gail met the full force of Russell's gray gaze. His eyes were bright and intense, staring down at her. He didn't look as debauched as he should, she thought. He looked tanned, fit and healthy…too damned good for someone as bad as he was rumored to be.

"Gail Little," she said, holding out her hand. "I've heard a lot about you."

Dumb. Was that really the only thing her mind could come up with?

Russell laughed as he took her hand and kissed it. "Uh-oh, that doesn't sound promising. I know precious little about you, but I look forward to hearing your story from your own lips."

She licked her lips and stared up at him. Her eyes tracked down his face to the sharp blade of his nose and then the full, sensual mouth underneath. *Lips*…the word echoed in her mind, and all she could do was stare at his. She gave herself a mental shake. She wasn't going to be the latest to fall for this charming playboy. He was messing up her plans, and there was nothing fun about that.

Russell Holloway wasn't sure what type of woman he'd expected to be matched with, but he knew he hadn't anticipated Gail Little. She was beautiful, with her thick black hair brushing her shoulders and her big brown eyes that tempted him to get lost in them. Her figure was curvy and generous. If he were honest, she was exactly what he wanted physically. And she was classy. He couldn't remember the last time he'd met a woman like her.

"I'm Russell Holloway," he said, though he could tell she recognized him. She'd said that she'd heard of him.

"I know." Then she shook her head. "Despite how it may seem, I'm usually a bit wittier."

He chuckled. "First meetings can be a bit nerve-racking."

"Yes, they can."

She stared up at him and then flushed. "I don't know what to say."

"Then say nothing and let me enjoy the view. You're a very beautiful woman."

"I don't know about that. Should we take our seats at the table?"

"Not just yet," Russell said, linking her hand through his arm, leading her out of the ballroom and into the hallway.

He'd already arranged for the camera crew to follow them. Every detail had to go off smoothly. Russell had signed up with the matchmaking service to improve his reputation.

The Kiwi Klubs had had stagnate growth for the past

two years. They had started as destination clubs similar to Club Med. Attached to each of the hotels was an exclusive A-lister nightclub where people went to see and be seen. Russell was making a profit but he wanted to try something new, and the real money in destination vacations was in families. He wanted to open a family-friendly resort, but with his reputation that was easier said than done. He had a chance to buy a well-known family vacation company but the owner was balking at selling to someone like Russell—not from a business standpoint but from a reputation-based one. So he'd decided to try to change his image.

He'd already arranged with Willow and Conner Mac-Afee, Matchmakers Inc.'s owner, to give Gail a preview of the Gustav Klimt exhibit that would be opening here in the Big Apple Kiwi Klub on Wednesday. As a personal friend of Russell's, Conner had suggested participating in the show as a course of action to help Russell out.

"Where are we going?" she asked. "I think we are supposed to stay where we were."

"Afraid to get in trouble?" he asked.

"No. I just like to follow the rules," she said.

"I don't."

"Shocker," she said.

He laughed. She gave the impression of being very sure of herself and confident. Those were traits that he'd been hoping for in his match. "Don't fret, Gail, this side trip has been preapproved."

"Good," she said.

"Here we are," he said, opening a door that led into the mezzanine atrium. The hotel area was very modern and had large expanses of open wall space with a glass dome inspired by Van Gogh's *Stormy Night*. The floor was made of marble.

"This exhibit is opening on Wednesday, so we will be the first to experience it."

When he'd approved the design, he'd specified that the atrium be used to display art. He had wanted to capture the feeling of the Metropolitan Museum of Art and replicate it here. If he was going to get families and couples into his hotels, then he needed to give them something special.

"I love Klimt's work. I have a print of *The Kiss* hanging in my bedroom at home," she said.

Russell thought it interesting that Gail had chosen that piece to hang in her bedroom. In it, the man was completely wrapped around the woman, holding her face in his hands as he kissed her neck. Klimt's style was very sensual.

"Have you ever been kissed like that?" he asked.

She glanced up at him, a bit of shock in her eyes. "No. I don't think so. But I'm sure you have."

He arched one eyebrow at her. She didn't seem to like him very much. "A gentleman doesn't kiss and tell."

"But then, you never have been a gentleman," she said almost sharply.

"That's true," he acknowledged. "I'm not exactly the kind of man who's been circumspect in my relationships. But that's why I'm here."

"Truly?"

"Yes. I'm not on this show to play games with you, Gail. I'm looking for a match just like you are." He knew if he was going to be successful in changing his reputation, it had to start with Gail. If he couldn't convince her he wanted to change away from his bad boy image, the viewers at home wouldn't buy it either.

"I'm sorry if I jumped to conclusions," she said.

"You should be," he said, flirting with her.

The PA motioned for them to move, and Russell put his

hand at the small of Gail's back and steered her toward another framed picture. It was a portrait of a high-society woman. They stood in front of it for a long time.

"She reminds me of you," he said. It was a sensual portrait of a fully-dressed woman with an open bodice, just starting to reveal herself to the viewer.

"Did I mention that I don't fall for practiced lines," Gail said.

"What makes you think that was a line?" he asked.

"She's so sexy," Gail said.

"You are too," he said.

Gail gave him a *yeah, right* look, and Russell realized for the first time that he was dealing with Gail's future as well as his own. And though he'd decided to do this purely for business reasons, he was determined to give her the very best of himself—however little that might be.

He reached over to touch her face, but Gail drew back. Getting past his reputation was going to be harder than he'd expected. It had been too long since he'd moved in any circles other than those inhabited by his decadent friends.

"She's mysterious like you, as well. There is more to you than meets the eye," he said.

"And you're all flash, aren't you?" she asked.

"I'd like to hope not. Otherwise I'd be pretty boring."

"Well, no one has ever called you boring," she admitted.

Russell turned them both back toward the end of the hallway. He'd forgotten the cameras were there. He rarely let anyone distract him from his surroundings and was a bit surprised that Gail had.

"Okay, cut. Great job, you two. Jack, come on in," Willow said.

Jack joined them, and Russell was reminded that this was definitely a TV show. Jack shook his hand and Gail's.

"You two are doing great," he said.

"Thanks," Russell replied.

"Okay, we're ready to start shooting," Willow said from across the room.

"Now that you've finished your first date, what do you think of Matchmakers Inc.?" Jack asked.

"They saw what I wanted even though Gail isn't my normal date," Russell said. "I think that the matchmaker was very intuitive."

"And you, Gail?"

"Well, Russell is definitely the last guy in the world I would have expected, so in that respect they found me a man I couldn't find on my own."

Jack laughed and then Willow called, "Cut."

"Jack, we'll need you to finish shooting the intro. Russell and Gail, you are free to go back to the dining room, where a crew will tape you talking and eating." The crew started heading back in that direction.

"That should be exciting," Gail said, turning sharply and walking across the atrium.

"What's your hurry?" Russell asked.

"I want to talk to Willow before we film any more."

"Why?" Russell asked.

"I just need to confirm some details with her," Gail said.

"Are you going to try to back out of this?" he asked.

She shrugged. "Don't take it personally, but I'm not sure that you are at all the right person for me. I'm sure that this would be interesting viewing—the whole opposites attract thing—but I want more than interesting viewing."

She started to walk away, and Russell realized anew

how hard changing his reputation was going to be. "I'm not doing this for ratings."

She stopped and glanced back over her shoulder at him. "Why are you doing it?"

"We all have to grow up, and I'd say it's definitely my time."

He saw something change in her eyes and knew he had her. She wanted to see if he really was just the playboy, or if there was something more.

"Fine. I won't say anything to Willow until after this date. But I'm not going to make it easy on you. Finding a husband is my goal for this year, and I don't want to waste my time with someone who clearly isn't marrying material."

Clearly, this wasn't going to be as easy as Russell had hoped.

Two

Since the beginning, when Willow had decided to take Gail's personal life and make it into a reality television show, Gail had had a niggling doubt in the back of her mind that this wasn't going to work out. But she'd forked out a lot of money to the matchmakers, and she really wanted to find a man to share her life with.

Willow had thought the show would be intriguing because a lot of successful men and women were finding it harder to meet someone. Willow said that with the 24/7 workday, it was inevitable that no one would have time for courtship.

Gail agreed, which was why she'd gone to a matchmaker. But she'd never expected a man like Russell Holloway to need one. He could snap his fingers and have any girl he wanted at his door.

Russell wasn't the man for her. Of course, he was sexy as hell...but she wasn't looking for sexy. She was looking for the guy in the Ralph Lauren ad, she thought, the one with perfectly styled hair, wearing those polo shirts and standing in front of a mansion in the Hamptons. She wanted someone who could look the part and give her the fantasy of the perfect life that she'd always craved.

She wanted to relax and enjoy her time with Russell, but she was under the gun, so to speak. Her biological clock wasn't just ticking, it was winding down faster than most of her peers'. She had to see if Russell was going to be the right man for her. Could he be? Now she was beginning to wonder.

She was seated at a private table, waiting for him. He'd had to take a call before they started shooting. Gail had pulled out her iPhone, but really she'd told her assistant, J.J., to handle all emergencies tonight. She knew she'd never have a chance at making this a success if she was distracted with work…. Her mind began to wander.

Was there more to Russell than met the eye? She knew there had to be, but thanks to years in publicity, she knew that usually what was beneath a shiny surface was less than appealing.

Russell rejoined her, and there was a lot of movement around them as sound techs and makeup people made them both camera ready.

"If my mates saw me with this makeup on, they'd never let me live it down," he said.

She had to smile. "It's just part of the package for being on TV, part of the glam life all celebs have to endure."

"Never thought I'd be part of any 'glam life,'" he said.

"Why not? You seem very at home in the jet set." Just this morning, she'd seen a picture of him on a yacht with two Spanish royals on one of the gossip sites she monitored for her clients.

"It's not really my thing," he said. "I like to travel and

I ski and yacht and go to club openings, but a lot of that is for my business. To keep it in the public eye."

"Yet you get a lot of newspaper and internet coverage," she said. She didn't follow him, so she had no idea when the intense media scrutiny had started, but she'd be willing to bet it had been there since he'd become successful in the hotel world. He had looks that no woman would resist.

"I do, but I really don't court that," he said.

Their food was delivered, and Gail found herself unable to stop looking at Russell. She had met so many people who'd needed to have their images cleaned up that she freely admitted she often saw the worst in someone. But she wanted to give Russell a chance, not simply to be fair to him, but also for her own sake. She'd invested a hell of a lot more than money in these dates; she'd kind of thought of them as her last chance.

"You're staring at me," he said.

"You are a very pretty-looking man," she said, being glib because that was easy when she didn't want to be honest.

"Pretty…isn't that a word for girls?" he asked.

"No. Boys can be very pretty." And he was, with that classic jawline and thick brownish-blond hair. But he was also a bit on the rugged side, thanks to that square jaw and a small scar on the bottom of his face. His face had character, but she wasn't sure if it was good. He had the build of a boxer and carried himself like a man who'd lived life—a very upper-crust one, but still, there was more to him than money.

"Well," he said, lifting one eyebrow sardonically, "thanks, I guess."

She smiled at him. He was an easy man to talk to, and though she was giving him the fifth degree in the hope of catching him out in a lie, she liked him. "I keep looking for some indicator that you are being honest with me."

"And?" he asked.

"I'm simply not sure yet. But I think it's making me overanalyze your every action," she admitted. But if she was honest, she did that with everyone. She'd always spent a lot of time thinking about why people did things. It didn't bring her any closer to really understanding them, but she tried.

"Then I'm not doing my job," he said. He leaned in, and she could smell that one-of-a-kind, spicy aftershave of his. "Am I boring you?"

"No, you are not boring me at all. Tell me why you are here," she said. It was a question she'd originally planned on asking her date before she knew it was Russell. In fact, she now made the snap decision to treat him the way she would have treated John Doe if that's whom she'd been matched with. No need to change just because he was Russell Holloway, international billionaire and playboy.

He leaned back in his chair and looked into her eyes. "It's time to settle down. I set out to make my fortune and a name for myself. I think we can both agree that I've done that."

"I'm not buying that as the entire story. There must be more," she said.

He laughed and tipped his head to the side, studying her, and she felt a little exposed for a moment, as though he was trying to see past the makeup and the facade to the real woman underneath. "The truth is that I like the party lifestyle, but it has lost its charm. I want to have a partner I can share all my life with, not just a couple of days."

She wanted to believe him. Who wouldn't? It was every young girl's dream to have a playboy like him say he wanted to settle down, and to be the lucky one he chose. "I can understand that, but marriage?"

"Why do I seem so debauched to you?" he asked.

"You don't," she said, realizing she was being harder on him than she would have been on any other man. And she knew it was because she was mad. Mad that she'd been matched to this man and now had to make the best of the situation.

"I'm sorry. Tell me about your family," she said.

"I had a traditional upbringing, and though my parents are gone, I know they wanted me to get married and have kids someday."

He had a pensive look on his face, and he turned away from her for a moment. She felt bad about the way she'd been questioning him. He obviously had a reason for going to the matchmaking service just as she had, and she should respect that.

She cleared her throat, and he turned his attention back to her. "You have kids, right?"

"No," he said. "There have been paternity suits that I have settled out of court, but I have no kids."

"Why not just make a family of those blended children?" she asked. What did he mean by settling paternity suits but not having any kids? She wanted to know more but this first date wasn't the time to ask questions.

"It's not feasible, since they aren't mine," he said.

"What do—"

"Enough questions—it's my turn. Why did you go to a matchmaker?" he asked, turning that direct, silver gaze of his on her. Suddenly she wanted to go back to being anonymous. She wanted to be the one in control, and she wasn't the least bit interested in sharing that control with him.

She fidgeted a little in her chair. She didn't want to tell

him about herself. "The simple answer is that it's the next step for me. I have a successful business and a good life."

"Sounds idyllic, but since you are here with me, something must be missing," he said.

"Yes," she said.

"It makes sense," he said. "And I understand where you are coming from."

"Do you?" she asked. It was hard for her to believe that she had much in common with this man. Odd to her that the two of them were at the same point in their journeys. But they were here together and, no matter how wrong that felt to her, she decided she'd make the best of it for now.

"Yes, when I was young I knew what I wanted and went after my goals with single-minded intensity. I worked hard and played hard and then one day…"

"You woke up and realized that you had everything?" she asked.

"Yes. But I wasn't satisfied."

"Me either," she said. Maybe she didn't want to see the man behind the image. Because now that she saw him expressing the same doubts that she had, she was starting to like him.

Like was too tame a word. She was attracted to him and wanted to find something—anything—that would give her a reason to stay on this show with him. The legal reason—the contract she'd signed—wasn't enough. But hearing him express himself this way…it was appealing.

"You're staring at me again," he said. "I'm trying not to let it go to my head, but you're making me feel irresistible."

"You'll have to get used to it, if you keep surprising me."

"Then I will, because I intend to keep you off balance," he said.

"Why?"

"That's the only way I'm going to get to know the real Gail," he said.

"And that's important?" she asked. She wasn't too sure she wanted anyone to know the real woman she was.

"Infinitely," he said. "I think that is the only way that you are going to let me know you trust me. I mean, really trust me."

"I don't trust easily," she admitted. "I guess that's another reason I've gone to a matchmaker."

"You've been burned by a man before?" he asked, leaning closer.

"Yes," she said, putting her head down and remembering that past love. Joe hadn't meant to hurt her—she was still sure of it—but he'd been too much into what Joe wanted to never realize that he was stepping on her dreams to achieve his own.

Russell nodded and took her hand. "I know there isn't anything I can say right now that you'd believe, but I do want to be very sure you understand I'm not like any other man you've had in your life before."

"I already knew that," she said with a grin.

"It's my pretty face, right?" he asked with a sexy smile that sent shivers of awareness down her spine.

"Okay, that's a wrap on dinner. Let's get you two up to the rooftop," the director said. The crew all bustled around them, and Gail realized she'd had enough. This matchmaking thing was going to take some getting used to. Add to that the cameras, and it was her definition of a nightmare.

Jack came back over and spoke to them again about their impressions of the first date. Gail was unsure what to say. She mumbled something and then thankfully was motioned off camera so Jack could talk to Russell. She stood to the side watching Russell and hoping this wasn't a huge mistake.

Had she really thought she'd find Mr. Right like this? Through a matchmaking service that she'd found off an internet ad? But, really, what had her alternatives been? She'd dated all the guys she knew. Willow and Nichole had even tried fixing her up, but that had led to nothing permanent.

"Are we going to jump?" Gail asked.

"Not a bad idea. I guess that's how we will get some ratings for the show," Russell said. "I can see the headlines now. Respectable woman pushes rogue Kiwi playboy off roof in hopes of finding a better match."

Gail had to laugh. "I won't push you...yet."

"I guess I better step it up in the charm department," he said.

Before she could answer, Kat was back and taking her by the arm. "Chat on camera, guys. We need you on the roof now."

They were escorted to a private elevator and soon were on the rooftop helipad, where a chopper waited for them. "Is this for us?"

"Surprise," Russell said. "I thought an evening ride over Manhattan would be nice."

"I am surprised," Gail said. "I've always wanted to do this."

"Good. Also, cameras can't come with us, so we will have some time alone to get to know one another."

Gail didn't say anything else as their microphones were removed and they were escorted to the chopper. She saw the cameraman at a distance, no doubt filming them so they'd have something to show later, but she was relieved that they were going to be alone.

Russell gallantly helped her into the chopper and was

seated next to her a short time later. He handed her some headphones, which she donned, and then she adjusted her microphone. "I'm sure I look pretty glamorous with these on my head."

"You look great," he said.

In a matter of minutes, they were in the air and flying over Manhattan. Russell's voice was soft and intimate in her ears.

"When I first came to the States, I wanted to make my mark here. We started in Vegas because that suited the Kiwi Klubs' reputation, but I wanted to own a building in New York City," he said.

She looked over at him. "How did you get started?"

"With a small run-down hotel in Sydney," he said. "I won it in a high-stakes poker game."

"I though you were a New Zealander from the South Island?"

"I am. I left home when I was sixteen and never looked back," he said.

"I didn't see any of that on the internet when I was reading up on you," she said. "I'm embarrassed to say, I only know the gossip I've read about you."

He shrugged. "That's the easy stuff to know."

"But is it true?" she asked. "I've been in PR long enough to know that sometimes bad publicity can work in your favor."

"Exactly," he said. "I'm known for having rich and famous friends and for being a bit of a player, and that is exactly what my clientele wants."

"So why change now?" she asked. "Is this more than a publicity stunt?"

"Of course it is. I'm not going to get married as a stunt," he said.

"Many have done it before. Even if they weren't just

for show, marriages of convenience have been around for centuries."

"I'd find it very convenient to have to look at you at breakfast every day," he said in that flirty way of his.

"Me, too, but I need more sustenance than flash," she said.

"Don't we all. It's easy to think that something or someone flashy has what you need, but after a short while you find that's not true," he said.

She glanced over at him. Surprised to hear something so...well, *deep* from him.

He arched an eyebrow at her. "I'm not just a playboy."

She smiled at him. "You couldn't be and be on the cover of *Fortune* magazine."

"True. What about you?"

"Me?" she asked. "I'm not flashy at all. This is me at my most flashy."

He chuckled. "I'm not shocked. You strike me as someone who is very sure of herself and where she is going."

She shrugged one shoulder. "I love to have a plan and then execute it. But when I have to depend on someone else...well, let's just say sometimes things get messed up."

"Like this?"

She bit her lower lip. She didn't want to lie to him, but then she had nothing to lose. Russell wasn't the kind of guy she usually went for, so being brutally honest wasn't going to cost her anything. "Yes, like this situation with you. I mean, I planned to go to the matchmaker and find the perfect guy. I have a checklist in my head with all his qualities."

"And I don't measure up?" he asked. "That's not fair, Gail. You don't know if I have those qualities yet."

"You're right. But you are flashy," she said with a grin. "And I'm a bit afraid to risk getting to know the real man."

"I can understand that. I'm coming at this from the opposite point of view. If you aren't the woman I think you are...then I'm screwed."

She laughed at how he'd said that. "I guess we both are."

He reached over, took her hand in his and lifted it to his mouth, rubbing his lips over the back of her knuckles. "I don't want that. Let's start over. I'll try to be more the man of your dreams and you can..."

"Yes?"

"Give me a chance and not judge me so harshly."

"I will try. It's one of my worst faults," she said, liking the way her hand felt in his.

"What is?"

"Not being able to accept failure."

"In others?" he asked, rubbing his thumb over the back of her hand before slowly letting it go.

Chills spread up her arm, and she knew she wanted to keep touching him. It was unexpected. She didn't know why and couldn't really explain it, but there was something about Russell Holloway that made her forget about lists and plans.

"And in myself," she said softly, almost to herself. But she knew he'd heard her because he nodded.

"I'll try not to let you down," he said.

And just like that, she was hooked on giving him a chance. She wanted to guard her emotions, to warn her heart to be careful where he was concerned, because her common sense told her there was more to Russell's move than just his wanting to change. But she couldn't help herself. For these next six weeks she wanted to be the kind of girl who'd allow herself to be caught up in a man. Even if she knew he was at his core a bad boy who would probably break her heart.

* * *

Russell knew that he was luckier than many men. He had his secrets and more than his share of hardships, but life had been good to him. And this was one of the moments when he realized he'd gotten lucky. He needed a woman like Gail and here she was, dropped into his lap.

Her skin was soft and smooth and he liked touching her, holding her hand. But he didn't want to crowd her. She smelled nice and clean, a pretty floral fragrance that he knew he'd remember long after he left her tonight.

"Thank you, Russell," she said.

"For?"

"This ride. It's really nice being up here, and I needed some time away from the cameras."

"I did too. I'm not used to conducting my dates in front of an audience," he said. Even though most of the women he dated were famous and they always had their pictures in the tabloids, Russell did try to avoid the spotlight.

"Me either. In fact, this is the first date I've been on that has felt this…high profile," she said. "Not at all what I expected."

"Is it on your list?" he asked.

"What list?"

"The Mr. Right checklist," he said. He liked the forthright way she spoke and how she always looked him straight in the eye when she talked to him. It made him aware that she was weighing everything he did and said. He needed to be careful to watch himself around her.

"Well…it's not real. Just a bunch of feelings and qualities that I think a man should have that would be compatible with mine."

He tipped his head to the side. "That's a checklist."

She shrugged delicately, drawing his gaze to her shoulders. They were left bare by the sleeveless dress she wore.

Her arms were toned and muscled, so she must work out, he guessed.

"You're right. It is a list. I'm looking for someone with a good job."

"Easy! Check one off for me."

She smiled at him. "I'll give you that."

"What else?"

"He has to be…committed to the person he's dating."

"Ah. That one will be harder to convince you of, won't it?"

"Yes. You aren't exactly known for monogamy."

"I am here, aren't I?"

"Yes. So that one is a maybe," she said.

"What else?"

"Um…" She hesitated, then a pretty pink blush spread up from her neck to her cheeks.

"What could be next?" he asked. "Why are you so shy now?"

She wrapped her arms around her waist and looked out at the skyline of Manhattan. He saw the reflection of her face in the window of the chopper as she absently brought her hand up to toy with the charm on the gold necklace she wore.

"I have to be attracted to you. A healthy sex life is on my checklist."

"When the time is right, Gail, you will have no doubts that I can fulfill your needs on that count."

She turned back around to face him. Her thick black hair with the headphones on it made her seem smaller somehow. In the intimacy of the chopper, she didn't seem as tough as she had in the ballroom when first seen her. Her mouth was full, and he couldn't help but keep his eyes on her lips. He wanted to taste them. He needed to kiss her just to prove to himself that, even though she felt different to him, she wasn't. He desired her. He knew that, but he wanted it to be just the normal lust he'd feel for any attractive woman.

Somehow though, in these close quarters with just the soft sound of her voice in his ears and her leg brushing his, it felt different. He felt different. He wanted to imagine he could check off all the qualities on her Mr. Right checklist, and he didn't know why that mattered.

He leaned in close and she just stared at him. The microphone was in front of her face, and he reached to push it up and out of his way. He did the same with his mic, and then touched her face. Her skin was smooth and cool to the touch.

He let his thumb move lower to touch her lips. He traced them: the small indentation at the top and the full, fleshy lower one. Then he closed the small distance between them and kissed her. Just a simple brushing of their mouths at first, and then he slipped his tongue in over her teeth until he tasted her.

He tipped his head to the side; he wanted more of her. The thought that she was just like any other woman disappeared in an instant. This was more than lust. He lifted his hands, tangling them in her thick hair as he tried to get more out of the kiss. Gail's hands fell to his shoulders, softly at first, and then as she moved closer to him, her grip got tighter.

He pulled back and took a deep breath. She said something, but he couldn't hear it because her microphone wasn't in position. He brought it down and she shook her head. "I didn't expect that."

"I didn't either."

She wrinkled her brow. "You were the one who kissed me."

"I was trying to prove something to myself."

"What?"

"That you were like every other woman I've ever kissed," he said.

She narrowed her gaze. "That's—

"Don't get your back up. You weren't. I don't know why," he said, genuinely perplexed. One of his good friends had married last year and Russell, while happy for him, hadn't understood how one woman could be that important. Now he had an inkling of what Cam Stern had been experiencing and Russell didn't like it for himself.

"Is that supposed to be a compliment?" she asked.

"Hell. No, it wasn't. I don't know what it was supposed to be. I only know that I have no idea how to proceed with this."

"Why not?" she asked.

He shook his head. He wasn't supposed to be this attracted to his match. But his blood was pounding in his veins and he had to shift his legs to make room for his growing erection. He wanted her. He wanted her right now. But that wasn't going to happen tonight. He needed to ensure that this matchmaking thing worked first, and sleeping with her tonight would pretty much send her running for the hills.

Three

Gail didn't know what had happened, but somehow in the last thirty minutes, Russell Holloway had started to become real to her. He was no longer that bad-boy cad whom she could keep her distance from. Instead she'd kissed him.

Oh, yes, she had. That was the most daring thing she'd done since skinny-dipping in high school. She shook her head; she had become a very staid person. In fact, it had been almost seven months since her last kiss.

Now her lips still tingled from the contact with Russell's. And she wanted more than just a few kisses. She wanted to feel his strong chest against her breasts and his arms wrapped around her.

She had a feeling that Russell knew how to use his body for maximum effect, and she was definitely ready for more. But that wasn't smart. She prided herself on making the "right" choices, but now she wanted to just forget that and do what *felt* right.

So what?

She'd been smart her entire life, and look where it had gotten her. She was alone and doing silly things like signing up for matchmaking services and reality-TV shows. She wanted something—someone—different, and Russell certainly was that.

"You're staring at me again," he said with that little half smile of his that she was getting very used to seeing. He used it as a shield to seem open and friendly, but she knew it was a mask.

"That is entirely your fault," she said. "If you'd just act like I expected you to, then I could walk away and pretend I gave this a chance."

"Where would you walk to?" he asked. "If you are on this show, I'm guessing you are out of options."

"Very true," she said. "I guess I'd go back to my safe little world where everything fits neatly in its place."

"So I no longer fit in my place?" he asked her.

Frankly, she wasn't too sure what she'd do with Russell in his place. She wasn't cut out to date a jet-setting playboy, and no matter what the matchmaker thought, Gail knew he wasn't right for her.

"No, you don't," she said.

"What am I doing wrong?" he asked.

She nibbled on her lower lip and tasted him. "Kissing me."

"You didn't like it?" he asked. "I can try to improve my technique."

"I liked it too much," she said. "Don't be offended—"

He leaned down and arched one eyebrow at her in a way that made her feel as though she was amusing him. "Saying that pretty much guarantees I will be."

She smiled at him. "I guess so, but I expected your kiss to be practiced and kind of mechanical...."

"Glad to disappoint," he said.

She wrinkled her nose at him and mock-punched him. "I'm not letting my guard down, no matter how charming you act. I'm not sure about you."

"I wouldn't expect you to let your guard down. But there is one thing you should know."

"And that is...?" she asked.

"I don't lose," he said with a full-on, smug grin.

She wasn't too sure she wanted him to look at this as some kind of competition, and it was telling that he had done so. "I don't want you to lose. In fact, I want us both to get what we want."

He leaned back against the seat and crossed his arms over his chest, glancing out the window as the chopper pilot made his way back to the helipad on top of the Big Apple Kiwi. "That came out wrong, didn't it?"

"Only if you think of me as a prize," she said. "We're both feeling our way here. I'm not judging you."

He shook his head and leveled that steady gray gaze of his on her. "I think you are. You'd have to be. Otherwise, how will you be sure I'm not the player you've read about."

That insight was enough for her to continue to relax her guard. He knew that he wasn't just starting a new relationship and maneuvering through the normal obstacles that most couples experience. They had the added pressure of his being so unlike her Mr. Right.

She knew that she'd designed her list based on a fictional guy. Her father had divorced her mother when Gail was eight, so she only had vague impressions of him at home. Her mother had dated but never remarried, so Gail was pretty much left with movies and books to form her opinions of what she wanted in a man. Well, that and the men she'd dated, who'd left her wanting more.

"I'm aiming for a win-win here," she said at last, because, if she was honest, she had no idea what else to say.

"Me too," he said. "Once we land, do we have to do more camera work?"

"I'm not sure. I think they will tell us when we come down. Why?" she asked.

"If not, will you join me for a nightcap?"

She would have said no just twenty minutes ago, but now she wanted to spend more time with him to talk to him, and get to know his point of view. See how he really viewed the world. His public image was different from this private man, and she was determined to find out how much so.

She took a deep breath. It was easy to say she wanted to change and was willing to put herself out there, but the reality was so different. In her fantasy date, the man was everything that Hollywood and romance novels had groomed her to expect. But Russell was a mixture of those fantasies and reality.

She had to decide if she was ready to step out of those expectations and into Russell's world. She was. She wouldn't have signed up with a matchmaker otherwise. "Yes."

"Good. I knew that this was going to be a good thing," he said.

"Matchmaking?" she asked. "It's strange. I'm really not sure if it's going to work out or not. When I saw the ad for the service, it was New Year's Eve and I'd had a little too much champagne."

"And a bad date?"

She shook her head. "Nope. I was all alone and I resolved that I wouldn't be next New Year's Eve."

"Well you've gone a good route to find a mate. Match-making is an old tradition," he said.

"Even in Australia?" she asked. She wasn't that well traveled and didn't know what the customs were in other countries.

"I'm from New Zealand," he said. "But, yes, even there. Some of the women in my town were mail-order brides."

"Did you have any doubts about doing this?" she asked. She had been unsure as soon as she'd signed up. Writing the check had been easy, but as soon as she'd walked out the door of Matchmakers Inc., she'd started to feel so vulnerable and scared. At least the fee had been refunded once she'd been selected for the TV show.

"Lots of them, but then I thought, if a woman was brave enough to do this, I could handle it. Having another person pick a date for you isn't any worse than meeting someone in a bar," Russell said.

"I've never met a guy in a bar. Most of the men I dated were from work or classes."

"Somehow that doesn't surprise me," he said. "You don't seem like the type of woman who'd allow a man to pick her up in a bar."

"Why don't I?" she asked.

"You wouldn't have time to ask all your questions. Most men are looking for a quick score," he said.

He looked over at her, and she wondered if she'd revealed something she shouldn't have. She knew she didn't always say the right thing with men. But then she took a deep breath as the chopper banked for its landing, and she saw her own reflection in the window. She was on a matchmaking reality television show with a billionaire playboy.... There was nothing familiar about this scenario, and she was going to just let it play out.

"What are you thinking?" he said, his voice intimately deep in her ears, thanks to the headphones.

"Just how unreal this entire thing is," she said. "Not reality at all."

He laughed. "I agree. But I don't mind it. Dating hasn't worked out for either of us in the real world, so this might actually work."

She wasn't betting on it. They landed and took off their headphones, as the pilot turned off the helicopter.

"Do we have to tell them we kissed?"

Russell caressed her arm and linked their fingers together. "That can be our secret."

With those words, he made them a couple. They had a secret that was just between them and, in a night of showy emotion and put-on romance, it was the first genuine thing to happen.

"Okay," she said. "I like the idea of that."

"Good. I like the idea of you and me," he said.

She did too. But why? She wanted to figure out what it was about Russell that drew her in so deeply, but she had a feeling that the emotions he brought to the fore in her weren't going to be logical.

"Ready to face the cameras again?"

"Yes," she said. And she was definitely ready to get to know this man better, once filming stopped for the night and they were on their own.

She really liked Russell when they were alone.

Russell listened to the producer talking to Gail, and every once in a while, he heard her laugh. The sound was full of joy, and he could tell that she was enjoying whatever they were talking about. She was relaxed with Willow and her guard was down. Russell realized he still had a long way to go to get to know the real Gail Little.

"How's matchmaking going for you so far?" Conner MacAfee asked as he came up beside him.

"Not bad," he said.

"Good," Conner said. "You know Matchmakers Inc. has a one hundred percent success rate, right?"

"Do you?"

"Yes, we do."

"Did you do anything differently for us because of the TV show?"

Conner shook his head. "No way. We can't compromise our policies, even for a show. I'm hoping to get some business out of this, and I can't if we don't do what we normally do for our clients."

"Point taken. Do you know anything about Gail?" he asked Conner. He figured it was a fair enough question, given that she had heard of him.

"No. I really don't get involved in the matching. I just run the company," he said. He straightened his tie and glanced around the room. "I have to use my MBA from Harvard somehow."

"Don't brag," Russell said with a grin.

"What's the use in having one if you can't tell people about it?" Conner said.

"Why do you own a matchmaking company?" Russell asked. His friend was one of the smartest business minds he'd ever encountered. Russell had always thought it was an odd thing for Conner.

"It was my grandmother's business and I inherited it. I figured it wouldn't make money and I could take it as a tax loss, but in fact the opposite was the case," Conner said.

"The market can be unexpected. I'm trying to diversify now to make sure we have more of a toehold in other segments," Russell said. That had been one of the reasons why he'd agreed to be on the show. He needed potential investors to see that he was a changed man.

"No kidding. We added an exclusive wife-finder for some of our more eccentric customers," Conner said.

"What does that mean?" Russell asked.

"We vet the woman and send her to the client, and he approves her and marries her without any dating. It's a very new service and a niche market. But a very profitable one."

"That's interesting," Russell said. He guessed that everyone was scrambling in this new economy to figure out ways to stay ahead.

"Do you need anything from me?" Conner asked.

"No. I'm good. Poker on Thursday night?"

"Definitely. I want a chance to win back some of my money."

"Good luck with that. The cards favor me and always have."

"I know. I remember when we first met and you'd win enough money at the tables in Monaco to make your payroll."

"Those days are long behind me," Russell said. "But my ability at the poker table hasn't diminished."

"It might have. I feel the need to remind you whose country you are in," Conner said.

"I haven't lost yet," Russell said.

"That only means you are due for a fall," Conner said as he walked away. Russell watched his friend leave and took a deep breath. The air was chilly this evening but not cold. He suddenly felt a sense of peace he hadn't felt in a long time.

The production crew left the rooftop as a group. He and Conner made their way toward the elevators, with Gail and Willow following them. They were still talking.

"I got a call from a friend of yours," Conner said, turning to the women.

"Mine?" Willow asked.

"Yes, Nichole…I can't remember her last name. She wants to interview me about Matchmaker Inc."

"She works for *America Today* so she's legit," Willow said.

The elevator arrived.

"Do you want to chat about it quickly?" Willow asked.

"I'd like that," Conner said. "See ya later, Russell."

Russell waved goodbye to his friend as the doors opened. Dylan, his executive assistant, was on the elevator, a concerned look on his face.

"Hiya, boss. We have a situation," Dylan said, stepping out of the elevator.

"I'll leave you to it," Gail said, backing away from the two men.

"Wait, Gail. Are we still on for that nightcap?" he asked.

"Yes. The lobby bar?"

"Sounds good. Twenty minutes?"

"Yes," she said, getting on the elevator.

Russell waited until the doors closed before asking Dylan, "What is so important it needs my attention?"

"Penny Thomson is in the lobby demanding to see you. I tried to get her to wait in my office, but she wouldn't."

Great. Not what he needed this night, but he'd handle it. "Please make sure that Gail is taken care of until I'm done with Penny."

"I'm happy to, boss," Dylan said.

"Never mind, I'll talk to her. You tell Penny I'm on my way, but I will only meet with her in the office, not in the lobby," Russell said.

He took the elevator to the lobby and, once there, noticed that Willow had rejoined Gail and the two were talking.

"I'll try."

Dylan walked away, and Russell made his way to Gail. "I'm sorry, but I think my situation might take a little longer than anticipated. Can we meet in forty-five minutes instead?"

She flushed and looked at Willow. "We're having a drink. Is that okay?"

"Yes, that's fine. We want to capture the phases of your relationship, not every second. Enjoy yourselves."

Gail turned back to him with a slight smile on her face. "I'll be down there in forty-five minutes, then."

"Good."

Russell left the women and headed down to the lobby and the office behind the check-in desk. Dylan was standing outside of it when Russell approached.

"I always thought Penny would be nicer in person," Dylan said. "Sorry about that, sir. I should have kept that to myself."

"You probably should have, but I happen to agree that she can be a bit of a bitch."

Dylan nodded and then walked away.

Russell opened the door and saw Penny sitting on the edge of the desk. She had her iPhone in one hand and was delicately tapping out a message with the tip of one French-manicured fingernail.

"It's about time you got here. I've been tweeting about the inconvenience of waiting on a former lover."

"Nice. Good to see you too, Penny."

"Yeah, right. You made it clear you didn't want to see me again," she said.

She was a Hollywood starlet so beautiful that she'd floored Russell the first time he saw her. It had been impossible to think of anything but sex. But, after spending two days in bed with her, Russell knew it had been a mistake. Penny was vapid and so self-absorbed, it was impossible for her to be aware of anyone else.

"Stop tweeting. You always get yourself in trouble with that."

"Well, this time, Russell, you're the one who's going to be in trouble."

"Why, exactly? I thought we ended things amiably."

"Sure we did. But it turns out we have a few unresolved issues."

Russell realized as she talked that he couldn't wait to get away from her and back to Gail. He liked Gail's freshness and the way natural sensuality imbued her every movement, as opposed to Penny's in-your-face sexuality.

"Like what?"

"I'm pregnant," she said.

Russell shook his head. He'd settled a paternity suit when he was twenty-four and, ever since then, every time a past lover became pregnant he'd had to deal with this. "I'm not the father."

"I'm not so sure about that, Russell, and I'm going to be tweeting about it unless you do what you should," Penny said.

Penny's timing couldn't be worse. This was exactly what he didn't want to deal with today. He wanted to get back to Gail and continue courting her and wooing her. But instead… "I'm going to need to see proof you're pregnant, and then we need to do a paternity test."

"I don't know why. The baby is yours, and if you don't cooperate, I'm going to make life very difficult for you," she said.

He knew she meant it. He had to handle this delicately, because Gail was his chance at the future he wanted to have, and Penny was part of a past he was trying very hard to distance himself from.

Gail waited in the lobby bar for Russell, feeling just a little self-conscious that she was by herself. Honestly, she'd thought she'd mastered sitting alone in public a long time ago, but the truth was she hadn't. She didn't like it.

She felt someone watching her and glanced up to see Russell leaving the back office with his hand on the shoulder of a woman who looked familiar. Gail leaned forward and recognized her as Penny Thomson, rising Hollywood star and Russell's ex. Gail watched them for a minute before deciding that he wasn't the kind of guy she wanted to get to know better.

She knew any guy she dated would have an ex, but with another man, she wouldn't be competing against someone like Penny. This was a mistake, she thought. Her gut had said so from the moment she'd recognized Russell, but the romantic in her had been wooed during that chopper ride over Manhattan. Just because he had money and knew how to make the right reservations, it didn't mean he was capable of being the man she needed in her life. And Gail was on a tight timetable. She had these few months to find a man if she wanted to execute her "family" plan, including husband and, eventually, children.

Gail lifted the glass of soda water that she'd ordered and took a sip, trying to be disinterested. But she couldn't be. Russell and Penny looked perfect together. That would make great TV, she thought. The pretty blonde starlet and the ruggedly handsome man. Not at all like her and Russell.

She'd had enough of this. She was going home and she'd figure out a new plan in the morning. For tonight, she needed to get away from the Kiwi Big Apple and the man who'd almost made her…what? For a little while, she'd forgotten that she was really just a plain Jane. For a little while, she'd forgotten her common sense. Forgotten what was painfully obvious right now—that there was no way Russell would be interested in her, because he was used to a class of women that was out of her league.

She wasn't putting herself down, but was being realistic. She was never going to dress that overtly sexually or spend as much time on hair and makeup as Penny did. She was a normal woman with a job and a life. Not a sexual plaything whose sole purpose was to be seen on Russell's arm.

"I thought you were meeting Russell," Willow said, coming up to her table.

"I was," Gail said, tearing her eyes away from him to look at her friend. "He's over there."

Willow glanced at the couple and then back at Gail before sitting down. Willow had thick black hair that fell almost to her waist when she left it free, but normally she pulled it back in a ponytail. She was tall—almost five-eight—and had striking features. Staring at her friend, Gail almost thought Willow would look better on Russell's arm than she herself would.

"What's that about?" Gail asked, gesturing to the couple.

"I don't know. I think…he's not right for me. I can't keep doing this for five more dates. I know that it will screw up your show, but I just can't."

Willow nodded. "I get that. I will talk with Conner and ask that they get another match for you."

Gail shook her head. "No, I don't think that will work. I don't like having something so important out of my control."

"Then why did you sign up for it?" Willow asked. "You

were the one to start this—I mean everything, including the show. What's different?"

Gail took a deep breath. "I think I could really get hurt. I never considered that part in my plan."

"What part?"

"Emotions, Will. I could easily fall for Russell, with all his charm and bad-boy ways, but I don't know what he's doing on this show. He could be using me…. He probably is, and I have no way of shutting off my emotions."

Willow reached over and gave her a one-armed hug. "I'm not going to lie to you. I want you to keep dating him, because he's different than your usual guy and I think you need that. But I don't want to see you get hurt either."

Gail thought about that image in her head of the man she'd wanted to find, and realized that now she saw Russell. She liked him. He was funny and self-deprecating and oh so good at making her believe he wanted to change. But she'd just seen the proof with her own eyes. Even if he wanted to change, he wasn't going to be able to. He had past lovers who would always be a part his life. And Gail didn't know if she could deal with it.

"I'm jealous," Gail admitted to Willow.

"Of…?"

"Penny," Gail said. "Did you see them together? They belong with each other. I'm not as pretty as she is—"

"You're prettier," Willow said.

"And you're one of my best friends. You're biased."

"True, but I'm not going to lie to you. Yes, she is pretty in a very polished sort of way, but you have never been able to see how lovely you are. And I think that Russell will see that. He already has. He didn't have to invite you for a nightcap, did he?"

"No," Gail said, thinking about that kiss on the chopper. There was an attraction between them. Was she just a novelty to him? Someone different? She didn't know, and she didn't want to wait too long to find out.

"I…I think I'm going to have to back out of it," Gail said. "I can't take a chance that Russell is playing a game and using me as a pawn."

"Fair enough," Willow said. "I'll talk to Matchmakers Inc. and we'll find another couple to take over your slot."

"No," Russell said, surprising Gail and Willow as he walked up to their table.

"No?" Gail asked. "I don't think you get to decide for me."

"She has a point," Willow said. "We only want you on the show if you both are interested in going forward."

Russell pulled a chair up and sat down with them. "That makes perfect sense, but I'm not about to let Gail back out of this without at least talking to me," he said, turning to Willow. "Will you give us until the morning to let you know?"

"Yes," Willow said. "But I don't think Gail is going to change her mind."

"If I can't convince her to give me a chance, then it will be better to end it now," Russell said. "Let's get out of here."

Four

Russell needed Gail more than ever. The meeting with Penny had convinced him that, if he had any chance of changing his reputation and by default the reputation of the Kiwi Klubs, he needed someone like Gail. But his conscience wouldn't allow him to simply use Gail. He was going to have to be honest with her. And frankly, that scared him. He was used to behaving a certain way so that the public and the people around him believed him to be a playboy.

"I'm not sure that you can convince me to change my mind," Gail said, as they entered his penthouse apartment on the top floor of the Big Apple Kiwi.

One wall was floor-to-ceiling glass making the sweeping expanse of the city a backdrop for the apartment. She'd seen pictures of places like this in *Home & Garden* magazine, but frankly it felt staged. She didn't feel comfortable in the apartment or with Russell.

"If I can't, I don't deserve you," he said. "What can I get you to drink?"

"I'm getting tired, so I should skip the alcohol," she said. "It will put me to sleep."

"Fair enough. The living room is over there," he said, gesturing to the leather couches grouped together in a casual seating area. "Have a seat while I get myself a scotch."

She did as he directed, and Russell went to the wet bar to pour himself two fingers, neat. Gail looked lovely and a little lonely as she sat on one of the big, stuffed leather couches. His apartment was clearly a man's domain, and seeing her here made him realize the changes he would need to make to welcome a woman like her into his life.

He took a deep swallow of his drink and then set the glass down before going to join her. Convincing her he wanted to change was easy; he knew he'd done that already and had actually made her see beyond the tabloid reputation. Convincing her that he was really going to change would be harder. Hell, he wasn't even sure of it himself.

"This is a nice place," she said as he sat down.

"Thanks," he said.

"Has it been featured in any decorating magazines?" she asked, glancing around.

"Two. My decorator tries to use it to drum up business," Russell said.

"And has that worked?"

"So far it has. She's going to decorate my new home in the Hamptons for a twenty percent discount. I bet this place isn't as welcoming as your home," he said.

"But it suits your needs," she said. "You look very at home here."

"I am," he said. "Gail, I don't want you to back out of

the matchmaking now. I really need a woman like you in my life."

She shook her head. "You might want to think that, but I saw you tonight with Penny, and she fits you and your lifestyle."

"You have no idea how wrong you are. Penny is fun," he said. He refused to say anything bad about Penny, but wanted Gail to realize that Penny was used to playing a part…just as he was. "We are too similar. I need a woman like you, who forces me to be honest."

"Sounds like you need a mother," she said.

"That's not true. Most people—women—give me a pass. They accept my charm and my flirting with every woman as just the way I am. I have a feeling you wouldn't," Russell said, lifting one eyebrow at her in question.

"You've got that right. I'm not interested in a man who can't commit."

Russell knew that. He needed that. He needed Gail. He liked her, he wanted her and she'd be perfect for his image. Gail just had a totally respectable look. She was hardly the type of woman to be caught sunbathing topless on his yacht. Yet he sensed a passion in her, so it wasn't that she was a prude. Just that she was circumspect—something that had been lacking in his personal relationships up to this point. "Good. I'm too used to getting my way."

"Hence this conversation," she said. "Russell, I'm sure you're sincere in wanting to change, and maybe even in wanting to find a woman to spend the rest of your life with."

"But…?" he asked. He felt he should interject something to convince her to stick with the matchmaking, but he actually had no idea what argument would convince Gail to stay. She was still too much like a stranger to him.

"I'm not sure I'm the right woman for you. I don't know that I can help you make that change. But I do know that I like you. I can see myself easily falling for your lines, and if it turns out you're lying…"

"You're convicting me of something before I've even done it," he said.

"Based totally on your track record," Gail said. "Look at Penny tonight. What was she doing here?"

"She…she has a problem and she thinks I can help her," Russell said. How was he going to tell Gail that Penny thought she was pregnant and he was the father? That would be enough to send Gail running for the hills, but if he explained how he knew he couldn't be the father… It was too much for this early in the relationship.

"Tell me about it," Gail said.

"I'm not sure what is really going on. With Penny there's always a lot of drama and bold statements," Russell said.

"I can understand that," Gail said. She leaned back against the cushions. "I'm used to dealing with clients that are like that. But this isn't a business deal for me—this is my life and my future."

"I figured you have some experience of these sorts of things, being in PR. Right now, Penny's very excitable, but I think once she has some time to think, everything will be sorted out. I get that this is personal. It is for me too. I'm not playing a game with you."

"Are you sure?" she asked. "I want to believe you."

"Then believe me," he said.

"Do you need my professional help?" Gail asked. "I would take you on as a client even if the dating thing doesn't work out…. I'll even give you a twenty percent discount."

"Ha-ha. You are too generous," he said. "But I don't

need your professional help right now. I want your personal help, Gail. I want you to give me a chance to be the man of your dreams."

He felt a little hokey saying those words, but with Gail he knew they were important, and even though he was in uncharted territory, he was willing to go with his gut. It was his gut that had brought him his greatest business success, and he trusted it now to help him with Gail.

"Ugh!" She stood up, walked over to the windows and put one hand against the glass as she looked out. In the reflection, he saw the perplexed look on her face.

"What?" he asked, striding over to her.

She turned to face him, crossing both arms over her waist. "I know that I should say no and walk away now before we get too connected, but I can't."

"Why can't you?" he asked. He knew it was because he was saying the right things. He had always had good instincts about what a woman needed to hear in the beginning of a relationship. It was as they continued moving forward that he would run into trouble.

"Because you are total temptation for me, Russell," she said. "Don't let that go to your head. I just can't seem to resist the thought of really getting to know you."

"Good," he said. He knew that as they spent more time alone, he would be able to win her over. He'd always been good at knowing what to say to other people; it was how he'd convinced his backers to initially invest in his business. But with Gail, he knew he was going to have to do more than just say the right things. He was going to have to actually do the right things, and that was going to be hard.

He sat there staring at Gail and knew he was going to do whatever it took to get her to believe him, because without Gail, he'd have nothing but the empty existence he'd been living. And he didn't want to be stuck there any longer.

Gail didn't know if she was going to be up to the challenge of Russell, but then no man in the past had even made her want to try, and he did. She wanted to pretend it was just lust and attraction, because then she could say it was hormones and walk away. But there was more to her attraction to Russell than that.

"I will continue on the show and with our matchmaking dates, but only if you are completely honest with me, Russell. If I catch you out, I'm not going to give you any more chances."

She didn't trust easily to begin with, and a man like Russell—well, he just made her even more wary of believing him. He was used to playing fast and loose, and she wasn't. She felt off balance, and while part of her was excited by it, another part was warning her to run away.

"And I assume I can expect honesty from you at all times," he said.

"Yes, you can. I'm used to being on my own and keeping who I am very private, but I'll try to be open with you," she said.

Russell smiled at her, and she felt a little thrill run through her body. "I'll help you."

"Okay. So, that's settled. I think it's time for me to go home." She wanted to be back in her sanctuary with her comfy chairs and her quiet music. She wanted the scents of her home to soothe her, as they did every day when she returned.

"I don't want to let you go," he said.

"Well, I have to. I'm tired and I have an early appointment with a client. But I enjoyed tonight. It was different," she said.

"Indeed. I enjoyed your company, Gail," he said.

She liked the way her name sounded on his lips. His accent was part of it, but there was also the implicit intimacy in the way he talked to her. She felt special and singled out, and she liked that just a little too much.

"Thanks," she said. "Um…I guess I'll see you at our next date."

"I think so. I don't want to wait a week. If I call you, maybe we can find some time together," Russell said.

Gail nodded, but she knew that she needed some distance to figure out how to get to know Russell better without letting him too close to her.

"Call me," she said. She began walking to his door, but he was there first. He put his arm around her and held the door closed.

"Am I so scary that you have to run away?" he asked.

She turned under his arm so that she was facing him. He was so close she could see some stubble on his jaw. He smelled of expensive cologne and a natural male musk that was intoxicating. She thought how easy it would be to just give in to him in this moment. But she knew that she'd have to wake up in the morning, and she'd have regrets. She hated that feeling in her gut when she'd made a bad decision.

But there was no reason she couldn't at least touch him, now that they were away from the cameras and alone. She reached up and rubbed her finger over the light stubble on his jaw, liking the abrasion against her skin. She put her other hand on his chest and slowly slid it around to his back. He stood there, leaning over her, one hand against the door, the other hanging loosely by his side, and let her have her way.

"I'm not scared of you, Russell," she said, hoping that by saying the words out loud they would become the truth. But she knew that she was truly afraid of herself. Afraid of her own fantasies of Mr. Right, which had been in her heart and mind for so long that she was a little too eager to meet the man who would fulfill them. And there were parts of Russell that easily checked those boxes for her.

He leaned in closer. The spicy scent of his aftershave surrounded her, as did his body heat. She felt the exhalation of his breath against the hair at her temple, and she closed her eyes for a second. Pretended she didn't know his reputation and that he was just a man—a very good-looking man she wanted. Pretended there was no ticking clock for her to find Mr. Right. Pretended she could kiss him and then walk away.

She closed the gap between them and rubbed her lips over his. A light, gentle kiss was her intent, but Russell parted his lips, and she couldn't resist sneaking her tongue inside for just one taste. That was what she told herself. She'd kiss him quickly and turn away.

But his taste was addicting and one small kiss wasn't enough. She pulled herself closer to him and felt his hand come around her back. His hand was at her waist, squeezing her carefully as she rose on tiptoe and pressed her breasts against his chest.

He felt so good…too good. She didn't want to back away. She wanted to stay in his arms tonight and every night. And every night was the problem. She pulled back and moved away from him. Her lips were tingling, her skin was sensitive and her pulse was racing.

"Good night," she said, determined to leave now, before she did something completely stupid, like jumping in his arms and begging him to make love to her.

"I guess you really want to go," he said. "Is there nothing I can do to convince you to stay?"

She shook her head. There were things he could do, but she'd regret it in the morning, and she knew better than to give in to that type of temptation. Russell was dangerous to her because he could make her forget the reason she'd signed up with a matchmaker in the first place.

"You'd have to be a different man," she said at last.

He nodded and tightened his mouth as he stared down at her. He tucked a strand of hair behind her ear and leaned down so their eyes were level. "I will show you I can be."

He put his hand on the small of her back and walked her to the elevator. He rode down with her, and when they got to the lobby, he asked the concierge to call for his private car.

"I can take a cab," she said.

"Never. I take care of my women," he said.

"I don't want to be one of your women," she said. And that was the problem with Russell as far as she could see. Gail would always be viewed by the world as one of his women. Not his woman. She had to figure out how she felt about that and if she was strong enough to go into a relationship with him anyway.

"You made that clear when you left. But I'm not about to let you go home in a cab when I have a car."

"I'm being difficult, aren't I?" she asked at last.

"A little," he said.

"It's my nature. You asked me if I was scared of you earlier, and I said no. I'm really not. But I am a little unsure of myself because you tempt me to forget common sense, and I'm not about to do that."

"When the time is right, we'll figure it out. Until then, I'll have to woo you. But don't forget, I'm playing to win."

It was all she thought about. That and the fact that, if he

won, she didn't want to be the loser. She didn't want to be standing alone at the end of these matchmaking dates with a handful of memories and a broken heart. She wouldn't allow it.

"I heard that the first time. I think you shouldn't view relationships as something you need to win," she said.

"Why not?" he asked. He seemed to genuinely want to make this work, and she felt bad that she was putting up obstacles.

"Because then you make everything into a best-of competition, that's not a way to build something."

"I'll consider what you said. There's my driver. Good night, Gail."

"Good night, Russell," she said, walking away from him, wishing she could dismiss him from her mind as easily.

Russell spent the morning in meetings and the afternoon doing some promo spots for the show. He'd hoped to see Gail, but it was just Willow and a cameraman following him around the hotel to show him in his everyday world. When shooting wrapped for the day, he pulled Willow aside.

"Do you have time to join me for a drink?"

"I have about fifteen minutes," she said.

"Good." He led her to the VIP section of the bar, which was empty at this time of the day. Russell signaled one of the waitresses to bring them some drinks.

"What did you want to talk about? Gail already called and said she'd be continuing on the show."

"I assumed she had, or you wouldn't be here now," Russell said. "I wanted to ask you about Gail."

"I don't know what I can tell you," Willow said, shaking her long hair. She reminded him a little of Cher back in her younger days, before she was famous on her own. Willow had impressed him as being very smart and tenacious in getting what she wanted.

"She's so guarded, and you two are friends, right?" Russell asked. He'd seen the way they were together and was asking just to hear her confirm it.

"She's one of my best friends. And she is guarded. What do you want to know?" Willow asked. The waitress stopped by, and Willow ordered a Diet Coke and Russell asked for Perrier.

At night, this bar was jam-packed with people. It had rich, dark carpet with an abstract design. The VIP area was lined with banquettes where A-listers could sit obscured from view from but still seeing everything that was happening. It was a world and an environment he knew well, and Willow looked out of place in her jeans and T-shirt. Russell suspected Gail wouldn't be that comfortable here either.

As soon as the waitress left, Russell turned back to Willow. "I want to know…everything. But that's not going to happen, is it?"

"No. If she wants you to know something, she'll tell you," Willow said. "I don't think I can be of much help."

"She's different, Willow. I want to know the best way to get her to open up to me. If she stays guarded…well, neither of us is going to get what we wanted from the matchmaking."

The waitress dropped off their drinks, and Willow took a long sip of hers. "You have to get her to relax. In your case, I'd say she's going to have to forget all the stuff she's heard about you over the years, and that's going to be hard. But once she starts seeing the real you, she'll drop her guard."

"Okay," he said. He had no idea who the real Russell

was. He'd spent so much time pretending to be whatever was needed to make money and be successful, Russell the man had gotten lost. But did that really matter? He didn't need to know who he was to woo Gail. He needed to know what Gail was looking for on her mythical Mr. Right list. "Thanks for that."

"I suspect you already knew that," Willow said.

"I did. I was hoping you'd say jewels or expensive presents would help."

Willow laughed. "That would be easier, wouldn't it? But she has her own money and doesn't really need *things*."

"What *does* she need?" he asked. "Do you know what is on her list of qualities for a man?"

"That's the million-dollar question," Willow said. "She's not open about that, even with her friends."

That was very interesting. So this list of hers was highly personal. It reassured him that she wasn't out talking about it with anyone. He was going to have to get her to trust him completely to find out what was in her heart and soul. And he instinctively knew he'd need to win both to convince the world that he'd changed.

"How long have you known each other?" Russell asked.

"Since grade school," Willow said, leaning back in her chair and smiling. "We grew up together."

"Wow, that's a long time. Most people don't tend to keep in touch over the years. I guess friendship is important to you both," Russell said.

"It is. We've always been close, and it's harder to maintain that relationship as we've gotten older, but we try," Willow said.

"That's good. I don't really…" Russell didn't know why he'd allowed the conversation to go down this path. He didn't want to talk about his growing-up years. In fact, most days he just ignored them.

"You don't have friends from your childhood?" Willow asked.

He thought about the isolated ranch he'd grown up on in New Zealand and the small town where everyone had known his story. His parents had died in a fiery car crash when he was sixteen. He'd been old enough to be considered a man and had started supporting himself by playing cards. He'd always been lucky, and he'd turned that luck at the table into the basis of his fortune.

He hadn't had friends and hadn't looked for them. He'd always wanted so much more than that place had to offer, and leaving it behind had been very easy to do.

"Not really. I'm not into that. I'm always looking for the next business goal," Russell said.

"Is that what you're doing now?" Willow asked. She was very direct and stared into his eyes when she asked him a question.

Russell had been looking at Gail from the angle of what she could do for him and his business. He'd known it all along, but there was no way he could admit to that now.

"I'm looking for a change. Maybe I want a little of that commitment you all have," he said.

She arched both eyebrows at him, and he had the feeling that if he crossed her, he'd be in big trouble.

"Is that what you said to Gail to convince her to stay on the show?" she asked.

"Didn't she tell you?" He was trying to piece together the woman that Gail was. Did she share the intimate details of her life with her closest friends? Or did she keep secrets?

"Actually, no, she didn't elaborate," Willow said, giving him a hard stare.

"Then I won't either. Thank you for your time, Willow," Russell said.

"You're welcome," she said, standing up and stretching. Willow didn't look anything like Gail, and he wondered at the bond of their friendship. In his experience, women tended to surround themselves with similar types. But these two didn't seem to have anything in common.

Russell walked her back to the front of the hotel. As he said goodbye, Willow turned abruptly and poked one finger into the center of his chest, forcing him to back up.

"Don't hurt my friend," she warned.

"I don't intend to," he said. He wanted Gail happier than she'd ever been before, because that was the only way he was going to know that he'd won her over. And winning was all that mattered now.

When Willow left, he stood there in the middle of the Kiwi Klub's hotel lobby, watching the people come and go around him. He'd worked hard to be successful, and it was apparent to him that he'd achieved what he'd set out to do. And he knew that he'd achieve what he wanted with Gail, because he wasn't a man who accepted failure.

He had his eye on the ball, and it wasn't just one goal he had in mind. He was going to convince the head of the Family Vacation Destination company to sell their controlling shares to him. He was going to make damned sure that Gail understood he wasn't playing around with her. It was time for him to move into the next phase in his life, and she was just the woman to help him do it.

Five

Gail didn't question her desire to know every detail about Russell Holloway, but when she found herself running a Google search on him for the fourth time in a single morning, she knew she needed to call him.

She took a sip of her Earl Grey tea and leaned back in the chair. She wanted to find answers easily, some sort of information that would make her feel safer about dating Russell. But the truth was there wasn't anything on the internet that could do that.

She wasn't going to find the information she wanted by reading articles about his childhood in New Zealand or when he'd made his first billion with the Kiwi Klubs. She wanted…what, exactly?

She knew but she just didn't want to admit it. She wanted to hear his story from his mouth. So without overanalyzing it any further, she picked up the phone and dialed his number.

"Holloway," he said, answering his phone on the first ring. His voice was strong and all business. She almost hung up, but she hadn't called him for nothing.

"It's Gail," she said, feeling nervous all of a sudden and a little shy.

There was a pause on the line, and Gail had second thoughts. Oh, this had bad idea written all over it.

"Well, hello, beautiful," he said, his voice softening and the charm she remembered from their first date returning.

"Beautiful?" she said.

"To me you are."

Gail knew she wasn't in the same league as Penny, so she dismissed his compliment. He seemed to be the kind of man who used endearments for everyone.

"I have some questions for you."

"Shoot," he said. "I'm an open book."

"Yeah, right."

She wanted to see his face when she talked to him about his past. There was a lot about him she didn't know, and she was tired of her fruitless searches. Who was the real Russell? "I was hoping we could meet and talk in person."

"I'm booked all afternoon, and have a VIP coming in tonight that I can't pawn off on my duty manager."

She smiled to herself. This was one match between them that she was going to win. "You're a workaholic. That is not on my list of qualities in Mr. Right. I'm going to have to make a note of that."

"Well played. I can give you ten minutes, but it has to be at the Club," he said.

"I'll be right there," she said.

"Text me when you get here," he said.

"I will. Thanks, Russell," she said, preparing to hang up the phone.

"You owe me one, beautiful," he said in that deep, husky voice of his.

"Stop calling me that," she said, even though she liked the sound of it. Endearments and compliments made her uncomfortable. She didn't think of herself in those terms, and hearing him say it… "Are you mocking me?"

"When?" he asked.

God, why had she started asking him about this? She didn't want to discuss her lack of attractiveness with one of *People*'s Sexiest Bachelors.

"When you call me beautiful," she said at last, hoping her voice didn't sound as small and vulnerable as she felt.

"No, I'm not," he said. "Why do you think that?"

"No reason," she said. She should have learned her lesson a long time ago, she thought, about keeping her thoughts to herself. "I'll see you in a few minutes."

She disconnected before he could say anything else. She should have kept her insecurity to herself, but she didn't know how to do the dating thing and pretend to be someone she wasn't. In PR it was different, because she knew the rules and scripted what others said. But for herself, she always shot from the hip and spoke from the heart.

She left her office and headed for the Kiwi Klub. When she got there, she texted Russell but didn't have to wait in the cutting-edge lobby long for him to show up. He walked toward her in a pair of casual slacks and a button-down shirt, left open at the collar. He was talking to a slim man with thick hair and glasses, but the man left as Russell approached her.

"Hello, Gail. So nice to see you again," he said, putting his arm around her and giving her a small hug.

"Hello, Russell," she said, hugging him back and pretending that this was normal for her. But it had been a long time since she'd been so comfortable with a man that they exchanged hugs.

"We can go to my office to chat," he said, leading the way.

"Sounds good. I'm sorry for the short notice, but I was doing some internet research on you—

"Man, I hate Google. No privacy at all anymore," he said, stopping to hold open a door to a hallway marked Private.

"True enough for people who are in the public eye. I have relatively little info that isn't work related on there," she said. She felt smug about her totally gossip-free life for a moment, but then remembered that it could also come off as somewhat boring.

"That's not true. I found some pictures of you from high school," he said.

She blushed, remembering her big glasses and how she'd looked back then. "How on earth did you find them?"

Russell shrugged one shoulder. "I have my ways. Here's my office."

The office was luxurious by anyone's standards, with a big walnut desk dominating the center of the room and dark paneling on the walls. Hanging at different points around the room were photos of Russell with various celebrities.

"Have a seat," he said, gesturing to the leather guest chairs.

She took her time walking to one of them and then sat down, surprised when Russell sat in the one next to her. Now that she was here, what was she going to say? In her head she'd had the idea that if they were face-to-face, she'd be able to see past the facade of his reputation to the real man—especially without the cameras rolling—but right now she wasn't sure.

"I…I sort of had a plan, but I'm not sure I can ask you the questions I wanted to," she said.

"Why not?" he asked.

"Because they're intrusive," she said. When she wasn't with Russell, it was easier for her to think of him as an object. As someone that she could ask personal questions of and not worry about how he felt. But now, sitting across from him, she realized how nosey she was being.

"Ask away. I'm planning to do the same to you."

"You are?" She had figured that he wouldn't be that worried about her. She didn't have a reputation at all, except in her professional life as someone who got the job done. "But I'm the normal one."

He laughed at that. "Good to know how you're thinking of me."

"I didn't mean it that way. Just that I'm the one who you'd expect to see on a dating show. You aren't."

He leaned back in his chair and casually sprawled his legs out in front of him. He was a tall man, long and lean, and she was distracted by him. "I'm counting on you to help me seem like a man who is moving on. I can't be that if you have skeletons in your closet."

She didn't have anything controversial in her past, so that didn't bother her. And hearing him say he had doubts about her was oddly reassuring. It made him real to her in a way that all the questions in the world wouldn't have.

"Fair enough, I guess," she said, wondering what kind of questions he would have for her. "You can go first."

He shook his index finger at her. "No way. That's not how this works. You called me and demanded this meeting."

"Fine," she said, sighing. Then she mentally reviewed

the questions she wanted answered. Most of them involved his past relationships. She wanted to try to find a pattern in how he'd behaved, so she'd have an idea of what to expect from him.

"Why did you settle that paternity suit?" she asked.

"Which one?" he asked.

Though he didn't move, he no longer appeared relaxed. After a moment he leaned forward and laced his fingers together.

"Was there more than one?"

"Yes. I've settled three. I'm going to tell you something that I won't discuss in public or with you after this…."

"Okay," she said. Three paternity suits—wow. That was more than she'd expected. And she really didn't know what to make of that information. Did that mean that he didn't want children?

"I am not the father of any of those children, but the women were all friends of mine who needed a hand. I have a reputation as a player and enough money to take care of all my needs."

"So you just helped them out?" she asked.

"I did," he said.

"Why would you do that? Were the kids yours but you just didn't want to be a dad?" she asked. "I'd think you'd want to clear your name and move on."

He shrugged and looked away from her. "The first case was a girl I'd grown up with and I'm not really sure how it happened—maybe a slow news week or something, but the story made headlines and the longer I played it out the more customers we had at the Kiwi Klubs. So I let it go on and then settled it. The press lapped it up and the new customers I'd found stayed."

"So it was just a press stunt?" she asked. She should

have expected that. Wasn't that the way most of her clients would have reacted?

"It became that, but my intent was to just handle it and move on," he said.

"What about the kids?" she asked. "Do you see them?"

"No. They know I'm not their dad. I don't talk about them or the situation ever," he said.

"I don't like this," she said.

"I can't change it," he said. "Would you rather I lied and made up some sweet story about always wanting kids so I helped out to get to know the babies?"

She shook her head and glanced down at her lap. But, yes, she would have preferred that. She was starting to like Russell, but this...this didn't jibe with her image of what Mr. Right should be.

"Liar," he said, not unkindly.

"Sorry, you're right. I do want you to have acted for a different reason," she admitted.

"Is that on your Mr. Right list?"

"No. I don't want a man with kids. I have a friend who's divorced with kids and every guy she dates has a problem with the kids. I think it's a complication I don't need."

"You're trying to make this match based on an image rather than what it really is. No one is going to be as perfect as the Mr. Right in your head," he said. "I'm not going to lie to you about this. It's easier for me to let the media and the public think I'm shallow."

"You are shallow," she said.

"Am I? Don't just assume everything I do is for my own pleasure."

"Isn't it?" she asked, questioning what she knew about him. He was saying one thing, but a part of her wondered if there wasn't more to his settling paternity suits than he'd let on.

He arched one eyebrow at her. "I think I've answered that. My turn to ask you a question," he said, leveling that cool gray gaze on her.

She had no secrets, the way he did, so she didn't know why she was so concerned about what he would ask. Except that she didn't want to let him really get to know her until she was sure about him. She wanted to protect herself and her heart, but after his honesty, she couldn't lie.

Russell was glad that Gail had asked to see him today. He wanted to know more about her, but wouldn't have pursued the information this way. Not the way she had. But thanks to her curiosity, he now had carte blanche to find out whatever he wanted.

This was the only time they'd had together that wasn't part of the television show or setup dates. She looked professional and polished, but not the way she had on the show. Her hair was pulled back, revealing her long neck and her high cheek bones.

He couldn't stop looking at her. This was the real woman, he thought. She wore a sundress belted at the waist and looked very Hamptons casual to him. She was successful and wore the trappings of it well. No other woman he'd ever dated had pulled off the look that she had right now. She was…well, understated and sophisticated, and he could easily see her on his arm at a business dinner or as his hostess at a party.

"What do you want to know about me?" she asked, her voice low and husky as she waited for him.

He really didn't think she had any skeletons, but his questions were all very personal and intimate. "Do you like for a man to seduce you slowly?"

She blushed and shook her head. "I should have known you would ask something about sex."

"You should have. I'm attracted to you, Gail, and I intend to have you soon."

Her eyes widened as she looked at him. "I like a slow seduction that gives me time to get in the mood. I've never had a lover who could turn me on with just one touch or one look."

He intended to change that. He wanted to be the man who knew her well enough to push her buttons effortlessly, because she already did that for him.

"Have you?" she asked.

That question caught him off guard. He'd kind of expected her to retreat when he turned the conversation to more intimate matters, but then Gail had yet to react the way he'd thought she would to anything. "When I was a teenager, a girl just had to bump into me to turn me on, but as an adult with my hormones under control…no, no woman has been able to turn me on with just a glance."

"Interesting," she said. "Do you think it's because we both use barriers to keep others at bay?"

"Probably," he said. "I didn't think you'd admit to the barriers."

"Why not?" she asked. "I know better than anyone that I don't like to let people too close. I've always been this way."

"Why do you think that is?"

She shrugged as if she didn't know the answer, but in her eyes, he saw the evidence that she was very aware of why she did it. She wasn't interested in sharing her deepest, darkest secrets. She kept them hidden for a reason.

"Tell me," he said.

"It's not something I want to share this early in a relationship," she said and turned away from him. He could see that she didn't want to expose herself to him. It was one thing to pry into his life—he was in the gossip magazines—but she was just a normal, average girl with her own fears. "It's too private."

He almost let her have her way, but he was in this to win, and he knew he'd never win Gail over if he let her set the terms and boundaries of whatever developed between them. "Asking me about the paternity suits wasn't?"

"Touché," she said. "Somehow it felt different because your business is all out there, you know?"

"I can see how it would seem that way, but it's still personal."

She nodded and shifted so she was facing him. "My parents had a very nasty divorce when I was eight. I know it doesn't sound traumatic, but each of them would watch me for any little upset and blame the other one for my sadness. Eventually, I just learned to keep all my emotions bottled up. And then that turned into keeping people at arm's length."

"How does that translate to keeping your distance?"

"My dad gave me everything I wanted, and my friends were aware of that. I had a lot of people start hanging out with me to get whatever they could. That's one reason why Willow and I are such good friends. She didn't care about the parties or the stuff—she just liked hanging out with me."

"Early on you learned to trust your gut," he said. "Willow is a good friend and she's earned your trust."

"Yes, she has."

"I intend to do the same thing, Gail. I don't need your money, and I'm not going to use your emotions against you," he said. But he felt a twinge as he acknowledged to himself that he needed her to fall in love with him so that he could convince the public he'd changed. Gail wasn't the kind of woman who would ever pretend convincingly that she loved a man. He'd have to win her over, heart and soul, and that was exactly what he intended to do.

But he promised himself he'd give her the world. Make sure she had everything she wanted, and he wondered if her father had perhaps told himself the same thing when he was vying with Gail's mother for her affection.

"Why are you looking at me like that?" she asked.

"I just don't want to be another reason why you keep people away," he said. "I want to be the reason why you look at life with new eyes, beautiful. And I'm not going to be satisfied until I'm convinced that you do."

Gail had never intended to tell Russell about her parents, but she felt that it was important to keep things even between them. Her sense of fairness was deeply ingrained, and she just couldn't shift away from it.

"I won't let you be a reason for me to keep people at bay," she said. "That's why I went to the matchmaker."

"There is still no guarantee," he said.

"Are you trying to tell me you are using me?" she asked. "I think you're very good at reading what people want."

"No, I'm not using you. I can read a man when he sits down across from me in the boardroom or at a poker table, but I can only see if he is hiding something. Women are different...unpredictable."

She looked askance at him. "Only a man would say that."

"Damned straight," he said. "Women think they are so easy to understand."

"We know we are complicated," she said, with a grin. "We just think that men should get that and not be afraid of the challenge."

"I'll do my best. Do you have any more questions for me?" he asked.

"Have you heard any more from Penny?" she asked. The starlet had been quiet since their encounter the other night, but since she was a part of Russell's past, Gail didn't want to ignore her.

"Not yet. Don't worry about Penny. She is definitely part of my past. And you, Gail, are my future," he said.

She felt a little thrill go through her. She'd never been called that before, and even though she suspected he was saying it to make her believe they would have a successful match, she wanted to believe it. She wanted a man who said the right things and turned on the charm with her. Russell was very good at that.

"Well, I hope she knows that, "Gail said.

"She does," Russell said. "Stand up for a minute."

"Why?" she asked, suddenly not too sure of herself.

"Something you said earlier is bothering me," he said.

"What?" He made her feel…just made her feel more alive and, conversely, more insecure than she ever had before.

"Stand up and I'll tell you," he said, rising and holding out his hand to her.

She took his hand and allowed him to draw her to her feet. He led her to the corner of his office, where a large gilt-framed mirror hung over an antique credenza. He stood behind her, and she saw how inadequate she looked on his arm. Whereas Penny looked like the perfect little Barbie to his Ken, she looked like…Barbie's less glamorous, generic cousin.

She tried to turn away but Russell enfolded her in his arms from behind. She liked the feeling of being surrounded by him. She leaned her head back against his shoulder and stared up at him.

"Look in the mirror, Gail," he said.

"I don't want to," she said, shaking her head and looking down.

"Why not?" he asked, taking her chin in his hand and tracing the curve of her jaw, then slowly caressing her neck and shoulder bones.

"We don't look like we belong together," she said.

"That's the problem," he said, leaning down to kiss her so softly that she thought she might have imagined it.

"Look again and let me tell you what I see," he said, his tone so inviting that she was tempted to do just what he asked.

She swallowed hard and then turned to look at them in the mirror. She loved the way his gray eyes were so sincere as he looked at her. And she wondered how she could have thought he was shallow. He had more substance than most men she'd met, and she realized how hard he must work to keep up that image.

"See how perfectly we fit together," he said. "I have thought of nothing else but how it will feel when we make love. You feel just right in my arms."

"You do fit me just right," she said. "You're not too tall, and when I kissed you…your mouth was…you tasted good."

He smiled at her in the mirror, and she didn't feel as awkward as she had a few minutes ago.

"Your eyes are big, bottomless pools of dark chocolate that I get lost in," he said.

"Even with the glasses?" she asked.

"Especially then," he said. He pushed her glasses up on the top of her head and rubbed the bridge of her nose, then drew his fingertip down to her lips, where he traced the outline of her mouth before putting her glasses back on.

"When I look at you, I see the most beautiful woman in

the world. The only woman I want and the woman I need by my side. I know that we are just beginning this relationship, but already I feel like you belong to me."

She had no answer for that and she wished she did. But she looked at them again in the mirror and then felt his hands loosen the pins in her hair until it fell around her shoulders in long, curly waves.

"Gorgeous. Why would you wear your hair any other way?" he asked. "You have a natural beauty that other women would kill for."

She shook her head, feeling the soft weight of her hair on her shoulders. She wanted to believe him when he looked at her hair, but she'd spent her life in a straight, smooth hairstyle world, and she knew that this crazy mass of curls didn't fit in. "My hair is a big frizz, but I'm glad you like it."

He pinched her side lightly. "Why won't you just believe that you are gorgeous? You have to get that negative self-image out of your head. You are beautiful, Gail, and before long I'm going to have you believing it too."

"I…I hope you can do that, Russell, but it is going to be hard," she said. Her entire life she'd felt too big, too curly, too dark to really fit in with the popular, beautiful girls. It didn't matter that she'd gotten out in the world and become successful—her inner mirror was always dialed to that look that she knew she'd never be able to achieve.

He turned her in his arms, his hands cupping her face. "I will not be satisfied until I've gotten you to see yourself as I see you."

She couldn't really think as he lowered his head and kissed her. It wasn't a tentative first embrace, as the previous kisses had been. This was the kiss of a lover intent on having his woman. And she could do nothing but surrender to him. She needed this from him. She wanted him.

Her skin felt sensitized and her breasts suddenly felt fuller. She leaned in so that she could rub them against his chest. His hands slid down her back to her waist, and he held her closer to him.

She leaned into him and forgot to breathe, losing herself in a swirl of sensations that centered around Russell's body and his mouth moving over hers. She knew that this was dangerous, because he was finding chinks in the wall she'd always used to protect herself, but she couldn't help it. He was more than she'd expected to find in any real man, and she felt herself starting to fall.

Six

Russell didn't want to stop kissing Gail. She felt more than right in his arms. He knew with a gut-deep instinct that this was the one place where he felt the most comfortable being honest. It didn't matter that he had business goals he needed her help to achieve. Even if all that disappeared, he'd still want Gail.

Her waist was tiny; he was able to span it with his hands and lift her more fully into his body. Her full breasts brushed against his chest as he lifted her onto the credenza. He kept his mouth moving over hers.

He pushed one thigh between her legs and felt her shift as her legs parted for him. He moved closer as her hands slid up and down his back, drawing him in. His blood ran heavier in his veins as he hardened for her.

Her touch was light and sure as she reached lower to cup his buttocks and draw him in even closer. He inched her skirt up her thighs, feeling the muscled smoothness of her legs.

The knock on the door startled him, and he drew back, pulling his mouth from hers. She started as well, her eyes going wide, but her pupils were dilated with the onset of lust and her lips were wet and swollen. He cussed under his breath.

"Who is it?" he barked toward the door.

"Dylan needs you in the lobby, Russell," Mitsy, his assistant, said through the door.

"Dammit," he said under his breath, but he stepped away from the credenza and helped Gail off it. He didn't want to go. He wanted to stay here in this office with the door shut and this woman in his arms. "I'll be right there."

"Wow. That got out of control," she said. She reached for her hair and started to pull it back into the tight bun she'd had it in earlier. Her lips were swollen and her pupils were still dilated with passion.

To his way of thinking, it hadn't gotten nearly as far out of control as he would have liked. "Leave your hair down. It's incredible."

She nodded and left it hanging around her shoulders. The curls were thick and soft, and he reached for her before realizing he couldn't kiss her or hold her right now. He had to go take care of the situation in the lobby.

"Will you have dinner with me tonight?" he asked. "I can't wait to see you again."

"I've got tickets for the basketball game," she said. "Want to join me?"

Basketball wasn't his thing, but Gail was, so he'd make the sacrifice. In fact, he thought that the corporation had a box at Madison Square Garden. "Yes. I'll pick you up."

"Sounds good," she said. "I never intended for that to happen. For you to kiss me like that."

He laughed. "I did."

She just shook her head at him. "I'm sure you did. Made me forget all the things I wanted to say."

"Good. You talk a lot," he said. But he liked it. She didn't sulk in silence. Instead, she just said what was on her mind. It was a different experience for him.

"Too much?" she asked, playfully.

"Not at all," he assured her.

He led the way past his assistant, and for the first time outside of the business world, he felt a sense of peace. That wasn't the right word exactly, but he was at home where he was with the person next to him. From the first moment he'd seen her, he'd known Gail was different, but now he was realizing just how much.

"I'll see you out," he said.

"I can take care of myself," she said.

"I have no doubt about that," he said. "But I like doing things for you, Gail."

"But you have to go take care of your business."

"Okay. Let me know what time to pick you up tonight," he said. Then he remembered he was hosting a dinner for the Family Vacation Destination hotel group. "Oh, hell, I just remembered I have a VIP event tonight. I can't make it to the game."

"I remember you mentioning it now," she said with a shy grin. "I forgot in your office."

"Me too. All I could think about was you. You go to my head."

"You do the same to me," she said.

"How about I stop by for a nightcap when I'm done?" he suggested. He hoped she'd say yes, but had no idea if she would.

"Okay. Just text me when you're done." Gail felt a little giddy at how well coming to see Russell had turned out.

She was feeling better and better about matchmaking. But all of that changed when she stepped out of the back office and saw who was waiting for Russell in the lobby—Penny Thomson. Just like that, Gail was reminded that the man she thought was being honest with her had a long track record of dealing with the opposite sex, and he had learned more than one trick.

"We need to talk," Penny said, as soon as she saw him enter the lobby. His grip on Gail's arm tightened.

"In a minute," Russell said. "Gail, are we still on?"

"You really don't want to keep me waiting, Russ. I have news, and I'm tired of you playing with me," Penny said.

Gail didn't like the way the other woman was talking to Russell, but she wasn't going to interfere. "Call me later."

"I will," he said.

Gail walked away, though she wanted to stay and see what was going on and how Russell was going to handle his ex-girlfriend. Given what he'd told her and his history with women, the situation was going to probably be a big PR nightmare. And Gail was going to be dragged into it.

She hailed a cab as the entire afternoon swirled in her mind. The quiet, sharing conversation they'd had. The kiss that had made her want to believe everything he'd said. And then there was his ex-girlfriend. What was Gail going to do? She felt as if, from the moment she'd signed up with Matchmakers Inc., nothing was under her control.

The drive to her office felt longer than it ever had before. She didn't know what she wanted anymore. She knew that this matchmaking wasn't going to work out. And she had so craved that family she'd had in her head. That picture-perfect image that it seemed fate didn't have in store for her. It hadn't been hers as a child, nor would it be as an adult. Maybe if she was lucky Willow and Nichole would have children some day and she could be their auntie and spoil them.

The cabbie pulled to a stop in front of her building and she got out after paying him. She hated giving up on her dream, but she knew better than to keep pursuing something when it was clear that it was a losing prospect. And she knew that she was giving up on more than just her dream of a family—she was also giving up on Russell.

Russell was beyond over Penny. But he knew that he couldn't just keep pushing her away. As soon as they were out of view of the public, he took her wrist in his hand and drew her to a stop.

"Never speak to Gail like that again," he said, warning her for the last time. He'd put up with a lot of bad behavior from Penny, but he wasn't about to let her interfere with what he had with Gail.

"Is that her name?" Penny asked, tossing her blond hair around her shoulders. "She seems like a nice girl, Russell, not your normal type of woman."

"You've got that right," he said. She was different and that's why he needed her. But this afternoon, he hadn't been thinking about all the reasons he needed to change his reputation.

"Maybe I should warn her of the kind of man you are. How you use up everything a woman has to give and then you just move on," Penny said.

"I didn't use you up. You dumped me, remember?" he asked. "You were the one who was ready to move on to someone more Hollywood."

"Semantics. You were ready to move on, you just didn't want to say it first," she said.

Russell knew that was true, but he would never have

dumped Penny. She was fun and had, until this moment, been someone he truly liked. "What happened, Penny?"

"I told you before. I'm pregnant. The baby is yours, and you're going to have to do your duty by me," she said.

"Did you arrange for the paternity test?" he asked. He knew the results would reveal he wasn't the father. He was infertile, but that wasn't something that any women knew. He'd kept that close to the chest, knowing that virility in a man was still prized in this day and age.

"No. As soon as I do that, you know it will show up on the news. We should handle this between us," she said, then turned those big blue eyes up at him. "Come on, baby, just do the right thing here."

"If you're honest with me, I'll do whatever I can to help you," he said. And he wasn't lying. He wanted to help her out in any way he could.

Indecision flitted across Penny's face, and for a moment he thought that maybe he could get her to talk sensibly to him.

Then she shook her head. "I am being honest. You're the one with something to hide."

"From who? I'm not hiding anything," Russell said. As much as he wanted not to be faced with another paternity suit, he wasn't going to be blackmailed by Penny.

"Gail, isn't that her name? She's not going to want to be in a relationship with a man who has your kind of drama."

"I don't have any drama. I have an ex-girlfriend who has trouble letting go," Russell said.

"Russ, I'm asking you to just give me the money I need and I'll walk away."

Russell wondered what was going on with Penny and made a mental note to investigate. "Do you need money?"

"Never mind," she said, looking away from him. "I can't talk to you when you're being difficult. I'm scheduled to be on Jimmy Fallon tonight—if I haven't heard from you before then, I will be breaking the news of my pregnancy."

"Penny, it's not my baby," he said.

"I don't see it that way. And the world will definitely believe me, Russ," she said. "You have my number."

She walked out, and Russell turned and punched the wall. He wasn't going to let her get away with manipulating him like that. But he knew Penny well enough to guess she wasn't bluffing. If she said she was going to tell the viewing public he was the father of her unborn child tonight, then she'd go through with it.

He also wasn't going to be able to keep Gail in the dark. Suddenly the VIP guest he had coming into the hotel tonight didn't matter. He needed to sort out his personal life, and he had to do it now.

He knew that Gail was going to the basketball game, and called the concierge to find out what time the game started. Then he called his assistant in.

"Get me Dylan. Cancel all my appointments for the afternoon and try to get Gail Little back here. I'm going to be on the phone," Russell said to his assistant Mitsy as he walked into his office.

"Yes, sir." Mitsy sat at a desk that had two computers on it and more gadgets than most people would be comfortable handling. She was the hub of his international business and went with him wherever he traveled. She had no life outside of working for him and freely admitted she was happy that way.

Russell approached this latest problem with the same calmness he faced all adversity. He wasn't about to let Penny throw off his plans for the future of his Kiwi Klubs or for Gail. When Dylan arrived, they discussed the evening's VIPs and what needed to be done. Then he called his PR agent, but he knew he was going to need Gail at his side.

As Russell was headed to the game, the concierge got back to him with the information on the Kiwi Klub's corporate booth. Mitsy hadn't managed to get in touch with Gail, so Russell was left with trying to find her at Madison Square Garden during a basketball game. Not an easy prospect, but he had a connection at the Garden and paid for a message to be played on the JumboTron. So he wasn't surprised when, shortly after his message ran, his cell phone rang and it was Gail.

"You wanted me to call you?" she said.

"Yes. Can you meet me in my suite? I have to talk to you and it couldn't wait," he said. This was not the way he usually handled this sort of thing, but he felt that he had no choice. The last thing he wanted was for Gail to hear about Penny's claims on late-night television.

"I…I thought you weren't going to be able to come to the game," she said.

"Circumstances changed. Please join me," he implored, using his most persuasive voice.

"I'm on my way," he thought he heard her say, though it was hard to hear her in the crowd. "Is something wrong?"

Russell knew he didn't want to discuss Penny on the phone with her. But lying wasn't an option either. "I don't think it's going to be a big problem, but I need to talk to you in person."

"Hmm…that's not the no I was hoping for. I'm on the elevator to your suite. I'll be there in a minute," she said. "I hope this isn't going to interfere with me watching the game."

"Thank you for coming up here," he said. "I'm sorry to say, I think it will definitely tinge your game watching tonight."

"No problem. The least I can do is listen to whatever you have to say after you answered all of my questions this afternoon. I was teasing about the game," she said, disconnecting the call.

Russell looked around the corporate suite. It was fully stocked and set to his specifications. His favorite scotch was at the bar, and he went over to pour himself a drink.

The door behind him opened, and he glanced over his shoulder to see Gail standing there in a pair of skintight jeans and a slim-fitting Knicks jersey. Her thick hair was up in a ponytail, and she looked good to him.

This moment made him realize that he didn't want to let her slip away, and he knew without a doubt that the problems with Penny were jeopardizing his future with Gail.

She knew as soon as she saw him that there was a problem. He had the same look in his eyes that her celebrity clients had when they'd been caught doing something they shouldn't. She put aside her thought that he was here for a date and realized that he must need her professional help.

"What's up?" she asked, trying not to worry, even though the last time she'd seen him, his ex-girlfriend had been with him and it hadn't seemed that she was just dropping by to catch up.

"Let me get you a drink first," he said, going to the wet bar and taking down a highball glass.

"Am I going to need one?" she asked, half joking. Russell was serious, not the playful lover he'd been in his office earlier, and she wondered what exactly the problem was today.

"I don't think so. But what would you like?" he asked, holding the empty glass up.

"Perrier, no ice, but a twist of lime," she said. She watched as he made her drink.

"Tell me what's going on," she said.

Russell brought her drink to her and then gestured toward the leather sofa that faced the windows overlooking the court. She took a seat and waited for him to sit down next to her.

"I mentioned earlier that Penny was being a little dramatic about our breakup, and she's taking it to another level tonight," Russell said.

"I don't know why that concerns me," Gail said. "We've only been on one date, and I know I was asking you about her, but it's fine with me—

"She's going to tell a late-night talk-show host that she's pregnant on his show tonight, and that I'm the father," Russell said.

"Oh, well. Is that true?" Gail asked. She'd known. Hadn't she had that feeling in her gut that things weren't going to work out the way she wanted them to?

"No, it's not true," Russell said. "I just felt you should hear it from me instead of the news."

"Thank you," she said, taking a sip of the Perrier. The fizzy drink was soothing, but right now there was nothing that could calm her racing mind. She wanted to know more, to demand that Russell explain to her why Penny was telling the world something that he said wasn't true. But she also knew that this was the excuse she'd been looking for to get away from Russell. To retreat back into her private, safe little world.

"What are you going to do to counter her claim?" she asked. Why was he so confident he wasn't the father? She'd have to ask him about that later.

"Nothing. The last thing I want to do is get into a mudslinging match with her. I don't have to defend myself to the public," he said.

"That's not the best idea. I think we should call Willow

and let her know as well. She'll want to use the contro-
versy around you to promote the show," Gail said. And just
like that, Russell went from being a potential mate to a
client. She knew how to handle this problem for him, and
it would make him safer to be around. She could manage
his PR nightmare and "date" him on the show without letting him get too close.

"I really don't want to do anything about it," he said at
last.

"You are going to have to. You said you went to the
matchmaker to find a mate and move into a new phase
of your life. You can't do that with Penny saying you're a
jerk. That isn't going to help things," Gail said. She was
also thinking of herself and of the show. This could affect
all of them, and they couldn't just let it ride.

Russell swallowed what was left of his scotch, then
rubbed the back of his neck. "I don't want this to affect
you and me."

"Too late. It already has," she said. "To be honest, I
thought something like this might happen when Penny
showed up again."

Gail was making notes in her head of what needed to
be done. "I can try to get you on a morning talk show. But
I'm going to have to get started on this right now. Have
you been working with a PR firm?"

"No, I haven't. Why?" he asked.

"We need to draft a message for you and send out a
press release. I think it would be best if you just had one
consistent message. What do you think it is?"

"That Penny's lying," Russell said.

Gail laughed out loud. Many of her clients had the same
reaction to news they didn't like. They wanted to just
issue a statement saying it wasn't true and never discuss

it again. But that kind of silence just bred more rumors in the media. "That's not going to work."

She toyed with the situation in her head. "Maybe something along the lines of, when your relationship with Penny ended, you both agreed to go your separate ways, but she's trying to continue… No, that won't work. I think you should say that you—

"I will say whatever you tell me to, but I don't want this to affect you and me, Gail. You're important to me," Russell said.

Gail knew that. He wouldn't have rushed across town to talk to her if she didn't matter to him. But she saw this as her out. It was her safety release and she was going to take it. She'd had doubts about Russell from the beginning, and using this one event as an excuse was going to let her protect herself.

"We can't continue like nothing happened," Gail said. "We have to stay on the show, because that will help you maintain the semblance of a real relationship and show a better side of you, but that's it."

"That's it?" Russell said, leaning closer to her. "What do you mean, that's it? I hope you don't think that we are over because of this."

"Yes, I do," Gail said.

"No. That is not what is going to happen. We are not going to pretend to date. We are going to really date. And I'm going to manage the problems with Penny the way I have in the past. I'm sorry if you thought I called you up here to do your professional job, but what I really wanted was to be with the woman I can't stop thinking about."

"Oh, really?" she asked, giving him a hard look that would have stopped a lesser man.

"Yes. I hate that anything from my past might hurt you

in any way, and I wanted you to hear from my lips that there is nothing to her claims," Russell said.

Gail stared at him, torn between what she knew with her mind and what she wanted with her heart. It was hard, because she liked Russell. He was no longer just some tabloid playboy, but a real man to her. She wanted to believe, him but she was afraid.

She'd still try to keep him in her life by agreeing to continue the show. She knew that she was going to be careful when it came to her emotions, but she was not going to let him walk away from her. She needed him.

She liked the way he made her feel, and she had seen a different woman in the mirror this evening when she was getting ready. She was starting to see herself through Russell's eyes.

"Okay I'll try my best, but I think you're going to have a hard time managing this without releasing a statement. I don't think I should be repping you, because that doesn't seem right."

"Fine, I'll do whatever you suggest, as long as you continue to give the matchmaking and our dates your real devotion," he said.

"I will," she said. "Will you?"

"Hell, yes. Starting right now. Thanks to Penny, we get to have dinner together and watch the game."

"We do?" she asked.

"Yes," he said. "The executive chef from my restaurant has prepared dinner for us, and the staff here will be serving it during the first quarter."

She nodded, no longer feeling that Russell needed her to manage his PR crisis, but that he was wooing her. What was he up to?

Seven

Russell spent the next three days being kept at arm's length by Gail. She'd send him information for the press releases that the PR firm she'd suggested should use. And she couldn't help but send him recommendations for shows for him to call into, but personally she stayed away. He didn't blame her for wanting to stay out of the maelstrom that was produced by Penny's pronouncement on late-night TV.

Even Willow and Conner had pulled him aside to make sure that he was still going to stay on the matchmaking show. Russell didn't like it, and had sent his lawyers around to Penny to see if they could figure out how to get her to stop going public with everything.

His board of directors weren't too pleased with him either, and Family Vacation Destinations decided to decline his bid for their resorts. As far as his plan to add the launch of a new chain of Kiwi Family Klubs to his existing Kiwi Klubs, he wasn't exactly on track. So he'd called Dylan into his office for a daylong meeting to figure out the business aspect of pushing past the mess Penny had created by telling the world he was a deadbeat dad.

He didn't let himself dwell on the problems with Gail. They had their second taped date this afternoon, and he had a feeling that once they were alone, he would be able to convince her to let go of whatever apprehensions she had.

"The board will come around as soon as they see this quarter's profits, but we need to have the Family Vacation Destinations owners here—we need to show them the improvements we have made at this resort to make it more family friendly."

"I'm on it, boss," Dylan said. "The new kids' zone hires are ready for a meeting with you. Once we have your approval on the events and the budget, we are ready to implement the plan."

"Sounds good. Make sure Mitsy gets that on my calendar for this week. Do we have anything else that I need to handle right now?"

"I think that's it," Dylan said. "Will you be reachable by phone later?"

"I have my second matchmaking date, so my phone will be off for a few hours. I'll check in when I can," Russell said.

"Where will you be?" Dylan asked.

"Montauk Yacht Club."

"Sounds good. I can handle everything here," Dylan said. "I've learned a lot in the last few weeks."

"I know you can do it," Russell said. "You are a good assistant."

"Glad you noticed. I'm planning to ask you for a raise at my next review." Dylan laughed a little as he said it.

"If you get Family Vacations Destinations deal back on track, I'm going to give you a huge bonus."

"I was already motivated, but now I really won't let you down," Dylan said.

Dylan was easy to deal with since he was young and hungry. He wanted to move up the corporate ladder, and the word *no* wasn't part of his vocabulary. To be honest, Russell knew that Dylan would burn out one day, but for now, everything was exactly as he needed it to be.

"I know you won't. Thank you, Dylan."

"No problem, boss," Dylan said as he gathered his papers and left the office. Russell leaned back in his chair and glanced over at the credenza and mirror where he'd watched himself kissing Gail. He'd hated the interruption at the time, but if he'd had a clue that she was going to put so many barriers between them, he would have been damned sure to keep her in his arms then.

Russell changed into casual clothes for an afternoon of sailing. He had arranged for the chopper to take him to the heliport in the Hamptons and had invited Gail to join him. She'd agreed, which he had taken as a positive sign.

Gail was waiting at the helipad on top of the Big Apple Kiwi Klub when he got there. She wore a pair of Bermuda shorts that hit the top of her knees and showed her legs off. Her sleeveless casual shirt was open at the collar. She had on a pair of designer sunglasses, and her hair was left to hang around her shoulders.

He wanted her. He was tired of waiting to make another move until things were just right between them. It wasn't like him to wait. He'd been trying to do whatever he could to please her, and he had a feeling he was failing. But now, more than ever, he needed to get control of the situation and of Gail. He was going to be the only man he could be around her. He was tired of playing a part.

She turned around as he approached and gave him that forced half smile she'd been using since she'd heard about Penny. "Oh, hello, Russell."

"Hello, Gail. You look lovely today."

"Thank you," she said, pushing her sunglasses up on her head. She wore contacts today; he could tell because she wasn't blinking to try to see him.

"You look nice too, but a little tired," she said. "How are you holding up with the media stuff?"

"Fine. It's a little demanding, and I'd rather be working than sending out press releases, but I'm following your advice on this," Russell said. She'd actually been a bit of a godsend, in that without him asking she'd acted as a go-between with the PR firm, leaving Russell free to do his business. It had made him realize what a good partner she was for him.

"You should. I'm very good at what I do," she said.

"I wish you'd stop treating me like a client," Russell said.

"Right now, that's all I can do. I want you to be able to move on and get the past behind you. Then you and I will have this great friendship we can build on," she said.

"That's bull," he said.

"What?"

"You don't want to build on this. You just want to keep me in a nice, neat corner where you don't have to reveal any more of your vulnerabilities. But I have news for you. We both went to the matchmakers for a reason, and that hasn't changed. I'm the man they thought was right for you, and despite the problems I'm dealing with, I think that I'm still the right match for you."

She smiled at him, and it was the first genuine expression he'd seen from her in days. He was glad to see that she still reacted to him when he made the effort. He wanted her. He didn't want to think about problems in the work-place, but instead wanted to focus on those long, tan legs of hers.

"You would say that, because you're all ego," she said.

"Just stating the facts," he said, wrapping an arm around her and hugging her close. She fit perfectly under his shoulder, and he realized that he wasn't going to be able to wait much longer to have her. He craved her touch, and he wasn't going to be satisfied until he had a lot more of it.

The chopper pilot arrived, and they were on their way to the Hamptons in a short while. They didn't talk, but Russell didn't let that bother him, as she kept her hand in his during the entire ride. He knew he'd have to keep being his usual, blunt self if he had any chance of getting her to fall for him. Being meek and letting her set the tone wasn't going to give him what he wanted.

And, though in the back of his mind he wanted to believe that he still just wanted Gail to help out with improving his reputation, he knew that he really just wanted Gail.

He liked the feel of her small hand in his.

The TV crew was waiting for them when they arrived at the Montauk Yacht Club, which had been named one of the top marinas in North America. It looked like the enclave of the rich and famous that it was.

Gail felt herself relax as soon as she saw Willow. Her friend was busy giving directions to the crew, and Russell stepped away to take a call, leaving her by herself.

She had tried to keep things all business between them, but every night her dreams were haunted by him. She had never been this turned on by a man. The week since they'd had their first date had been packed with things that kept her busy, but underlying that had been thoughts of Russell and a longing to be in his arms again.

Kat the production assistant came and got her. After she'd spent a little time in hair and makeup, Gail had her first inkling that this date wasn't going to be an entirely intimate one between her and Russell. Gail and Russell were positioned on the sundeck for the filming. The yacht was an Oceanfast 48 with four decks. There was a crew of ten and the yacht had a top speed of sixteen knots. Gail had no clue how fast that was, but since the captain had mentioned it, she thought it might be fast.

"Kat?" Gail asked as the PA finished adjusting her microphone.

"Yes?" she answered.

"Um…will you take a picture of Russell and me with my iPhone once he's ready?" Gail didn't feel silly asking. She knew she wanted something private of Russell that no one else would see. Something that wasn't a broadcast image or part of a promo package.

"Sure," Kat said with a smile. "You two make a nice-looking couple."

Russell arrived a few minutes later and was seated next to her, and for a minute Gail felt the family image in her head merge with reality.

"Do you mind if Kat takes a picture of us?" she asked Russell.

"Not at all," he said, putting his arm around her shoulder. They turned toward Kat and she snapped a photo of them with Gail's iPhone. She took her phone back and tried to slip away from Russell, but he kept her where she was, at his side.

"Why a photo?" he asked as Kat walked away. The sound people were doing a check, but no one was really paying much attention to the two of them.

"I just wanted to be able to remember this moment," she said.

Before Russell could respond, the production crew was moving around them and getting set up for their shots. They were given directions on how to sit and where to look.

"We're going to film you exchanging some small talk, and then we'll cut and remove all the microphones, and you can head out for your date. When you come back in, we will have you both record private video journals with your thoughts. Any questions?"

"Where's Jack?"

"In L.A. filming one of his other shows. We'll have you both chat with him via the magic of editing," Willow said.

Gail was beginning to feel as though the taped dates were routine. She was grateful that the producers—not just Willow—had agreed that the dates needed to have some privacy. It was hard to get to know someone when the cameras were rolling and they were both careful of what they were saying.

She wondered if this was what regular matchmaking would be like. Just staged dates and then feedback to the matchmaker? But she'd never know. This experience with Russell had convinced her that if he didn't work out, she was going back to her normal life.

"None here," Russell said.

Gail shifted away from Russell so she'd be in position as she'd been directed, but then she couldn't think of a thing to say once the cameras started rolling. Russell was watching her, and she nibbled on her lower lip.

Should she mention the media attention he'd been receiving, or how she'd signed a big A-lister as a new client? Should she talk about the times they'd seen each other since their last official date for the show? She really wished she'd taken a moment to ask a few questions of Willow, instead of just looking at Russell and lusting after him.

"It's a gorgeous day," she said at last.

"Yes, it is. Did you grow up near the water?" he asked.

"Not really," she said. "I'm from Texas…near Dallas. There were a few lakes near us."

"You don't have an accent," he said.

"Only when I'm home," she admitted with a laugh. "It didn't take me long to realize that if I was going to make a living talking to people I was going to need to be understood."

"Good point. When I first came here I realized that my accent was a novelty, but that I needed to know the idioms of American English if I was going to be successful."

"Exactly—we're speaking the same language, but sometimes we can't be understood," she said.

"A little bit like men and women," he said.

"True," she said, smiling at him. "Have you had that problem in the past?"

"Mostly I've learned to just sit back and let ladies talk. It's my experience that I don't get into as much trouble if I keep my mouth shut."

She had to laugh at him and the way he'd said that. She realized that she'd almost forgotten they were being taped. Russell had a way of commanding all her attention and making her forget everything else.

"You haven't been too quiet with me," she said.

"I'm trying a different tack with you," he said.

"Why?" she asked.

"You're too sassy. If I give you your way all the time, I'll lose myself," he said.

She shook her head, knowing he was teasing her. And she liked it. She liked seeing his big eyes twinkle as he tried to get a reaction out of her. "With that big head, you'd never get lost."

That startled a laugh out of him. And the director called, "Cut!" They were separated to have their microphones removed, and then the crew was gone, and it was just Russell and her and the yacht crew, who had been instructed to be discreet, according to Willow.

Gail went back to the bench seat as the boat ride got under way. She'd been out to the Hamptons for charity events in the summertime, but she'd always been working. This was the first time she could just relax.

Russell walked toward her holding two glasses, and she swallowed against a suddenly dry mouth. What she'd both wanted and dreaded for the past few days was about to happen. She was alone with Russell.

She'd told herself that he didn't need the distraction of getting involved with her while he was still dealing with Penny. But she couldn't resist her own desires any longer. No matter what happened today, she was going to go with it. She was going to stop worrying about the future and just enjoy this man who seemed to like her.

Normally Russell wouldn't even consider spending this much time away from the office when there was a deal in jeopardy, but it hadn't taken him long to decide that this afternoon he needed to leave his phone off. He knew that in the long run, winning over Gail was the more important project.

He handed her a glass of champagne and then sat down next to her. With the wind blowing through their hair, it was hard to have a deep conversation unless they sat close together.

"That was awkward," she said.

"How?" he asked. "I thought you were poised, as always."

"I had no idea what to say," she said. "I wasn't sure if I should mention the stuff that we've done away from the cameras."

"I think whatever we say will be fine."

"You think so? I've never been in a situation like this where I don't know what to do, you know? I'm used to being in charge and doing what I want."

Russell could honestly see that. It fit with her need for control. "We are still the decision makers, Gail. We can say no to anything they suggest."

"I know, but I figured I wasn't getting results being in charge…maybe it was time to let someone else decide things."

"I'll be happy to do that for you. Just put yourself in my hands," he said.

"I have a feeling we're talking about two different things," she said, biting her lower lip.

Russell didn't know if that was true. He could tell that Gail wanted him, and he was tired of playing games and pretending he didn't want her. The crew of the yacht were discreet, which was what Russell paid them to be. Now that they were underway the crew wouldn't bother them unless he summoned them. So in essence Gail and he were completely alone.

"I'll take care of you," he promised. But he wasn't sure that she could believe him. After everything that had happened, he knew he was battling, not just the fact that she didn't know him well enough to trust him, but also the fact that she'd seen some negative things about him.

"I don't need you to," she said.

"Yes, you do, you just don't trust me to," he said, gently.

Everyone wanted someone to watch over them. And he knew that Gail was no exception.

He stretched his arm out behind her on the seat and drew her into the curve of his body. She went there willingly, and he squeezed her to him. Her hair was stirred by the wind and brushed his neck and cheek. The strands were soft and smooth, and he lifted a hand to toy with one.

"I like this," he said.

"What?" she asked, tipping her head back to look at him.

"Holding you," he said. "I didn't know if you were ever going to let me again."

She reached up and weaved her fingers into his hand where it rested above her shoulder. "I didn't know if I would either. I really don't think this is wise."

"What?"

"Being with you. But I can't stop thinking about you. I hated being all business the last few days. "

He leaned down to kiss her, not wanting to let another opportunity to taste her go by. He'd realized a long time ago that life was too short to put off what he wanted for someday. His dad had done that but had ended up dying young. Never getting to the someday he'd been waiting for.

That was one of the reasons that Russell had never hesitated to do something when he felt the urge. And right now, his gut was crying out for more of Gail. He pulled her up and onto his lap.

She wrapped her arms around his shoulders and tunneled her fingers through his hair. He liked the feel of her on his lap. His erection stirred, and he ran his hands down her back to her waist, brought them together and then stroked his way up her front, cupping her breasts in both his hands. She moaned and shifted her shoulders so that her breasts moved in his hands.

He pulled his mouth from hers and looked down at her. Her skin was flushed with desire and her lips were once again swollen.

This time they were away from the office and the world. There was nothing to stop him from touching her.

She rubbed her hands down his chest. "I have had a lot of fantasies about what you look like with your shirt off."

"Have you?"

"Yes," she said. "You feel so muscled and I remembered the way your arms felt around me. I dreamed I was sleeping in them last night."

"I dreamed of these luscious breasts of yours pressed against me as I slid in and out of you."

She shivered in his arms. "I want you, Russell."

"Good."

She shook her head. "It's not good. I'm normally not this sexually aware of a man. It frightens me a little."

"It shouldn't. We are well suited to each other," he said.

She tilted her head a bit. "Does that mean you'd take your shirt off if I asked you to?"

"Yes."

"Consider yourself asked," she said.

He unbuttoned his shirt but didn't pull it off. She reached into the opening to touch him. Her fingers were cold against him but her touch was sure. She moved her hands up toward his neck and then pushed the sides of the shirt open so she could see his entire chest.

She leaned closer as she stroked her fingers down his sternum, lingering over the birthmark that was to the left of his nipple. Then she traced his nipple with her fingertip before leaning forward to kiss him.

He shuddered as her mouth met his chest and a shot of

pure energy went from through him. She shifted around on his lap until she was straddling him. Her fingernail traced the path further down his sternum to his belly button, and she circled it, making him harden even more. He was straining against his zipper. He breathed in deeply and all he could smell was Gail. He tunneled his fingers into her hair and tipped her head back, taking her mouth with his. He plunged his tongue deep into her mouth and, stroking deeply, moved it back and forth against her tongue. He couldn't kiss her deep enough to satisfy the ache her touch had stirred in him. He would never get enough of her, he thought.

But he was damned sure going to try.

Eight

Gail shifted on Russell's lap to let her fingers touch him more intimately. It had been almost a year since her last lover and, until Russell, she hadn't realized how much she missed the touch of a man. He smelled so good, and with the sun beating warmly on them, the sea breeze blowing around them and the relative isolation of being out on the water, she felt free. Free from the normal worries and doubts. Nothing could mar this.

Russell let her set the pace. She caressed his chest, which was warm and lightly covered in hair. She liked the way it tingled under her fingers as she ran them over the pads of his pectorals and down his ridged stomach. He had a tan, making her suspect he spent some time outside without his shirt on. The birthmark by his right nipple fascinated her with its shape, and she kept going back to touch him there.

"Unbutton your blouse," Russell said, his voice deep and husky with passion.

His commanding tone sent a pulse of liquid heat through her body. She shook her head. "I'm not sure I should."

"Do it. Now."

She nibbled on her lower lip and leaned in. "What are you going to do if I don't obey you?"

He arched one eyebrow at her. "Why wouldn't you obey me? It's what you want."

It was what she wanted. She leaned back on his thighs looking down at him and then scanning the horizon. There were no other boats in the area. She brought her hands to the first button and slowly undid it. She felt Russell's gaze on her as she moved to the next button. But she only pushed it through and then peeled the fabric back so he could get a glimpse of her lacy bra underneath.

"Are you teasing me?"

"Yes," she said. Russell made her feel more feminine, more alive than she had with any other man. He made her very glad that she was a woman and that she could excite him. She knew she was successful in turning him on because his erection nudged her under her hips.

She slowly undid the next button. "Is this what you wanted?"

"Almost," he said. "You are driving me out of my mind. I can't wait to see you naked."

"Do you like what you've seen so far?" she asked. She suspected he would because of the way he'd been with her up until this point, teasing her with kisses and his touch.

"Hell, yeah," he admitted. "But I'm desperate to see more of your body, beautiful," he said.

"Yes," she said, slowly unbuttoning the rest of her shirt. She held the blouse closed and leaned down to kiss him.

His mouth moved under hers with a smooth surety that made her know that Russell was still in charge of this. And she didn't care. She liked the feel of his tongue as it swept into her mouth. And she realized that even in just those short minutes they'd been apart, she'd missed the taste of him.

He slid his big, warm hands around her midriff and unfastened the back of her bra, before drawing her forward until her breasts brushed his naked chest. He pushed the fabric of her shirt off her shoulders and then leaned back to look at her. The sun was warm on her exposed skin, but the breeze was cool. She felt comfortable and safe on his lap with him watching her.

She wore a La Perla bra made of expensive lace that had a pretty, swirling pattern on the cups. He traced the edges of the demi-cups down to the V in the middle and back up the other side. "Beautiful."

She wanted to believe him when he called her that, but wasn't sure if he was merely referring to the exquisite lingerie she wore.

"You like pretty things on your body."

"I do," she said, even though it wasn't a question.

"If we go down to the stateroom will you take off your shorts and let me watch you?"

An image formed in her mind. "Will you keep your shirt off?"

"And probably take off a lot more," he said.

"Then, yes. I will do that."

"Good," he said, lifting her in his arms and carrying her across the deck. He walked down the few stairs to the galley, and then down a hallway to the master stateroom. Once inside, he set her on her feet and closed the door.

She stood there, feeling a little awkward now that he wasn't touching her. She wrapped her arms around her own waist, unsure what to do. But Russell banished her uncertainty with his touch, running his hand from her shoulder down her arm and taking her hand with his. He led her to the porthole windows where a chaise was situated. He leaned back on it.

"I'm ready."

"For?"

"I want to see if your panties match your bra. I want to see you, beautiful."

She nodded. She'd never undressed in front of a man before. Well, one time with one lover—they'd both stripped down quickly in front of each other, but she didn't think he'd even been looking at her. Certainly, he hadn't been staring at her the way Russell was.

"I've never done this before."

"You don't have to do it now, if you don't want to. But I want to see that pretty body of yours," Russell said. "I can undress you if that would be better."

She shook her head. She didn't want to miss this experience with him. She stood a few feet in front of him, where the sun shone through the porthole. She toed off her deck shoes, then put her hands at the waist of her shorts and unfastened them. She remembered how going slowly before had given her confidence and excited Russell, and she did it again.

After taking her time to lower the zipper, she pushed the shorts slowly down her legs. With a swivel of her hips, they fell to the floor. She stepped out of them and walked over to him. When she was close enough for him to touch, he reached out and stroked his hand down the outside of her thigh and then sprawled his fingers to clutch her.

"You are killing me," he said, drawing her closer between his legs. He wrapped his arms around her waist and kissed her belly button. She felt the warmth of his tongue and lips as he dropped kisses from her waist all the way down to her lower abdomen. He then used his tongue to trace the elastic band of her lacy thong along each of her hip bones.

She melted and her legs went weak. He lifted her up and pulled her onto his lap. She rubbed her center over the hard ridge of his erection, but it wasn't enough. She was empty and aching and needed more from him. She needed it now.

Russell was running his hands up and down her back. He found the fastener for her bra and undid it. Then very slowly he drew the straps down her arms and caressed his way from her back, up over her shoulders, and then down the front of her chest, until he was cupping both of her breasts in his hands. He palmed her nipples, abrading them lightly. She shivered in his arms.

He rubbed his thumbs in circles around both of her nipples as he leaned up to kiss her. His mouth was delicious. There was no other way to think of it. When he kissed her, she wanted to stay in his arms forever and let the sensations slowly sweep over her. He moved his hands to her back and drew her closer until the tips of her engorged nipples rubbed against the hair on his chest.

She shifted her shoulders and rubbed back and forth against him. She couldn't help moaning at how good it felt to have him touching her like this. She let her head fall back as she felt his mouth against the base of her neck. He dropped languid kisses against her exposed flesh. She felt the edge of his teeth as he scraped them against her neck and then suckled the base of it. Shivers spread throughout her body.

She reached between them, rubbing her hand up and down the ridge of his erection. She reached for the button of his pants but he stopped her.

"Not yet."

"Why not?" she asked, wanting more of him and wanting it now.

"Now I'm teasing you," he said.

He put his mouth back on her neck and slowly moved down her chest to the globes of her breasts, using his tongue to trace his way from the base of each breast to the tip of her nipple. But these were only teasing brushes of his tongue, nothing more. Finally she couldn't stand it another second and put her hands on his shoulders and shifted around until the tip of her nipple was pressed against his lips. He tongued her and she moaned his name. She wanted him. Now. She was tired of waiting and of denying herself.

He put his hands on her waist and held her to him as he suckled first one nipple and then the other. His fingers sprawled wide at her waist, and his hands roamed down to her buttocks to cup her backside. Using his grip on her waist, he shifted her back and forth over his erection. That hard ridge rubbed her in almost the right spot and she felt herself moistening, readying for him.

She reached between them again, unfastening his belt and then undoing his pants until she could reach her fingers inside and stroke him. She reached lower to brush her fingers over him.

He groaned her name. "Wrap your arms around me."

She did and he stood up. His loosened shorts fell to the floor, and he stepped out of them as she wrapped her legs around his lean waist. He walked them to the bed. She undid her legs and slipped down his body.

She pushed his boxer briefs down, carefully pulling the band over his erection. Then she pushed them down his legs and brought her hands back to him. She stroked him from tip to base and back again. He widened his stance to give her more access, and she continued to caress him as he did her.

He pulled her back to him and up over his lap. "I want you."

"Me too," she said.

"Good. I knew from the moment I saw you that I'd have you in my bed."

She hadn't been as sure.

He reached up and undid her hair until it fell around her shoulders. "Shake your head for me."

She did and felt him stir between his legs.

She shifted over him until the tip of his penis was at the entrance to her body. She started to move him, but he stopped her. "Are you on the pill?"

"Yes," she said. "And I know we are both healthy, since Matchmakers, Inc., ran a screening."

"I'm glad, because I don't want anything to come between us. I want to feel your warmth around me."

"I want that too. Enough playing around," she said.

"Yes," he said. He put his hands on her waist and positioned himself at the entrance of her body once more. He controlled her and entered her slowly, inch by inch, until he was fully seated inside of her. She threw her shoulders back and shuddered at the feel of him filling her. She tightened around him and he groaned deep in his throat.

"You feel so good," he said.

"Yes, you do too," she said.

He reached between their bodies and flicked his finger lightly against her clitoris. And she came. Just like that. With no warning, everything in her body convulsed in one second. She couldn't stop rocking her hips against him. Trying to take more of him. Then she leaned forward to find his mouth.

He broke away from the kiss and whispered hot words

in her ear. Once again, she felt the tingles spreading down her spine. "I'm going to come again."

"Not yet," he said. "Wait for me."

She didn't have to wait long, as she felt him tighten his grip on her waist, driving up into her. "Now."

She started spasming around him as he pulled her head to his and kissed her long and deep. She felt his release inside her body. He kept pumping into her and she shuddered around him, riding the crest of her orgasm until she collapsed against him.

She rested her head against his shoulder and he held her close to him as he rolled on to his side. She cuddled close to him as he swept his hand up and down her back.

"Thank you," he said.

"You're welcome," she said. She wrapped her arms around his shoulders and hugged him to her, finding the notch of his neck to rest her head for a few minutes, she wanted to rest in his arms. To let this moment turn into forever. She liked the feeling of him around her. He was warm, and she felt safe in his arms.

"I guess we should head back up to the deck," he said. "Do you want to wash up first?"

That broke the mood for her. She'd been feeling warm and happy with him, but now he was all business, and her heart broke a little. She didn't love him, but she'd thought...she'd thought this was more than a little afternoon sex. She saw now that it wasn't.

"I'll go first," she said, pushing herself up and moving to gather her clothes. "My blouse is upstairs. Will you get it?"

"Gail, are you okay?"

She nodded. She didn't want to talk about this. Not now. "I'm fine."

He cursed under his breath. "What did I say?"

"Nothing. Just get my blouse, okay?"

"I'm not going to let you brush this aside. We can't stay down here for too long. We're supposed to be back to the marina in thirty minutes."

"I know," she said. But she hadn't been thinking of the time or the show or anything except Russell. "Actually, I didn't. I lost track of everything except you."

But she doubted that he could say the same. He'd had one eye on the clock, and now they had to clean up and get back on deck before they returned to the marina. She hated this. She wished she'd thought more about the emotions that would be stirred up by going to a matchmaker and being on a reality TV show. It didn't matter that she'd thought she could control her reactions and be logical about this. The truth was she'd never be.

"I'm going to wash up."

"Gail—"

"Not now, Russell. I have to get back to normal, and then I can talk about this. Please get my blouse."

She walked to the head and closed the door behind her. It felt like a luxury bathroom—in fact, it was actually bigger than hers at home. It had a large garden tub and a shower big enough for two. She glanced at herself in the vanity mirror and saw her swollen lips and the redness on her neck from his kisses. She looked well loved. There was no way anyone would see her and not know that she and Russell had had sex.

She used a washcloth to wipe between her legs and then pulled her clothing on slowly, piece by piece. She put her hair back into the bun, and with each motion felt a bit more like herself. Except that she didn't have her blouse. She had to stand here in her expensive bra. She'd purchased it because she liked feeling sexy, but now she felt small and used.

It wasn't anyone's fault. She had expected…hell, she hadn't really thought about anything except making love to Russell. She'd wanted him and she'd had him, but she hadn't thought of the consequences.

There was a knock on the door. "Your blouse is on the bed. I'll meet you on deck."

"Thanks."

She waited a few more moments before opening the door and then quickly donned her blouse and buttoned it back up. The bed had been straightened and the room looked as it had when they'd entered it. No trace of them remained as she walked out the door and back up to the deck. Russell stood at the front of the yacht, looking out over the water.

She admitted to herself that her feelings for Russell scared her. Making love to him had only made her realize how vulnerable she really was. She wanted him to be that fantasy man she'd envisioned in her head, and that was a heavy burden for anyone, because fantasy was never going to equal reality. No matter how hard she tried to make it so.

He glanced over at her and smiled tentatively. She knew she'd thrown him too by the way she'd left the bed. But she couldn't help that. Russell was used to women and relationships that were fluid and changed on a dime, while she was used to…nothing, she thought. She'd never had a relationship with a man that had been real.

Russell was going to break her heart. She was honest enough to admit that to herself. She couldn't be around him and not fall a little for him, with his smoldering, sexy gaze and his easy charm. And he made her feel…beautiful. But now she realized she had to feel beautiful by herself, because depending on Russell was only going to lead her down a path she was afraid of.

Nine

As soon as they docked back at Montauk, the camera crews were waiting. Gail felt exposed and raw and wanted to get away from the prying eyes of the TV show she'd signed up for. Russell put his hand on the small of her back, and she looked up at him. Despite the fact that she wanted the distance from him at this moment, they presented a united front.

"I can't do this right now," she said.

"We have to or Willow will know…" he said.

"I…I'm going to say that I'm seasick. You can talk to them. Be charming and tell them what they want to hear. You are good at that."

"Yes, I am. I'm sorry."

"Don't be," she said. "The problem here is me."

"Gail—

"I can't."

"Yes, you can. You are trying to run away again. I'm not going to let you," he said.

"I'm not running."

"Yes, you are. We both signed up for this, and it's hard. I'm not denying that. I'd have loved to spend the rest of the afternoon in bed with you. If we'd been on my yacht, I would have told the captain to keep us at sea until we both decided we wanted to go back to the real world. But we don't have that choice on a date that was set up for us by a television show."

She nodded. "I get that. I just…I forget sometimes, and you never seem to."

He pulled her close and wrapped his arms around her. "One of us has to be aware of that stuff. I'd like nothing more than to just lose myself in you, but I don't want you to be embarrassed by anything that happens between us, and I want it to stay between us."

She pulled back and looked up at him. "I guess you haven't had a lot of privacy in your relationships."

"Try none," he said. "You are different to me, Gail, and I don't want to let anything screw this up."

"Okay. I'm sorry I overreacted," she said.

He shook his head. "You didn't. I was abrupt and should have handled that better. I have no excuses, except that you make me react like a primal man. All the charm and sophistication I like to think I've accumulated over the years melts away when I'm with you."

She couldn't help but smile at that. She liked the thought of having that kind of power over him. It made her feel more equal because Russell made her vulnerable without really trying in the same way. She reacted to him as though he was the only man in the world made for her. And she knew that had to be because of all the emotions she'd built into the matchmaking thing. She didn't want to believe that it was Russell who was responsible.

"How was it?" Willow asked as she came onto the boat with the camera crew.

"Good," Gail said. Luckily, the sound tech was busy putting on the battery pack and wireless mic, otherwise she might have been forced to lie to Willow. A brief "good" was all she could manage. She hadn't intended on what had transpired between her and Russell. She shook her head and almost laughed out loud, but stopped herself.

"You okay?" Russell said, coming up behind her and putting his hand on her waist as he leaned in closely.

"No, but I'm faking it," she said and turned to him with a brilliant smile. "Is it working?"

He gave her a wry half smile. "Not when you smile like that. Right now it's not reaching your eyes as it usually does."

"I'm trying."

"And I appreciate that. I'm sorry, Gail. I shouldn't have—"

"No," she said. "Don't say any more right now. I can't deal with it and I might start crying."

Damn, she wasn't a crier. But her emotions were all tangled up, thanks to an afternoon of having sex with a man… whom she'd never expected to have sex with. A man who was charming and sophisticated and all the things she'd never expected to find. A man who was standing next to her, looking like he wanted to be her Prince Charming. And even though she'd learned a long time ago that she had to stand on her own, she wanted to lean on him. She wanted to feel those thick, comforting arms around her once again.

"You are going home with me after this," he said.

"I can't. I have a client meeting," she said. Her life went

on. This date was just one thing on her calendar today. And she'd deliberately scheduled something else so that she wouldn't be tempted by Russell. Damn, that had back-fired. Big-time.

"We'll discuss this later," Russell said, as the director came over to them and gave them staging directions.

Gail was grateful for Russell, who took control of the postdate interview and did most of the talking, covering for her. She was trying to regain her equilibrium. Slowly she realized that what had panicked her was the fact that she'd felt as if she was like every other woman he'd slept with. But she knew that she was different. And Russell, for all his playing with the opposite sex, insisted that he saw her differently. By his own words, he wanted to be different for her, too.

She knew she was different with him. She'd never been that turned on by a man. Never come twice before, and never wanted to immediately crawl back into bed with any of her lovers. But Russell brought that out in her. She wanted him again.

"Gail?" he asked.

"Yes?"

"I asked if you'd like to go sailing again on my yacht. Maybe for a weekend where we didn't have to rush back for filming," he said.

"I'd like that very much," she said, speaking directly to Russell and looking into his eyes.

"Very good, I don't feel like we had enough time out there today," he said.

"Me either," she agreed. She wanted a lot more with Russell, and it didn't matter if every time she did some-thing with him, she panicked. She was tired of hiding away from her own feelings, and she wasn't going to do it anymore.

* * *

Russell hadn't realized how gratifying it would be to step in and take care of Gail. He knew that she'd felt vulnerable when they'd returned to the Long Island Yacht Club and having him take control of the interview had helped her out. He'd never been a woman's hero and had never really wanted to be…until now. He wanted to do whatever he could to ensure that Gail would see her Mr. Right when she looked at him.

"That's a wrap. We'll see you both next week for your third date," the director said, and walked away.

"I have to talk to Willow and then I'm actually meeting my client at his home here in the Hamptons. So I won't be on the chopper with you on the way back," she said.

"I'll wait for you at the yacht club. Text me when you're ready," he said.

"Are you sure?"

"Definitely," he said. "I'm still hoping to talk you into going home with me."

"Fat chance," she said. "I need to process everything that happened."

"Process? Don't overthink it," he said. "Relationships aren't like business deals."

"I agree," she said. "But if I don't want to end up an aching mess, then I have to be sensible."

Within ten minutes they were both out of their microphones and free to go. Gail lingered, talking with Willow, as Russell waited to the side. His phone rang and he glanced at the screen, cursing under his breath as he realized it was Dylan.

"Holloway speaking," Russell said.

"Dylan here. I'm sorry to bother you, but I have Malcolm Addington of the Family Vacation Destinations group here in the lobby. He is asking if you can have dinner with him and his wife tonight."

"Give me a moment," Russell said. Malcolm had provided him with the excuse he needed to ask Gail out again. A date mixing business and pleasure was something that he suspected she wouldn't say no to. "Sorry to interrupt," he said, approaching her.

"It's okay," Gail said. "What's up?"

"A business dinner, and the other guy is bringing his wife…. Any chance you'd be available? I can accommodate your meeting," he said.

"I'll leave you two to work it out. Call me later," Willow said before she walked away.

Gail tipped her head to the side. "This feels like a setup, but I know you wouldn't lie about business."

"You're right. This dinner is kind of crucial. I'm trying to win this guy over to doing a merger. And I think you could help," Russell said.

"Okay, I'll do it. I can dine anytime after seven-thirty. I have to run to make my appointment. I'll meet you at the yacht club bar when I'm done."

"Thank you, Gail," he said.

She nodded, and he watched her walk away. Knowing her more intimately now, he couldn't help staring at her. He wanted her again. He hadn't been exaggerating at all when he'd told her that he wished they'd had more time together. He thought he'd covered his panic well by explaining his actions the way he had. But he knew deep inside that Gail had gotten too close. He wanted to be what she needed from him so that he could win her over, but he hadn't realized that he was creating a vulnerability in himself.

He, who never got attached to anyone, actually wanted

to keep Gail with him. Not just for today, but for the foreseeable future. And that was damned scary.

His iPhone chirped at him, and he glanced down at the screen to see a text message from Dylan asking about dinner. He typed his response.

Tell Malcolm yes and make a reservation for four at the Rooftop Restaurant.

A moment later, he received a reply from Dylan.

Will do.

He walked up to the club and entered the air-conditioned bar area. He went to a corner table and ordered a Foster's. He was halfway through his second drink when he glanced up to see Conner walking toward him.

"How are the dates going?" Conner asked.

"Good—I think they are going very well," Russell said.

"Great. Um, my crew found something of yours on the boat," Conner said, and held out a lacy, delicate thong. The one that Gail had looked so lovely in.

"Thanks. I'd appreciate it if you didn't say anything more," Russell said.

"No problem," Conner said. "I didn't think about asking you to use your own yacht. The *Happily Ever After* is owned by Matchmakers Inc. We use it a lot for dates."

"That makes sense. Why are you telling me this?" Russell asked.

"Because I don't want to be ungentlemanly and say something I know I shouldn't," Conner said with that big grin of his.

"Good idea. Join me for a drink?" Russell invited.

"Love to," Conner said. "Let me go and order something. What are you drinking?"

"Foster's."

"Gone native?" Conner said with a laugh.

"I'm a Kiwi, not an Aussie," Russell said. But Conner was already walking away. Russell didn't dwell on it. Instead his mind drifted to Gail. He still couldn't figure her out. He wondered if he really needed to. He was kind of winging it with her and seemed to be doing okay, by his own estimation.

But he'd nearly lost her today. And that kind of mistake couldn't be made again. His problem was he didn't know many men who were in long-term committed relationships. And those he knew he wasn't going to ask for advice.

Conner returned and they talked about the America's Cup and the Americans' chances of winning this year. Conner knew the team captain and the conversation was enjoyable, but Russell couldn't concentrate on it. He was waiting. Every time the door opened, he refused to glance over and see if Gail had returned, but everything in him was anticipating the sound of her footsteps.

Finally she walked right up to their table. "Hello."

"Business done?" Russell asked.

"Yes."

"Do you know Conner MacAfee?" Russell gestured to his friend.

"Not personally. Nice to meet you," Gail said.

"The pleasure is all mine," Conner said, standing up. "I'll talk to you later."

Conner walked away, and Russell stood up. "Are you ready to go?"

"Definitely," Gail said.

He put his hand on the small of her back and directed her toward the entrance. And as they walked, he felt the eyes of other men on them and the answering primal need to stake his claim. To let everyone who saw them know that she belonged to him.

* * *

Gail had taken her time getting ready for her date with Russell. Things had changed and she wanted him to think it was no big deal. She was fairly sure that Russell didn't realize how out of character it was for her to sleep with a man on the second date. But she felt as though they'd known each other for much longer than they really had. There was something about Russell that made her feel more comfortable in her own skin than any man ever had.

She knew that was dangerous because she kept dismissing things that were red flags. Normally she would have stuck to her guns about not seeing him again tonight, but with Russell, she actually wanted to see more of him. She wanted to break plans with other people and do whatever he asked.

Damn, she was an idiot. She wasn't going to let him mean that much to her. She'd promised herself to be smart about this entire matchmaking thing. But one look into his light gray eyes had her swooning like a teenager in a Taylor Swift song.

She donned the new dress she'd purchased on her way home from work. Nothing ordinary or average tonight. She wanted Russell to be wowed, and she was pretty sure he would be. While she'd never feel truly pretty, she knew she looked good in the empire-waist sundress. Her shoulders were toned and her hair—which she left hanging around her shoulders in soft curls—looked perfect. Not a bit of frizz. Now, if she could just get the contacts in, she'd be ready to go.

The right one took her almost twenty minutes, and she lost the first one she tried to get in. She glared at her own face in the mirror. "Stop psyching yourself out."

But no amount of glaring made the stupid contact easier to get in. Finally it was in and she moved on to her left eye, which was always easier. Her mother swore that it was a mental thing, but Gail didn't care—she always got her left contact in with no effort. It was silly.

Finally she was ready and looked at herself in the full-length mirror in her bedroom. With her sandals on, she was taller, but that was not a problem because Russell was so tall. She looked almost as good as she did when the hair and makeup people helped her get ready for the TV show.

Suddenly unsure, she nibbled on her bottom lip. Was she fooling herself? Did the dress cling too much to her hips? Should she change?

She glanced at the clock and thought of grabbing her old standby black dress, but then shook her head. Feeling the weight of her own hair against the back of her neck, she remembered the way Russell had looked at her with her hair down in the mirror in his office. He found her attractive. Why would she doubt him?

She grabbed her clutch and left her bedroom before her doubts could influence her. She took the elevator down to the lobby of her apartment building and asked the doorman to get her a cab. A part of her knew that this was just fantasy. That what had happened between her and Russell that afternoon was making her see him through rose-colored glasses.

He was still a man with a lot of problems from his past tying him down. He was still someone she wasn't sure she wanted to trust. Yet her body wanted him, and her mind was slowly catching up.

The cab pulled to a stop in front of Daniel Boulard's restaurant on the Upper East Side. She'd never been here before but had of course heard of it. Who hadn't?

She calmed herself down, but when she walked into the lobby and saw Russell waiting for her in his dinner jacket and dress pants, her heart beat a little faster.

He looked good all the time, but dressed up, he looked great. He was meant to wear a dinner jacket, because it emphasized the width of his shoulders, and the white shirt accented his tan. He was yummy and dreamy, and when he looked up at her, she thought, he's mine.

He smiled at her, and she felt a tingle run through her body. She walked over to him and leaned up on tiptoe to kiss him. He hugged her close. "You look great."

"Thanks," she said, blushing. All the doubts she'd had and the frustration with the contacts melted away. She'd put herself through that to get this reaction, she thought. And it was all worth it.

"Malcolm and his wife are running a few minutes late. Would you like a drink while we wait?" he asked.

"I'm good for now," she said. "Tell me about Malcolm and what you need from me tonight."

"Just be yourself," he said. "He is a key player in a company I'd like to acquire, and he is one of those men who doesn't just let his pocketbook rule his business decisions. He wants to make sure I will keep the core of his company the same, and my values up to this point aren't what he has in mind."

"But you're changing," she said, wondering how much the matchmaking dates were being motivated by this business goal. She felt a little twinge of disappointment as she realized why Russell wanted her here, but he hadn't lied to her. She was the one who'd made it into something else in her head.

Those damned rose-colored glasses. She wished that this would be enough to make her see him as he really was, but she suspected it wasn't. Her heart was ruling her impressions of Russell now, and her mind had little to say, except to warn her that she was going to be hurt.

Ten

Malcolm and Ashley Addington were easily sixty years old, but looked at least ten years younger because they were fit and fashionable. Russell wondered why Malcolm would even consider selling the controlling shares in his corporation. But that wasn't his concern tonight. Convincing the father of four that Russell had changed from player to family man was his goal. And Gail was doing her part in making him seem like a changed man.

Russell normally would spend all evening trying to keep the subject on business, but having Gail at his side made a huge difference, and for the first time he realized why Malcolm was insisting on having a family man at the helm of his corporation. They talked about everything except business, and Russell was adept at keeping up with the conversation.

"How did you two meet?" Malcom's wife asked.

"Through a matchmaker. In fact, you will be able to see the details of our courtship this fall on a reality TV show."

"You're kidding," Ashley said. "I've never known anyone who was on those shows before. How did you even get on there?"

"The matchmaking service we'd both chosen is part of the show," Russell said.

Malcolm leaned across the table to look directly at Gail. "I can guess why he'd need a matchmaker, but why did you choose one?"

Gail blushed and looked at Russell. He reached over and took her hand under the table and squeezed it. She appeared to relax a bit.

"I wasn't meeting a lot of men who were good relationship material. Mostly I'm a workaholic, since I own my own company," she said at last. "But having a family is the next thing on my list. And I didn't want to waste any more time dating Mr. Wrong when a matchmaker could find me Mr. Right."

"Looks like you were successful," Ashley said. "You and Russell make a lovely couple."

"Thank you," Russell said. He didn't want to give Gail a chance to say anything about how he was less than perfect.

"You know, at first, Ashley, I wasn't sure Russell was a right fit for me," Gail said.

Russell wanted to groan or kick her under the table. Malcolm would love to hear her doubts about how he'd never be the right kind of man to settle down with. It would give the other man the excuse he needed to end the business discussions they'd been having.

"I can see that," Malcolm said. "Russell, you do have a certain reputation with the ladies."

"He certainly does," Gail agreed. "But once I got to

know the real man, well, it was easy to see that he was as ready for a change as I am."

"Really?" Malcolm asked.

"Yes," Gail said, looking over at him and smiling. "I think he's still got a way to go to be Mr. Right, but he's getting there."

Russell relaxed, truly relaxed for the first time that evening. He stopped worrying about Malcolm's impressions of himself, and Gail and took a deep breath as her confidence in him surrounded him. That was all he'd wanted from the beginning. Winning Gail over was hardly a done deal, but he was closer now than he'd been before, and he couldn't help the feeling of satisfaction that spread through him.

"It goes without saying that you are my Ms. Right," he said.

"Definitely," Gail said, then turned to Ashley. "Never let them see you sweat, right?"

"Oh, definitely. Malcolm still believes I wake up looking like this every day," Ashley said with a cheeky grin.

"And she still believes I have a six-pack," Malcolm said, rubbing the top of his belly. Which made both of them laugh.

Gail looked over at Russell, and he saw in her eyes that she wanted what the other couple had. That happiness that came from being so close to another person and being accepted for just who you are. He wanted that too, though even a week ago he'd have scoffed at the way Malcolm and Ashley were together. Since then, he'd changed.

"Shall we order dessert?" Russell asked.

"Definitely," Malcolm said. "And then I'll ask the ladies to give us some time alone to talk business."

"Well, you know my no-dessert rule," Ashley said. "I heard there is a nice view from the bar, so Gail and I can go get something yummy to drink there while you two discuss business."

"That sounds lovely," Gail said. "I want to know more about the decorator you mentioned earlier."

Russell stood when Gail did and dropped a kiss on her cheek. She hugged him and went up on tiptoe to whisper in his ear. "Knock 'em dead."

He squeezed her close. There were no words to express how grateful he was for what she'd done tonight. He doubted she even realized how much she'd helped him out, but he knew he owed Gail a lot.

"I intend to," he said.

She walked away, and he sat back down with Malcolm.

"You found a keeper."

"I did."

"I didn't believe you could change," Malcolm said. "I've been wary that you'd take our chain and turn it into another of your 'singles' vacation destinations. No matter what your assistant said, I've seen the way you operate."

"Well, I can understand that," Russell said, leaning back against his chair. "I'm in business to make money, and until this point in my life, I only knew one way to do it."

"But having Gail is making you see the world in a new light?"

Russell nodded. "The changes are kind of all happening together. I approached your corporation for a buyout at the same time I signed up for the matchmaking service."

"Why?" Malcolm asked. "You're not just using her to convince me you've changed, are you?"

Russell knew that Malcolm wasn't stupid, so he had to be careful how he answered that question. "I...I'm not going to lie. That was my initial thought, but once I met Gail, it was no longer about business."

Malcolm laughed a big, loud laugh that echoed around

the room. Several diners turned to look at them. "Caught in your own trap?"

"Definitely. And women aren't like business," Russell said.

"They certainly aren't. Lord knows Ashley has given me more trouble than any hotel I own," Malcolm said. "But she's worth it."

"I can see that. How long have you two been married?"

"Thirty-five years. She's the reason I'm stepping down. She wants to enjoy more time together and travel with me, instead of me working while she explores different places."

Russell wondered if he'd ever get to that point with Gail. Right now he was barely able to see them as a settled couple one year from now. But thirty-five years together? That was more than a lifetime.

"I think that's a great idea, and I am definitely the man to sell your shares to, so that you can enjoy your life and not worry about your business."

Being with Ashley made Gail keenly aware of how badly she needed this matchmaking with Russell to work out. Since they'd met, she'd been on a roller coaster of emotions, and tonight she'd seen how much he needed her to move his business deal forward. She shook her head as she thought about that. It worried her that he might be using her.

Again, she thought. She'd had a million different worries since she'd been matched with Russell, and this one was nothing new. He was so different from anyone else she'd met that it was hard to really understand what he wanted and how he acted.

"So…" Ashley said, as they had their Baileys-on-the-rocks, seated at the floor-to-ceiling window with a view of the city below them.

"So?"

"What's it like to date someone like Russell?" Ashley said. "Sorry if that's too forward, but Malcolm is so staid and always has been. I want to live vicariously through you."

Gail took a swallow of the Baileys and wondered exactly how to describe Russell. "I don't know what to say. It's sort of scary, because he has this reputation, and I'm just little old me. I worry that I'm not enough to keep him satisfied."

Ashley shook her head. "You're plenty. He was staring at you tonight when you weren't looking…. I've seen that before in men who are smitten."

Gail didn't doubt that. Even though Russell was selling it tonight, she knew he wasn't faking all of it. He did like her.

But his behavior gave her pause. She knew he wanted Malcolm and Ashley to see what they needed to see. And that was a couple in love.

"Russell is complicated."

Ashley nodded. "I can see that. Malcolm is too, but in a different way."

"How do you mean?" Gail asked. She was ready to hear about someone else and get the spotlight off her and Russell. She didn't want to have to lie to Ashley; she liked her.

"He's very strict about family time, and it's hard with all the kids. They have their ideas about what they want to do as adults, and our son Keir wanted to take over the company, but had other ideas about what direction it should go in…." Ashley shook her head. "Sorry."

"It's okay. Right now, since we are in the beginning of our relationship, I just assumed that once we were as settled as you and Malcolm, things would just be good all the time."

Ashley laughed. "They are good. Better than good. But it's hard once you have kids, because they add a new dimension to every decision you make. You'll see someday. Malcolm compromises a lot, because family is at the core of everything he does."

"Did you know that when you married him?"

"Yes. I wanted to be a stay-at-home mom and have him take care of me and our children, and he always has."

"Sounds perfect," Gail said. She knew that wasn't the relationship either she or Russell desired. Though she wanted kids, she knew that she still needed her career. It was too much a part of who she was for her to give it up.

"Do you really want to know more about my decorator?" Ashley asked.

"Not really, but it seemed the right thing to say."

Ashley laughed. "I've had to do so many of these wife chats, I understand. I did want to ask you a little more about what you do."

"Ask away," Gail said. "I own my own public relations firm and give my clients advice on what to say and when to say it."

"Does it work? I've often wondered how celebs get into trouble if they have people like you working for them," Ashley said.

"It only works if the client listens to you. My company is usually hired after the client has said or done something out of character for them. So, like a sports figure who gets caught in a compromising situation, or an actor who badmouths a director. Stuff like that."

"What do you to fix that?" Ashley asked.

"We can't fix it, exactly, but we do damage control. Show them in the light they used to be in, maybe get them a guest spot on *Dr. Drew*. Something to show that they know they screwed up. Let's face it, we're all human and we all make mistakes."

"Very true. And I like to see celebs like that," Ashley said. "Makes them seem more real."

"Yes, it does," Gail said, knowing that Russell was like the celebs she dealt with. If she'd been his PR person, she would have definitely recommended he find a woman like herself and do some sort of public courtship to "fix" his image.

Gail didn't want to think that Russell was using her, but tonight she really had no choice. She wondered if she'd have the guts to confront him on it.

Russell helped Gail into his waiting car and then slid in next to her. She'd been quiet since they'd joined back up together, and he wondered what she was thinking.

"Thank you."

"For what? Dinner was nice, but I doubt you are thanking me for that," she said. She seemed pensive and very closed off to him. It wasn't what he'd expected, since the evening had gone beyond his expectations and, if he was honest, he wanted her to be happy and celebrate with him.

"For tonight. You were spot-on and exactly what I needed in a partner."

"I kind of picked up on that," she said.

He stretched his arm along the back of the seat and toyed with a strand of her hair as the driver maneuvered them through the crowded city streets. "I appreciate everything you did. Malcolm is a nice guy, but he has some odd ideas about his business and won't sell—"

"I know. I got that from the first moment we met him. And Ashley confirmed it when we were alone. Did you know he won't even let his son take over?"

"I didn't know that," Russell said. "Why not?"

"Something about not following his vision," Gail said. "Are you playing a game with me, Russell?"

"No. I am ready for a change. As I've said a million times to you. When are you going to believe me?"

She shook her head. "When you stop surprising me. First it was your starlet ex-girlfriend, now it's a man who will only sell his company to a settled man. Every time I think I have you figured out, it's something else."

Russell really didn't have an answer to that. "You're just as a complex. Maybe even more so, because all of my issues are out in the open, and you play yours close to the chest. Slowly letting me see a bit of you and then pushing me away again."

Gail nibbled on her lower lip and turned in the seat so she was facing him head-on. "I'm not trying to tease you."

"I know that. Starting a relationship is hard for anyone. We both are complex people, and we have to do it on camera and in the middle of things that keep coming up. It's hard."

"It is hard. And you're right, I do play things close to my chest. It's just that every time I decide it's safe to trust you, something else comes up that makes me leery again."

Russell wished he had the words to assure her that everything would be okay, but he didn't know that, and he wasn't about to lie to her. "I wasn't acting tonight. I think we make a really good couple."

"I think we do too. But I'm not sure that means we should be a couple. You know, there are women out there who act as corporate wives," Gail said.

"There isn't another woman I want by my side, Gail. You are the one who understands me, and we fit together."

She blushed. "We do fit together."

He smiled at her. "Not just physically but also socially.

We were good together tonight. There aren't a lot of couples who are that in sync with each other."

He'd seen that enough in his friends and even with the other women he'd dated. No one fit him as completely as Gail did. And that was something he wasn't going to let slip away.

"We are in sync. I'm kind of surprised, given the lifestyles we both have led."

Russell was too. "Maybe that's why we were matched to each other."

"You have a point. From the beginning, I've been trying to figure out exactly why we were matched up."

Russell smiled at her. "Sounds like you. What have you come up with?"

She shrugged her shoulder and looked back out at the street. "Nothing, Russell. Until tonight I couldn't see whatever the matchmaker saw in us. Until we were at that table chatting with another couple—a real married couple—I didn't have a clue of why we were together."

"And after dinner, you figured it out?" he asked. He didn't care why they were together, but he knew it was important to Gail. He just wanted them to stay together and to be happy. He liked her, he needed her. And as far as he was concerned, he'd hit the lottery when he'd been paired up with Gail. She was everything he wanted in a woman and potential wife, and so much more.

"I think I did," she said.

"Tell me what you figured out," he said.

"I figured out that we are the same on some level. We both know how to socialize, and we have similar tastes."

"And that was enough for the matchmaker?"

"No, we also each have something the other one needs—I have the reputation and stability that you needed, and you have that romantic hero quality that I've long wanted."

Russell didn't like the way that sounded, and had the feeling that Gail didn't see those things in a positive light either.

"We have what's missing in each other," he said. "We complete each other, Gail, and I don't know why you can't see it."

"How do you mean?"

"You're cautious where I'm adventurous. I'm wild where you are calm. And that's what makes us fit together. You want to be adventurous, but have always been afraid, and you've always wanted to be a little bit wild, but were scared you might lose yourself. But, now that you have me in your life, you can be those things and know that I will keep you safe."

Eleven

Gail chose a relatively tame outing for their next filmed date. It was a pizza-making class that she'd been wanting to try but only couples could book.

"Pizza, eh? I don't know that I've ever made one," Russell said, as they entered the kitchen area with a view of the Hudson River at their back.

"Do you cook?" she asked.

"I'm single—what do you think?" he countered.

"I bet you can make one or two things and that's it," she said. She figured a bachelor like Russell wouldn't have to cook for himself too often.

"You'd be right. If I can toss it on the grill or in the microwave, then I call it a meal."

"That sounds a bit limited," she said.

"After tonight, I'll be able to make pizza with the best of them," he said.

"Okay, people, let's get the lights set up and you two

into makeup," Willow said, as she entered the room. "Kat, I need you to confirm that everyone in the class tonight has signed the waiver to allow them to be filmed."

"I'm on it, boss," Kat said.

Willow went off to tell more people what to do, something that Gail realized her friend did really well. And she and Russell were sent to their respective hair and makeup people. She was almost getting used to how she looked when she was done up for the show. But she'd asked them to stop straightening her hair, which they had agreed to do.

Soon she was wired with her microphone and directed to a cooking station. Other couples were trickling in and, as she waited for Russell, Gail smiled at some of the men and women who were glancing over at her, making her feel a little self-conscious. Finally Russell walked up beside her, and Gail breathed a sigh of relief—until she heard some of the people talking among themselves about Russell.

"Oh, ho, this is going to be a fun night," she said. "I guess I should have chosen something where we'd be alone."

Russell put his arm around her and squeezed her close. She tried to ignore the fact that he soothed some of her nerves with that simple little touch.

"Nah, this is going to be perfect," he said.

"What makes you say that?"

"The fact that you picked it," he said with that sexy grin of his.

"May I have everyone's attention, please," Willow said, moving to stand in the center of the room. "Chef David will be out in a moment, and your class will begin. I need you all to just act natural and try to ignore our cameras.

We are going to tape the session uninterrupted and then edit it, so that we don't interrupt the class."

"What are you filming?" a man on the other side of the room asked. "Will we be on TV?"

"We are filming a reality dating show, and you might be on TV, but we won't be filming you up close," Willow answered. "Any other questions?"

Willow moved over to Gail and Russell's station. "For you two, just do what you've been doing. We are going to have a camera on you both, and we will be recording your conversations. The focus of this episode isn't learning to make pizza, but rather on your date, okay?"

"Yes," Gail said.

"Of course," Russell answered.

Willow moved away, and the chef came in and started the class with a brief lesson in the history of pizza. Then he talked about where he came from in Italy and how they made it there. The chef was from Naples.

"Have you ever been to Italy?" Russell asked.

"No. I'm hoping to go on a Mediterranean cruise next summer, but I'm usually busy and so are my friends, so…"

"You work too hard," Russell said.

"Ha. That's a laugh coming from a workaholic like you. Have you been to Italy?"

"Yes, Rome and Venice," he said.

"Do you have Kiwi Klubs there?" she asked.

That surprised a laugh out of him, and he shrugged. "In fact, I do. But I did take some time off to sightsee while I was there."

She was going to ask him more about it, but the chef was having them take a bowl with prepared dough in it out from under their table.

"I will now show you how to toss the dough," Chef David said.

He tossed it in the air, expertly expanding it with each successive toss, working the dough until it was the right size for the pizza mat on the table.

"Now you try it," Chef David said.

"Right," Gail said under her breath. "Why don't you go first?"

Russell picked the dough up, and after a moment of stretching it, he started tossing it. With each toss it remained the same size. She watched as he got more frustrated at the dough. "Damn, it's harder than it looks."

"Is it?" she asked.

"You have a try," he said.

He handed her the dough, and she started to toss it in the air. It was hard to get it to stretch, so after three unsuccessful tosses, she put the dough back in the bowl.

"Let's try pulling on it," Russell said.

They each got a side of the dough and stretched it until a big hole opened in the center, and Gail started laughing. Russell looked up at her and laughed too. What had struck her as funny was that they were both so successful and used to making things happen, this stupid pizza dough should have been a snap, but it wasn't.

Russell was concentrating on it as though he could will the dough into the right shape. Chef David heard them laughing and came over to offer some additional guidance.

But even he had to shake his head at the pathetic way their dough looked. They formed it as close to a pizza shape as they could on the tray.

"Thank you," Russell said after the chef walked away and they were alone.

"For?"

"Tonight. It's fun and silly and just the release I need from all the pressure that has been hounding me."

She smiled at him. "I'm glad."

But, inside, she wasn't too sure about that. She was still scared of caring too much about Russell. Tonight he was that guy she needed him to be, but she'd heard the comments of the other participants. Everyone knew that Russell was the love-'em-and-leave-'em bachelor type, and Gail wanted to believe she wasn't heading for a heartache, but wasn't too sure.

When the class was over and they were all allowed to take their pizzas to the patio outside the cooking school, Gail was surprised to see paparazzi waiting for them. Russell's face got tight and they both tried to ignore it, but reality was setting back in. Russell wasn't the carefree guy she needed him to be. He had real problems, and the only reality between them was the matchmaking show. They wrapped up the evening with a quick chat with the host. But Gail slipped away while Russell was still talking to Jack. She needed to escape and figure out if her feelings were real of just another part of this show.

Russell knew that last taped date hadn't ended as well as he'd hoped. He had thought long and hard about what he wanted to do on his next date with Gail, but the constant barrage of media attention and the problems with Penny kept him from being able to select the date he wanted. So he settled for walking the Appalachian Trail near Sunrise Mountain in New Jersey.

"I don't know about this," Gail said, as they were fitted with microphones before the hike.

"I'll protect you," Russell said.

"I'm sure you will try," she said. "But what about bugs and stuff?"

He laughed nervously. He was very afraid that, when the television show ended, Gail was going to walk out of his life without a backward glance. "You'll be fine."

She looked like a city girl in her walking shorts and newly purchased hiking boots. She had her thick hair braided down her back and a pair of cute designer sunglasses perched on the end of her nose. He wanted her.

He wanted to take her out into the woods and find a secluded place to make love to her, but with the cameras rolling that was impossible. Far away from the pressures of both of their jobs and lives. He needed to be buried in that long, silky body of hers, so he could hold her and pretend that she was his.

"So, for filming," Willow said, "I'm thinking we will do a shot of you guys here at the start of the trail and then one at the summit. I'm sending two of our crew up the mountain ahead of you so they can do some long shots. I want the date to be yours, but I need some good footage too."

"That's fine," Russell said. "Do they need a map? Or do they know where they're going?"

He had spent a month hiking the trail last year before he'd started dating Penny. He'd needed to get his head together, and hiking had helped. Once he'd grown in his beard and spent a few weeks out here, no one had recognized him and he was just another man, another hiker.

"It'll be okay," he said to Gail.

"It's just not my thing," she said by way of explanation.

"Pizza making wasn't mine but it turned out okay," he said.

"Until the end of the night," she reminded him.

"That's the beauty of this place. No paparazzi out here. Too much work for them," he said.

She laughed, as he'd hoped she would. "Okay, tell me what to do…. You've done this before, right?"

"Yes, I have. I know what I'm about in the outdoors," he said.

"That's right. You grew up on a farm, didn't you?" she asked.

"A ranch," he corrected her.

"Okay," Willow said, interrupting them. "Go ahead and start hiking."

As they got underway, Russell wanted to be alone with Gail, instead of having the cameras there. He hadn't had a chance to talk to Gail in days. But he wasn't going to have privacy right now.

"How have you been?" she asked.

"Fine."

"Really?"

"No," he said. "The media are making some demands on me, and I still have a lot of work to do. There hasn't been any time to chat with you."

She reached out and snagged his hand, twining their fingers together. "You can always call me."

He squeezed her fingers and lifted their joined hands to his mouth, brushing his lips across the back of her knuckles. "I've missed you."

"Why?" she asked.

"You just treat me like a regular guy. And there's no chaos when you're around," he said.

She blushed. "That's sweet."

Now he felt like an idiot. He didn't want to be sweet. He wanted to be…whatever she really needed from him, and he knew on an instinctive level that he wasn't. It didn't stop him from trying but, he knew he was missing the boat.

"I'm sorry."

"For what?"

He thought about it for a minute. Finding the words to tell her that he knew he wasn't the man she wanted was harder than he'd thought it would be. "For not—ah, hell, I don't know. I just wish that my life was more normal for you."

She chewed her lower lip as they continued walking, and then she stopped. "I know that I haven't been very easygoing about everything that is happening in your life right now, but that doesn't mean I regret meeting you or these dates."

"Good. I don't either," he said.

He led them up the trail, and when they reached the peak, he pulled her into his arms and kissed her. The camera crew was waiting and caught the entire thing on tape, but Russell didn't care. He had found something with Gail that he'd never expected, and he wasn't about to change his attitude and let her slip away.

She was his. And it was time for Gail and everyone else to know that.

Gail spent the next week trying to just relax and let her fears dissipate, but it was hard. She knew that Russell wasn't the type of man to ever need a matchmaker. The last two dates they'd had were fun, and she'd fallen just a little bit more for him on each occasion, but it was the time away from the camera that was making her wonder if he was sincere and that worried her. Was she seeing the real man or the man he wanted her to see?

"Why are you frowning?" Nichole asked as she took a seat next to Gail and Willow at the Blue Fish. It was rare that the three friends got a chance to catch up.

"Was I?"

"You know you were. Don't make me ferret the truth out of you. I'm a reporter—that's what I do for a living."

"I know. I'm not sure—"

"Don't say another word," Willow said. "I need a drink

and I don't want to miss any of the gossip." She got up and went to the bar.

"You won't," Nichole reassured her. "Don't think you're getting out of telling us what's going on, Gail."

"I know I'm not. So much has happened since last month."

"For me too," Nichole said. "I've been researching Matchmakers Inc., and I talked my boss into letting me do a story on Conner MacAfee. Have you met him?"

"Yes. He and Russell are friends," Gail said.

"What did I miss?" Willow said, as she returned to the table with a round of drinks.

"You didn't miss anything," Gail said with a laugh. "Nichole is doing a story on Conner MacAfee."

Willow sat down on the seat next to Gail and plopped her wineglass on the table. "I'm exhausted."

"You always are," Gail said.

"Running a production is stressful. You and Russell have been great."

"Thanks. We try to do our best," Gail said.

"Okay, so back to whatever I interrupted," Willow said.

Gail took a long swallow of her Pinot Grigio, letting the dry wine soothe her nerves. "I don't know what we were talking about."

"Liar," Nichole said. "She was frowning. Something is bothering her."

Gail shook her head. "I'm…I don't want to talk about it."

"It has to be Russell. Tell us about him," Nichole said.

"I wonder if I should tape this for the show," Willow said.

Gail kicked her under the table. "Can I please have one thing in my life that is private?"

"It was just an idea," Willow said. "He's a very public man."

Gail leaned back in her seat. "That's part of the problem. How much of dating me is for real, and how much of it is for show?"

Willow put both elbows on the table and leveled her ebony gaze on Gail. "He signed up with Matchmakers Inc., the same as you did. And we didn't ask for him, he was the man the matchmaker picked for you."

"Why?" Gail asked. She knew that Russell had explained it, but it was hard for her to believe that a man as dynamic as he was would be the perfect match for her. How could that be? They weren't the same—they were like oil and water, and that didn't seem like a peaceful way to live.

"I don't know," Willow said. "But I do know that when I watch you two together, something just clicks. Whatever your fears are, are you sure they are based on Russell? And not your own doubts in men?"

Gail couldn't answer that. She knew she had issues. She'd been battling them all along and trying to be as open and trusting of Russell as she could be. Was she making a big deal out of nothing?

"That's why I'm frowning, Nic. I can't figure this out. No matter which way I look at this, I'm still unsure."

Nichole reached over and patted her hand. "I don't blame you. That's why I've stopped dating."

"Yeah, right," Willow said. "I saw you in the club the other night with a guy."

"That's sex, ladies. Not dating," Nichole said with a laugh.

Gail shook her head. Nichole was wild and had a joie de vivre that she'd never had. "You'd be better suited to Russell."

"No, I wouldn't. We'd bore each other in no time. Sex is a temporary bond. But you are building, or want to build, a relationship. That takes something different."

"It takes trust," Gail said. And that was where she struggled. If she could simply trust Russell and ignore her doubts there would be no problem. "Enough about me. Tell me what's going on with you two."

"Willow let slip that I'm hooking up with a hottie, so I guess I have nothing new to say."

"Who's the hottie?" Gail asked.

"A young photographer at the paper. He is Spanish and likes older women as lovers.... He said that to me. I was like, hey, I'm only thirty. Then I realized, girls, we're thirty!"

Gail laughed at the way Nichole said it. "I already knew that."

"Me too," Willow said. "But then Gail and I aren't out there dating like we're still twenty-five."

"Hey, one of us has to enjoy life while you two are busy putting your nose to the grindstone. You can live vicariously through me."

Gail laughed as she knew Nichole intended them to, but a part of her was worried about her friend. Where Gail wore her lack of trust on her sleeve, Nichole hid hers deep behind a wall of superficial dating and a lifestyle that seemed wild and carefree. But Nichole had her secrets, just the same as Gail did.

"How many more dates do you have?" Nichole asked.

"Two. We are nearing the end, and I for one will be glad."

"Will you keep seeing him?" Willow asked.

"Yes," Gail said. "I think I will. He's been so busy with a business deal and that bad press from Penny, that we are hoping to enjoy some quiet time once filming stops."

"That's good," Willow said. "We want to see some big romance at the end. The other producers are urging him to ask you to marry him."

Gail swallowed hard. She wasn't sure she wanted that to happen on camera. "That doesn't seem right."

"I know. Russell said he'd ask you when he was good and ready."

Gail felt a little better, and the fear that had been riding her abated a little. Maybe she and Russell really were meant to be together.

Twelve

Poker night with the boys was always one of Russell's favorite occasions, but he had a date with Gail and, for once, he was anxious for the game to end. He shouldn't have been surprised; he wanted to spend every minute he could with Gail—she was all he thought about. And thanks to the producers of *Sexy and Single*, now all he could think about was asking her to marry him.

He didn't know if six dates were enough to ask her to spend the rest of her life with him. He wasn't entirely sure he wanted to commit himself to Gail now because of how busy he was, and he knew that, if he asked her to marry him, she would expect him to be a good husband.

Tonight he was playing at Conner's penthouse apartment with Conner, Gerald McIntyre and Les Wells. Gerald and Les were friends of Conner's. They went outside to smoke cigars after an hour of playing, and Russell contemplated leaving the game. He'd broken even, but that wasn't how he normally played. He liked to win at poker, as he did at everything, but he was distracted by Gail.

He still wasn't sure he'd figured out what she needed from Mr. Right. Plus, how was he going to juggle that on top of the new merger, which appeared to be going through? At least he had a little thank-you gift for Gail for her part in making that happen.

"Just because you look at your watch doesn't mean time will go faster," Conner said.

"Am I that obvious?" Russell asked.

"Yes. What are you rushing off to?" Conner asked.

"A woman."

"Gail?"

"Yes."

"Good. I take it you're pleased with your match?" Conner asked, taking a sip of his rye whiskey.

"Very pleased. I wouldn't have thought an interview and a questionnaire would do the job.... Well, who does think that matchmaking works?"

Conner laughed. "You'd be surprised at how much more is involved than that."

"Have you had a hand in any of the matches?" Russell asked.

"Not at all. My assistant tells me I'm not intuitive enough," Conner said with a laugh. "My grandmother said the same thing. She's the one I inherited the business from."

"Did you believe her?"

"Hell, yes. I barely know what I want, much less have the ability to guess what a woman wants," Conner said, shaking his head. "I have no idea how you are managing Gail so successfully. Why did you want to give up the single lifestyle?"

Russell wasn't too sure how honest to be, but this was

Conner, and he'd been in the same situation as Russell before. "I was getting bored with it. After so many years of serial dating, every woman was becoming the same. I wanted...something different."

Conner nodded. "I hear ya. Sometimes I think I should give it a whirl."

"You should," Russell said.

Conner arched one eyebrow at him. "My mother says the same thing. She's anxious for grandbabies. Do you have kids?"

"No."

"What about those paternity suits?"

"Just lump-sum settlements to help the mothers. I'm not the father."

"Why would you do that?"

"The women were friends.... They needed some help and I was in a position to help them."

"Really? Why would you do that?" Conner asked.

"To be honest, it was to help my business. I was just starting out when the first suit came up. Had just made my first million and the lawsuit brought people to the Kiwi Klub like you wouldn't believe. The kids weren't mine," Russell said, thinking that at some point he was going to have to tell Gail that he was sterile. But right now, he had bigger problems.

Conner looked at the glass door leading to the balcony as if to make sure they were still alone. "Why not just do that with Penny?"

"She is insisting the baby is mine. And it's not. As soon as she's honest with me, I'll help her out."

"Does she know that?" Conner asked.

"I've told her as much," Russell said.

"What does Gail think about that?" Conner asked. "I

can't imagine she's too happy with the thought of you giving money to Penny."

Russell and Gail didn't talk too much about Penny. They had dealt with the paparazzi when they had to. And Gail had offered him her professional opinion on the matter, but he'd been frank with Gail and let her know where he stood. "I think she's fine with it. We've discussed Penny and my past suits."

Conner shook his head. "You're a better man than me."

"Doubtful," Russell said.

"I would never settle a paternity suit," Conner said. "My mother would be livid. She'd want to raise the kid as a MacAfee."

"That's the difference between you and me. You were born with a silver spoon in your mouth and have the generations of family waiting for you to give them an heir. I am the orphaned son of a down-on-his-luck rancher.... No one questions me."

Conner nodded. "I envy you. Someday I'd like to just walk away from my family and my name. But I think it would kill my mother."

"She's in ill health?"

"No, but my sister and I are all she has left. And she relies on me far more than you'd imagine."

Russell wondered what that would be like. He sort of envied Conner and that legacy he had. His family had the big mansion in the Hamptons, and he had a family history he was proud of. Russell imagined that was what he'd have with Gail. But he knew there'd be no child to pass that on to, and that worried him a bit, because, as he'd come to know Gail and in talking to her about Penny's situation, he'd realized that she wanted a large family one day.

And while he could give her anything else in the world

she desired, a family of her own was beyond his reach. "I'm glad you have each other."

Conner nodded, but the other men rejoined them and the game play resumed. Russell wasn't as anxious to get to Gail as he had been before. He was afraid for the first time that he might not be holding a winning hand with her after all.

Gail left her friends and headed uptown toward home. Russell had asked if he could come over tonight, and she'd said yes. She'd been pretty successful in not sleeping with him again. Not because she hadn't wanted to, but because she'd been afraid that if she did, she'd have to admit she was falling in love with him.

She let the night doorman know that Russell would be coming by and to let him up. His last text had said he'd be leaving ten minutes ago, so she felt she might be just ahead of him.

They'd been busy between their on-air dates, and there simply hadn't been a lot of time to get together. When he'd texted earlier tonight, asking if he could stop by, she hadn't wanted to deny herself the chance to see him and be with him again.

Despite what she'd said to Willow and Nichole, she really had no idea if she and Russell would see each other after the show ended. She suspected they'd both say they wanted to continue dating, but they were very busy people and, for her part, Gail knew she was still afraid to let Russell in. Still afraid to really trust him, and being in love... falling in love, wasn't going to help that in the least.

She let herself into her apartment and turned on the lights in the living room. She kicked off her shoes in her bedroom and then slowly walked through her empty place. Her dreams had been changing over the last four weeks as she'd come to know Russell. Now, instead of that faceless man she'd fantasized about for years, she saw Russell standing next to her. She saw him as the husband and father in her little perfect-family image.

The doorbell rang, and she felt her heartbeat speed up as she went to let Russell in. His hair was rumpled and he smelled faintly of cigars. But he smiled when he saw her and stepped over the threshold to take her into his arms.

He kissed her long and hard, and the doubts she'd had subsided. She'd missed this, she thought, closing her eyes and resting her cheek on his shoulder. When they were apart, it was easy to entertain her doubts, but when she was in his arms, she felt like she'd found that thing she'd always been searching for. She was afraid to admit to herself that being in his arms felt like home.

"That's more like it. I can't believe it's been two weeks since I've held you like this," he said.

"Me either. Do you want a drink?" she asked, leading the way to the living room.

"No, I'd like to hold you in my arms," he said. "I've missed that, beautiful."

"I've missed you," she said. "But I see you've been busy. Every alert I get for work has at least one mention of you or Penny in it."

"Yes. She is going ahead with her plan to blame her pregnancy on me."

"Has she had—"

"I don't really want to talk about her," Russell said. "Sorry to interrupt you, but I have some good news."

She smiled at him, even though she suspected he wasn't sorry at all. He didn't like talking about Penny or the negative media she'd generated for him. "What's your good news?"

"Malcolm has accepted my offer to buy his shares. In

a short while—maybe two months—I will be the controlling owner of Family Vacation Destinations."

"That name stinks. You're going to have to change it," Gail said, "But congrats. I know that is what you wanted."

"Yes, the name will be changed," Russell said, reaching into his pocket. "I wouldn't have convinced Malcolm without your help, and I want to say thank-you."

He held a small blue jewelry box out toward her, and she hesitated. "Your thanks are enough, Russell. I don't need a gift."

"Please accept this. I want you to know that helping me out with Malcolm and Ashley was a big part of closing this deal. And it had nothing to do with our courtship."

Courtship. It was an old-fashioned word, but it made sense in thinking of the arranged dates they'd been on. "In that case, I'll be happy to accept it."

She took the light blue Tiffany box from him and opened it to find another velvet box inside. She tipped it out into her hand and then opened the hinged lid. Lying there were a pair of earrings. Chocolate pearls encircled by diamonds. They were beautiful. She hadn't received a gift like this from a man in a long time.

"Thank you, Russell."

"You're welcome," he said. "Put them on."

She did and then swept her hair up so he could see them. "Gorgeous, but then, I knew they would be. I know that our dates with the matchmaker are ending.... Well, we have two more, but I don't want to stop seeing you."

"Good," she said. "I know we're both busy."

"Not too busy for each other. I know you had your reasons for going to the matchmaker, and I don't think they've changed."

"They haven't."

"Do you think I can be your Mr. Right?" he asked.

Gail didn't know. She wanted to say yes, but there was still a part of her that wasn't sure.

"I guess not," Russell said.

She shook her head. "You are Mr. Right in my eyes now, but I'm scared, Russell, because I don't know if I'm trusting you because of your charming ways, or if you are the real deal. And I don't want to get hurt."

"How is this different from how you felt when you first saw me?" he asked. "Haven't you seen that I'm not the same man who was a serial dater?"

"Yes, I have. And the way it's different is that I really care for you now, and I don't want to risk being disappointed by you."

"Then let me take care of you. I'm not going to let you down, Gail."

She shook her head, but he kissed her and then made love to her on the couch, and all her objections disappeared. All she could think about as he held her close was that she wanted to always be in his arms. No matter what the consequences were.

Thirteen

Gail hadn't had a man sleep over in a long time. And Russell wasn't just any guy. The way she felt about him was more intense and, honestly, she wasn't sure how to act this morning. She had the usual fears—morning dragon breath, hair that was more than tousled, thanks to its being curly and tending to stick out all over the place, and of course no makeup. She didn't have great skin like her friend Willow, and usually when she woke up in the morning she had sheet creases in her cheek.

Maybe she could creep out of bed, make herself presentable and then get back in.

"Morning," Russell's low voice rumbled under her cheek.

She was curled around his body, her head resting on his chest. She had felt his arms around her all night, and that had been nice. Well, more than nice, she thought. She'd never slept as soundly with someone else in her bed.

"Morning," she said, not tipping her head up toward him. "I should go and get you some coffee."

"You should? Why?" he asked, stroking his hand up and down her bare arm.

"Don't you want one?" she asked, realizing she was out of practice in waking up with a man.

"I do, but I will make you a cup. I didn't get much of a tour last night, but I think I can find the kitchen."

"Okay," she said.

He tipped her head back and she stared up into his light eyes. They were becoming so familiar to her, so dear to her, and she knew that if nothing worked out between them, she'd always cherish this memory. He leaned down and kissed her. His mouth moved slowly over hers, until her eyes drifted closed and all the fears that had been circling around in her head disappeared.

His hands smoothed down her back and cupped her buttocks, drawing her into his body. "You feel good first thing in the morning."

He rubbed his beard-stubbled chin against the top of her head and hugged her closer. She sighed and let herself relax into him.

"That was a big sigh," he said.

"I know."

"What are you worrying about now?" he asked.

"Everything," she said, pretty sure that covered it all.

He laughed. "Damn, woman, you even wake up worrying?"

"Yes, I do," she admitted. "I wish I didn't, but that's the way I am."

"You need a man to lean on so you don't have to worry so much," he said quietly.

"I do," she admitted, looking up at him. She wanted to

believe he was that man. But she still wasn't one hundred percent sure, and she doubted she ever would be.

"What am I going to have to do to prove myself to you?" he asked.

She just shook her head. "I wish I knew. I keep waiting for this feeling inside of my stomach to settle down."

"That's excitement," he said. "You don't want that to go away."

But she did. She didn't like feeling as if she was caught up in a hurricane, and that was exactly what life with Russell was like. "I'm not sure."

"I know. Why don't I get you some coffee while you shower, and then we can share a cab to your office?"

"Why my office?" she asked.

"Because I am seeing you to work today, after giving you a proper morning with your lover," he said.

She knew it was silly, considering the age they lived in, but the word *lover* always gave her an illicit thrill. "Why do you put up with my doubts?"

"I have them too, and until they are abated for you, I know we aren't where we need to be in order to move forward."

She bit her lower lip and sat up next to him, bringing the sheets with her to keep covered. "What do you mean, 'move forward'?"

"I mean marriage," he said. "It's a bit hard for me to get my head around, but I can't see a future for you and me where we are simply live-in lovers. I know you want more and I think I do too."

"Think? Well, I'm not going to say yes to marrying you until you're sure you want it," she said. "People who feel trapped in relationships end up wrecking them."

He nodded. "I suspect that's why you're still worrying

about my level of commitment and I'm still not sure what it is."

"I think you're right," she said, feeling better about being with Russell than she had thought she would when she woke up this morning. "Ugh, I forgot about my hair. Is it crazy?"

"Yes," he said with a wicked grin. "But I love it. You look as if you've had a very enjoyable night."

She shook her head, reaching out to pinch him. "You were supposed to say no."

"Why would I? I assume you'll see yourself in the mirror. And to be honest, I like you this way. It's the real you without any of the barriers of makeup. It's just Gail Little, and I like her."

Those few words soothed away the last of her early-morning worries. She realized that Russell had a tendency to do that. He always found a way to say the right things to make her feel at ease, even in the oddest moments. "Thanks."

"Thank you for last night and for the last month. When I went to the matchmaker, I honestly believed I wasn't going to find anything different than I had experienced before. But you surprised me, beautiful."

"You've surprised me too."

"In a good way?" he asked, arching one eyebrow at her.

She studied him for a long minute. "Yes, I think so."

"Damned by faint praise," he said as he swung his legs to the side of her bed and stood up in all his glorious nakedness. "Maybe coffee will help win your heart."

She doubted coffee would help. "Stand there for a minute and maybe that will help."

"Like this," he said, putting his hands on his hips and turning to face her fully. She skimmed her gaze over his muscled form and could only nod.

He was a very good-looking man, and this morning she felt very happy and lucky to call him hers.

Russell didn't really know what he was going to do with Gail. He knew the producers of the show wanted him to make some romantic gesture on their last date, and he wanted to fulfill his obligations to them, but a bigger part of him wanted to blow Gail's mind. Defy her expectations.

She'd entered into the show and the matchmaking with the expectation that she'd find a man who'd marry her. But he knew he wasn't the guy she wanted to spend the rest of her life with...or at least he hadn't been in the beginning. And to be fair, he'd gotten what he wanted from Gail when Malcolm had agreed to sell his shares to him. But Russell still wasn't ready to walk away from her.

He'd meant what he'd said to her earlier. He couldn't see them simply living together. He needed to know she was bound to him, and that nothing from his past was going to come between them and take her away from him.

He heard the shower stop and realized he hadn't finished making the coffee. Gail made him question things that he'd always taken for granted. Take this morning—he had never had to assuage a woman's worries after a night with him. But she was different. With each day they were together, he was learning more and more about how different they were.

"Do you want to get a shower?" she asked from the doorway. She was wearing a summer suit and had her wet hair pulled back in a tight bun. She couldn't have looked more different from how she'd awakened in his bed if she'd suddenly shaved her head. She was all professional now, and he was still in his boxers.

"I guess I will. I'm afraid I never got the coffee made," he said.

"That's not a big deal. I'll take care of it while you're cleaning up."

There was awkwardness between them that he could tell she felt as well. They weren't close enough to be doing these intimate daily rituals, yet he wanted them to be. He knew that only once they started waking up together every morning would he really get a feel for what was coming between them.

"Have you ever lived with a man before?" he asked her.

"No, I haven't. I'm… There just hasn't been anyone who I wanted to spend all my time with."

"For me as well," he said. "Though I have had women live in my houses, it never felt like this does."

She gave him a very shy smile. "Is that good?"

"Yes, it is," he said, noticing she wore the chocolate-pearl-and-diamond earrings he'd given her. Some of his own doubts disappeared. He knew himself well enough to know that he was going to make Gail his completely. Now that he'd acknowledged he couldn't be happy with anything less than marriage, he was going to do everything in his power to make that happen for them.

"I don't need coffee," he said.

"Well, I do," she admitted. "I'm a wreck until I have at least one cup."

"Then I'll leave you to it. I'm going to bring over some stuff so that, when I spend the night here from now on, I'll be able to shave."

"Don't you think you should ask?"

He closed the gap between them and put his hands on her hips to draw her in close to his body, forcing her to tip her head back and look up at him. "No. You like to be difficult."

"I do," she admitted with a grin. "I think everyone has made your life too easy up until you met me."

He pinched her ass and then leaned down to give her a long, deep kiss. His erection stirred again, and he swept her up in his arms and carried her back to the bedroom.

"I just got dressed," she said.

"Would you like me to stop?" he asked, tracing his finger over the lines of her face as he set her on her feet. She had delicate features, but usually she acted like such a powerhouse that he didn't notice it until they were alone like this.

"No, I was just being silly."

"Good," he said. "I wanted to make love to you as soon as we woke this morning, but you seemed to want to get out of bed."

"I was unsure what to do," she said. "It's been a while since a man slept over."

"I'm glad. I don't like the thought of sharing you with anyone else. Even a memory."

She looked up with a quiet stillness that he knew meant utter sincerity from her. "There is no other man that can compare to you."

His ego and his erection grew at those words. He pushed her back on the bed and came down next to her, cradling her in his arms. Telling her with his caresses just how much she meant to him.

He slowly undressed her and saw that she had another fabulously sexy matching bra-and-panty set. He vowed that he'd unlock that latent sensuality that she kept hidden beneath conservative suits and tidy hair. He wanted her wild and aching for him.

And he set about arousing her until she was begging him to take her. He pulled her over his lap so she could ride him, with her thick hair falling around them in a veil and her pretty breasts bouncing with each gyration of her hips. He leaned up and suckled one nipple and felt her tighten around him. He jerked his hips forward, jetting his completion and calling her name.

When they were both spent, she fell forward in his arms, resting her head in the crook of his neck. He held her tighter than he intended and knew deep in his soul, he wasn't letting her go.

Gail showered with Russell and then they got dressed together. She tried not to let the feeling of joy that was swamping her right at the moment get to her, but it was hard not to. Russell had turned out to be absolutely perfect for her in a way that she'd never expected.

On the elevator ride down in her building, she hugged his arm to her and smiled up at him.

"What was that for?" he asked.

"Just because," she said, not ready to admit to him what she was just acknowledging to herself. She loved him. It was overwhelming, and when she looked at him, the truth just stared back. He might be a billionaire jet-setter, but he was also the man who had won her over with his honesty and his charm.

He squeezed her back. "We're good?"

"Very good," she admitted. Finally admitting how she felt about him put to bed all the doubts that she couldn't figure out. It was as if worrying over Russell had just been a way to mask what she really felt.

They reached the lobby, where Russell gestured for her to walk in front of him and she did. Turning back to smile at him as the doorman opened the lobby doors to the street, she stumbled, and Russell reached for her arm to steady her.

As flashbulbs exploded around them.

A cacophony of words barraged them, as cameras, microphones and paparazzi surrounded them. She couldn't understand a word they were saying as Russell wrapped his arm around her, guiding her to his waiting car. His driver had the backseat door open, and Russell hustled her into the car. The door closed solidly behind them, and there was an almost unnatural silence in the interior.

"What was that about?" she asked, feeling dazed and a little scared.

"I'm going to find out now. I'm sorry, Gail, but I need to go to my office."

"That's okay. You can drop me off at mine," she said.

"I wanted this morning to be about you," he said.

"It's fine," she said, but she knew that it wasn't. While they'd been alone in her apartment, it had been easy for her to pretend that they were meant to be together. But this was the first time in her life that she'd been surrounded by a swarm of photographers, and she knew that was a normal occurrence in Russell's life. She hadn't considered that. She'd been living in a little bubble of her own making, and it was time for her to be serious about her emotions.

Loving Russell wasn't a neatly tied package, and she was coming to realize that it actually brought about more complications than she would have guessed. He was on his phone, and she didn't even pretend that she wasn't listening to his conversation.

"They were outside of her apartment, Dylan. I want to know who gave them Gail's information," Russell said.

He was angry. His body was tense and his free hand clenched in a fist. Gail had the first inkling that she really was important to Russell. That helped her calm down. He had been right earlier when he'd said that she needed someone—well, him—to take care of the things she worried about.

And her earlier fears about hair and morning breath

seemed so inconsequential compared to this. She should have been worried about their lifestyles, as she had been in the beginning. But Russell had done such a good job of wooing her and making her forget how different they really were.

She felt the sting of tears behind her eyelids and turned away, fumbling for her sunglasses. It didn't matter how the information about her had gotten out in public. Now that she'd seen that swarm, she knew that, despite her feelings for Russell, she couldn't live like that. She never wanted to be in that situation again.

"You okay?" he asked.

"No," she said. "I'm sorry, Russell, but I can't handle this."

"It's fine. I'm going to find out who leaked your address and we'll take care of that. They won't bother you again."

"I don't think you can control it."

"Hell. I will do what I can to make sure you feel safe. I think it might be best if you move into my place for the time being, and I will hire a bodyguard to travel with you."

She shook her head.

"They will not be as bad from now on," he said.

"It doesn't matter. I can't do this, Russell. That's what I'm trying to say to you. Keep the bodyguard and all of your threats for the paparazzi. I'm not going to be part of your life anymore."

"You can't decide that unilaterally," he said. "We are in a relationship and both have a say in what happens."

"I know. It's just that today I realized, no matter how you are with me in private, I'm always going to be dealing with your past, and I'm just not up to that, Russell. I want to be. I wanted my feelings for you to make everything okay, but they won't—they can't."

"Coward," he said. "You are bailing based on the

chance that you might be hurt, without seeing that you are running away again. Hiding behind those barriers you have put in place to keep yourself safe. But you can't see that you are withering behind those walls, Gail."

"You might be right. I'm afraid and I thought that maybe… It doesn't matter. The truth is I'm not really the right woman for you, and you're not the right man for me. I want quiet time with you and being able to be in public without being followed, or worrying that something from your past is going to spring up to interfere with our lives again."

Russell ran his hand through his hair. "Penny is going to be taken care of, and that threat will be gone. There's nothing in my life to warrant attention, not going forward, not with you."

She shook her head. "I can't. The driver can just let me out here," she said, realizing they were circling the block where her office was.

Russell signaled the driver to stop. "I never figured you for someone who'd run away."

"It's funny, I've always known that I would."

She opened the door and got out, closing the door and walking away without looking back. She didn't even realize she was crying until she was in the elevator on the way up to her office. She knew she wasn't just mourning her short-lived love and happiness with Russell, but also the death of the dreams she'd secretly harbored for her entire life.

Fourteen

The hotel was bustling with activity when he entered the lobby. The doorman greeted him and people waved and smiled, but Russell wasn't in the mood to keep up the image of the good-natured owner today. He was ready to explode and didn't know what pissed him off more. The fact that Gail had walked out over something so ridiculous, or the fact that he'd let her.

He was tired of dealing with the mess that Penny had stirred up. It was time to put an end to it. He'd done what he could to help her out, and in the past he would have let things ride, but he wasn't about to let Gail back out of the relationship they'd been building.

He walked into his office to see Dylan on his phone, Mitsy on her phone and two lawyers waiting in the guest chairs. He signaled the lawyers to enter his office and came to a halt when he realized that he needed to know the exact details of what was out there in the press. He wanted to fight it, but he had to know what he was up against.

"Do you know what's going on? Why were there photographers at my girlfriend's apartment this morning?" he asked Jack Monroe, his lead attorney.

"Near as we can tell, Penny's filed a palimony suit against you, alleging that you won't acknowledge her or her child. She has named Gail Little as the 'other' woman."

This was worse than he had thought. "What are the options? I want her stopped and this to end."

"We can take care of it, but it's not going to be pretty, and Ms. Thomson will understand that you will never give her anything."

"Do it. She might cost me a merger as well as Gail. I want her stopped, and I don't want to have to deal with anything like this again."

"Understood. We will file the papers necessary to stop her."

"Good. I don't want to hear from you until you have results," Russell said, then realized how abrupt he was being. "It's not your fault. Sorry if that came out wrong."

"Not a problem," Jack said. "We are used to dealing with stressful situations."

"Thanks," he said.

The two men left, and Russell wasn't alone for a minute before Mitsy walked in. She was dressed in a sunny spring suit that made her seem cheery. Knowing his assistant as he did, he suspected she'd dressed that way because of what was going on today.

"What's up?" he asked her.

"Malcolm is on the line and he's not happy," Mitsy said. "I've been as placating as I could be, but he won't listen to me."

Russell nodded and then smiled reassuringly at his assistant. "Thanks for doing what you could. I'll talk to him now. I need a bouquet of wild flowers sent to Gail. I will email you the message I want on the card."

"Yes, sir. Anything else?"

"Probably, but for now I'm good," he said.

She left, quietly closing the door behind her, and he walked over to his desk and picked up the phone. He stared at the blinking light where the call waited and tried to get his feelings for Gail out of the way so he could simply be a businessman again. He could do this. He'd wined and dined this man and made him see the world from Russell's perspective. All he had to do was somehow convince him that this latest blowup with Penny was just water under the bridge.

"Holloway," he said, unable to keep his lack of patience out of his voice. After all he'd done to assure Malcolm he was a changed man, Russell found himself right back where he'd been six months ago, when Malcolm had first refused to sell to him.

"Damn, boy, you know how to rile up the women, don't you?" Malcolm asked. "First, Ashley and I want to make sure that Gail is okay."

Gail wasn't okay and frankly, Russell had a better idea of how to finesse Malcolm than he did how to win Gail back. There was no way she was going to believe that his past wasn't going to pop up from time to time, and Russell knew very well he couldn't control how someone else acted.

"She's fine. I'm hiring a bodyguard to keep the paparazzi away from her."

"Good thinking," Malcolm said. "I assume that the stuff we are hearing about you is all untrue?"

"First of all, the child isn't mine, Malcolm, which is something that I've told Gail. I am not abandoning the baby or its mother," Russell said. "We were through long before I met Gail."

"I'm going to need more information than that or the deal is off," Malcolm said.

Russell thought about it long and hard. He really didn't have time to explain himself to Malcolm. He should be at Gail's office forcing her to talk to him, but this was business.

Malcolm said something else, but Russell had stopped listening. Business. He was going to end up all alone if he kept giving priority to things like this. Yes, he wanted to move into a new market segment, and his board had demanded it, but he needed to get his personal life in order first.

"Malcolm—sorry, mate, but I've got to go to Gail. This entire thing is a mess, and I can't leave her alone."

"Hell, boy, I think you might have really changed for this woman. We can talk later," Malcolm said, hanging up the phone.

Russell walked out of his office. "Forget the flowers, Mitsy, I'm going over there myself. Dylan, hold down the fort until I get back. The only one I need to talk to is my attorney. I'm not available to anyone else."

"Yes, sir," Mitsy said.

"I've never been in charge before," Dylan said.

"You've done it a thousand times, just not by yourself. You have my confidence, and I'm sure you can handle anything," Russell said.

He walked out feeling like a new man. This crisis had put in perspective for him what was really important. It wasn't a new market in the hotel industry. It wasn't his reputation as a jet-setter. It was one woman who didn't give a crap about any of that.

One woman who'd made him realize that being with

her was all he really needed, and he hoped he hadn't left it until too late to tell her and convince her that he needed her.

Gail couldn't really be upset or blame anyone else for what had happened this morning. It was just that she'd been focusing on Russell and thinking if she was able to trust him, then she'd get what she wanted from the matchmaking. But all of a sudden, none of that mattered. The truth was that they were just too different, and no amount of dating or assurances from Russell was going to change that.

She'd spent her entire life in PR but had never really known until today that you couldn't change perceptions. Not really. There was always going to be one little thing from the past that would continuously come up and make a mockery of whatever new life you thought you'd built.

Truth was, she just wasn't meant for a husband and a family. She saw that now. She'd have to trust another person—a man—with every part of her being. If she couldn't trust Russell, whom she really did love, then perhaps she just wasn't wired to trust anyone.

Her assistant, J.J., was sitting at his desk when she walked in. "You are on the ticker. I mean big-time. Several of our clients have sent sympathetic emails, and one of them volunteered to punch any photographers who bother you."

"Thanks," Gail said. She felt wounded and wasn't truly sure what to do next. This was out of her realm of what was acceptable.

J.J. stood up and came over to hug her. "What can I do?"

"I don't know," she said, then shook her head and forced herself to stop feeling everything. She'd deal with this.

This was what she'd made a career of. "Actually, a cup of tea would be great, and then I have to make some calls. I need you to deal with anyone new today. I'm not talking to the press, and I have no comment on anything involving Russell Holloway."

J.J. nodded. "I can handle that. In fact, if you want to go home…"

"I can't. They know where I live," Gail said. That hurt a lot because her apartment had been a sanctuary for so long. She'd made it into the perfect little homey place where she went to dream, and now those dreams were sullied.

"Okay. I have a friend with a place on Long Island—I can call him if you'd like," J.J. offered.

"Thanks. Let me see what I can come up with first," Gail said, realizing she didn't want anyone to know where she went. Maybe she'd head to her grandmother's house in Florida, where she wouldn't have good internet reception, and her grandparents would make her fattening food and just love her. And the quiet of the swamp could soothe the feelings of heartbreak that were sweeping through her.

She knew she couldn't blame Russell. From the beginning, she'd tried to keep herself from falling for him. But how could she not, when he had so many of the qualities that she'd always secretly wanted in a man. She knew now that she'd been destined to fall for him from the beginning.

Her iPhone rang, and she glanced down to see Russell's picture on her screen. It was the photo of the two of them she'd had Kat take that day on the yacht. She hit Ignore and turned her chair away from her desk to stare out the window at the building next to hers. It was all brick on this side, and she just stared at that wall, hoping that somehow she'd easily fall out of love with him. That somehow she'd figure out how to bow out of a show that her friend was producing, and that by some weird miracle, she'd be able to continue her business without ever having to talk to anyone again.

She shook her head. She was being melodramatic. But she was just going to allow herself these few minutes of being a little down, and then she'd figure out a plan.

She pulled out her Clairefontaine notebook and ran her hand over the smooth paper. She liked the blank page, because she knew she had infinite possibilities of where her plan could take her. She picked up her fountain pen and decided to treat herself as she would a new client.

She'd advise her client to get out of the spotlight. So she jotted that down. She'd advise her client to try to ensure she was never in that situation again. She put that down next, and then couldn't help but add get rid of the negative influence. That got a frowny face next to it.

She wasn't sure she wanted to get rid of Russell.

She closed her eyes and remembered this morning when she'd realized that she loved him. Just because she'd only now acknowledged the feelings didn't mean they weren't strong and very real. God, she wasn't sure she was going to be able to get over him.

A part of her didn't want to. She wanted to have Russell in her memory—no she didn't. She wanted him in her life. She wanted him to be the guy she'd come to know, and not a man who was ruled by past girlfriends and media crises.

She drew a line across the page and started on a different plan. A plan that would fix Russell's troubled past once and for all. A plan that would give her what she wanted from him.

She wasn't sure where to start, but the ex-girlfriend seemed the best place. She wondered how much of this was maliciousness and how much of it was simply a broken heart. If she was honest, she had no idea what type of person Penny Thomson was. It was funny to her that someone she'd never met could have so much influence over her own life.

She'd go and visit Penny, she thought. But before she could even do a Google search for her address, her office door opened and Russell stood there.

Russell walked into Gail's office. He had made her a promise, back in the beginning when they'd met, that he was in this relationship to win. And he wanted them both to be winners. He wanted to have her by his side when he faced down trouble from his past or triumphs in the future.

Being on the phone with Malcolm had solidified everything for him. He wanted this woman, not just in his bed and in his arms at night, but also in his life. Episodes like this morning's wouldn't have happened if he hadn't been hesitating to make her his, really make her his.

"What are you doing here?" she demanded.

"We kind of weren't done talking earlier," he said.

"I was. There isn't anything else to really say," she said.

"There's a lot more. You didn't give me a chance to tell you how foolish I thought you were being to run away."

She tipped her head to the side and shook it. "I seem to recall you mentioning that."

"I did, didn't I? But that wasn't what I really meant."

"What did you mean?"

He stepped into her office and closed the door behind him. He took a deep breath and realized that this was the most vulnerable he'd been since his parents had been killed in that fiery car crash.

"I don't want you to walk away from me," he said. "I can't live without you."

"You can't live without me, or you can't grow your business without me?" she asked.

"I couldn't care less about my business right now. I cut Malcolm off and told him I had to make things right with you before I could even consider his issues with my reputation."

"But you talked to him?"

"Don't. Stop trying to twist everything around so I'm the bad guy. I'm not," he said, and as his focus narrowed to just Gail, he knew what he had to do. What he had to say. And that knowledge only came with the soul-deep certainty that she was the woman he'd been waiting for his entire life.

"I love you," he said. The words just came out without any real planning.

Her eyes widened and she shook her head again. "You don't. Just a few hours ago—"

"A few hours ago I was trying to figure out how to spend more time with you. For the first time in my adult life, getting to the office was the last thing I wanted to do. I don't care about new deals and making more money if I don't have you by my side. You make it all worthwhile."

"I do?" she asked.

"Yes, you do," he said, walking around her desk and spinning her chair to face him. He drew her to her feet and into his arms.

"I don't know…. I'm afraid to believe it. Just this morning I realized how much you meant to me…. I love you, too, Russell."

He kissed her with all the passion and determination in him. He'd been so afraid that his inexperience with love would make him say or do the wrong thing. But this was Gail, and he was coming to realize that he knew her best.

She wrapped her arms around his waist and rested her head against his chest. "I've been busy thinking of what I needed to do. I was going to fix your problem with Penny."

Russell lifted her up and sat down in her chair, then settled her on his lap. "Making a list?"

"Of course, that's the way I operate. I did just sit here and feel sorry for myself for a little bit. But then I figured I had to do something or I'd go nuts," she said.

He pulled the pad of paper toward him and saw her first list. "I'm sorry."

"Sorry?" she asked, looking up.

"Yes, I haven't been completely honest with you," he said.

He saw all the color leave her face and knew that he hadn't come close to clearing all the hurdles he had to convince Gail that he was her Mr. Right.

"What else could there possibly be?" she asked.

And he tried to find the words. Well, of course, the actual words were easy, but he tried to think of a way to say them. A way to tell her that if she stayed with him she'd never have her dream family. But he couldn't skirt the truth any longer. He couldn't pretend to be something he wasn't. And if he'd learned anything from the entire fiasco with Penny, it was that secrets could definitely hurt his future.

"I'm sterile," he said, opting for simplicity. There really wasn't any other choice.

"Pardon?" she asked.

But he knew she'd heard him. She put one hand to her throat and then leaned her head forward.

"I know you want a family—"

"It's why I went to a matchmaker. My body is on a short clock. It won't be long before I won't be able to conceive.... Maybe fate is trying to tell me something."

"Adopt?" he said, throwing out the option he'd considered.

She gave him a sad sort of smile. "I think you might be

right. I can't fall out of love with you, Russell. God knows I've been trying to make that happen since I first realized you weren't the shallow playboy you seemed to be."

"Really?" he asked, afraid to believe it. "I know you can do better than me, but I promise you'll never find a man who loves you more."

She was so close that he could see the pretty colored rings of her iris and realized that her eyes weren't just brown, but had a lot of gold in them, too. He squeezed her closer, thankful that he'd found her. That the matchmaker had the good sense to listen, not only to what he'd said he wanted, but to truly understand what Russell had needed.

"And I'm sorry for this morning," he said.

"How could you have avoided that?" she asked.

"I should have taken you to my place, where I could have protected you better. We would have used the underground parking garage."

She shook her head. "They would have been waiting there. We can't put off the inevitable. I think you need to talk to Penny."

"I've already sent my attorneys to deal with her, and I can promise you that she won't be bothering us anymore. I'm moving on to a new life with you, Gail. And the problems of the past are going to stay there."

"Are you sure you want that?" she asked. "I'm never going to want to party every night. You've only had a glimpse of what I'm really like."

"We will take our time and get to know each other better. But I already know the most important thing of all."

"And that is…?"

"That I love you and you love me. Everything else will fall into place."

"Promise?" she asked.

He looked into her deep chocolate eyes and kissed her

for a long moment before lifting his head. "I promise. Do you believe me?"

She put her arms around his neck and leaned in close to whisper in his ear. "You are the only one who I would believe."

Russell laughed and hugged her even closer to him. Thankfully, he'd found the one woman in the world who could tame his bad reputation and claim his wild heart.

Epilogue

The last date for *Sexy and Single* arrived, and Gail was a little sad to know that it was ending. She and Russell were living together and working to figure out their future. Russell had closed the deal with Malcolm, who had been impressed when Russell had hung up on him and put his personal life in front of business.

Gail was impressed, too. She knew that Russell would always be dedicated to his business, but it was nice to know that when it mattered he put her first.

Penny had come clean about using Russell to try to manipulate the father of her baby into marrying her. But once she'd stopped trying so desperately to find a man to marry, she had realized she would be fine on her own. She was giddy with the anticipation of having her baby, and Gail was a bit jealous of the other woman, who had come to her house to apologize in person for being such a witch—Penny's words, not Gail's.

It was almost time for the date to begin. Gail went into the confessional after her hair and makeup were done and turned on the camera.

"This is my last date with Russell, and though it didn't go as I'd expected, I couldn't be happier with the results. Matchmaking might not be right for everyone," she said. "But it was for me."

She turned off the camera and was led down the hall to the same exhibit hall where they'd had their first meeting. Just reflecting back on it made her smile. She'd been so sure that the Kiwi playboy was Mr. Wrong then. But Russell had proved to be so much more than just a fictional made-up guy could ever have been.

She was directed to sit at the table set for dinner. There was a champagne stand next to the table with a bottle chilling in the ice. She glanced around the room and saw Willow, who waved at her, and the rest of the camera crew, but Russell wasn't here yet.

Then he entered wearing a white dinner jacket and black pants. His smile was a thousand watts when their eyes met, and he walked straight over to her.

"Action," Willow called.

Gail admitted to herself that the camera was one thing she wouldn't miss. Still, she smiled up at Russell as he walked to the table, and he arched one eyebrow at her. "I never thought that we'd get to this."

"Me either," she said, unable to control the joy that was bubbling up inside her. "I thought you were going to end my dreams for finding a husband."

"I guess that means I won," he said with a cocky grin.

"You might think so, but I believe we are both winners," she said.

"Not yet," he replied, getting down on one knee next to her chair.

He took her hand in his and dropped a kiss on the back of it.

"Gail Little, will you do me the honor of being my wife?" he asked.

"Yes!" she answered, wrapping her arms around his shoulders to hug him. He grabbed her around the waist and lifted her out of the chair, hugging her tightly. She tipped her head and he kissed her. In that embrace she felt all of her hopes for the future and all of his love tied together.

Slowly Russell lowered her to her feet and pulled a box from his pocket. He took a ring with a large marquise-cut diamond from the box and put it on her finger.

"I hate to admit it, but the matchmaker really knew her stuff when it came to you and me," Russell said.

"I agree."

They sat down to eat dinner and Gail didn't let go of Russell's hand the entire time. When Willow finally called cut and production wrapped, Gail breathed a sigh of relief. Doing a TV show wasn't her thing.

"You look relieved," Willow said, coming up to her after the microphone had been removed. Russell was a few feet away having the same thing done to him.

"I am. It's not that I regret doing this, because I wouldn't have met Russell without it, but I am so glad it's over," Gail said.

"I can tell. Thanks," Willow said.

"For what?" Gail asked her friend.

"For letting me take your matchmaking idea and turn it into a TV show."

"Did I have a choice?" Gail asked with a cheeky grin. She couldn't help smiling, because she was simply happy with her life.

"No," Willow said with a laugh. "I never thought it would really work. I mean I've been surprised by things before, but a matchmaker? I didn't think you and Russell were suited at all."

Gail agreed. "Russell says that we fill in the missing pieces in each other."

"Aw, isn't that sweet. You complete each other," Nichole said with a tinge of sarcasm as she joined them.

"We do. I don't care if it sounds a bit hokey."

Nichole nodded. "I agree. That was just jealousy on my part."

"Jealousy! From you? The hottest dater in the tristate area?" Gail asked. "Trouble in noncommittal paradise?"

"No," Nichole said. "Just envy. I sometimes wish I had a permanent guy in my life."

Six months ago Gail would have felt the same, but today luckily she had found a man who would make her happy for the rest of her life. That didn't mean that the relationship with Russell wasn't without its ups and downs.

Russell waved at her from across the room and Gail smiled at him.

"Earth to Gail," Nichole said, waving her hand in front of Gail's face.

"I'm here. I was just…"

"Daydreaming about your fiancé," Willow said. "I'm so happy for you."

"Me, too," Gail said.

Russell walked over to her and the other women moved off. But Gail didn't pay any attention to them. "What were you talking about?"

"You," she said.

"Good. I was talking about you. I called my mates back home and told them that I had finally found a girl to love."

"You told them that?"

"You betcha. I am not afraid to tell the world how I feel

about you, beautiful. You've given me more happiness than I'm sure I deserve."

She smiled up at him. "You've done the same for me."

* * * * *

THE PRODIGAL COWBOY

KATHLEEN EAGLE

For All My Relatives

Chapter One

"Looks like he ain't coming."

Bella Primeaux glanced up from the news report on her smartphone display. The cowboy claiming the next bar stool was half-shot and full-ugly. She didn't know him, wasn't interested in knowing him, and there was no point in sparing him more than a glance. She pressed her elbows against the bar and swiveled two inches to the right, turning a cold left shoulder.

"What's that you're drinkin'?"

Bella glanced right. Another one was moving in. She was book-ended by Crude and

Rude. Experience told her that if they got no satisfaction, their type would go away.

"What does that look like to you, Loop?" the one on the right asked the one on the left. "Seven and seven?"

Loop? Bella swallowed the urge to laugh. She'd interviewed a rodeo cowboy named Rope who'd given a shout out to his brother Cash and his friend Spur. But *Loop?*

"Looks like tea." Loop was perceptive.

"Is that some of that Long Island iced tea? You wanna try some, Loop?" Rude signaled the bartender. "Bring us three more of these."

"Lemme try hers first," Loop said as he reached for Bella's glass from the left.

She slipped her phone into the woolen sack that hung over her shoulder on a braided cord. He could have her drink. She was leaving anyway.

"Is it whiskey and tea?" Loop sniffed, slurped and slammed the glass on the bar. "It's just tea."

"And it's yours now, Loopy," said a new-comer to the growing group.

Bella turned to her left, and her glance traveled quickly over the glass in the one called Loopy's grubby hand, past the full-ugly face to a faintly familiar one that loomed in the shadows above Loopy's cowboy hat. Familiar, fine looking, and frankly unsettling. It had been years since she'd seen the man, but he wore the years as well as his own straw cowboy hat. Surprising, considering where he'd spent the last couple of those years. His hat was battered, and his jeans and T-shirt had seen better days, but he made them look camera ready. She'd lost what little touch she'd had with high school friends, and Ethan Wolf Track was no exception, but she'd never quite shaken her interest in what he was up to. Generally it was no good.

But his smile was as disarming as ever.

"Sorry I'm late, Bella."

Loopy peeked over his shoulder and then turned back to Bella with a whole new brand of interest in his glazed eyes. "Why didn't you just say you were with Ethan Wolf Track? Hell, man, we were just—"

"Long Island iced tea all around. Loopy's buying." Ethan's hand appeared on Loopy's shoulder. "Right, man?"

"It's just tea. There's no whiskey," Loop said.

"Long Island iced tea isn't made with whiskey or tea." Ethan jiggled his hand rest. "You been living under a rock, Loopy?"

"Same as you."

"Nah, look at the difference." Ethan laid his hand on the bar beside Loopy's. "You need to get yourself some sun, boy."

Bella glanced between the two faces. The "boy" couldn't have been any younger than the man, but he didn't take exception. Ethan was still *the man*. The memory of a younger but no less commanding Ethan letting the boys know who was boss flashed through her mind.

"Iced tea for two," the bartender announced, landing the glasses on the bar with a thunk. "As for the other two, you want another beer? It's the same price as tea."

"No beer for these horses, Willie," Ethan said as he claimed both glasses. "Tricky, ain't it, Loopy? Pullin' the wagon and riding it, too?"

"You got your parole officer, I got mine. Far as I'm concerned, beer don't count," Loopy grumbled. "And it's *Toby*. That's a Toby Keith song, 'Beer For My Horses.'"

"Not without Willie," Ethan said as he glanced at Bella and gave a nod toward a corner booth. "Not on my wagon."

Bella was off the bar stool, but she wasn't looking for a booth, and the man and his boys could do what they pleased with their wagon. She wouldn't be vying for a parking spot at the Hitching Post. She'd already crossed the place off her list of possible sites for her report on Rapid City's hottest singles' hangouts.

"Would you rather go someplace else?" Ethan asked her quietly.

She looked up, taken by the change in his tone. He was speaking for her benefit alone, and he sounded sincere, even hopeful. Tension drained from her shoulders as she shook her head. "We can catch up right here."

As she neared the high-backed booth, she saw a big book lying open on the far side of the table beside a cup half-filled with black coffee. She slid into the near side, her back to the room.

"Looks like he ain't comin'," she drawled as she checked her watch.

"Maybe he's still working on his story." He set his glass on the table and dropped his hand over the book, which he closed, swept off the table and deposited on the seat beside him in one quick motion. His eyes danced. "Better be a good one, huh?"

She shrugged, subtly acknowledging that he was playing along. "You were here all along. All I saw was the hat."

"It serves many purposes." He pulled down on the brim, shadowing all but the generous lips and their slight smile.

"I'm surprised you remember me."

"I watch TV."

"So...you don't actually *remember* me."

"Really took me back when I saw you sitting on that bar stool. You sat in front of me in—what class was it? English?"

"History."

"History. Don't remember any names or dates, but I never forget a woman's back. You have a small—" he hooked his hand over his shoulder and touched a spot near the base of his neck "—beauty mark right here."

"*Beauty* mark?" She laughed. "It's called a mole."

"Not in my book."

"Which book is that?" She wondered about the one he was sharing his seat with.

"History. My favorite class. Liked it so much, I took it twice." He dropped his hand to the seat as he leaned back, grinning. She imagined him patting that book as though he wanted to keep a pet quiet. "You were there the second time around."

"No wonder you had all the answers. You'd already heard the questions."

"I didn't hear anything the first time." He leaned closer, getting into the reminiscence. "We did a project together. Remember?"

"I wasn't going to mention it. You still owe me."

"I do?"

"I bought all the materials. Actually, I did all the work. You were going to come to my house the night before it was due, but you never showed up."

"Forgot about that part." He arched an eyebrow and cast a pointed glance at her watch. "How do you keep getting mixed up with guys like that?"

"I'm not meeting anyone," she confessed.

"Then what the hell are you doing here?" He pulled a dramatic grimace as he glanced past her.

She shrugged. "Checking the place out."

"For what? This ain't no singles' bar, woman. This is a hole in the wall."

"Maybe I'm not single. Maybe I'm here doing my job." She gave herself a second to rein in her rising tone. "And maybe I didn't need to be rescued."

"In the old days, you wouldn't've said *maybe*. Once you got to talkin', you were as sure and self-determined as any girl I ever met." He gave her the no-bull eye. "I don't know about the rest, but you're not married."

"That doesn't mean I'm single."

"I think it does." He took a drink of his tea, then looked at her again. "So how much do I owe you for labor and materials?"

"Since it was a required class, I think you owe me your diploma."

"I showed up for the report. I had all the facts and figures. Hell, we got an A, didn't we? Can't do any better than that." He shook his head. "We'll have to come up with something else. You sure don't need my diploma."

"And you sure have a better memory than you first let on." She gave a tight smile. "I guess we can call it even. Being Ethan Wolf Track's history project partner raised my lowly underclass social status a notch."

"What were you, a sophomore?"

She shook her head.

"Freshman?"

She smiled and nodded.

"How did you get into that class as a freshman, for God's sake?"

"I took a test. Actually, I took several. They had a hard time coming up with a schedule for me." She lifted one shoulder. He had his muscles, she had her brain. "And you were a senior and the captain of everything."

"You were smart. It didn't take a test to figure that out. You were goin' places." He glanced around the room. "Better places than this."

"I go where the story is. Or where we think it might be." She tested out a coy look as she sipped her tea. "Stay tuned."

"Do me a favor. Give me a heads-up if this place is gonna be raided. I try to stay out of trouble these days."

"By doing what?"

"I guess you could say I'm a cowboy."

"Like your brother?"

"Not a rodeo cowboy like Trace. A working cowboy. A ranch hand. I work for the Square One Ranch."

She had no idea where that was, but he seemed to think the name of the place spoke for itself, so she made her usual mental note. *Find out. It could lead to something.*

"So you're one of a dying breed," she said. "I did a story on a guy who calls himself a cowboy for hire. He says he has more work than he can handle. Do you ride a horse or an ATV?"

"What's an ATV?"

"All terrain…" She caught the smile in his eyes. "You know, vehicle."

"Those kid toys? Couldn't call myself a cowboy if I rode one of those things. Hell, I was raised by Logan Wolf Track."

"He trains horses, doesn't he?"

"He does, and so do I. I'm training a mustang right now. Entered up in a contest." He winked at her. "Gonna win it, too."

Déjà vu on the Wolf Track wink. She'd been on the receiving end of one or two of those babies years back, and the experience had given her the same tummy tickle that was *not* going to get a smile out of her now.

"You're talking about the competition they're running at the new Wild Horse Sanctuary near Sinte?"

"The wild horse program is pretty new, but the Double D Ranch has been there forever," he reminded her. "I hired on for a couple of summers when I was a kid, back when old man Drexler was running it. Now it's his daughters."

"I know. I've been reading up on the place." She took a breath, a moment's pause. They'd been playing a circuitous game, and she'd just landed at the foot of a ladder. One person's connections could be another person's rungs. They could be fragile, but as a journalist, she was weightless. Most sources had no idea she'd gotten anything from them.

But Ethan Wolf Track wasn't most sources. Sure, he'd been a source of adolescent anxiety and disappointment, but hadn't that been his job back then? It was up to the captain of everything to teach the princess of nothing not to expect too much. Bella had always been a quick study.

Still, he owed her.

"I think it's wonderful, the way the Drexlers have worked out a deal with the Tribe to set aside some of that remote reservation land for more sanctuary."

The Tribe being her people and Ethan's adoptive father's people. Logan Wolf Track was a Lakota Sioux Tribal councilman. Ethan looked Indian, too, but she'd never asked him about his background. Everyone knew that his mother had left Logan to raise her two boys, whom he'd legally adopted—just up and left and never came back—but nobody asked too many questions. It wasn't their way. Ethan and his older brother, Trace, were Wolf Tracks.

"Are you working on a news story?" he asked.

"I've been digging around." She folded her hands around her glass and studied the two shrinking chunks of ice. "There's definitely a story there—one that goes back a ways—but I'm looking for the details on my own. It's not the kind of assignment I'm likely to get from KOZY-TV."

"Why not? They don't like mustangs?"

"They're fine with mustangs. They don't like digging around."

"Isn't that how you come up with news? Dirt sells."

"But sleeping dogs don't bite, and the suits at the station—such as they are here in good ol' Rapid City, South Dakota, you know, not exactly coat and tie—they don't want to get their business-casual clothes torn." She ignored his quizzical look. "Let's just say they don't pay me to dig." She smiled. "But it's fun, isn't it? You dig?"

He chuckled. "Postholes, yeah."

"When you were hiring out as a kid, did you ever work for Dan Tutan?" The change in his eyes—quizzical to cold—was barely discernible, but it was there. "You know, the Drexlers' neighbor."

Oh, yeah. He knew.

But he shook his head. *Interesting.*

"There's a story there," she said with a smile. "Big-time rivalry. Maybe some political back-scratching going on that could affect Indian Country. And that's where I come in. Like I said, strictly on my own." Was he ready for the kicker? Timing the kicker was Bella's journalistic specialty. "Tutan wants the leases that went to the Double D for the sanctuary, and he's got a friend in D.C.— Senator Perry Garth."

He stared at her. Or *through* her.

Perfect timing.

"South Dakota's beloved Senator Garth. Tutan and Garth go way back. And Garth is on the Indian Affairs Committee, as well as the Subcommittee on Public Lands and Forests."

"Politics." He shook his head. "You just cruised past my point of interest. My story's in the training competition. My interest is in the horses." He drank half of what was left in his glass in one deep pull.

"I just thought…because Logan is on the Tribal Council…"

"That's *his* story." He set the glass down and smiled as he slid to the end of the booth. "You wanna talk politics, you're followin' the wrong Wolf Track." He glanced toward the bar and its deserted stools. Remote control in hand, the bearded bartender was surfing channels on the screen above the Bud Light sign. "Looks like your fans have moved on."

"I doubt that pair watches much news. They know *you,* though."

"Yeah. You need a name to drop in low places, you're welcome to use mine." He gave her his signature wink again. Damn if it didn't give her the same deep-down shiver. "You decide to do a story on wild horses, look me up."

And *damn* if he didn't walk out first, taking the book she hadn't been able to identify.

Ethan sat behind the steering wheel of his pickup, parked in the shadows across the street from what had once been the Hitching Post. The neon had given up the ghost on the letter *H,* so it was now the *itching Post.* The sign had called out to him the first time he'd seen it. He'd finally had his freedom back—most of it, anyway—and it had some weight to it. He was itching to do something different with his life, but damned if he knew what. So he'd answered the blinking call of the itching Post. He'd claimed a bar stool, wet his whistle after a long dry spell and gotten himself wasted. *Stupid* drunk.

The next morning he'd looked at himself in the mirror and scratched his face. He'd scratched his neck, his shoulder, dug all his fingers into his hair, looked in the mirror again and nearly busted a gut laughing.

The sign said itching post, you idiot. Not scratching post.

If he'd learned one thing from spending two years behind bars, it was that the word *freedom* pretty much summed up everything a man had to lose. Freedom was living. Two years without it and you had a foot in the grave. Deadwood. Reviving that foot meant getting a leg up somehow. He hadn't been quite ready for South Dakota. He still had some growing up to do.

He'd gone to Colorado—as good a place as any that wasn't South Dakota—and taken up his parole officer's suggestion that he continue on the path he'd taken with the Wild Horse Inmate Program. Ethan had answered correctly—*yeah, I like that idea*—but mentally he'd added that the prison program couldn't claim credit for anything except maybe backing him into the right corner, the one that gave him a clear view of where he'd

come from and where he might go. He'd spent
most of his life within earshot of a horse barn,
which might have been why he'd taken horses
for granted, along with every other promising path he could have taken instead of the
one that had cut off his slack.

Before the horses—before Logan Wolf
Track—his life was hazy. He'd been Trace's
little brother. They'd had a mother, but she
was part of the haze. Even after she'd married
Logan, her part of the family equation was
hazy. *Muddy,* more like. He remembered the
sound of her voice and the way she'd drawn
out certain words so that South Dakotans
looked at each other and shrugged. An accent, they'd called it, but to him it was the
sound that settled an unsettled mind. *Mom's
here.* He couldn't picture her face, but he still
felt an odd sense of relief when he heard her
voice, even though it was only in his head. He
was up to his neck in hot water, hot *muddy*
water, shrouded in early-morning haze, but
he wasn't alone. He could hear her. She hadn't
gone away.

And neither had that stupid kid. God, how
he hated that quivering, shivering little boy
who still clung to the soft tissue of his in-
nards. He was pitiful, that kid. He had to get

tough or get dead, that kid, and he'd damn sure better not show his face. Keeping that kid quiet had been a full-time job. Ethan needed all the help he could get, and he'd assigned roles. Whether they knew it or not, every person, place or thing within spitting distance had a part to play, and he'd taken it all for granted.

Including the friendship he might have had with the woman who'd just stepped into the spotlight under the itching Post sign. Of course he remembered her. Straight-A student with a straight body and a straightforward approach. She would go places and do things, and she wasn't letting anyone get in her way. Not that his charm was lost on her, or that he wouldn't pass up the chance to use that to his advantage, but there was an air of dignity about her that gave her some protection from guys like him.

But not from guys who had no use for dignity.

Tom "Loopy" Lupien and his forgettable sidekick were back in play, following Bella out the door. Two colorless figures casting long shadows across the dimly lit sidewalk. He'd thought they were gone. Must have been hiding out in the can.

"Hey, did the Wolf make tracks?" one of them called after her.

"You need a ride?" the other asked. In this light it was hard to tell one from the other, but it didn't matter. Any friend of Loopy's had been scraped from the mold underneath the empty barrel.

A remote-control lock chirped, headlights flashed, car door opened and shut, engine roared. Bella was safe. Ethan smiled to himself. No-nonsense Bella.

No sooner had she turned onto the street when another engine fired up. An old Ford pickup—even older than Ethan's rattletrap Chevy—emerged from the lot behind the building and followed her car.

Damn. Loopy wouldn't be able to bring any prey down himself. He was a scavenger. The other one must've been driving. Between the two of them, they could do some damage.

Ethan joined the parade. When they reached a one-way residential street, Bella parked her little white Honda on the curb near the front entrance to a modest two-story apartment building. Ethan peeled away from Loopy's tailgate, pulled over to the opposite curb, and watched Loopy and his pal roll past Bella's parked car. They'd taken the hint. Ethan chuckled. *My job here is done.*

Bella hopped out of her car, slammed the door and turned toward Ethan's pickup, gripping some kind of bag made out of blanket material with a string handle—was it a purse, or a grocery sack?—under her arm.

"Hey! I carry a .38 Smith & Wesson, and I know how to use it!" she shouted across the street. "So whatever you're thinking, think again."

Her face was hidden in the shadows, but her hands were steady, her shoulders squared and her long black hair shone blue-white under the streetlight. He didn't know who she thought she was talking to, but she wasn't bluffing.

And he loved it.

He was thinking, *I've got your back.* Not that she needed him, but he was there, just in case.

Hell of a woman, he told himself as he watched her stand her ground. She was on TV, but that was just a job. It wasn't her life. Pretty cool. Cool enough to get the message without some big explanation to go with it. Whatever her interest was in Senator Perry Garth—the man who'd helped put Ethan away for two years—it was of no interest to *him*. Neither was any rivalry between neighbors, nor tribal politics. Ethan was looking for a new life. He wanted the kind of freedom Bella had—the opportunity to chart her own course, to do a job and then some, and that some could be more than what somebody else was willing to pay for.

The last time he'd seen her, she'd been a sweet young girl with a big brain. He'd assigned her brain a role, but the girl was sweet and young, and she'd had that straight body and those big ideas. Sure, she'd had the hots for him, but back then she'd been more appealing walking away from him in a huff than looking up at him all wide-eyed and innocent. She'd had some growing up to do.

She turned and mounted the steps to the front door.

I've still got your back, Bella, but I can appreciate your front now, too. Turn around. Let me see those pretty eyes.

No such luck. She pushed the door open and disappeared.

Ethan grinned as he shifted out of neutral. Yes, sir, little Bella Primeaux had grown up just fine.

Chapter Two

The tiny reservation town of Sinte, South Dakota, hadn't changed much, but the house Bella had grown up in looked different. In only five years weeds had taken over Ladonna Primeaux's flower beds. A swing set occupied what had been the vegetable garden, and an old Jeep had muscled in on the shrub roses that still more or less lined the driveway. Mom had fussed over that yard the way some women gravitated toward babies. With her gone, it looked like most of the other yards in the neighborhood—a cottonwood tree or two, a bunch of kids' toys, maybe a deck and some struggling grass.

Bella could hear her mother now. *Don't ever let your yard go, Bella. All it takes is a little interest. People who take an interest, those are the interesting people. They're the ones you always want to talk to.*

Ladonna Primeaux was an interesting person. Everyone thought so. Bella had been certain of it. Her mother was as knowledgeable as she was opinionated, which was fine by Bella. Nothing wrong with having opinions if you had the knowledge to back them up. Mom was also dependable, practical and psychic. It wasn't always easy being the only child of a woman who was constantly one step ahead of the one Bella was about to take. But she'd followed the deep imprints of her mother's footsteps until there were no more.

The home they'd shared wasn't there anymore, and the house alone gave no comfort. No point in lingering, hoping for more than memories. Bella didn't need guidance or approval anymore—she knew who she was and where she was going—but with her mother's death she'd been cut off at the roots. She was growing as a journalist, but every time she looked at her résumé, she felt like a fraud. Maybe not on the outside—she had the look, totally—but deep down she was missing something.

Her KOZY-TV News assignments rarely touched on Indian issues, so she'd started blogging as Warrior Woman, and her site was gaining followers. But the comments from people who claimed to be Native were few and far between. Maybe they were out there but just weren't saying so. Or maybe they weren't even there. Maybe what was missing was new growth. Her interest in Lakota issues was real, but what about Lakota life? What about the home she'd left as quickly as she could and the mother who'd encouraged her daughter to fly while she'd remained in the nest? What about the remnants of those severed roots? Deep down they were still there, like shorn whiskers creating an itch that needed attention.

Guess what, Bella, you're not a kid anymore. You need to touch up your roots or grow some new ones.

A stop sign and two right-hand turns took her to Agency Avenue. The old Bureau of Indian Affairs building with its spacious offices had been turned over to the Tribal government, and the BIA had moved into the building once occupied by the Tribe. Sign of the times, Bella thought as she took in all the changes. There were more windows, fewer walls, and the colors of the four directions— red, white, black and yellow—had replaced BIA green and tan. There were new names on the directory. Indian names. But there were no office numbers, and so she asked the receptionist whether Councilman Logan Wolf Track was in the house. *He's around here somewhere* was the old familiar answer. Monday-through-Friday casual.

"Of course I remember you." Logan greeted her with a handshake when he came out to greet her. He was lankier than his son but not as tall, not quite as handsome. "Full scholarship to a fine college on the East Coast, right?"

"University of California at Berkley."

"I meant West Coast." He smiled easily. "I remembered the important stuff. Full scholarship, terrific college and Bella Primeaux. Your mother was so proud of you we could hardly stand it."

She lifted one shoulder. "Sorry about that."

"Hey, just kidding. We're all proud of you." He glanced through the plate glass that separated the sparsely furnished lounge from a small parking lot. "And we sure miss your mother. She was something else, wasn't she?" He turned back to Bella, assuring her with a nod. "In a good way."

"She was the best nurse Indian Health ever had."

"She sure was."

"She could have been a doctor." It was something she'd always thought, but she couldn't remember saying it out loud before, giving due credit, open admiration. She'd felt it, but she hadn't said it within range of her mother's ear. What kind of range did Ladonna Primeaux's hearing have now?

"She was a damn good nurse."

"Yes, she was." *But she could have been a doctor.* She'd said so herself, many times. What she'd never said was that she'd had a child to feed. "I ran into Ethan the other night."

"Where?"

"In a bar," Bella said, an answer that clearly surprised Logan. "Rapid City. I live there now."

"I watch you all the time on TV." He lifted one shoulder. "Well, not every day, but whenever I watch the news."

She smiled. It was good to be watched and even better to be acknowledged. She owed him something in return. "Ethan's following in your footsteps."

"How's that?"

"Training horses. He mentioned the wild horse training competition. He says he's going to win the big prize."

"I hope he does. Help him make a fresh start. Hope he's not spending too much time in the bars." He glanced away. "I haven't seen much of Ethan since, uh…"

"Since he went to prison?"

"He told you about that?"

"He didn't have to," she said quietly.

Logan gave a mirthless chuckle. "Made the news all the way out to California, did it?"

"The news is what the media makes it, and I'm part of the media now. I know these things." She smiled. "All we talked about was high school and what we're doing these days. He gives you credit for raising him to be a cowboy."

"A cowboy? That's down to his older brother, Trace. Although outside the rodeo, I'd say Ethan's the better hand when he's of a mind to be. They're both good, mind you, but Trace goes in for a wild ride, and Ethan… well, he's wild enough on his own."

"He was drinking iced tea."

"In a *bar*?" Apparently even more surprising. Bella nodded. "Straight iced tea."

"I saw him at the Double D earlier this summer," Logan recalled. "First time in two years. Said he was entering the training competition. Said he was working for a rehab program."

"He told me he was a ranch hand. Square One Ranch. Something like that."

"Square One?" His tone put the news on par with tea in a bar. "That's a program for kids in trouble. Hell, that's right outside Rapid City. I didn't know he was living that close by. He didn't, uh…" Logan's wan smile spoke of a father's discomfort with being the last to know. "He didn't say."

"I thought it was a cattle ranch. That's interesting." What was left out was always more interesting than what was said. Bella added it to her mental file marked *Ethan*. Also interesting was the way she'd filed him under his first name.

Maybe because it was an old file. She was just realizing how far back it went and how carefully she'd kept it up. No surprise that he'd joined the army after he graduated. No surprise that he'd been gone awhile and come back home. No word of his military experiences, which was also no surprise. The return to Indian Country was never questioned. But he hadn't stayed around long, and the next Ethan Wolf Track news flash had been surprising. *Dirt sells,* he'd said, and if she'd been a little further along in her career, she might have tried to track him down. Not because he was in trouble—no surprise there, either. Not because the story involved a woman—most of Ethan's stories undoubtedly involved women. But there was an odd political connection.

Ethan Wolf Track and a senator's daughter? Now that was interesting. And Bella would have bet her new mobile phone that what was left out was far more interesting than what was reported.

"He's pretty sensitive about Senator Garth, isn't he?" she asked.

"Couldn't say." Staring out the window at a young couple getting into a pickup with a washing machine in the bed, Logan didn't blink. No sensitivity there. "Ethan spent two years in prison for taking Garth's car. His daughter was the one who took it, but she wouldn't stand up for him. I'd say he was sensitive about *her,* but I'd just be guessing." He turned to give Bella a what're-you-gonna-do look. "Too damn stubborn for his own good."

"He said he worked over at the Double D when he was a kid."

"Couple of summers, yeah. Like I say, Ethan's a good worker. I'll bet he's real good with those kids in the Square One program."

Bella wondered why Logan seemed so clueless about his son. If she were still alive, Ladonna Primeaux wouldn't be betting or guessing, she would be asking. On the other hand, Bella herself wasn't exactly being subtle about fishing for clues about the man's family, and he was trusting her with what few he had.

A twinge of guilt pushed her to switch tracks.

"The Double D took some grazing land away from a neighboring rancher, didn't they? I know some of it was public land, but wasn't there a Tribal lease, too?"

"Yep." Logan smiled. He liked this topic. "We decided the Wild Horse Sanctuary took precedence. The Lakota are horse people."

"But Senator Garth has a longstanding friendship with Dan Tutan, who is—"

"My wife's father." His smile broadened. "We just got married. Haven't told Ethan yet."

"So, uh…"

"Whose side am I on? The horses' side. So's my wife. I haven't heard any objections from the senator. What's he gonna do? The Tribal Council determines how the land will be used nowadays. It's called self-determination."

"That term is so twentieth century," Bella teased.

"Yeah, well, some of us go back that far."

"All of us do. The whole relocation program and termination of reservations policy in the 1950s, and then the switch to Indian self-determination in the 1970s, seems like it was only yesterday." She smiled. "We studied it in our high school history class. Ethan sat behind me."

He laughed. "Now that must've been interesting."

"It was unsettling." She folded her arms beneath her breasts and held on tight as she glanced away. "What was interesting was twentieth-century American Indian history and how we're supposed to finally have a say over what we do with our lives. And our land." And the fact that Ethan remembered the mole on the back of her shoulder.

Bella shifted her stance, cleared her throat

and her thoughts, and turned back to the Lakota leader. "So you don't think the senator can interfere with the Wild Horse Sanctuary? He sits on a couple of key committees."

"Let him sit."

"I was thinking of doing a story." He gave her a look that that reinforced his suggestion. If the story had to do with Garth, she was wasting her time. She gave a diffident shrug. "Maybe a series on the Tribe's involvement with the Wild Horse Sanctuary."

"Involvement?"

"In a good way," she added hastily.

"Kind of a *feel-good* story about Indians and horses? That always works. Sally'll take all the TV spots she can get. You know Sally Drexler—I mean Sally Night Horse—is the woman behind the whole program. You talk about a white tornado…" He chuckled. "That's from an old TV commercial. White tornado."

"Must've been before my time."

"Mine, too. Even before self-determination, but around here some things are as timeless as Indians on horses. Especially now that you've got YouTube." He grinned. "So I say go for it. If you need me, I'm in."

"Thank you." She smiled. "Actually, it

wouldn't be for KOZY-TV News. My suggestions there fall on deaf ears. They hand me an assignment, and I make it happen. Whether it means anything to anyone…" She glanced away, gave her head a little shake and turned back to a man who was known for having good ears. "That's what I was doing at the bar the other night. I was looking for different types of singles' hangouts. The place is called the Hitching Post. Doesn't that sound like a place to connect?"

"Depends on your idea of hitching, I guess. Never really got the hang of hangin' out. But Ethan…" He shrugged. "I don't know, Bella. If you're asking me about—"

"I'm not," she said quickly. But she *had* asked, and she shouldn't have. "I only meant to say that I'd run into him. You know, just saying."

"Not telling." He smiled indulgently. "Just saying."

"Do you know anything about Square One? Is it a good program?"

"It's pretty new, but they're building a good reputation. We've had some kids placed there through Tribal Court."

"Why don't we go out there and take a

look? You haven't seen much of Ethan lately, and I'm looking for connections."

"I'm not much of a connection, Bella. I don't think Square One qualifies as a singles' hangout, and I don't qualify as a single. My wife's coming home for good pretty soon. The army's letting her go."

"Her choice?"

"Yeah." Again he grinned, but this time it was purely for personal pleasure. "I'm gonna be a father again."

"Congratulations. Wow." Apparently he'd wasted no time. "So how about it? Do you have some time today?"

"I do, but if Ethan's there, I'm not gonna show up uninvited. He only let me visit him once when he was in prison. Took me off his visitors list after that."

"Why would he do that?"

Logan shook his head. "I married his mother, and he took to me right away. After she left, he was different. For a while we thought sure she'd come back. His brother and I did, anyway, but Ethan never asked about her. Never jumped for the phone the way Trace did, never expected any more from her. He kinda became his own little man, you know? He got a little older, he tried to find his father. We didn't have much to go on, so it didn't pan out. Far as I know."

"You helped him?"

"Did what I could. He had a picture and the little bit his mother told him. The guy was part Indian. Don't know where he was from, though. Ethan looks a lot like the guy in the picture. I don't know what would've happened if we'd found him."

"Ethan didn't seem like one to dwell on the past. History didn't interest him all that much."

Logan smiled wistfully. "Don't let him fool you. He's as smart as they come." He punctuated a cocked finger with the cluck of his tongue. "Ethan's your connection to Square One."

Without a GPS Bella would have missed the turnoff to Square One Ranch. The sign stood so low to the ground that the dancing heads of the tall crested wheat grass obscured the small print. *Rebuilding Our Lives From the Ground Up.* The two visible roofs turned out to be a hulking old barn and a spanking-new two-story box. It wasn't until the access road took a dip that she saw the small ranch-style house that had to be a good place to start searching for someone in charge of the operation.

An attractive young blonde opened the front door before Bella mounted the steps. Bella knew the routine. Country dwellers saw visitors coming a mile off. At half a mile they had the vehicle categorized—known or unknown, in-or out-of-state, on target or gone astray. In good weather they met you outside. In bad weather they opened the door just enough to check you out with eyes that challenged your motivation, not to mention your common sense.

But Bella had an advantage. "I've seen you on TV." The woman offered a handshake. "Shelly Jamison."

"Bella—"

"Primeaux, right? You're even prettier in person."

"Thank you. I'm aiming for professional."

"You've hit that target, too, but my observation stands." Shelly tucked her hands into the back pockets of her jeans. "What can I do for you?"

"Show me around and tell me about your program."

"You think we might be newsworthy?"

"I met with a councilman from my reservation. He suggested I come out and take a look."

"Tribal Courts have sent us a few kids since we started the program." The hands came out of the back pockets and the arms were quickly folded up front. "We haven't had any complaints."

"And you still don't." Bella shaded her eyes with one hand so she could offer an un-squinty smile. "Councilman Wolf Track said you were doing a good job here."

"Wolf Track? We've got a Wolf Track on the payroll here." Shelly glanced toward the weathered barn as her shoulders relaxed and dropped a full two inches. "Hell of a good worker."

"Ethan," Bella supplied. "I went to school with him."

"He can't be on the Tribal Council, can he? He hasn't been... I mean, he keeps busy around here, like, 24/7."

"His father's the councilman."

"He never mentioned that. You don't think that's why we get... I mean, we didn't hire Ethan as a favor to any—"

"His father didn't know he was working here. Really, I'm not here to, um, dig up any dirt." Recalling Ethan's words, Bella almost smiled. "KOZY loves a feel-good story, and I thought we might find one here. Ethan has been—"

"I know where he's been." Shelly grabbed a chunk of hair that had strayed from her low ponytail and hooked it behind her unadorned ear. "You tell anyone who asks, Ethan Wolf Track is doing just fine. The boys really look up to him. Tell the truth, he's quickly becoming indispensable around here."

"I'm not here on any kind of assignment. I've heard only good things." Bella followed the direction of Shelly's gaze toward the hulking barn. Noisy swallows darted in and out the tiny doors of the clay row houses tucked under the edge of the gambrel roof. "I'm interested in the wild horse part of your program, and I thought maybe I could take a tour." She lifted her shoulder. "And if Ethan's around, I'd like to say hello."

"Oh, he's around. Dependable as they come, that guy."

Bella smiled. "If anyone asks, I'll relay the message."

"I don't know anything about Ethan's family." Shelly stepped down to ground level, putting them on par, height-wise. "It's just that good help is hard to find when you're paying in hot dogs and beans."

"There must be other rewards," Bella prompted.

"You get to be around wild things. Wild kids, wild horses and what's left of wild country." Shelly moved into the shade of a tall cottonwood, and Bella followed suit. "Wild hearts attract each other."

"How's yours?"

Shelly grinned. "I'm the maypole they all get to dance around. I have to crunch the numbers and find the wherewithal."

"I like that image. This could be a good story, and KOZY isn't the only media outlet I can access." Bella smiled. She didn't mind throwing her TV connection into her pitch. Most people—local people, anyway—were dazzled by it. If they had nothing to hide they eventually opened their doors. Sometimes they couldn't resist even if they *did* have something to hide. Besides, everything she was saying was true. "Do you have time to show me around?"

Of course Shelly did.

She led the way with a "follow me," and they started toward the barn. "The bunkhouse is new." She pointed toward what might have passed for a truncated no-name roadside motel—plain white, no-frills. "Kitchen and commons area downstairs, bunks upstairs. You wanna see inside? Nobody's there now except the cook."

Bella shook her head. "Another time. Who paid for the improvements?"

"We qualified for a government grant and scored some private funding, as well. We get community support, too. People come in and teach whatever skills they have to offer." Shelly glanced over her shoulder. "TV reporting must require all kinds of skills."

"You mean, besides talking to the camera?"

"Are you kidding? You're talking to thousands of people."

"I don't think of it that way," Bella said absently as they rounded the corner of the bunkhouse and headed toward the barn.

"I'd be shaking in my boots and tripping over my tongue," Shelly said.

"You get used to it. The scary part can be trying to get information out of people who don't want to talk or pictures of things they don't want you to see."

"We tell the kids, once you find out what a relief it is to come clean, you'll never want to—" They turned another corner and ran into an old flatbed farm truck with its hood up, one guy standing and another guy squatting next to the front tire, and one pair of boots sticking out from under the orange cab.

"Did you guys run over somebody?" Shelly called out. She glanced back at Bella and nodded toward the two faces now turned their way. "There's your man." She raised her voice. "You've got a visitor, Wolf Track."

"You patted her down, didn't you?" Ethan wiped his hands on a rag as he rose to his feet. "Was she packin'?"

"Packing what?" Shelly asked.

"A .38." Grinning at Bella, he touched the brim of his straw cowboy hat in salutation. "Smith & Wesson, right?"

Bella's eyes widened as she and Shelly approached the truck. "That was you?"

"You saw the pickup that cruised past? That was trouble."

"You followed me?"

"Trouble followed you. I followed *them*." Beneath the bent brim of his hat a smile danced in his dark eyes. "You don't wanna tip your hand out on the street like that, Bella. Some people might find a Smith & Wesson even more tempting than a Bella Primeaux."

She returned a level stare. "Neither one was

there for the taking. As I said, I know how to use it."

"If you really knew how to use it, you wouldn't be giving away your advantage by broadcasting it."

"This sounds like an interesting reunion," Shelly injected, amused. "I'm guessing high school sweethearts."

"No. Never." Bella laughed. "I was a lowly underclassman when Ethan was the cock of the walk."

"The *what?*" Ethan said.

"You were the captain of everything except the cheerleading squad."

"And our little two-man history team." He winked at her, and she wondered whether the gesture had become pure reflex. "I dropped the ball on that one. It was your leadership that got us on the A list."

"Well played, captain. Credit your team-mates. We'd love to hear a play-by-play. Sounds like the makings of an excellent lesson in humility." Shelly slipped an arm around Bella's waist. "Please stay for sup-per so the boys can watch their hero recover whatever he's fumbled."

"Thank you, I will." Bella gave Ethan a sweet smile. "I'm interested in seeing how a cock walks the straight and narrow walk. We already know how he talks the talk."

"You *do* know a cock is a rooster, right?" Ethan said.

"Of course. My mother had one. Beautiful plumage. But the hens got tired of him, and the neighbors complained about the crowing." She shrugged. "So we ate him. I made a tiny dance bustle out of his tail for my little cousin."

It took a moment, but Ethan burst out laughing. The boy standing near the truck joined in, and the one underneath called out, "Whoa!"

"Are you watching what you're doing there?" Still chuckling, Ethan returned to his duty. "Has the oil finished draining from the filter?"

"How am I supposed to tell?"

"Use your eyes, Dempsey. See anything dripping?"

"Out of the *filter,* Dempsey, not your face," the other boy jeered as Dempsey scooted out from under the cab.

Ethan tapped the scoffer's barrel chest. "You're not gonna make it as a comedian, so you'd better learn to make yourself useful for something else." He reached through the cab window and drew out a box. "Step two."

"I gotta get back under there?" Dempsey whined.

"What do you say, Bongo?" Ethan laid a hand on the big boy. "You wanna do the oil filter?"

Bongo chuckled as he glanced under the hood. "Does it go on top?"

"No, you gotta get down and dirty."

Dempsey laughed. "Good luck gettin' him back out."

"So that was our automotive program," Shelly said to Bella as she turned her toward the barn. "The next stop on our press tour will be the henhouse. One of the few centers of serious, steady, no-bull productivity on the place. Besides the kitchen, where we have another woman in charge. I swear, Bella, the testosterone…" With a smug smile she glanced back. "Carry on, boys."

Ethan looked up at Bella as he sank down, butt to boot heels. "You stay for supper, me and the boys'll show off our table manners. We just learned that passing is our first option."

"Yeah, but Bongo still wants to run with the bowl."

"Shut up, Dempsey," Bongo called out from under the orange cab.

"Count me in, Shelly," Bella said, amused,

hesitant to move on. "I'm really interested in your program." To be honest, she felt favored, much the way she had the day Ethan had tapped her on the shoulder in history class and pointed his finger in her direction and then his own. *You're with me on this one.*

"I'm interested in her .38," Dempsey said, loud enough to be heard.

"Jeez, Dempsey, what's wrong with you?" Bongo asked.

"You *do* know a .38 is a gun."

"Sure, I do. And I figure she can read the No Firearms sign out at the gate. You're just rude, Dempsey. Ahh!" Bongo kicked both legs in the air. "Something's dripping on me!"

Ethan tipped his head and leaned to one side. "Is it hot?"

"No, but it don't taste too good."

Dempsey leaned back against the truck and howled.

"Maybe you'd better keep your mouth shut and get done, Bongo," Ethan said. "I gotta get cleaned up for supper."

Folding dining tables flanked a large pass-through window that separated the kitchen from the commons area. Two worn sofas, a card table, a TV and a few chairs furnished the opposite end of the great room. The setup was a small version of the commons at the Indian boarding school Bella had attended before her mother decided she should come back home and go to little Sinte High School. It was not Bella's choice—the South Dakota mission school had a good reputation for preparing kids for college—and she remembered questioning her mother's judgment, even accusing her of being selfish, which had turned out to be true. Her mother jealously guarded those years, claimed them as *her* time. But what she really meant was *their* time, and Bella had had no idea how short the time would be.

She wondered how many of the two-dozen boys who lined up at the window and came away with plates loaded with meat and potatoes would be taken home by their parents if and when the state stepped aside. They behaved like the boys she'd gone to school with, jostling for position, be it in suckling, pecking or batting order. Dying to get noticed, an expression a few of them would take literally if they found no other way. But here they were allowed to be boys while they learned to be men. If they could, and if they would. She'd reported on more than a few who did not.

"You really are their hero," Bella noted after Bongo and Dempsey had taken the long way around the tables to congratulate Ethan for "scoring."

"Yeah, they think I'm bad," he said with a smile.

"Which is good."

"In their eyes, maybe. Should I leave it at bad, or should I admit to a generous helping of stupid?" He shook his head as he cast a glance at the fluorescent fixture overhead. "I don't know, Bella. I'm new at this job, and I'm kinda wingin' it. You never know what's gonna work with these gangsters."

"They don't seem like gangsters."

"A couple of them are here because they won't go to school. They'd rather sit in a hole and smoke weed." He scanned the tables behind her. "Some have done worse."

"What's worse than throwing away your best chance to climb out of a weedy hole?"

"How long have you been reporting the news? You tell me."

She drew a deep breath as she ran down her mental list. She'd interviewed hardheads in all shapes and sizes. "Throwing away your next best chance on top of the first."

"Which is why they're back to Square One.

It's a good option for kids who are open to this kind of rural life."

"Is it good for you?"

"It's perfect for me. Tailor-made." She gave him an incredulous look, and he laughed. "No, I'm serious. I've got a place to stay, but I'm free go. I get to eat and sleep and shower whenever I feel like it. I'm doing something useful, and they pay me for it. Plus, they let me keep a horse here." He winked at her. "I'm makin' progress."

She poked at her mashed potatoes with her fork. "I went to Sinte this morning to do a little research."

"Research?"

She nodded without looking up. "I spoke with your father."

"If you're interested in horse training, Logan's your man."

"I'm interested in the story *behind* the horses."

"How much time you got?" He gave her a sly grin. "Some 'tails' are longer than others."

It wasn't much of a joke, but the way his eyes sparkled, she had to reward him with a laugh.

"And some kicks are harder on the gut

than others," he added, the sparkle fading. "So watch yourself, okay?"

The smile fell from her face. "Are you talking about Logan?"

"I'm talking about poking around behind the horse. I'm talking about being in the wrong place at the wrong time with the wrong questions." He sipped his coffee, studying her over the rim of the cup. He set it down slowly. "With all this interest in sleeping dogs and horses' asses, have you thought about doing something useful?"

"Like what?"

He frowned briefly. "Maybe go back to school for veterinary medicine."

She laughed. "You know, I never had a dog, and I've never really ridden a horse."

"No lie?"

"I try not to do that, either. So I bet you're thinking, an Indian girl who's never had a dog? No way."

"I'm thinking, a girl who's never been on a horse? That is heartbreaking."

"I didn't say I'd never been *on* one. I got on, got scared, had a very short ride."

"End of story?"

"Well, I've always loved horse stories, but you get up there, and the horse raises his head right away and starts prancing around, and you're so high off the ground..." She could almost feel the prickly tummy-to-toes *whoosh* just thinking about it. "I was six years old. That was my one chance, and I blew it."

"Stick with me, Indian girl." He cocked a forefinger at her. "I'm all about second chances." He smiled. "You want one?"

She stared at him. She knew that come-on look, the charismatic smile, the reflexive wink—she'd seen it all, generally directed at someone else. But she'd only been favored a time or two, and her adolescent self had yearned for *once more, Ethan. Look at me that way again, and I'll follow you anywhere.*

Thank God he hadn't. She would be in a fine mess now, wouldn't she?

"Tomorrow's my day off," he said. "Come back in the afternoon and let me take you riding."

"Today was *my* day off."

"That's right," he recalled. "They don't pay you to dig."

"They do, but only in certain places. They're called *assignments*. I'm very good about getting my assignments done before I go back to digging in more fertile—" she demonstrated, sinking splayed fingers into air serving as ground "—loamy ground, dark and loaded with secrets. In my business, there is no right or wrong question, only true or false answers."

"Ask me no questions, I'll tell you no..." His smile was slight, almost sad. "Truth is, I've got no answers. I'm still looking."

"My mother told me once that she was taught not to ask questions, but eventually she decided it was no good to hang back." She sat back in her chair, listening in her mind's ear, reciting word for word. "'We live in a world full of people who love to give answers. They might not be generous with anything else, but they have answers to spare. If you don't ask, they think you're not interested. And if you're not interested...'"

"I'm interested. I'm asking." His smile turned inviting. "Would you like to go out with me sometime?"

"What time tomorrow afternoon?"

"Whenever you get off work."

"I have some flexibility in my schedule. I could try to move some things around." She pulled her woolen shoulder bag into her lap and fished out her phone. "What's your cell number?"

"I don't have one."

"So you don't have a phone number?"

"No numbers." Ethan looked straight into her eyes and gave the two words—*true words*—a moment to sink in. They were heavy enough to crush her *no wrong questions* theory. And then he smiled. "I'll be here all afternoon. Come when you can." He smiled slowly. "Just call out my name."

Chapter Three

Bella's interview with the chairman of the Rapid City Autumn Art Festival had gone well. Carson Watts described the juried competition and made a point of mentioning several of the Native artists by name. The city was gaining a reputation for galleries and shops specializing in American Indian art, and the annual festival in the fall rivaled the one that marked the beginning of tourist season in early June.

Of course, holding the art show the same weekend as Pumpkin Fest didn't hurt, Watts admitted. You had your pumpkin catapult and your beer garden with the oompah band going full tilt downtown, while the east end of Main Street hosted the more "genteel" residents and visitors. What he hadn't said—but she knew—was that his brother-in-law was the head honcho of the pumpkin party, and his own wife had chosen chairmanship of her brother's quilt show committee over her regular fundraising assignment for the art festival. Bella had interviewed the Pumpkin Fest planners earlier in the week. They'd had her cameraman sampling German beer and opining on brands of bratwurst. She had laughed off the offer of beer for breakfast and thought better of telling the friendly group how much she hated bratwurst.

With the community celebrations covered, Bella had convinced her producer to let her take a look at the Double D Wild Horse Sanctuary for a possible story about the training competition, which would come to an end in another few weeks with some kind of performance. She was reminded that a story about the competition had been aired and that it would make sense for the same reporter to do a follow-up.

Or maybe it didn't really matter.

Go ahead, Bella. And since the wild horse place isn't too far from the reservation, why don't you check with your sources there? See if there's anything interesting going on.

She would take that as an assignment.

Her car rumbled over the cattle guard at the gate to the Double D Wild Horse Sanctuary. It had once been a cattle ranch, and she passed a few Herefords grazing alongside their white-faced black calves as she sped down the gravel access road toward an imposing white house. Upon closer inspection the place became less imposing. It was big, but the white paint needed refurbishing. The Office sign told her the house was more than a home, and the wiry old cowboy standing on the porch looked like a fixture worth investigating.

He rattled down the front porch steps on bowed legs, pumping his elbows like a flightless chicken as Bella approached. She read *Where have I seen you?* in his eyes and cheerfully introduced herself. She enjoyed being recognized.

"I'm looking for one of the *D*'s—whichever Drexler sister is in charge today."

"No more Drexlers. We got Night Horse and Beaudry, but no Drexler. Both girls are married now."

Bella smiled. "Are you Night Horse or Beaudry?"

"Me? No. Gosh, no, not me." Blushing, the little man adjusted his straw cowboy hat and did a little boot scoot in the dirt. "Them girls are like my own kin. Hoolihan's the name." He stuck out his hand. "Everybody calls me Hoolie. The girls are around here somewhere. Pretty sure Sally's over by…" He nodded toward the barn. "Here, let me show you."

Bella followed the old cowboy, whose friendly chatter reached the ears of a lovely blonde, who appeared in the open doorway leaning heavily on a sturdy cane with a tripod base. The woman shaded her eyes with her free hand and then flashed a huge smile.

"Well, I'll be damned. The paparazzi have finally tracked me down."

Bella recognized the former Sally Drexler from the original KOZY interview. The new last names would come naturally soon enough.

"Where's your camera, Miss Primeaux?" Sally laughingly demanded as she emerged from the barn. "I'm ready for my close-up."

"What've you done now, girl?" Hoolie chided. "I told you, my film star days are over, so don't be signing me up for any more of them promotional videos."

"You're our most authentic-looking relic of the Old West, Hoolie." Sally turned to Bella as she pulled off her work gloves. "You do a story on the Double D, you get Hoolie in the picture for free. For a donation, he comes with woolly chaps." She offered a handshake. "Sally Night Horse." She glanced at Hoolie, grinning. "I love saying that. *Sally Night Horse.*" To Bella she added, "We're newly-weds."

"Not me," said Hoolie.

"Hoolie turned me down years ago," Sally said. "You KOZY people sure are quick. I just sent the email this morning."

"What email?"

"You know, where it says *Got news? Contact us.* I told them they oughta be setting something up for the grand finale of our training competition." Sally patted Bella's shoulder. "And here you are. My favorite reporter, too."

Bella frowned. "My producer didn't say anything about an email."

"Thought of it on her own, did she? I'm sure glad she didn't give it to the guy who came out here before. He didn't know a mustang from a unicorn. Have a seat." Sally gestured toward a wooden bench on the shady side of the barn and then proceeded to beat Bella to the far end of it.

Bella hesitated. Whatever physical strength the woman lacked, she more than made up for in vitality and sheer will. She seemed to fill up more than physical space. She had considerable personal presence.

"Come on, take a load off. Mine's heavier than yours, so humor me." Sally patted the empty space beside her. "Sit down and tell me what you need. We've got pictures, we've got stories, we've got facts and figures. It's been one hell of a ride, and we haven't even gotten to the best part yet. I mean, *I* have, but that's because I've met my soul mate. And I've only nibbled around the edges of that discovery. The ride gets better and better. There's so much more we can do here."

"I'd better get to haulin' that hay," the old cowboy muttered, edging away.

"Are you blushing, Hoolie?"

"It's my farmer tan." He lifted his cowboy hat. He was ruddy below the eyebrows, pale and polished on top. "It ends right here. See? Don't you be signing me up for any stories with pictures, Big Sister." He replaced his hat and tugged at the brim in deference to their visitor as he backpedaled a step or two. "Never know what you're gonna say."

"I'm just sayin' it's all good." Eyes dancing, Sally glanced at Bella. *Between girls.* "And I'm still looking forward to handing over that twenty-thousand dollars to the winning trainer. Thank God I'm not judging. I've been getting pictures from the trainers. You should see some of the riders they've lined up to show the horses. You wanna show us a gentle horse, you put a kid in the saddle, right?" Sally took a deep breath and glanced heavenward. "I need more prizes."

"Maybe I could help you get some. Show me some of your pictures and I can find a way to use them. We do community support spots all the time."

"We'll take some of those." Sally nodded. "But what I really want you to cover is the competition. Show off the horses and the people coming from all over. If I had to make a choice..."

"Maybe we can do both. It doesn't hurt to try."

"I wanna show you around." Sally balanced her weight on the cane and levered herself off the bench. "The best view is from the back of a horse, but I need to rest up first for that."

"Start with the pictures," Bella suggested as she sprang to her feet. She wouldn't offer help unless she was asked, but she was ready. And, yes, she was also ready to ask a little and offer to listen a lot. "Tell me more about your program," she said as they headed for the house. "How you got started, what it takes to create a sanctuary. Talk to me about how you get the land you need and cooperation from all the bureaucrats that would have to be involved with something like this. And your neighbors. You must have some helpful neighbors. Not everyone wants a wildlife sanctuary butting up against their pasture."

Sally moved like a woman living in a body that couldn't keep up with her mind. Bella had seen the same frustration in her mother, and it scared her a little. Not the hint of impatience—she understood that—but the reality. It was a feeling she tucked away, to be studied later.

"Come on inside," Sally told Bella when they reach the top of the porch steps. She nodded toward a wheelchair parked beside a porch swing. "On days when the saddle's out of reach, that's my ride. MS." She reached for the screen door. "You know, multiple sclerosis. The last guy KOZY sent out was here for about ten minutes. One look at me, and he was after a whole different story. He wanted to put me in my wheelchair out in the corral, gather some horses around me and then mike me up. That's what he said. And you know what I said?"

"I know what *I* would have said."

Sally laughed. "And that's what I said, too. Not to mention, that chair is camera shy." She led the way through an old-fashioned foyer and nodded toward the first door past the foot of the staircase. "But I know a slacker from a doer. Glad they decided not to send a boy to do a woman's job this time."

The door led to an office whose walls were covered with pictures of horses—all sizes, colors, attitudes and settings. The heart of the matter. Sally probably spent more time in this room than she wanted to, so she brought her outdoor world inside. This was the Double D's hub. Her regular desk chair was probably the one sitting on the porch, but there were a couple of padded folding chairs and a day-bed, lots of room to roll around, a desktop computer, file drawers and desk trays galore, and an array of framed family photographs standing on shelves above.

Sally took a shot of a foursome down from

the shelf. "This is Hank and me with my sister, Ann, and her new husband, Zach. This was taken at their wedding. Hank was the soloist, and I was the maid of honor. That was just last spring." She flashed Bella a smile as she reached for another shot of four smiling faces. "And here's *my* wedding picture. We work fast here. You know this guy." She pointed to Logan Wolf Track. "He married my BFF Mary Tutan just a little over a month ago. Double wedding." She looked up, eyes dancing. "Me and Hank figured what the hell? Everyone else is doing it."

"It doesn't look like that's what anybody in this picture was thinking," Bella said of the four glowing faces. She glanced into a frame on the shelf above the wedding pictures.

"That's Trace Wolf Track," Sally said, indicating the man on the bucking horse. "Logan's adopted son." She took the picture down from the shelf. "You know him? Rodeo cowboy."

"I went to school with his brother."

"You know Ethan? He's one of our contestants. He's even better looking than this guy, if you can believe that. Have you seen him lately? He's like—"

"I met with Logan recently over at the

Tribal Office," Bella said, sparing the shot of Trace Wolf Track in action little more than a glance. She knew how to learn a lot by asking only a little, but it wasn't a two-way street. Seeing Ethan would not enter into this conversation. She was keeping that close. "Indian Country is one of my beats whenever my producer thinks there might be something newsworthy going on."

"Logan's been a big help to the sanctuary," Sally said. "Backed us on leasing some Tribal land, which gave us a leg up on getting a big tract of public land adjacent to the reservation. We'll be able to take on a lot more horses."

Bella set Logan's older son back on the metaphorical shelf. Now she was getting somewhere. "Your neighbor was running cattle on that land, wasn't he? Dan Tutan?"

"Damn tootin' he was. Poor guy's losin' it." Sally laughed. "In more ways than one."

"What do you mean?"

"I don't know, he's just…" Sally snapped a lever on her cane and telescoped it closed. "To all intents and purposes he lost his daughter, Mary, a long time ago, but now that she's married to Logan, the plot thickens."

"How so?"

"Let's just say ol' Dan better start tootin' a sweeter tune or he won't be bouncing that first grandbaby on his knee. Of course, if I get to be godmother—which I'm counting on—he'll have to go through me no matter what."

Sally hadn't told Bella anything she didn't already know, but a baby brother or sister for Ethan seemed like a pretty big deal. Since Logan and Mary had just gotten married and Logan had said he hadn't seen much of Ethan, she wondered if he knew. Or cared.

And why did she wonder or care whether Ethan cared? She was looking for a story about Indian land and Dan Tutan's good friend Senator Garth. Ethan Wolf Track figured in somewhere out on the fringe at best.

"Is everything signed and sealed on the leases?" Bella asked. "I mean, I've heard you might have some opposition."

"Just Tutan, but the Tribal Council already shot him down."

"Tutan has influential friends in Washington. One, anyway."

"Who?"

"Senator Perry Garth. I just wondered if you'd actually gotten anything on paper."

Bella read the message in Sally's eyes. *Of course I'm dotting the* i*'s.*

"The leases turn over in November," Sally said. "I don't care who Tutan's cozy with. D.C.'s a world away. The people I deal with at the regional Bureau of Land Management office, the ones who handle wild horse issues, they tell me renewal's in the bag. They need this sanctuary. They've got no place to put the horses they consider unadoptable. That's what we do. We give them a home where they can roam." Sally's grin was infectious. "You know, with the deer and the antelope. No buffalo. Wish I had some. Hank would love that. I don't suppose you've met my husband, Hank?"

"I don't think so."

"He's not from this reservation, but he has connections here. In fact, I think his father worked for Tutan some years ago, but I don't know much about that. We haven't talked much about... Did I tell you we got married at the Tribal building? In the judge's chambers. It was so cool. No fuss at all, just *bam*." Sally slapped the back of her hand into her palm. "Man and wife. Love it." She smiled. "I don't think Tutan's gonna give us any trouble. I think he's afraid of Hank."

Fear. Could be something... "Why?"

"They've had words. I don't know exactly what those words were, but they weren't friendly." Sally took another picture down from the shelf. Two young women—Sally and someone in an academic robe. "It wasn't so long ago that it was just my sister, Ann, and me running the place. We had Hoolie and a few high school kids working for us, some volunteers helping out. Then Zach Beaudry came along. Another rodeo cowboy. Have you heard of him?"

Bella shook her head. Rodeo itself held no interest for her, but she knew better than to show it. Listening—her strong suit—had always served her well. Talkers like Sally tended to ramble, dropping crumbs of information along the way. With any luck Sally would wander back and pick up the tidbit about Hank's father working for Tutan. Even if she didn't, Bella had sniffed the crumb and made a mental note of the scent.

"My husband works the rodeo circuit as a medic, so that's how he knew Zach." Sally perched on the edge of the big desk. "Life's funny, isn't it?" she went on. "Not much happens for the longest time, and then Zach's pickup breaks down outside our gate and the

Double D family starts growing." She gave a catbird's smile. "And 'Damn Tootin' isn't very popular around these parts. So I'm not worried."

"I don't know much about rodeo. The only name I know is Trace Wolf Track." And the name was clearly a connection to the horses, which were Sally's claim to the land. "Do rodeo contractors ever get hold of your mustangs?"

"First of all, they're not mine. And the people who adopt horses could use them that way, but I doubt it happens often. Good bucking stock is hard to find. You almost have to breed for it, and those animals are valuable and well taken care of, so if you're looking for some kind of scandal..." Sally's smile had gone cool. "I was a rodeo stock contractor for a short time years ago. I took good care of my animals."

"Oh, I have no doubt," Bella said quickly. "I'm interested in the making of a sanctuary, the commitment to providing at least some animals with the space to be wild. I could really get into a story like this."

Sally's eyes lit up again. "That's what I like to hear."

"But I have to convince my producer to let me do it."

"Tell your boss that first guy flat out offended me, and I don't want him back." Sally reached for a Post-it pad. "Better yet, give me the guy's name and number."

"Let me handle it." Bella reached into her shoulder bag—her ever-present office on a string—and poked around while she spoke. "You might want to check on the public lands leases. I've heard that one of their favorite tactics is to come up with a snag when it's too late to get it straightened."

"Whose tactics?"

"Bureaucrats. My mother used to say the word as though it had been soaked in sour milk." She produced a business card from her woolen bag. "If you smell anything fishy, would you call me?"

"I was gonna offer you lunch, but now…" Cautiously Sally took the card in hand. "Dead fish and sour milk?"

Bella smiled. "Damn tootin'."

Bella had called ahead, but she didn't know whether to knock on the door of the house at Square One or walk in. She hadn't seen an office sign anywhere. Or, for that matter, any sign of an office. She remembered knocking on the door of the Wolf Track home years ago, shoring up her courage with a bit of self-talk and going in search of Ethan. She'd gone over what she would say as she stood there on the front step, grateful that the log house was far enough out of town that no one would see her. Too far to walk. Too windy, too cold. Her mother was waiting in the car, keeping it running, keeping the heat on.

How did you end up with him as a partner on this project? Why don't you just do your part and let him twist in the wind?

Because it would be incomplete. Because I'd get laughed at. Not him. Me. *Because I thought we'd do this thing together.*

She could almost feel her mother's angry stare boring into her back as she headed around the corner of the house. *So who're you gonna team up with next time? Not some football hero, I hope.*

Oh, yeah, the heat was on.

"I got your message."

Bella was snapped back to the present and whirled around to find that this time the heat was coming from Ethan's eyes. They'd always made her a little nervous, made her feel as though he knew more than she did. Not that what he thought was terribly important, but he was older, wiser, more experienced, and he knew things. He had answers to questions she hadn't thought of yet—at least back then.

"I said I'd come."

"I said I'd be here." He adjusted his battered straw hat by the brim and smiled. "A man of his word meets a woman of hers."

"I hope we're really going to ride horses." She stuck out her right leg. "I wore my boots." With riding heels. Guaranteed to keep her feet in the stirrups.

"Pretty flashy." He gave a nod toward the barn, and she lowered her boot—a step, she hoped, in a useful direction. "Did you buy those today?" he asked.

"Last night."

"First pair?"

"First pair of cowboy boots, yes. They're not very comfortable." She picked up her pace. One step behind was not her way.

"You gotta break 'em in."

Her boots squeaked on cue. She glanced up at him, and they both laughed.

"I paid a visit to the Double D this morning," she told him as they approached a rail fence. "I'm going to ask if I can to do a feature on the competition. I want to tie it into land use and can't-we-all-just-get-along and stuff like that." She braced her arm over the chest-high fence and turned to him. "You say you're going to win?"

"Get along with who?" he asked, ignoring her question.

"Oh, you know, the farmers and the cattlemen, the cowboys and the Indians. How can you be sure you'll win?"

He gave her an incredulous look. "Damn, woman, let it go. That is *so* past history." He bumped her arm with his elbow. "To boot, we both already passed history." He tipped his head back and laughed. "Ah, funny stuff, Bella. Wait till you see my horse. He can go from zero to sixty and stop on a dime."

She smiled. "Turning your thrill gauge upside down is he?"

"My thrill gauge?" He laughed again. "It's pretty easy to thrill me these days. I get a kick out of simply turning a knob and pushing the door open." He demonstrated with a handful of air. "All by myself."

"No hands tied behind your back?"

"That was always my brother's favorite boast." He squared his shoulders and pitched his voice down low. "*Hell, I can do that with one hand tied behind my back.* So I always wanted to go him one better."

"I'll bet *that* was some competition." Bella rested her elbows on the rail and surveyed the pasture beyond. No horses. No cattle. Just grassy hills, clear blue sky. "I read about your conviction," she said quietly. "And, no, it wasn't *big* news out where I was, but it wouldn't have been news at all if it hadn't involved a senator."

"His daughter," Ethan amended. "Politics and sex, right? The only thing missing was money."

"Money's always somewhere in the mix."

"Don't look at me." He turned his back to the fence, which positioned him for a challenging look at her. "I stole a car and a girl. No money."

"There was money somewhere, Ethan. That's where the power comes from."

"I did the crime, I did the time, and now I'm done with it."

She frowned. "You pled not guilty."

"Against the advice of my attorney. Turned out I *was* guilty." Leaning back, he glanced past her, tucked his lower lip under his front teeth and gave a deafening whistle.

Bella turned toward the sound of pounding hooves. A stout buckskin galloped toward them, his mane flapping like a black flag.

"Impressive," Bella said.

"Damn straight." Ethan betrayed his secret, opening his hand to let the horse snuffle up a tiny brown treat. "Big Boy, meet Bella. She's a reporter. She's got a ton of questions. Help me show her some answers."

"I haven't asked you anything."

"I noticed." He slid her a subtle wink. "You're good."

"Yes, I am. Are you going to show me the dime-stopping routine?"

"Nope. I'm gonna take you out riding. Watch this." Ethan climbed the fence, lured the horse into position with another treat and a little sweet talk, grabbed a fistful of mane and mounted. He grinned at Bella. "How do you like my wild mustang?"

"Amazing. How long since he was wild?"

"How long since I whistled? A minute or two?"

"He's not wild. You've tamed him."

"If I turn him out of this pasture, he'll head for the hills and his band of brothers. He won't give me another thought until I go out there and run him back in."

She nodded at the unfettered horse. "Will he do that for anyone else?"

"No one else has tried. You want to?"

She shook her head. "I want a kid horse."

"The kids are out in the field. Meet me at the gate by the barn and we'll steal their horse for an hour or so."

She watched him ride away, loping the buckskin along the fence line. Quite a picture, she thought. Both magnificent looking, neither quite tame. Together they made a story, and she could stand aside and watch and listen and make notes. She could find that story and tell it in a good way, so that people would find it and feel it and value the lives they lived at the back of beyond. She had a role to play.

And she'd said she would do the horseback-riding scene, hadn't she?

Well, at least she looked the part. She opened the appointed gate and watched Ethan swing his leg high over the buckskin's head and slide to the ground.

He grinned. *Did you see that?* And she nodded, suitably impressed. The mustang had earned another treat.

"He took to this apple-flavored stuff right away, which is kinda surprising. It's generally an acquired taste." He scratched the horse's withers. "Ain't it, Big Boy?" He glanced over the buckskin's back and peered at the bright blue horizon. "So you've really never had a look at this country of yours from the back of a horse?"

"Country of mine?"

"Isn't this part of the land Warrior Woman blogs about? The Great Sioux Nation, she says." He flashed a knowing smile. "That's you, isn't it? Warrior Woman?"

It was her blogging handle. "How did you know?"

"I'm an Indian, too, Bella. I'm not sure what tribe, but it's in my blood," he told her. And then he disappeared into the barn with the horse following him as far as the open door. Within seconds Ethan reappeared carrying a saddle on his shoulder. "I know how to read sign."

"What sign?"

"The sign that somebody wants to be waited on. Saddle rack's in here."

"I don't have a horse."

"I'll get the horse. You get the saddle." He grinned at her as she walked past him. "Together, we're gonna ride."

Half a dozen saddles were shelved on wall pegs just inside the door. "Any saddle?"

"Any saddle," was the response from outside.

She eyed the hanging array of horse head-gear. "What about the other stuff?"

He appeared in the doorway.

She turned and quickly pulled down the nearest saddle. "Got one."

She thought he might take it from her—the damn thing was heavy—but he walked around her and selected two sets of headstalls with reins.

"So you use your tracking skills on the internet?" She followed him into the corral and dropped the saddle beside the one he'd brought out. "That's interesting. That's a topic worth exploring. Are you a hunter?"

"No. Never hunted. Never will. Lost my right to bear arms." He gripped the handful of tack and did a quick biceps curl. "Except these. These can go bare."

"They're quite impressive." He was wearing a gray T-shirt, and for the first time she noticed some ink peeking out from under his sleeve. On impulse she pushed his sleeve up and discovered a pair of hawks fighting in flight. "The artwork seems a little amateur-ish."

"You don't like that?" He glanced at it and shrugged. "Neither do I, but I'm stuck with it. Don't know what I was thinking." He offered a sheepish grin. "Literally. Nothing like a three-day bender for blowing the mind."

"Was that the first thing you did after your release from prison?"

"Hell, no. First thing I did was go around turning knobs and pushing doors open. Hold this." He handed her one of the headstalls. "Getting drunk was the first thing I did after I got discharged from the army." He spoke quietly as he approached the mustang. "And the second thing. Maybe the third thing. I lost count."

"But the army was *before*..."

"Yeah, before. But I did some stuff *between*. Check it out, Big Boy." The buckskin lowered his head and snuffled the proffered headstall. "I did road construction, worked for Logan, followed Trace around a little bit. Even took a few college classes."

"Where you met Senator Garth's daughter."

"And the rest is history." He turned to the horse. "The woman is a history freak, boy." Ethan lifted the simple, handmade-looking piece of tack over the horse's head. There was no bit to coax into his mouth. "What's past is present, they say. How're we gonna live with that, huh? You and me?" He glanced over his shoulder at her as he rubbed the horse's face. "So come on, tell me the truth. Have you really never ridden?"

"I just need a gentle, well-broke mount," she said, sidestepping the question. "Nothing fancy. No stopping on a dime or going on a tear." The closer the moment of getting on a horse came, the less she wanted to think about her long-ago but never forgotten experience.

He smiled. "I'll go wake your horse up."

"But first…" She shoved her hand in the front pocket of her jeans, pulled up the contents and flipped a glinting dime, which he caught midair. She nodded. "Prove it."

He laughed. "Yes, ma'am."

He flipped the reins over the mustang's withers, vaulted onto his bare back and put on a quick show for her. The horse leaped into action, skidded to a stop and reversed directions like a swinging door.

Bella knew little about training horses, but she was impressed. "How long have you been working with him?"

"Little over two months."

"And he was completely wild?"

"Came straight out of the hills." Ethan swung his leg over the horse's withers and slid to the ground. "Course he'd had a couple of human encounters. For one, he's a gelding. But I had no part in that, did I, Big Boy?" He patted the horse's shoulder.

"Who *did?*" she asked.

"Any doctoring these horses get is done by a vet. They try not to interfere too much when the horse is in the wild, but you need geldings for the adoption program."

Bella felt the urge to pat Big Boy, too, but she stayed put. "Did he come with the name, or did you give it to him?"

"That's just what I call him. There's gonna be an auction after the competition to benefit the sanctuary, and this guy will bring in big bucks. I figure naming rights go with him."

"And if you named him, you'd be hard-pressed to let him go."

"There's always another horse." He entreated her with a nod. "Come hold him for me."

"I don't…"

"Sure you do. You two have a lot in common. You're both observers."

She took one cautious step, then another. Ethan reached for her hand, uncurled her fingers with his thumb and drew her palm to the horse's big, soft nostril. It widened as Big Boy took her measure and found her acceptable. Ethan placed the ends of the reins in her hand.

The thing about animals smelling fear must have been an old wives' tale, Bella thought as Ethan walked away. Or maybe that was just predators. Animals driven to knock you down, step all over you and eat you alive.

"You wouldn't do that, would you, Big Boy?" she whispered. "We have that in common, too. We're gentle creatures. We eat plants."

Ethan emerged from the barn leading a small black horse. "This one's for you." He dropped the lead rope, and the horse stood patiently while he straightened the saddle pad and set the saddle.

"Does he have a name?"

"This is Sister Sara."

"She." Bella looked up and found Big Boy staring back at her. "A mare. We like mares. They're usually gentle, aren't they?"

"This one is." Ethan brought the mare over and traded reins. He watched Bella take quiet stock of the mare's response to her. One female sizing up the other.

"Would you rather do something else?" Ethan asked.

"No. Oh, no, I've been looking forward to

this. Obviously." She dug one heel into the dirt and tipped her toe toward the sky, showing off her new boots again.

"One step at a time, then. Step one is to mount up."

No problem—as long as Sister Sara didn't move. Ethan spoke to her while Bella got herself lined up, put mind over matter and pushed off. One smooth move. Victory.

"How's that feel?" Ethan asked.

She looked down at him. "So far, so good." Nobody was moving yet.

"Yeah?" He smiled. "You look good up there. You feel okay?"

"I do." Bella nodded quickly. "I do. We're steady. Nobody's nervous. This is a good start."

"Take the reins easy and find your contact point."

She felt a little jittery as she slid the leather straps through her fingers. Where was it, this contact point? Would it show the horse that she was in charge?

"Easy," he said softly, laying his hand over hers. "This isn't a lifeline. You don't hang on with these." He moved his hand to her thigh. Now she *really* felt jittery. "You hang on with these."

"I know. I know that."

He looked up and considered her face for a moment. She wasn't sure how much the hand resting on her thigh had to do with it, but her insides were all abuzz.

"Okay, just how bad was your experience?"

She lifted one shoulder. "I got dumped. Hard."

One corner of his mouth twitched. "I mean, with a horse."

"I've never been dumped by anything else." A little fake indignation calmed her nerves, and she smiled. "I got left in the lurch on a history project once, but since I landed on my feet, it doesn't qualify."

"How long is it gonna take you to forgive me for that one?" He turned to Big Boy, whispered something and reached for the top of his headstall.

"Forgiving is no problem. It's the forgetting. It just seems to jump out there when I need a good comeback. And what are you doing?"

"Turning my horse loose. I'm going with you." He slid her boot out of the stirrup, put his hand under her knee and lifted it toward the saddle swell. With a light touch on the saddle horn and a toe in the stirrup he swung up effortlessly and settled behind her. "Our Sister Sara's gonna take us both."

"She doesn't mind?"

"Doesn't seem to. Do you?" Bella shook her head. "We're just gonna amble along so you can get the feel of being safe on a horse. How's that?"

Bella nodded, and Ethan guided her foot back into the stirrup, then took the reins in his left hand and urged the horse through the gate and into a pasture that had been grazed down to crisp nubs.

"I remember sitting across from you in the library," he said, "working out the plans and looking stuff up. You were so damn serious, thought you knew it all, and if you'd been a little less bossy, maybe a little older…"

"What?" she coaxed.

"You mighta been in trouble. I remember going along for the fun of it, thinking you were way too smart, too cute, too mouthy and too young. What I don't remember is why I didn't show up that night."

She laughed uneasily. She could almost feel the inked wings of the birds on his arm fluttering against her shoulder. "*You* were serious about other things."

"I was living in the moment." He laid his

free hand on her shoulder. "You know what? You need to relax. How bad were you hurt?"

"I wasn't hurt. I was mad."

"At the horse?"

"Oh, that. I broke my butt."

He laughed.

She didn't. "Hairline fracture of the coccyx."

"Oh, yeah, that hurts. Sorry. No wonder you're tense." Slowly he began kneading her right shoulder. "Let's try to loosen you up some. Let me untie this knot so you can let your arms down." He rested his chin on her left shoulder and rocked it side to side. "This side, too. Stop thinking. You don't need a comeback."

No kidding. Tight loops began opening up, raised parts lowering, hung-up pieces sinking, and, oh, it all felt good in concert.

But she wasn't about to start singing.

"Shouldn't you pay attention to the road?"

"You've got the front seat." He chuckled soft and low, his breath warm in her ear. "Lean back and take the reins. Then you'll really be in charge."

"You're making me nervous."

"Take the reins in your left hand. You can still hang on to the swells with your right.

Not the horn." He touched the high pommel that anchored the saddle horn. "The swells."

"I don't want to make the horse nervous," she muttered, but she accepted the assignment.

"She's a kids horse," he whispered as he drew his hand back and slid it around her waist.

She quickly sucked in her belly and then half expected somebody to laugh at her. Who cared whether she had a waist? She was fine. She was healthy and fit. Her jeans rode her hipbones, and his hand had no business hovering around there. But it was warm and comforting, and she was pretty far out of her comfort zone. Still, with all the square inches of surface her body possessed, the only patch she felt at the moment was underneath his hand.

And then he moved it. "Lean back," he said, and he pressed her to him. "Relax and get into the flow with us." His fingers stirred. "Sister Sara ain't the nervous type, and she's got the sweetest rockin' horse lope. You wanna try it out?"

"Not yet."

"Is it me or the horse?"

She laughed a little. "It's me. I don't want to be afraid. Horses are *beautiful*."

"What about me?"

"You're beautiful, too."

"Do you want to stop being afraid of me?"

She turned her head quickly and found herself shaded by the brim of his hat and basking in the warmth of his gaze. "I'm not…"

He stopped her answer with a soft, sure kiss. Her words would have been meaningless, anyway. A hollow denial would be a waste of breath. Words stood no chance against a kiss, and his was pure and promising. She drew in the feel and the scent of him, meeting his kiss in kind.

Yes, I do.

He lifted his head and smiled down at her. "Give me time. I'll show you how."

She glanced at the horizon. Time was easy. There was nothing to it. Being together was something else.

"Talk to me," he said. He nudged the mare, and she picked up her pace. "Tell me about your college days. What was it like for you? Was it hard?"

"Very hard, and very good for me, thanks for asking."

He rested his chin on the top of her head,

staking a claim. "You always talk cute when you're nervous?"

"I rarely do things that make me nervous. This is out of character for me."

"You go on TV. Most people would be shaking in their boots."

"Would you?"

"Hell, yeah. God knows what I'd say. But you never miss a beat. First time I saw you, I said, *hey, I know her.*" He chuckled. "But I didn't, did I?"

"What did you *think* you knew about me?"

"You were always one to speak your mind, but only when you had something to say. I thought down deep you were pretty shy." His hand stirred against her midriff. "Pretty. And shy."

"It's not down that deep."

"When you read about me going to prison, did you say, *hey, I know him?*" A beat passed, and then another. "If that's what makes you nervous—"

"It's not," she assured him. "I didn't say anything. I just kept reading. One thing about not speaking up until you have something to say is that you get to hear more, maybe see more, than you would otherwise. That's how I knew you, not from something I read."

"And you liked me."

"No, I didn't. I had a crush on you, but that's not really the same thing. I was beneath your notice until you needed me to get you through a required class."

"Needed you?" He snorted. "I could've done that thing myself."

"But you didn't have to."

"And you know damn well I noticed you."

"You teased me."

"Of course I did. I was a cocky eighteen-year-old. And you were, what, fifteen? Believe it or not, I don't go around lookin' for trouble."

"That's my job."

He laughed. "You're doing just fine, Bella. Whatever hurt I caused, you rose above it. And now I'm the one who gets to polish up his image when he says, *hey, I know her.*"

"No apology for calling me Bella the Fella when one of your buddies said I needed to grow a pair?"

"Aw, jeez," he groaned. "I said that?"

"I was fifteen and flat as a board."

"What did you do? I know you didn't go home and cry."

"I threw a pencil at you, but I missed. And then I went home and grew a pair."

"A very nice pair. I noticed, Bella. I definitely noticed." He laid his free hand on her shoulder again, then rubbed it down over her arm. "You've relaxed. You notice the difference in Sister Sara? No resistance."

"I'm doing better?" She smiled. "And I'm not freaking out inside. I'd like to try it on my own." She glanced up at him. "Next time."

"We're havin' a next time?"

"I was thinking of blogging on you."

"I don't think I've ever been blogged on. I notice you're pretty good at it."

"You won't find better."

"Why don't we pull over to the side of the road and you can start now. Does it hurt the first time?"

"I'm betting you're pretty thick-skinned."

"Only in some places."

"I'll make a deal with you," she said. "Come over to the studio when you have a little time. If I'm on a story, you can tag along if you want to. And then I'll start doing you. Blog style."

"You make it sound real tempting, but I've been out of circulation for a while now. I'm what you'd call fresh fish. You throw the net over me, I'll be taking you for one crazy ride."

"Throw the net over you," she mused. "I

like that. It's quotable. Where's a pencil when you need one?"

"You're still using pencils? Don't they get hung up in the net?"

"Still funny after all these years." She turned to look up at him. "With your looks and my brain, we might actually be a team this time."

"You've got looks, lady. Good looks. *Great* looks."

She flashed him a smile.

"Hey. You're supposed to say something back."

"*Of course* you have a brain, Ethan. It's all in the application."

Chapter Four

Ethan had never been to a television studio, and he didn't know what he was expecting, but it was something a little grander than the building KOZY-TV shared with a veterinary clinic and a real estate office. The station occupied the lion's share of the space, and it was flanked by an impressive tower, but the news desk was smaller than it looked on TV, and the weatherman stood in front of a solid green backdrop instead of a map. Bella called it magic. Ethan added the word *tricks*.

There were wires and cables hanging from the high ceiling and strung across the dark floor, lots of equipment on wheels, messages and images dancing on big and small screens, and two monster cameras. The cameras looked cool. Everything else was disappointing, like shaking hands with the actor who played Ironman and realizing his hand was half the size of yours.

Bella introduced two behind-the-scenes people who showed him how their gadgets worked. It was one computer, two computer, three computer, four. "More machines, fewer bodies," the young engineer said. "The station manager says if I can grow an extra ear and another hand, I'll have a job for at least five more years." He nodded at a pretty young woman hurrying past with an armload of file folders. "But she won't."

The woman skidded to a stop, neck arched. "Won't what?"

"Marry me," the young man said.

"In your dreams, Richard."

Richard grinned as they watched her disappear bit by lovely bit down a flight of stairs. "What I could do with another hand," he said under his breath.

Bella was already moving Ethan on to the next tour stop, but he tapped the man's shoulder in passing. "Machines can't replace a man's hands, no matter what anyone on TV says."

He left Richard laughing his headphones off.

"I'll show you how we switch over from news to weather," Bella was saying as they stepped into a den of rubber snakes on the dark news set. "Hey, Paul, is Darryl here?" she asked an older man who was monkeying around with a big camera. "I want him to meet Ethan Wolf Track." She turned to Ethan. "Darryl Brugmann is the—"

"Sports guy." A bright-eyed fellow with a spiky haircut appeared with a firm handshake at the ready. "Any relation to…"

"His brother." Sports guy was a short guy. Ethan grinned. "I caught Trace's interview with you a few months ago."

"Your brother's a hell of a bronc rider. What's your event? Rodeo usually runs in the family, and you look like a bulldogger to me."

"Nope. I got no interest in wrestling a steer to the ground just to let him up again. The rodeo genes went to my brother. I got the hand-me-down overalls." Ethan shoved his hands in the back pockets of his jeans. "I'm a workin' man. A cowboy, at least for now."

The sportscaster looked up at Bella. "Interesting. Are you doing something on cowboys? Or overalls?"

"I'm showing a friend around the studio before I go out on assignment."

"How far do you have to go? I'm covering a game tonight, and I need the new Betacam with the good tripod."

"I'll use the old camera," Bella said cheerfully. "I don't need a tripod."

"And I get John."

"I don't need John. I have a workin' man right here." She threaded her arm though Ethan's and around his back, smiling up at him. "Right?"

"Right. You don't need John." In the face of all the fancy equipment, he felt damn good about edging John out of the picture.

"What they say about working cowboys must be true," Darryl said. "Kinda like a Swiss Army Knife." He looked Ethan up and down, checking to see whether he was the deluxe model. "Your brother sure can ride."

"He sure can." Ethan smiled. He was standing there with Bella Primeaux's arm around his waist.

Brugmann gave a snappy salute and turned on his heel. "Have fun, kids."

"You think you like somebody," Ethan

mused as he watched the little man make his swaggering exit. "And then you meet him in person."

Bella smiled. "Darryl thinks he's a big fish in a small pond. The only part he's got right is the size of the pond."

"Maybe you need to stop messin' with fish and find yourself a real man." Before she could slip away, Ethan slipped his arm around Bella's shoulders and gave her an affectionate squeeze. "Not a John, though. You don't want a John." He frowned. "What does John do, anyway?"

"He's our cameraman. We're down to one. The way the station's been cutting the budget, I'm surprised *I* still have a job." She patted his midsection. "Are you any good with a camera, cowboy?"

"I can point and shoot."

"That's all I need. Otherwise I have to shoot myself."

She was walking him toward a set of stairs. He hoped they led to the great outdoors. "Sounds like your job is harder than it looks."

"It depends on the assignment, and this one could get weird. We're going to talk to a dog breeder."

Ethan stepped back and let Bella take the stairs first. "We're talkin' puppies?"

"Puppies by the cageful. An affiliate in Boston got this lead on what they think is a mill shipping puppies out east. Apparently the owner agreed to let us take a look, so maybe it's a legitimate breeder." She turned when she reached the top of the stairs. "South Dakota doesn't require a license, so legitimacy is in the eye of the beholder."

"I can't shoot puppies," he teased as he stepped onto the landing. "Sorry. That's just wrong."

"I doubt we'll get to see many puppies. If these people are the kind we think they are, I'll give you a nice reward for full-face shots of any of the people. What would you like?"

"Like a prize at the fair?" He smiled hungrily. "Something from your top shelf."

She gave him a quick lesson on the hand-held video camera and loaded the necessary equipment into her car. Ethan offered to drive so that she could use the GPS on her phone to find the place, which was pretty far out in the sticks. When they got there, the gate across the access road was locked.

Bella was back on the phone. "Hello, this is Bella Primeaux from KOZY News. I have an appointment for an interview with Mrs. Mosher. The gate's locked." She lowered the phone almost instantly. "They said to wait."

"Somebody's coming." Ethan appraised the approaching vehicle. It was a Hummer, for God's sake, bearing down on Bella's angelic white Honda. A South Dakota farmer with a Hummer? "I've got a bad feeling about this, Bella."

"Welcome to my world. You never know when something interesting might turn up"

"No, this is a feeling I've had before. Many times. Same world, different neighborhoods." The Hummer pulled over on the side of the rutted road inside the gate, and Ethan positioned the Honda for a quick return to the highway.

Whap. Whap. The Hummer's two front doors slapped shut.

"Good thing I'm not alone." Bella took the camera out of its case and presented it to him like a newborn baby. "Remember to hold steady and keep rolling. Don't shut it off unless we're getting back in the car. I'll keep them talking, so they'll forget about you."

Ethan glanced toward the gate at the sound of somebody rattling chains. The way the creeps were crawling up his back, they might have been jerking on his. The smaller of the two gatekeepers emerged first, while the other one took care of the chain, lock and gate. Neither one was in a hurry to welcome anybody.

"What do you want me to do if it gets weird?" Ethan asked quietly as they got out of the car.

"Keep rolling."

The face of the younger man working the gate was partially obscured by a sweatshirt hood. The smaller guy—billiard-ball bald and bearded—strolled ahead two paces as though he was in charge. Ethan stepped back and turned the camera on.

"Mr. Mosher is unavailable," the bald guy said.

"*Mrs*. Mosher booked the appointment," Bella said, her tone friendly. "She said she welcomes the opportunity to show off her dogs."

The droopy hood shielded the younger man's eyes, and his lips barely moved. "Mr. Mosher likes his privacy, and he has the final word."

"Which is *no trespassing*. And no—" Baldy's hands shot out and snatched the camera "—pictures."

"Give that back!" Bella shouted.

Hoodie grabbed for Bella, but Ethan shoved him to the ground before he could get a firm hold on her. She staggered, caught her balance and went for the camera again. Baldy threw it down on the blacktop and raised a booted foot over it.

"No!" she screamed.

"Bella, leave it!" Ethan shouted. Hoodie was trying to get up. Ethan was forced to give him a swift kick in the ass before he could prevent Baldy from booting the camera. "Stay down or I'll break something," Ethan warned.

"You and me both." Big words spoken in a wary tone as the older man glanced at his prone partner and took a step back from the camera, giving the lie to his own statement. He pointed his finger at Bella. "No pictures."

"Elaine Mosher agreed to an interview with KOZY," she repeated with commendable calm.

"Well, her husband musta disagreed," Baldy said. "He's trying to make a living here, and you news people just wanna make trouble. That's what you do."

Ethan stood between Bella and the two flunkies. "Where's your phone, Bella?"

"In the car."

"Get in the car," he told her gently.

"That camera's checked out to me, and I'm not going anywhere—" trusting Ethan's upper hand, she leaned over to pick it up "—without it."

"You'd better hand it over, or I'll have to take it," the bald man said.

Ethan laughed. "You and what army?"

Baldy glanced at Hoodie, who was picking himself up off the ground. "You're the one threw it down," Hoodie muttered. "It's busted anyway."

"Get in the car, Bella."

"We gotta get the camera," Baldy said. But he didn't move, and Hoodie's hesitant step was unconvincing.

"Come on, punk." Ethan offered a cold smile. "Try me again."

Hoodie took a moment to consider. He turned his eyes from Ethan's, glanced at the camera and rubbed his carbuncled jaw with an oily hand. "You didn't get nuthin', and that thing's busted anyway."

Baldy pointed to the cattle guard that stretched between the gateposts. "Cross this line and you're on private property."

"Is that a fact?" Ethan eyed each man in turn. "I don't see anything that's gonna stop me from taking the lady wherever she wants to go. Bella?"

"I'm done with this for now," Bella called out from the car.

"How 'bout you two?" Ethan asked. "You done?"

Baldy glared at Hoodie, who shrugged as he backed off. "We'll just tell him they didn't have one," Hoodie said. "Or tell him it's busted. That's the truth."

The two men turned and started walking back toward their mighty Hummer. "You're about to get more than a kick in the ass," the older one said.

Ethan returned to the car, smiling. "I got mine in first." He closed the door and glanced toward the camera. "Sorry. I didn't see that coming. You didn't tell me this was hazardous duty."

"I didn't know it would be hazardous."

He glanced at the camera she was cradling in her lap. "Is it busted?"

"I don't know. I turned it off, but now I'm afraid to turn it back on. I'll leave it to the techs."

Ethan had never been so glad to pull a car away from a driveway. If it had been just him, he would have stood his ground, no problem. But he was no brawler, and Bella was no brawler's broad. "You shouldn't be going out alone on something like this."

"It sounded like just another assignment." She tugged at a wisp of hair escaped from the clip at the back of her neck. "It wasn't supposed to be like this. We arranged for an interview. We were surprised they agreed, but that seemed like a clue that there wasn't anything going on. But I think there was." She turned in her seat. "I think we got something, Ethan."

"You need a bodyguard more than a cameraman."

"I'm sorry. I really didn't—"

"Hey, nothing to be sorry about except the camera, which was my fault. They ever send you out to that place again, give me a call." He chuckled. "Hell, who'da thought reporting the local news could be that much of a rush?"

"There's obviously a story there. The Boston affiliate might even send somebody out."

"Is that good? Would you get to stay on it?"

"We'll see." She lifted a shoulder. "Commercial dog breeding isn't regulated as strictly here as it is in, say, Massachusetts. But cruelty is cruelty."

"They're not gonna blame you for the camera, are they?"

"I hope we got some pictures. If we did…" She studied the camera for a moment and then looked up. "Would you like to come over for supper tonight?"

"What, *you* owe *me* now?" He laughed. "If we got pictures, let's call it even."

"Okay," she said quietly.

"And start over. I gotta be somewhere at six, but after that, let me take you out for supper."

"You don't think I can cook?" She gave his shoulder a light jab. "Smart girls can't cook? Is that what you think?"

"Course not. Why would I…?"

"Is it true that smart girls can't dance?"

The line rang a bell right away, but he let her wait a moment for his guilty glance. "That's no way to ask a girl to dance," she chided with a smile.

He lifted his shoulder. "Did you dance with me?"

"Should I walk away and let him wonder, or dance with him and remove all doubt? Hmm." Squinting, she tapped her chin and then looked skyward. "Walk away, I told myself. Blow his mind. Nobody's ever done that to him before."

He smiled. "And?"

"I wasn't much of a dancer, was I? You would've remembered if I'd walked away."

"It was my turn to lead. I think that's what threw you off your game."

"I had no game," she admitted. "I was there because it was my cousin's birthday, and that was the only reason my mother agreed to let me go. That and the chance to take a picture of me in a dress."

"It was blue, wasn't it? The material felt real soft, but underneath you felt like you'd taken a bath in starch."

"Guess I was scared stiff."

He glanced, grinned, and they groaned in unison.

"Not anymore, though," she said gleefully. "Stood up to those two thugs today. Got the camera back. Asked you over for supper. I'm not even afraid of being turned down."

"I can be there by seven-thirty."

"Two-twelve."

"Can't stay that late. I'm a workin' man."

"*Apartment* two-twelve."

He grinned. "Just sayin'."

He was also a student. Ethan had done well in the correspondence courses he'd been al-lowed to take before his release from prison, and he'd been able to transfer a few of his credits toward a college degree, but now he sat uneasily in the back row of his first real class in nearly ten years. He wasn't the oldest guy in the group, and he sure as hell wasn't the dimmest bulb in the string. When they'd gone around the room introducing themselves, he'd simply given his name, mentioned his job, said he was training a mustang in his spare time. Nobody had asked him where he'd been for the past two years. He wasn't sure what his problem was, but he was uneasy with feeling uneasy. Come hell or high water, he could save himself as long as he took it easy. He was far from feeling any heat in this class, far from being in over his head.

So what was his problem?

If he was back to square one, if he was nothing unless he was easy, then where was he? *Who* was he?

That's what you're here to learn, Wolf Track.

It was going to be an interesting class. He'd tested out of all the bonehead stuff, so he was able to take a course that counted for something. An American lit class was a good bet for a guy who'd spent two years reading books like a fiend. He'd gotten the reading list ahead of time, and he'd already read everything on it, then started in on the list again. Take nothing for granted this time around, he told himself, even though his parole officer's advice was to take it easy, easy does it, *go easy on yourself.*

Hell, he'd never had any trouble going easy. Easy was no challenge at all.

It was time to try something different.

"Yeah, this is my second time with this one," he said in answer to the teacher's question about the assignment at the top of the list. "But I'm noticing some things I didn't see the first time."

"Something sure smells good."

It was the right thing to say when a guy walked into the apartment of a woman who'd just cooked supper for him, but it was also true. He wanted to tell her how pretty she looked with her sleek black hair falling loose behind her shoulders, but he decided to play it safe.

He handed her a bottle in a brown paper sack and grinned when she pulled it up by the neck. "I almost went for the box, but then it takes a while if you like it cold."

She read the label. "Pre-sweetened, and with lemon. Excellent choice."

"The clerk said it was the best they had."

They shared a polite laugh. He glanced from window to window—the big one with the sofa in front, the smaller one over the table with the white cloth, two plates, one candle—and back to Bella, who was watching him, waiting for something. Not a kiss, that wasn't it. "You've fixed your place up real nice. It makes you feel good when you walk in."

"Thank you. It's California thrift shop. I love color, and I want to be comfortable."

Colors. Right. He took another look. "Earth, water and sky. You brought it all inside."

She smiled. "I hope you like chicken."

"I'm lovin' this one already."

She gave a sweeping gesture toward the table. "Sit down. It's all ready. I'll fix the tea."

"Can I help with—"

"I want you to sit." She disappeared around the corner of a partition, but she kept talking. "I was just going to have water, so this is perfect."

Ethan sat down at the pretty little table and listened to the sound of cupboard doors gently opening and closing, kitchen tools softly clinking. Home kitchen sounds, not institutional. It sounded almost musical. He wanted to be part of it. If he hadn't quit smoking he would at least have been able to light the candle.

"Guess what?" she said as she set glasses of tea on the table. "No, I won't tell you. I'll let you see for yourself later." And she was gone again.

She returned with serving dishes, one steaming, one piled with chunks of crusty bread. He was salivating.

"I hope you like cacciatore."

"Is that chicken?"

"With vegetables and sauce. Do you like sauce?"

He was ready to jump into the dish. "I'm a sauce fanatic."

She turned on her bare heel. "I forgot the—"

He caught her hand. "We're gonna ride double in this chair if you don't sit down pretty soon."

She gave him a funny look, and then she laughed, lowering her shoulders by several inches. "Matches. They're right over here."

He let her go, but he held out his hand when she came back. She laid the matches in his palm, her fingertips lingering, inviting him to curl his around them briefly, just to say thanks.

He lit the candle, and she served him his

supper, candlelight dancing in her eyes. The food tasted so good he didn't want to talk. She looked so good smiling back at him across the table that he didn't want to eat. He wanted to look and taste and smell, and just be right where he was with this woman sitting across from him.

"Where'd you learn to cook like this?" he asked when they had finished their food and she finally allowed him to follow her into her neat little kitchen. "Your mom?"

"She gave me the basics. Meat, roots, corn, season with salt and pepper. In California I discovered variety." She nodded toward the serving dish as he set it on the counter. "Sauces. Lots of fruits and vegetables. I had a roommate who showed me what to do with it all. He'd grown up with all that fresh produce. Who knew herbs and spices started out as little plants?"

"You had a guy for a roommate?"

"Two. Two girls and two guys." Bella rolled her eyes and laughed. "My mother hit the roof when she found out, but it was already a done deal. I wanted to live off campus my senior year, and rent is really crazy out there. I was carrying a full course load and waiting tables as many hours as I could get."

"Sounds like you learned how to party."

"Did you hear the part about full course load and waiting tables?" So pretty, the way she lifted one shoulder as she turned on the faucet. "It was worth it. I loved having a lot on my plate. I lapped it up."

"It shows. You've filled out nicely."

"Thank you." She slid the dinner plates under a growing mound of bubbles as she slid him a second-thought glance. "I think."

"That's what I mean. You were always thinking, but now you look pretty while you're doing it. No matter what you have to say, it's a real pleasure for me to listen."

She laughed. "Why, Ethan, that's the nicest thing you've ever said to me. Also the screwiest."

"That's what happens when I shoot straight. It sounds screwy." He reached for the serving dish. Not much left. "What should I do with this? Toss it?"

"Oh, no. That'll be soup." She took the dish and scooped the contents into a plastic bowl. "That's the Ladonna coming out in me. Don't let anything go to waste."

"You called your mother Ladonna?"

"Only when she wasn't around. Which—" she gave a tight smile "—she isn't."

"You miss her?"

"More all the time. Don't you?"

He held up his right hand and wiggled a crooked middle finger. "I broke this playing football. She helped the doctor set it. I coulda sworn she was the doctor and he was the assistant."

She nodded, gave him a funny look as though he'd said something wrong. Or screwy. But all she said was, "Doesn't look like they did a very good job."

"I took the splint off too soon. Didn't wanna miss another game."

"Were you able to play?"

"Hell, yeah. I can always play."

The smile she offered struck him as sympathetic. He was open to all kinds of feelings from her, but sympathy wasn't one of them. He'd done the damage all by himself.

"Actually, I meant do you miss *your* mom? You must've been pretty young when she left."

He looked down at his bent finger. It had angered him a time or two, that finger. Jumped out there and made him look stupid. Caused him some trouble he could have done without. "I was five when she married Logan. Seven when she left."

"Left? I thought… I guess I assumed she died."

"She was just gone one day. I don't know what happened to her after that. I hardly remember her."

"If you were seven, you must remember—"

"I was seven, and I hardly remember her. Nothing else to report. End of story." He backed up to the counter and braced his butt against it, bracing for more even though he'd said there wasn't any. So far he didn't mind the questions, partly because he didn't have many answers. And partly because this was Bella. He felt good about her, didn't mind admitting, "I guess I thought everyone knew she walked out on us."

"Let's see, if you were seven, I would've been four or five. Ladonna would've been finishing up her nurse's training. We would've been living in Grand Forks, North Dakota." She raised her brow. "Either the news didn't travel that far, or it didn't make an impression on me."

"Damn. All this time I was embarrassed for nothing." He smiled. "Been tryin' like hell not to let it show."

"And you succeeded."

"Until now." He folded his arms. "Tell you what, though, I had a fine dad."

"Have."

"Have," he acknowledged quietly.

"So, do you want to talk dads now? That's where I missed out."

Good, he thought. *Over to you.* "What happened to him?"

"Killed in a car wreck. It wasn't until I was in high school that I heard he was drunk, *and* he was with another woman. Ladonna never told me that part. I had to hear it from one of the other woman's relatives." Her eyes challenged his. *See? So?*

"Maybe it wasn't true."

"I was a baby when it happened." She reached for his arm. "Let's go sit in the living room. Show-and-tell time. What's in your wallet?" She smiled. "Do you have pictures?"

"Of what?"

"Family? Friends? We're swapping stories. Time to look at pictures." She directed him to the sofa while she rustled around with some stuff on a bookshelf. "I'll bet you haven't seen a school yearbook in a while."

"You win, darlin'. Man, this is a comfortable sofa." He looked up, smiling as she sat down with an armload of books. "California thrift shop?"

"Rapid City furniture store. My one big splurge."

"Good choice." He rubbed his hand over the butter-soft leather. A school yearbook landed on his knees. "Do me one solid. Don't quote me on that blog of yours, okay?" He grinned. "Unless I said something intelligent."

They turned pages and revisited faces, and his own warm feelings surprised him. No regrets. No desire for do-overs. They'd walked the same halls, shared some of the same friends, or relatives of friends. Each had memories the other enjoyed hearing about, because there were shared ties to a place they were beginning to enjoy being from. Sinte was part of them.

The scrapbook Bella pulled out afterward was more personal. Memories mixed in with pictures of people and places—a nice little history book. It was something he didn't have, something he'd never missed, never thought about. Saving bits of the past made no sense to him. He decided it was a female thing, and he suddenly realized his life hadn't included females in ways that might make sense to one of them.

He looked down at the picture of a little headstone sitting in the middle of the big prairie.

"We always took care of my father's grave on Memorial Day," Bella recalled. "Ladonna never said anything bad about him. Never said much about him at all unless I asked, and then it was always kind of vague, some little tidbit she plucked out of nowhere. Like she was saying, I don't have anything to say about that, but here's something you'll like."

She brightened. "He named me. My father named me Bella. I found out what it meant. Beautiful. That made me happy for a long time. And then I put it together with my mother's name, and it made me so mad that they were both dead, and I couldn't ask them whether it was an accident or some kind of comment or curse. Or maybe it's a joke." She gave him a perfunctory smile. "What do you think?"

"I think you lost me. Had me at *beautiful,* lost me at—"

Her eyes widened. "Belladonna? *Deadly poison?*"

"Oh, yeah. Interesting." He slid his hand over hers. "Anyone ever suggest you might have a tendency to *over*think?"

"No. No one ever has. But, then, these are things I've never told anyone else." She squinted a little, second-guessing him. "Are you suggesting…?"

"No." He surrendered, both hands up. Whatever it was, he wasn't. "Not at all. I'm just catchin' up here."

"You have to wonder, right? Your parents are gone, and they took so many answers with them. So you think about what you have from them, you turn it over in your mind, and you wonder what more they would have given if they'd had more time. Don't you?" She didn't seem to notice him shaking his head. "Like when I asked—you know, the way we all do—where babies come from, my mother said they come from the seed a man plants inside the woman he loves. I liked the sound of that. It took me quite a while to come up with the next question."

"How does he do that?"

"Why does she let him?" She turned her palms up, empty. He didn't dare drop any of the words that sprang to his mind. "I mean, why doesn't she just plant it herself?"

He offered a lopsided smile. "I'm gonna say *because it's man seed* was not her answer."

"You're right. It was not." Her smile was

pretty indulgent. At least it was a smile. "She said the seed comes from the man a woman loves, and that love is like water and sunshine. It makes the baby grow. I liked the sound of that even better."

"It's beautiful."

"It doesn't sound screwy at all, does it? It's pure and simple, and it sounded like the straight, God's honest truth."

"Should've left it at that. I would've. I never asked." Ethan slid down and rested his head against the back of the sofa. "One day I got mad at Trace and called him a name that, you know, started with *mother,* and Logan heard me. He sat me down and told me that was about the worst thing you could call a man. Hell, I knew that. That was why I said it. But the look in Logan's eyes…"

He shook that sad look out of his head. "I never used that word again. Not around Logan. I don't remember exactly how old I was when he told me the facts, man-to-man. Simple, straightforward, but respectful, you know? It was good, coming from him."

"Your father—*biological* father—he was Indian, too, wasn't he?"

"Yeah. We had different fathers, Trace and me. She said mine was Indian. Never knew his name, but there was a picture of the two of them. I don't know where he was from, though. I kinda look like him." He chuckled. "Good-lookin' dude."

"Absolutely." Bella closed her scrapbook. "I'm glad you were with me today."

"So am I. Does that kind of stuff happen often?"

"I've been told to go away. I've had the door slammed in my face. But, no, nothing like what happened today. But that wasn't the end of the story. Did you catch me at six?"

"On TV?" He shook his head. "I was in…"

"That's right, you had to be somewhere." She glanced at the clock. "But it's just turning ten. You got pictures, Ethan. One full face and one sort of." She held her hand up to her eyebrows, shading her eyes. "But the really good part…well, you'll see for yourself," she promised as she reached for one of the remotes on the side table.

Within moments there she was on the screen, but the anchor, she said, was just teasing her story. "It'll be on at the end of this segment. It's big enough that it'll keep people in suspense for five minutes."

"You gotta be careful about going out to

places like that. You know how to defend yourself?"

She lifted one shoulder as she set the remote aside. "I really do own a gun."

"You don't carry it."

"But I know how to use it." Another one of those token smiles. "And I know a few moves."

"Show me."

"Not unless I have to."

"Good move to start with. Keep your weapon a secret." He leaned closer and lowered his voice. "Wait until I make a move."

"I thought we were friends. I don't have to defend myself against friends."

"Expect the unexpected, even from friends." He took her shoulders in his hands. "A word is the only defense you'll need."

Her soft smile was a welcome sign. Her hand in his hair was a sweet surprise, its pressure drawing his head down for a meeting of smiles, mingling of breath, mixing of impressions made by moving lips and fingertips. He'd been saving this kiss for a long time, guarding it, fearing for it, thinking long and hard about the look and the mind and the heart of the woman who could take it from him. *Expect the unexpected* sounded good, but he hadn't expected Bella. He couldn't have known how good he would feel giving her an experience that had all the magic of a first kiss. He wanted to draw her closer, but he was afraid he would scare her away. Let her invite him, and let him go easy.

She lifted her arms around his neck, and he turned his head to one side, lightly taking the measure of her lush lips with his, touching and tasting, catching her breath in his mouth, tickling her mouth with his tongue. And when he felt her tremble under his hands, he drew her to him and kissed her thoroughly.

She kissed him back. She'd dreamed of this kiss long ago, made it happen a hundred ways, cooked up a thousand dreamy details—some raw, some overdone—and she'd been a believer for the very long time it had taken to become a woman. She'd held out for the hundred ways and the thousand details, and here was the first, the way of the kiss. It made her breath falter and her insides flutter. It made her reach up and lean forward, part her lips and greet his tongue. It made her a believer again.

And then, when the greeting was complete, she kept her eyes closed and licked the taste of it from her lips. "I haven't been…"

"Neither have I." He kissed her again, briefly. "Take it slow?"

"Yes," she said without thinking, and then on the other hand, "No." And that sounded almost as ridiculous as what came next. "Surprise me."

"I thought I was."

"Not yet." She'd dreamed a hundred ways times a thousand details. It would take...

He shook his head slowly, his gaze affixed to hers, and she had no idea what he was thinking as he looked at her, his hands gently kneading her shoulders. His lips came down on hers softly again, and then came the turn of his head, the touch of his tongue, the warmth of his breath and finally more kiss, good kiss, much more kiss. She opened herself up to him and welcomed the taste and the scent and the feel of him.

Then he backed off, giving her a little breathing room, thinking space. She glanced up at the clock, and broke both the kiss and the mood as she sat up straight. "Oh, no, I think we missed it!" she exclaimed, turning to the TV.

He blinked. *Damn. Who the hell cared about...?*

"No, we didn't. Here it comes."

What she was saying didn't make as much of an impression on him as the sound of her voice, the way she held her shoulders, moved her hand. Oh, he got the gist of the report. He'd been on the inside getting the scoop firsthand. Anybody could see what was going down, and hey, he *did* get a little footage. But Bella looked terrific. The two thugs looked terrible. The camera mike picked up the few words that were exchanged before the picture did a three-sixty and went to black.

"Hot damn." Ethan slapped his knee. "My first—"

"Shh, here comes the good part."

Her rich, smooth television voice was truly the good part. It was familiar but different. Even more authoritative than usual. The raid that had taken place soon after her producer called the sheriff department was good, too, but Ethan was enchanted by the sound of her voice, the way it gave weight to the words and import to the story.

"It was a puppy mill," she told him. "I don't know why the woman said we could go out there and talk to her husband. She'll probably get in more trouble with him than with the law. The sheriff was able to get a warrant and get past the gate before they could cover up all the—" She pointed to Baldy and Hoodie walking across the screen in handcuffs. "Look. Serves them right. I guess those two tried to resist. The Moshers went quietly and made bail, but the two flunkies are still guests of the county."

"Who took these pictures? They didn't send you back out there, did they?"

"No, just John Carney, the cameraman."

"The real cameraman?"

"You're the real cameraman on this one, Ethan. You got the goods."

"I was about to, but then the news came on." They exchanged warm smiles. "That's really something, Bella. You uncovered a puppy mill. Where they...manufacture a lot of puppies?"

"It's like factory farming for dogs. We're running a follow-up tomorrow with a warning that it gets graphic. People from out of state answer ads for puppies, they don't realize what they're—"

"You and John?"

She frowned. "Me and John?"

"Doing the follow-up."

She smiled. Was he jealous? "I wanted to take you, but I really wasn't supposed to let you run the camera."

"What were you supposed to do?"

"I was supposed to get an interview. I

would have asked my questions from behind the camera. Budgets are tight in the news business these days. But, Ethan, this was too good. This is really going to make a difference, at least for those poor dogs. They've all been rescued by the Humane Society."

He touched her arm. "You could've gotten hurt. You shouldn't be going out on stories like that alone."

"Hey." She laid her hand over his. "It's almost never like that. It's not a dangerous job. Taming a wild horse, that's a dangerous job."

"What's in the follow-up?"

"They got some pictures of lots of skinny animals crowded into cages stacked in filthy, crumbling shacks. And that isn't the half of it, Ethan. Yes, those bitches are used as puppy factories. It'll have to be edited, but people will get the idea. And I'll be interviewing the sheriff and maybe talking with the affiliate that put us on to the story." She was glowing. "It's my story. And I probably wouldn't've gotten any video if you hadn't been there."

"You could've gotten hurt."

"Okay, I could've gotten hurt." She squeezed his hand. "But I didn't."

He leaned in for a kiss, prefaced with a whispered, "I'm glad."

Chapter Five

Ethan's kisses took Bella out of her head. Her whole being rushed to be where he touched her, and there were no loose ends. His kiss went on forever, and his mouth made hers sing without sound. His hand tucked under her shirt made her skin tingle from the middle of her back to her bare toes. All she had to do was feel the all-over excitement. It didn't matter whether he felt it, too. He did—she could feel it where their bellies met—but that was just part of the process. She didn't have to figure anything out or plan the next step. This was happening. She was unfolding, stretching out and connecting up, and it felt right. Where one kiss ended another began.

Until it didn't.

But he still held her and slid his fingertips lightly over her skin, and looked into her eyes like the besotted schoolboy he never was. She wondered how she looked to him. Like she would follow him anywhere? Because she would. No words required. All he had to do was lead the way.

He pushed a strand of hair back from her face and gave a reflective smile. "I can't stay tonight."

She bit back, *No one asked you to,* in favor of a matching smile. "It's okay."

"No, it isn't. You don't know me, Bella. And the thing is…" He withdrew his hand, pulled her shirt down in back as though he'd disturbed something on a shelf. "I'm ready to jump out of my skin right now, and that's not the way I want this to go."

"This what?"

"This…you and me. I didn't expect…"

"What didn't you expect? That I could give you—" she gave him a bold below-the-belt glance "—that?"

"Honey, I've been out of circulation long enough that even the slightest smell of a woman makes me so hard it hurts." He kissed her gently and touched his forehead to hers. "But that's not what I want. Not with you. Not tonight."

She kissed him back, a quick it's-fine-with-me kiss, and then freed herself. It really *was* fine.

"Can I ask you something?" she said quickly. Because asking questions was something she knew how to do. "The woman you went to jail for... Have you seen her since you got out?"

"Last time I saw her she was on the witness stand. Man, that was..." He gave a dry chuckle and shook his head. "And I didn't go to prison for her or because of her or anything like that. It was me. I was stupid."

"She said you drove off and left her after she told you to take her home and gave you the keys to her daddy's car." She glanced up at him. "That's what I read."

"She went off with somebody else and left me with the car." He leaned back and searched for the story on the ceiling. "We went to a party at somebody's cabin up in the hills. Craziest party I've ever been to, and that's just the part I remember. I didn't know anything about her father—didn't even know who he was—but it ended up that I had the car and not the girl whose daddy owned it. And the rest was my word against everyone else's."

"She's been in the news since. Her father's still trying to cover for her."

"She's a live wire, that woman. If you're lookin' for trouble, she can help you find it."

"Were you?"

"I was chasin' my tail back then." He reached for the straw hat he'd set on the side table, planted his elbows on his knees and toyed with the hat brim. "Tried playing football for South Dakota State, but they wanted me to take classes at the same time."

"Imagine that." Bella smiled even though he wasn't looking.

"Tried the army. I was fine with that for a while, but then I, um…" He shook his head. "Like I said, I'm not much of a hunter. Not with a gun, anyway. But, yeah, I was a lone wolf."

"Caught in a trap?"

"Nope." He glanced up, gave a self-effacing smile. "Paws on the ground, nose in the air, eyes wide open, nobody can touch this lobo. I got nobody to blame but myself."

"You sound like a totally rehabbed man."

He gave a nod and a wink. "One day at a time, kiddo."

"Kiddo?" She punched his arm. "I guess that explains why you can't stay."

"Hey, I don't call just anybody that." He laughed. "Okay, I don't call anybody that. I don't know where it came from."

"It goes nicely with that sexy wink."

"Now I'm totally deflated." He leaned over, took her chin in hand and kissed her, fast and firm. "I mean that, Bella. And this." He laid his hand on her cheek and kissed her again. Another kiss followed, and then another, each lingering a little longer than the last.

"Do you *want* to stay?" she whispered when he straightened, gradually separating himself from her.

"Absolutely." He clapped his hat on his head and pushed off, hands on his knees. "I need to get back to Square One."

"There's something to be said for showing up where you're expected." She stood, too. This close, this enclosed, she was keenly aware of his height and his powerful build. Ordinarily she would have stepped back, required space. But with Ethan, this close was not close enough.

"And it's not that hard," he was saying.

"Who knew?" Silly comment. Overused filler. Bella wasn't fond of filler.

"You did. Some people have to learn these things the hard way." He took a piece of her hair between two fingers and let it slide through until his hand reached her shoulder. "Believe it or not, what's happening between us is new for me." Gently he squeezed her shoulder. "Like I picked up an egg, and something soft and sweet hatched in my hand. I don't know what it is, but I damn sure want the chance to find out."

"You didn't have a female judge, did you?" She smiled. "Of course not. A line like that would've gotten you off with time served."

He laughed. "Time to reel in my lines and hit the road." He took a step in that direction, and then had a second thought. "If I can get the day off, can I take you out on Saturday?"

"This Saturday?"

He nodded, his eyes bright with promise. "You like rodeo?"

Not particularly. "Is your brother riding?"

"Yeah, and it's been a while since I've seen him ride. He's doin' real good. Heard from him last week. He has a new girlfriend." He smiled. "Sounds pretty serious."

"The marrying kind of serious?"

"I wouldn't be surprised." He shoved his hands in the front pockets of his jeans. "So how 'bout it? You date real cowboys?"

"Not so far." She looked at him quizzically. "Funny. I never thought of you as a cowboy."

"How *did* you think of me?"

"I tried not to. You made no sense to me. Or *for* me. But look at you now. You've got the boots, the Wrangler jeans, the hat." She jerked her chin, pursed her lips in the general upward direction. "That hat looks as though it could tell some campfire stories."

Ethan snatched it off his head and turned it over in his hands, as though he hadn't seen it in a while. "Logan gave me this hat, long time ago. Thought of switching to outlaw black, but I'm pretty attached to this hat."

"I never thought of you as an outlaw, either." She folded her arms. "What time Saturday?"

"We'd have to leave before daylight, drive down to Nebraska. It's a midday show."

"If you can get time off."

"I'll get the time off if I get back on time tonight. Part of my retraining program." He tapped her arm with his hat. "You're keeping me in suspense here, woman. My ego ain't what it used to be. But I'll tell you what, I know how to get the most out of a twenty-four-hour pass. After the rodeo, I'll take you dancing."

"Oh, that's a real incentive. You know how long I've avoided dancing?" He cocked an eyebrow, and she nodded. "Yes. That long."

"The wait is finally over, baby. Wolf Track is back."

She laughed. "So much for a bruised ego."

It took a little over seven hours to get to the rodeo on Saturday. Seven short hours. The road was empty, the sun rose in a clear sky, and the conversation was packed with upbeat memories and down-home anecdotes. Bella had the local history, and Ethan's curiosity knew no bounds. She didn't mind letting him steer. It was his pickup after all. His party. He'd trusted her with enough truth to test her acceptance, and she'd passed. It was the kind of test a good reporter handled well. She was glad he wasn't in this thing—*what's happening between us,* he'd called it—for anything more than dinner and a show. No bed-and-breakfast. That was a good thing, and she owed him props for good sense. She really did.

They met Trace and his beautiful blonde

lady behind the stock pens when they got to the rodeo grounds. The first moments were all about the brothers, all backslapping and inside joking. No matter where the years had taken them, they were close at the roots. Bella and the blonde exchanged smiles as the camaraderie spilled over.

"You remember Bella Primeaux?" Ethan asked Trace.

Trace offered an eager handshake. "I remember Ladonna Primeaux. The nurse?"

"My mother. I take it you broke some bones."

"Nothing major. Got carried out of the Sinte rodeo arena once or twice as a kid."

"He's got a hard head," Ethan said.

"Runs in the family. But don't tell my—" Trace reached for the stunning beauty he'd brought with him "—special lady." He introduced Skyler Quinn, who asked Bella the inevitable question about having met before.

"You get Rapid City TV stations on the other side of the Hills?" Ethan asked. He turned to Bella. "Easy for me to keep a low profile around you. I'm just the guy with that TV reporter."

"I know what you mean. I'm the guy with the Dairy Princess." Trace laughed at Skyler for groaning. "It's true," he said. "It's a woman's world. Guys were put on earth to carry the water."

"Well, break out the canteen, honey. The special ladies need to rinse off all that soft soap." Skyler winked at Bella before turning to Ethan. "Trace tells me you're training a horse for the Mustang Sally competition."

"I am." Ethan adjusted his hat. "Hear you and Trace are entered up, too."

"Just Skyler," Trace said. "I'm the coach. The only horse I'm entered on is that little black." He gave an over-the-shoulder nod toward the pen at his back. Bella glanced politely toward the fence. "Tomcat, he's called. Good match for me. High roller. He can get a little snaky, but we'll rack up the points." Trace tapped Ethan's arm with a loose fist. "Your big brother's headed for the finals again. Mark your calendar."

"I won't miss it this time," Ethan said.

"Damn straight you won't." Trace reached *up* to plant his hand on his *little* brother's shoulder. "So, you like your job? Start your classes yet?"

"Yeah, I do and I did." Ethan clapped his hands and rubbed them together, clearly eager to move on. "Let's get something to eat."

"Nothing for me until after I ride." Trace turned to Skyler. "You hungry?"

"You know me. I can eat anytime," she said.

"Right." The two of them exchanged an intimate glance. Yes, he knew her. "But my little brother needs food now, and I think I know just the place."

Ethan stepped back. "You can just point us in the right direction. Then we'll meet you somewhere later."

"Not so fast," Skyler said as she reached for Bella's hand. "We've got some getting acquainted to do." She met Ethan's gaze. "And some catching up."

Ethan tipped his hat, offering Skyler a cowboy salute. "Thank you, ma'am."

"You've had a long drive," Skyler told him.

"Not quite as long as yours," he said. "Did you come down from Newcastle?"

"I live closer to Gilette," Skyler said. Wyoming was big territory, small town, which meant that mileage was not an issue. "Trace has been helping me out with the ranch, and I've been helping him ride like nobody's watching." She caught Trace's eye and smiled lovingly. "Except me."

"Why don't Bella and I go get something to eat while you two get a room?" Ethan teased.

"Mind your manners, kid." Trace gave Ethan a backhanded slap on the chest. "She's determined to keep me off crutches."

"Good luck with that, Skyler. My brother enjoys the agony of victory."

"It sounds as though you've both been to the nurse's office," Bella said.

"Emergency services only. The mark of a real cowboy," Ethan assured her.

Trace tapped his brother's arm. "Let's ride. I'm on a tight schedule here."

"I parked my pickup—"

"Way the hell on the other side of the arena. Come on, kids."

Trace loaded the foursome into his shiny white club cab pickup, drove a few blocks and pulled up in front of a restaurant called Better Than Your Mama's Spaghetti. He glanced at each of his passengers in turn. "What do you all think?"

Both women approved, Bella saying that her mother never made spaghetti and Skyler that her mother wouldn't let her eat it.

"Works for me," Ethan said.

"I know how to fill up that hollow leg of yours," Trace told him. "I've eaten here a few times. The spaghetti can't hold a candle to mine, but it's pretty damn good."

"Wait a minute," Skyler said. "Didn't you tell me you were a lousy cook?"

"I forgot to mention the three exceptions." Trace ticked them off, starting on his thumb. "Enhanced peanut butter sandwiches, everything-goes-into-it soup, and excellent spaghetti."

"He's right," Ethan said as he followed Bella out of the cramped backseat of the pickup and onto the sidewalk. "Trace perfected all three—when he wasn't keeping me in line. Logan's right-hand man. Riding herd on me was a two-man job."

"Two men and a bottomless pot of spaghetti," Trace said. "Took a little time to get Logan on board the spaghetti train. Devoted to his macaroni, that guy."

"That's the way he is. Loyal to the end and then some." Ethan shook his head. "Loyalty is good for filling graveyards." He glanced at his brother. "I think I read that somewhere."

"He's been there for you, Ethan."

Ethan nodded.

"And now he's found a woman who deserves his loyalty. Our mother—"

"I know all about our mother. Far as I'm

concerned, a smart man doesn't put himself out there like that."

Bella took it all in. Trace was a rider; Ethan was a fighter. She wondered whether these were two more categories—*two kinds of people in this world,* Ladonna used to say—that deserved their own pages in her mental notebook. You found your niche at your first rodeo, and for the rest of your life you had it all figured out.

She slid quietly into a dark corner booth along the front wall, and Ethan slid in beside her. There were menus to be studied and water to be sipped, but the conversation was not over. Not until big brother said it was over.

"Cut Logan some slack," Trace instructed. "Every man gets one free pass on being a fool for love. Who was it that said 'Fool me once, shame on you. Fool me twice, you can't get fooled again'?"

"Somebody who got the quote wrong," Bella injected.

"Exactly." Trace cocked a finger and fired her a point. "But it's no shame to love somebody. Matter of fact, it's a shame if you don't. Maybe one quote doesn't fit all."

Ethan checked the front of the menu again. "Better than your mama's, huh?"

"She never knew what was good for her, little brother. You gotta pity her a little bit for her loss."

"I don't even like to think about her," Ethan said as he turned back to the list of entrées. "Why don't they turn a light on in here?"

Trace reached up and pulled the cord for the blinds, shedding considerable light. "I know what you mean."

He *thought* he did—Ethan would give his brother that much credit. And more. Hell, any credit to be had, Trace deserved it. He was a good man. He was Logan's true son in every way but DNA. If Trace didn't like to think about their mother, it was because of what she'd put him through, the hurt she'd put on him, the bad stuff Ethan didn't remember. Maybe he should be able to remember some of it, but he didn't. And the reason he didn't— he was just speculating here—was that he was like her, created in her image, *her* right-hand man. He shared in her faults. He—not Trace—was their mother's creature.

"So what's on the program?" Ethan asked. "Besides the next world-champion bareback rider."

"You talkin' to me?" Trace's De Niro was actually halfway credible. He drew a folded piece of paper from his breast pocket, set just below his sponsor's stitched-on logo, and tossed it on the table.

"Cowboy poker," Ethan announced as he scanned the program. "Thought they'd stopped doing that."

"You don't see it around here much. Hard to find takers after what happened down in San Angelo."

"What happened?" Skyler asked.

"What's cowboy poker?" was Bella's question.

"Some woman wasn't playing with a full deck, and she got her watermelon thumped," Trace said.

Bella and Skyler exchanged a look. "Colorful," Skyler said. "You mean she was—"

"I'm sorry, darlin'." Trace put his arm around her. "But there are some games women should not be playing."

"—*pregnant?*" Skyler's eyes widened.

"I picked the wrong fruit." Trace pulled her head to his shoulder. "Rest your worried melon right here, hon. No animals or unborn children were harmed. Some woman got kicked in the head was all." He turned to Bella. "They take four volunteers from the audience, sit them down at a card table in the middle of the arena, deal a hand and turn out one of the livelier bulls. Last player to leave his seat wins the pot. Which is what tonight?" He nodded at the paper in Ethan's hand. "Five hundred bucks?"

"That's what it says."

"You're right," Skyler said. "That's not a game for women. We're way too smart."

"How about five hundred pairs of shoes?"

She lifted one shoulder. "That might be different."

"Have you checked out the night spots?" Ethan asked Trace. "Bella's dying to go dancing with me."

"The Killer Hayseeds are playing at a place near the arena. I hear they're pretty good."

Ethan grinned at Bella. "What do you think?"

"I think Killer Hayseeds sounds like the perfect follow-up to cowboy poker."

Ethan turned his grin on his brother. "We're in."

Skyler and Bella watched the Grand Entry from seats Trace had chosen for their view of the arena and the bucking chutes. His event came first, and he'd invited Ethan to help him set his rigging. Ethan seemed pleased, almost touched, or as close to touched as Bella had seen him. From her convenient perch she watched the activity behind the chutes, watched the two brothers confer over the equipment, and exchange words and handshakes with other cowboys.

The proceedings became nothing short of operating-room serious when Tomcat was loaded into the chute. Ethan took charge of setting the rigging and making sure his brother's glove was sufficiently rosined and his grip was solid. When Trace nodded for the gate to be opened, Ethan turned cheerleader. Bella half expected him to tumble into the empty bucking chute.

Trace did his fans proud. Tomcat rolled and pitched, twisted and turned, but Trace was unshakable. His score put him on top in the standings, and when he joined them in the stands, Skyler's kiss apparently put him on top of the world.

"Where's Ethan?" Bella asked.

Trace turned to look behind him, then turned back, frowning. "Snack bar, probably. Like I said, hollow leg. At least I don't have to buy his ice cream anymore." He grinned as he took his seat. "You got any chores you want done, Bella, you can pay him in spaghetti and ice cream."

"He helped me with a dangerous assignment the other day, and he didn't charge me anything."

"Oh, yeah, one other form of payment works." Trace draped his arm around Skyler's shoulders and settled in. "He can't resist an adrenaline rush. What kind of danger did you treat him to?"

"He got to hold the camera," she said, and then she related the puppy-mill story.

"Those two were lucky Ethan was in a generous…" Trace suddenly leaned forward and peered toward the far end of the arena. "What the hell?"

"What is it?" Skyler wanted to know.

"Little surprise in store," Trace said with a chuckle, and then he sat back and tugged at the front of his hat brim. "I sure hope these Killer Hayseeds turn out to be as good as they say. Sounds like something you might name a bull, huh? You like country music, Bella?"

"It's okay." She hadn't figured out what Trace was looking at, but she was working on it. Two rodeo clowns were pulling a cart loaded with a plastic patio table and four chairs into the arena. "Is it halftime already?" she wondered.

"Wrong sport," Trace said. "We don't go for a lot of downtime around here. This is what you call your—"

"Audience participation time," the announcer said. "Please welcome our four volunteer gamblers, in for a round of cowboy poker!"

It was Bella's turn to lean forward. "That's Ethan."

Trace drew a deep breath. "Yep."

"Is he helping with the... He's sitting down at the table."

"And that's the surprise."

"Not really," Skyler said. "He's your brother."

"You won't catch me messin' with bulls, darlin'."

"Has he done this before?" Bella asked.

"I doubt it."

A gate slammed, and a couple of levers clanked in the chute area below. Bella looked down and saw white horns, chocolate hide, no daylight on either side of the animal crammed into the chute. It moved, and the whole enclosure rattled.

She eyed the arena. The clowns in their

droopy overalls and red suspenders were setting up the table for the four players. A moment later Ethan started dealing cards.

"The last man to remain seated wins the pot," the announcer said. "Five hundred dollars, winner take all. You ready for Ace High, boys?"

One of the men waved.

"I hope your hard head runs in the family," Skyler said.

The gate opened, the bull stepped out, and the game was on.

"This is crazy," Bella said quietly.

"I'm getting used to it," Skyler said.

The bull seemed to have eyes only for the smaller of the two clowns, who was jumping up and down like a string puppet. "Every bull wants a piece of Jackson," Trace said. "He's the best in the business."

The big brown bull lowered his head and shoveled the bullfighter clown out of the way.

"But so is Ace High."

"He's a bull," Bella said without taking her eyes off the action. "Bulls don't do business."

With a quick about-face, Ace High took a run at the closest player's hand. Cards flew, two chairs went down, and two cowboys scrambled in two directions.

Trace laughed. Ethan was still sitting there within spearing distance of a pair of horns, and his brother was laughing. "Forget the cards, bro. Save the jewels." He grinned at Skyler. "Hell, that's what I'd do."

On his next pass the bull took out the table, along with the third cowboy. Ethan was the last man seated. He stood to claim victory just as the big beast swung around, lowered his head and flew across the arena like a cannon ball, sweeping him ass over sawed-off horns.

Skyler and Bella shot out of their seats. The rodeo clown darted toward the bull as Ethan rolled out of its way and got to his feet. He gave his head a quick shake, recovered his hat and greeted the announcement that he'd won with a two-finger salute.

Trace laughed, slapped both his thighs and gave a victory whistle as he rose to his feet.

But then he shook his head and muttered, "Crazy kid," as he headed for the aisle. He turned and motioned to the women. "Let's go take inventory, see if he's all there."

"He's missing something upstairs," Bella said under her breath.

They met Ethan at the pay window. He'd already pocketed his winnings and was grinning to beat the band.

"Any blood?" Trace called out.

Ethan bent his arm and showed off a skinned elbow.

"Child's play." Trace turned a fake gut jab into a hearty handshake. "You coulda warned me, bro."

"And spoil my entrance?" Ethan shoved his hands into the pockets of his jeans, still grinning like a triumphant teenager. "Hey, remember when we entered the wild horse race at the Standing Rock Rodeo? This was like that. The kind of thing you do on the spur of the moment. You give it too much thought, you're gonna back out."

"You were about twelve, and I was—"

"Half as old as you are now, and what are you doing for a living?" Ethan tugged at his hat brim. "I rest my case, big brother. I know you won more than I did today, but I'm ridin' just as high as you are. Supper's on me."

"Supper? You just ate." Trace glanced at Bella as he slapped Ethan's gut with the back of his hand. "Can't fill him up, can't put any weight on him."

"I can wait a little while," Ethan said, all innocence. "Is there any dancing anywhere this time of day? Bella made me promise to dance with her."

"He's lying," Bella told Trace with a smile. "Dancing is the last thing I'd want him to promise me."

"What, then?" Ethan slipped his arm around her. "Make a wish, darlin'. I've got a pocketful of found money and I'm ready to spend it all on you."

Bella glanced at Skyler.

"Our first date I let Trace coax me onto a Ferris wheel. I'm afraid of heights." Skyler smiled. "Sometimes a little crazy doesn't hurt."

"I know where there's an old-fashioned jukebox," Trace said. "Take my mind off the final go-round."

The little hole-in-the-wall Trace took them to was enjoying some unusual late-afternoon business, thanks to the rodeo. Riders and fans mingled at the bar, traded change for tunes, and toasted winners and losers alike. Trace and Ethan made the most of the party atmosphere. They traded taunts and dance partners, told stories on each other and reveled in the rediscovery of each other's company. It couldn't last the way it once had, but that only made the minutes count more.

At least it did for Ethan. Not that he'd ever say anything that sappy, but he could tell that

Trace knew. Trace always knew how Ethan felt, even if he didn't know exactly why. Didn't matter. They might be two very different people, but they were brothers.

And Ethan knew how Trace felt about Skyler. He was glad to see that lovesick look in his brother's eyes. Trace would make a great family man—hell, he'd looked after his younger brother like some papa grizzly—and if he'd chosen Skyler, he'd chosen well. He always chose well.

Ethan nodded as Trace flashed him a thumbs-up across the dance floor. He was a mind reader, that guy. He could always tell when Ethan's head was totally in the game. The message was clear. *You're doin' good, little brother.*

Ethan leaned back and smiled at the lovely woman in his arms. "Did your mama teach you to dance?"

"Obviously nobody did," Bella said. "And my partners generally excuse themselves after one dance."

"Guess your previous partners were mostly tenderfeet. Or maybe they expected to lead."

"They should've said so." She laughed. "Okay, yes, my mother taught me to dance. 'In case you ever have to,' she said. I also know how to get out of a headlock or a moving car *if I ever have to*."

"Relax and follow me." He drew her close and pressed his cheek against her sleek hair. "All I wanna do is hold you. I won't be giving you a score." He could feel the effort it took for her to relax, but she did. A wave of release fell slowly from her shoulders, and she was finally pliable. "There. Now we're dancing."

"We are?"

"We are."

She rested her cheek on his shoulder, and after a moment she whispered, "I like dancing."

It was a start. Ethan hated to cut it short, but now that he'd come back down to earth, he had to follow through with his plan. One day off was all he had, and he was not going to blow the trust he'd earned at Square One. He couldn't stay to watch his brother take the final round in his event, but Skyler exchanged cell phone numbers with Bella and promised to call no matter how things went.

Trace would do well. He always did.

"Why did you do that poker thing?" Bella asked Ethan after they'd been on the road awhile. He was surprised she'd waited this long. They were only a few miles from the state line.

And there was only one honest answer.

"For the hell of it."

"How many times do you get to be a fool for fun?"

"What do you mean? I came away with five hundred dollars. How does that make me a..." He glanced at her and chuckled. "Okay, but it was fun to watch, wasn't it?"

"It was not."

"I heard you yelling for me."

"I never yell."

"Ha. You called my name."

"The same way I called my dog's name when she was about to get hit by a car." She folded her arms. "The dog had sense enough to move."

"You have a dog?"

"I had one when I was a kid. She was smart about cars." She turned her face to the side window. "But men with guns, not so much. She was killed by a hunter."

Ethan felt a chill crawl down his back. "A hunter?"

"My uncle used to take her hunting. I'm the one who should have had more sense. I shouldn't have let her go." She turned to him again. "Do you hunt?"

"Never have." He stared hard into the head-light path. "Never have."

"Three men in the house and you didn't turn out to be a hunter? What kind of an Indian are you, Ethan?"

"Wish I knew." Much better topic. "Hell, I don't much care who the guy was who, uh, planted the seed, but I wish I knew where he came from. You know, who his people are, whether they're hunters. Logan claimed me and gave me his name, but I can't claim his tribe. *Your* tribe." He flashed her a quick grin. "I want a tribe, hey."

"Hey." Bella smiled. "There's the Tribal rolls way and the Indian family way. You're in the family way."

He gave her an incredulous look, and they both laughed.

"Logan's been a good father, hasn't he?"

"The best."

"You and Logan have nothing but good to say about each other. It's none of my business, but I'll ask anyway."

"Because you're in the business of asking questions."

"Can't help myself, I guess." She cleared

her throat. "Why are you keeping your distance?"

"It's not *my* distance, it's…" He lifted his shoulder. "Space. I guess."

"You've got it." She gestured toward the Welcome sign as they flew past. "South Dakota has a good supply of space."

He let the hum of the pickup motor fill theirs. She was asking him a serious question, one he knew he'd created in Logan's mind. One that troubled his own.

"He was there during the trial," Ethan said quietly. "I couldn't look at him. I didn't want him to have to hear his name, the name he'd given me…"

It was a name that had fit him well. He never had to explain it the way Trace did. Ethan looked like a Wolf Track. The first time he'd written his name on a school paper, he felt like he was somebody. A boy with a man's name.

He'd wanted to do the name justice, but so far he'd come up short.

"It all seemed pretty unreal. I didn't take it too seriously. It was a party. A big steam-blowin' three-day bash. No one cared who anyone else was. I couldn't believe I'd be found guilty, couldn't believe I'd go to prison over something so crazy." He shook his head. "I didn't believe it until I heard those doors shut and lock behind me.

"And then Logan came to see me there. He never said anything one way or the other about what I'd done. He talked about anything but that. I couldn't let him keep coming to that place, getting locked down with me. I took him off my visitors list." He spared her a glance. "It was the least I could do, you know? Spare him that."

She nodded. "How did you cope with being locked away for so long?"

"I went home in my mind."

"But you haven't gone home since you got out. You haven't told Logan any of this, have you?"

He shook his head again. "I will. Soon." He gave her a lopsided smile. "Not that it's any of your business."

"I have a confession to make."

"Careful," he warned.

"No, I do. I've read everything I could find about your case. Police reports, court transcripts, newspaper reports. Anybody else's car, there's no way you would've spent two years behind bars."

"It wasn't about the car," he reminded her. "It was about the girl."

"Who came with the car."

"The car came with her."

"And they both belonged to Senator Garth, who's known for throwing his weight around."

"He's got plenty to throw." He reached for her hand. "Listen, Bella, it's over now. I came through okay. At least I think I'm okay. If you notice any screws loose, don't try to fix me yourself. Just walk away." He squeezed her hand. "Okay?"

"Walk away from what?"

"From trouble you don't need."

Chapter Six

He walked Bella upstairs to her apartment and waited without comment while she unlocked her door. But rather than turn to him, she pushed the door open and stepped inside.

From the scenes he'd watched and the pages he'd read, this wasn't the way your average, ordinary date was supposed to go.

He braced his forearm high on the door frame, just to show that he was cool right where he was. "How about a good-night kiss?"

She turned to him and gave him a not-for-prime-time look. "I'm not going anywhere. Are you?"

"It's after midnight." Which was prime time for old habits, but he'd knocked himself out to get his date home at a reasonable time.

"You don't get a full day off?" She moved in on him now. "You might be a little reckless, but I don't see any loose screws. And if you have any, well..." She touched his chest with tellingly tentative fingertips. "Look at me, Ethan. I'm not walking away."

"This is your place. Tell me to go now, and I will." His arm came away from the door frame, but it would have been unfair to touch her before he had her answer in words. "If I stay, we're going to make love."

"I know." She reached for his hand, drew him inside and closed the door behind him. "That's the kind of kiss I want. The let's-get-it-on kind."

"That's not what I said."

He took her face in his hands and kissed her gently, the approach of an unassuming supplicant. She lifted her chin, granting more access. He took her in his arms, kissed her hungrily, the approach of a hopeful guest. She slid her arms around his back and stood on tiptoe so she could serve him fully with ample lips and searching tongue. He drew a deep breath, replete with her heady scent, and he took in the taste of her, the welcome-to-me comeback from her mouth.

It was almost too much for an appetizer, but not enough, not nearly enough, to meet his needs. He touched his forehead to hers, eyes closed, hopes high.

"I said we'd make love if I stayed. Will you do that with me?"

"You'll have to show me how," she whispered.

He lifted his head. "You're—"

"Not a virgin, no. I've had sex." No more whispering. "I've never made love. I don't *think* I have." Her smile seemed apologetic. "I hope I haven't."

"You'd know." He smiled. If he knew Bella, she'd done some reading, too. "For once, you won't have to think." He kissed her with absolute purpose. She wanted him, whatever having him would mean. And she couldn't help speculating.

He chuckled. "I know what you're doing, darlin'. I can hear it. Stop thinking."

She lifted her chin and smiled. "Make me."

He made her take him to her bed without further discussion. By the light from the hall he was able to get his bearings. The fat candle and the book of matches on her dresser beckoned. He struck a match, touched it to the blackened wick and blew out the match flame as the hall light went out.

Good. He wanted to feel her, to be felt by her, but he didn't want her to see too much. Not this time. He couldn't be sure what she would think if she put the feel of him together with the look of him in the light.

He turned and found her seated in a chair, struggling with one of her new boots. He took the heel in hand and stripped it off, followed by its mate. His own worn boots came off with an easy swipe of the hand. She stood quickly and unsnapped her jeans, as though she was afraid any dithering might bring on doubt. His doubt or hers, it didn't matter. He would banish it. He stepped in, took the bottom of her shirt in hand and peeled it over her head. Her hands were momentarily out of the picture, just the way he wanted them. For now.

He knelt before her, slid her zipper down slowly, tucked his hands into the open vee and spread the fabric wide. She wore a cotton bikini. He pressed his smile to her belly, and rubbed his lips back and forth over her soft skin. Her splayed fingers crept into his hair. He felt a slight trembling in her hands.

He pushed jeans and bikini over her hips, and drew his hands down her legs. When he reached her ankles he lifted each one in turn, and she stepped out of her pants.

He skinned his shirt over his head, picked her straight up and stepped over to the bed. Then he kissed the top of each of her breasts, just because they were there, peeking over the cups of her bra.

He looked up. "You have condoms?"

"I said I've had sex. It's been quite a while, though, so...no."

"Yeah, me, too. But I have condoms." He let her slide along his body until they were face-to-face. "Hope they haven't expired."

Neither of them was in a laughing mood. He lowered her to the bed, and he hovered over her, kissing everything he could get his lips on without pouncing on her. He would go slow and take pleasure from giving her pleasure. He was almost certain he could do that. Take it slow. Give pleasure. Make love.

Her bra was fine and thin, perfect fabric for teasing nipples into tight beads while he rocked his hips against hers and coaxed her thighs apart. He took one nipple in his mouth and made the fine thin fabric wet, then pulled the strap over her shoulder, licked and suckled the tight bead until he could almost taste nourishment.

"Let me take it off," she pleaded, as though she'd outgrown the last bit of her clothing and it hurt to have it on.

He fully understood.

"Let me." He blew on her wet nipple as he reached under her and pinched the hook from the eye. She shivered.

"Is that good?"

She nodded.

He moved over her other nipple and treated it to the same mouth massaging and tongue lashing and pulling out of stops its twin had received. She called his name or, rather, moaned it, and the sound slithered into his ear and plunged straight for his groin. He propped himself on his elbows, used his hips to pry her thighs even farther apart and pressed his straining penis tight into the crevasse he'd created. Tight, but not too hard. Not too fast. No rush.

She thrust her hands into his jeans and grabbed his cowboy ass. Tough enough to break a knife blade, tender enough to bear the marks from her fingernails for days. Damn, it hurt so good.

"Take these off," she demanded.

"When I'm ready."

He slid down and kissed her midriff, farther down and kissed her belly, still farther and kissed the juncture of her thighs, and heard her breath catch and felt her suck everything in and hold every bit of herself at bay.

"I'm not ready," she whispered.

"Better than latex," he said, but he took her at her word and traced her slippery folds with a gentle finger as he moved over her. "Take my billfold out of my back pocket whenever you *are* ready." He nuzzled her neck and suckled her earlobe as he slipped his finger inside her. She gasped. "And then you can have my pants."

With his help she did what she was told, but he would not take his hand from her until she had come to the edge of wildness and given in. She started to shudder, and he would not let her stop, not without him deep inside, taking him deeper and making the wildness grow and scream and sing and burst open and pierce the dark with a shower of sparks.

She lay beside him quietly for long moments, enjoying the freedom to touch him anywhere she felt like it. And she felt like touching him everywhere. He was a beautiful man, and she took pleasure in his masculine physicality. She wasn't going to ask him whether the stories about prisoners beefing themselves up were true, but clearly he had taken care of his body. One day maybe he would tell her about the time he'd spent there, and maybe there would be some things she didn't want to hear. But she wanted to be the one he confided in. She wanted him to feel free, the way she felt free with him at this moment. Was that the effect of lovemaking? Trust and a sense of belonging?

No, she hadn't made love before. But now she had.

"Trace asked whether you'd started your classes," she said as she turned to him, knowing he was awake. He'd been touching her, too. "What kind of classes?"

"College classes. Right now I'm taking American lit and History of the American West. Thought I'd stick close to home this term."

She pushed up on her elbow and propped her head on her hand. "Are you just starting out?"

"Nope. I have a few credits in my jacket."

"Your jacket?"

"My record." He laid his hand on her shoulder and rubbed it back and forth. "I've got all kinds of records. My college record is the best one. I'm like you. Straight As."

"I didn't get straight As. I got some Bs." She rolled to her back and grinned at the shadow the flickering candle threw on the ceiling. "Three."

He chuckled. "You set a pretty high bar."

"I did not. You did, with your straight As. I don't like contests. Never did."

"You don't like to lose."

"Who does?"

"Admit it. You liked it all over when I won that poker game."

"Don't be silly." She turned to him again. "Okay, I did. But mainly because the bull hadn't broken your body into a whole bunch of pitiful pieces." She laid her hand on his smooth chest. "I like your body just the way it is."

"Even with the ink?"

"It's growing on me." She dragged her hand over the contours of his chest, over his shoulder and down his arm to his tattoo. His birds must have been sensitive. Either that or they were actually mating in flight. She smiled. "You're growing on me."

"Yeah, I know. Try to ignore it and maybe it'll stop showing off."

"How long can you stay?"

"You mean time-wise?" She laughed, and he growled and nipped at her shoulder. "I could just eat you up. Are you hungry? I'm starving. Let me make you some breakfast."

"At four in the morning?"

"I've never met an Indian who was such a slave to the clock."

If he didn't want to stay in her bed, so be it. She threw her legs over the side and reached for the French terry robe she kept hanging over the footboard. "I thought you said you'd met my mother."

"La—"

"Shh." She turned quickly and pressed her fingers over his lips. "No names. This would not be a good time to wake her." Silly, she thought as she slipped into her robe. Her mother would be the first to say so. But she wasn't so sure. Sometimes she felt a familiar presence, and she wanted to do the unthinkable. She wanted to call it back rather than send it on.

"You need to brush up on your traditionalism, Wolf Track." She shook her head. "Slave to the clock."

"I said I'd do the cooking. I like to eat when I'm hungry." He gave a dry chuckle. "Whenever I can."

"Are you an eggs-and-bacon man, or do you—"

"Hey." He reached for her hand. "I'm a happy man right now. A very happy man. If I fell short, it's because I'm a little rusty. I promise to do better by you next time." He drew her hand to his lips and kissed her palm. "There's that word again." He touched the tip of his tongue to the center of her palm and made her shiver. "Time."

She didn't know what to say, so she put her arms around him and kept him there with her body instead of her words. She wanted to banish all doubt, but she wasn't sure what it would take. Words wouldn't cut it. He wasn't fearless, after all, and she might just be the only person in his world who knew it. It took him a moment to return her embrace, and she could only guess why. Maybe he was thinking too much, or remembering or yearning for something more. Maybe lingering in bed didn't appeal to him. Or maybe he was just hungry.

One thing was certain. There was nothing rusty about Ethan Wolf Track.

"You okay?" he whispered cautiously.

She nodded. She wanted a next time. She truly did. And getting all clingy might scare him away.

Keep it light, Bella.

"And I promise you…" She gave him an awkward parting pat on the arm as she slid away. "You're not short."

It was a relief to hear him laugh.

So she'd had sex, but she'd never made love. He was beginning to wonder if he ever had. He'd sure given it his best effort tonight. It wasn't even an effort. It was more like a gift that he meant to give, to feel it taken and kept, but it kept coming back to him. Maybe that was why they call it *coming,* he told his suddenly overactive mind. It was a rush, all right, but not the kind that rolled over you and blew away. The feeling was still with him, like a new kind of hangover. The good kind, which was something he'd never had before. Something nobody in his right mind would question.

But this woman was the queen of questions.

"What made you decide to try college again?" she asked as he poured the last of the pancake batter into two spreading dollops.

"I didn't actually try college the first time." The hot skillet started the batter bubbling almost instantly. Somewhere in the back of his mind a voice told him to wait until the whole face was full of blisters. Man's voice? Woman's voice? He shook his head. "I tried sports and parties and hangin' out."

"That's the way you got through high school."

"You notice every little detail, don't you?" He scooped up the first pancake and flipped it, golden side up. "About the time I realized it wasn't working for me anymore, along came a recruiter. I signed up. I figured Logan would approve of the army because he'd done his hitch and he never complained." He flipped the second pancake. "Not that I was looking for his approval—I wanted to go my own way—but I wanted his respect."

"I'm sure you had it."

"I don't know."

"Well, you have mine. Has he seen you flip pancakes?"

"He's the master flipper." He slid a fresh hotcake atop each stack on the plates in waiting. "I had one little problem with being a soldier." He handed her the two plates. "I wasn't very good at shooting at people," he said airily as he turned off the stove.

"Understandable. Is that why you don't hunt? You're not a good shot?"

He joined her at the table, where she'd already set glasses of orange juice and a platter of bacon. It was still dark outside. There was something cozy about sitting down at the breakfast table before daybreak with a woman wearing a soft white robe and a smile on her face.

Something that made it feel okay to let the stories just keep on coming.

"I shot *expert* with every weapon they gave me. That's the highest qualification you can get. They thought they had a real Sergeant York on their hands." He took a drink of juice and then gestured with the glass. "You know about Sergeant York. You shoot *expert* in history."

"World War I hero."

"I tore up those targets like a human paper shredder. They sent me over to the Middle East. Fine. I'm ready, willing and more than fit for duty." He tipped the glass and studied what was left of the orange juice. "Until the first time I had a real human being in my sights," he told her quietly without looking up. He wasn't gonna quit now. "Couldn't do it. I shot over his head." He drained the glass.

He cut into the pancakes with the side of his fork, sopped up some syrup and shoveled the food into his mouth. It had no taste. He made a project of chewing and swallowing. When he looked up, she was waiting. No note taking, no disbelief in her eyes, no pity or judgment. She was listening.

He lifted one shoulder and tried to crack a smile.

"One time I put my weapon down and tackled a guy that needed shooting, sure as hell. I don't know why. Damn near got myself killed. Coulda gotten my whole unit blown to pieces. Went off the deep end, drinking, getting into fights. Ended up in psych. They sent me home with a general discharge." He glanced out the window. "Logan wanted me to appeal it, but I couldn't see it. Hell, stuff I did was flat out dishonorable. That's what they should have stamped on my papers."

"They must've given you some kind of treatment while you were in the psych unit," she said gently. Which was not really what he wanted. "Was there any reason why you couldn't…" He speared her with a look. *Say what you want to say.* "Other than the obvious? That the target is human."

"One doc said I wasn't crazy. Another one said I was. He didn't use the word, but that's what it boiled down to." He lifted one shoulder. "Pretty sure most of 'em thought I was fakin' it."

She didn't say anything, but she was looking at him pretty hard.

"If I was, I wasn't conscious of it. I wanted to shoot somebody. I really did."

She shook her head. "The only part that sounds crazy is you apologizing for not killing anyone."

"You can't run an army that way."

"You don't get VA benefits, then."

"I get medical. If I lose it again, they'll try to put me back together. But I don't get the GI Bill. You know, to pay for school." He poked at his pancakes. "I'd rather pay for it myself anyway. Let the real soldiers have the benefits."

"You'll earn yours like a real cowboy?"

He gave a lopsided smile. "Playing poker in the bullpen, yeah."

"Maybe with a little more psychiatric treatment you'd unlock some sort of—"

"Childhood trauma? No, thanks. Sleeping dogs, remember?"

"They're everywhere," she said as she reached for her orange juice. She hadn't eaten much. "We all go around stepping over our sleeping dogs."

"Which gives people like you some job security. You get to wake those dogs up and make 'em bark their fool heads off."

She smiled. "And free the puppies."

"Yeah. You do good work, Bella. You and Warrior Woman."

"How long have you been following my blog?"

"I wouldn't say I'm a follower. I don't get on the computer that much anymore. I started taking classes when I was, um…you know, in prison. I got to use a computer. Warrior Woman did a whole series on Indian gaming. Another one on water rights. I used some of that in one of my courses."

"How did you figure out it was me?"

"I'd see you on the news." He took after his breakfast in earnest, now that the focus was on her. "A couple of words here, couple of words there, you put two and two together…"

"You were taking math?"

"I was taking Research and Writing, Miss Smarty-Pants. You helped me get another A."

"You're welcome." Her smile went with the smarty-pants. Which he knew for a fact she wasn't wearing. She finally cut into her pancakes. "Have you seen any of the posts I've been doing on the latest court cases concerning payments on Indian land?"

"That wasn't one of my topics."

"Senator Perry Garth is one of my topics."

"Ah, Senator Perry Garth." He wagged a slice of bacon at her. "The senator in particular is not one of my topics."

"Why not?" She snatched his bacon. "He's trying to hold up the transfer of public land leases from the Tutan Ranch to the Double D Wild Horse Sanctuary."

"I thought that was practically a done deal."

"Practically." She took a bite of bacon, gave it a couple of chews, and then wagged it back at him. "Do you know what *practically* means in Department of the Interior terms? In Bureau of Indian Affair terms? If you get the right person pushing the buttons, you can slow a done deal down to an everlasting simmer. Just ask anybody on the Tribal Council."

"Never had much interest in politics, Tribal or otherwise. Like I said, not one of my topics."

"Water rights?" she recalled. "Tribal gaming?"

He shrugged. "Drinking and gambling."

She rolled her eyes. "Okay, what about the horses?"

"Now you're talkin'. Big Boy gets auctioned off, I want it to be part of something big. He's a hell of a horse."

"You're a hell of a trainer." She nodded at his empty plate. "Would you like more?" He flashed his palms in surrender, and she reached for his plate. "When are you going to show Big Boy off to Logan?"

"When we're ready."

"I want to be there. It's an important part of the story." She piled her nearly full plate on top of his empty one. "The Wild Horse Sanctuary story. There's so much to it, Ethan. Saving the horses is only the beginning. We're all related, you know. *Mitakuye Oyasin*."

"Yeah, I've heard that somewhere. I believe it." He smiled as he took the last of the bacon. "We shouldn't be shooting each other."

"On that observation alone you should qualify for the GI Bill. What are you majoring in?"

"Staying out of trouble." He licked the bacon grease off his thumb. "I haven't gotten that far yet. I just started taking classes. It's gonna take some getting used to."

"History and literature. Interesting choices."

"I figured I'd better pick things that would hold my interest. You know, to start with. I've got people advising me on courses and job prospects. I'm learning how to take people's advice, or at least consider it. I've taken some swings and chalked up some strikes."

"You've had at least one unfair call against you."

"Best advice I've gotten lately is not to dwell on things. Hell, I was hanging over the edge looking for a better view. Guess I'm lucky I didn't fall any farther than I did."

"What would you *like* to do?" She tipped her head to one side and gave him what he'd come to call the counselor look. "If you had a clean slate, what would you choose?"

"If I had a clean slate, maybe I wouldn't have much to offer. Maybe I wouldn't know anything." She scowled, and he shook his head. "I'm not putting myself down, Bella. I learn the hard way." He grabbed his empty glass. Something to study. "I think I could teach. The kids at Square One, I can relate to them. They're like Big Boy. You can't push them, but you gain their trust, you can lead them."

"Pretty obvious, those boys would follow you anywhere."

"I'd want to lead them to trust their instincts. The good ones. Like you do."

"I've never heard of bad instincts, have you?"

"Good point." He laughed. "Can I borrow it?"

"You talk to Logan and you can have it." She reached for his hand. "Just call him. Your instincts will take over, and the two of you will get past whatever's keeping you apart." She smiled. "And then I can get a few pictures of you working together for my story."

"I don't have a problem calling him."

"Yes, you do. But you'll get over it."

"Is that what your instincts tell you?" He drew his hand away and started gathering up what was left on the table. "You don't know everything, woman. As smart as you are, you've got some holes in your education."

"One less as of this morning." His eyes met hers, and she smiled. "I've finally made love."

Chapter Seven

"All right, woman. I called him."

And this was the first time Ethan had actually called *her,* Bella realized. The very first.

"And?"

"And the party's at his place. Logan's a big believer in working horses in a round pen. You know, the sacred circle. I don't have one over here, so I said I'd haul Big Boy down to his place. You're going with us."

"Is that an invitation?"

"You want pictures, you'll have to take them this time. I can guarantee your safety. And Logan and me...all is forgiven. I guess."

"You guess?"

"I told him I wanted him to take a look at my horse, and he told me to bring him on over. That's how it's done. No hashing over who did what last year or last century. You just move on."

"Whatever it takes. I'm glad you're—"

"The deal is, he helps me come up with a routine that'll really show the horse off, and I help him paint my old bedroom. He's getting it ready for his next kid."

"When?"

"I don't know. Couple of months, I guess. That's a woman's question. Or a reporter's."

She laughed. "When are we going? That's my question."

"As soon as you can. I got to work on time last weekend, so I'm golden."

"You sure are."

Moving on had always been his way, but these days Ethan was taking it at a collected walk rather than a headlong gallop. He was getting used to the pace. He thought he would have to sign his life away in return for the use of Square One's horse trailer, but Shelly didn't even bat an eyelash. "You're in charge of the horses, and the trailer goes with them. It's your call, Ethan. As long as you bring Bella Primeaux back to visit soon."

His call. He had a call, and suddenly he wasn't averse to using it. He wasn't locked up anymore. Pick up the phone and talk. No justification necessary.

It had been too long since he'd seen Bella. Four long days. He could tell she'd been watching for him—she was out the door the instant he drove up in front of her building— and the sight of her made his heart skip a beat. Her black hair, caught up in a ponytail, gleamed in the sun. She was dressed in jeans and a sweatshirt—there was an autumn chill in the air this morning—and she carried the tools of her trade in a bag that hung from her shoulder.

She was always prepared, ever mindful of the way the bits and pieces of the world around her connected up. He admired her mindfulness. At the same time, he was fearful of it, and he wasn't sure why. Maybe she would see things in him he didn't want her to see, though he couldn't imagine what that would be. She'd read up some on his crime, and he'd told her the rest. She liked him anyway. She'd made love with him anyway.

She was something, this woman. As soon as she hopped into his pickup, he had to kiss her. They talked a blue streak all the way to

Sinte, and by the time they walked in the Wolf Track front door, Ethan was feeling just fine about seeing the man who'd raised him.

"I'm ready to paint," he announced as he shed his denim jacket and tossed it in the old brown chair near the front door where he'd always piled his stuff when he came inside.

"You want to do that first?" Logan asked. "Or hang up your jacket."

"Just testing." Ethan grinned. "You always said, get the chores done first, then you can play," he said as he reclaimed the jacket.

"That's exactly the kind of recall I need," Logan said as he offered Bella a handshake. "Glad you could come. Mary's getting out soon, and I want everything to look nice when she comes home." He turned to Ethan. "If you still remember anything I told you, it must be worth using again. Probably should write it down so I don't forget. I just got a pair of reading glasses. You believe that?"

"And you're having a kid?" Ethan laughed. He was feeling downright comfortable. "Better not be using pin-on diapers, old man."

"I wear bifocals," Bella said. She glanced at Ethan as they followed Logan and the smell of coffee. "You didn't notice, did you? I used to wear glasses. Now I wear contacts."

"*That's* what's changed. I knew there was something," Ethan teased.

"It has nothing to do with age." Bella assured Logan as he handed her a cup of coffee. "Neither does maturity."

"Living proof right here." Ethan took a cup from the cabinet and poured his own coffee. He was home. "What color are we going with? Pink or blue?"

"White. But I've already primed it, so it won't take too long. Hasn't been painted since you moved out."

"Sure hope the primer covered everything up."

"That's what it's for." Logan led the way down the hall, bypassing a row of boxes that hugged the wall. "Couple of boxes I've been saving for you and Trace. Stuff I thought you might want. Trophies, books, pictures."

"No pictures," Ethan said. He turned to Bella. "*No* pictures." God only knew what kind of pictures of him Logan could dig up.

"Too soon, huh?" Logan laughed. "Good thing we have a basement. I guess a baby will mean a lot of stuff we've never had around here. But don't worry. I won't be throwing anything else away. Only moving it to… Remember this one?" He plucked a book from

the largest of the boxes and showed the cover
to Ethan first, then Bella. *Where the Wild
Things Are.* "One of his favorites. He used
to know it by heart."

"I still do, so you can keep it for my little
brother. Or sister. Wouldn't that be cool? A
little sister." He tapped his father's chest with
the back of his hand. "Hey, she's gonna look
a lot more like me than she does Trace."

"If she's lucky she'll look just like her
mother. Mary's beautiful. Hey, remember
this?" Logan dropped the book into the box
and turned his hand into a living puppet with
forefinger and pinkie as ears, middle fingers
tapping thumb to create a menacing muzzle.
"Track Man's coming after you."

Thank God Track Man didn't complete the
old routine by going for his armpit, Ethan
thought.

"Look at him." He jerked his chin, pointing his lips the Indian way. "Track Man has
a golden eye." His glance connected with
Logan's. "I'm glad you got a ring this time.
That's the way it should be. It should work
both ways."

Track Man fell apart as Logan laid his hand
on his son's shoulder—an earnest gesture—
and then playfully pulled the brim of his hat

down over his face. "You're about due for a new one of these, aren't you?"

"Nope. My dad gave me this one." Ethan adjusted the battered hat. "It goes everywhere with me."

"Well, put a drop cloth over it and let's get to painting."

Logan stirred the paint while Ethan showed Bella the view from his old bedroom window. The backyard was more than hobby-horse land. It was Logan's real home. In the horse world, Logan Wolf Track was a well-respected name. He'd developed training methods based on Lakota tradition. He'd even written a book about them. His sons had learned what they'd been willing to learn. Ethan told Bella he wished he had paid more attention as he got older, but before he'd gotten "too big for my britches" he'd followed Logan around the very pen they were looking at like a pup on the heels of its mama.

"Is too big for your britches anything like being a smarty-pants?" Bella asked.

"Nope." He slid her a flirty wink. "It took me a long time to grow into my paws, but the britches were another story. For a while there I never did have a pair that fit."

A few hours later, Bella stood on a rail

on the outside of the round pen while Logan leaned back against the inside, a pile of horse gear at his feet. They were watching Ethan work Big Boy on a lunge line. Logan had expressed his approval of Ethan's progress many times over with a simple nod. He reminded Bella of her mother. Sometimes a kid wanted a few words. You might have learned not to expect the effusiveness you saw in other parents, but you still wanted to hear words. You wanted the people around to hear those words.

They weren't kids, Bella reminded herself. As Ethan said, they knew how to read sign. Their people exercised the kind of patience and subtlety that mainstream society had forever misconstrued. She and Ethan couldn't afford to do the same. They were the bridge between two worlds.

"It's good to see him like this," Logan said. "It's been a while since he's seemed comfortable in his own skin. You must have something to do with that."

"I'll let you in on a little secret. I've had a crush on Ethan just about as far back as I can remember."

Logan glanced over his shoulder, smiling. "Probably not much of a secret, huh?"

"Oh, I think I kept it to myself pretty well."
She laughed. "Or not. Thought I did at the
time." She watched Ethan signal the horse
for a lead change. She only recognized the
maneuver because he had showed it to her
earlier. "You know he didn't steal that car."

"'Course he didn't. But you try going up
against a United States senator. Especially
one who's been a senator as long as Garth
has, and *especially* in this state."

Bella nodded, still gazing at Ethan. "Big
fish in a small pond."

"You got that right. I tried to talk to his
daughter after it was all over, see if she'd do
the right thing, but it was no go. Garth got
wind of it and threatened to charge me with
harassment or some kind of…" He turned his
head to her sharply. "Don't say anything to
Ethan. I don't want him to know. I knew I was
on shaky ground, but I had to try."

"Is Garth using that against you in any
way? Politically, I mean."

Logan lifted one shoulder. "I don't have
much to do with him politically. Have you
started working on that story you mentioned?"

"I've been nosing around. I know the Double D Wild Horse Sanctuary was granted the

use of some public land that Tutan Ranch livestock has been grazing for years."

"Tutan's permits ran out," Logan said. "Sally got her application in, and with the leases the Tribe switched over to her and the backing of the BLM Wild Horse Management office, her case was ironclad. She gets the land."

"Done deal, right?" Bella shook her head. "Except Garth's committee's thrown it into bureaucratic limbo."

"Oh, jeez." Logan scowled. "That's not what I need to hear."

"As far as I can tell, it's the transfer of the public land he's trying to block right now. But can he interfere with Tribal leases?"

"He can cause delays. You know how that goes." He turned to watch his son. "You don't think it's because of Ethan?"

"I'm betting it's about your father-in-law," she said. "Dan Tutan."

"You think he wants to get at me? Because of Mary?"

"You guys all have this idea that it's personal. Sally thinks Tutan's afraid of her husband."

"Hank?" Logan shook his head. "Tutan liked to give Sally a hard time, but she doesn't take crap from anybody. She was standing up to Tutan before Hank came along."

"I'm sure she was," Bella allowed. "But in a pond as small as South Dakota, all the fish have a way of bumping into each other. You've got your brown trout, your big white lake trout, and then you've got your cutthroat trout." She shook her head. "That's a lot of competition."

Logan burst out laughing. "Ah, that is *beautiful*." Ethan was approaching with his quick buckskin as Logan called out, "You got yourself a live one, son."

Ethan grinned. "The horse or the woman?"

"Both." Logan offered his hand for the horse's inspection. "You ready to saddle him up? What are you using on him?"

"Hackamore, like you taught me."

Logan watched Ethan sort through the gear he'd left on the ground. Then he reached for an unusual-looking length of rope he'd draped over the fence rail. "I made something for you." He held it out for Ethan's inspection.

Ethan rubbed the intricately woven rope between his fingers. It was made of multicolored strands—shades of brown, gray to near black, tan to blond. Tiny ends sticking out all along its length made it looked prickly, but when Ethan shook it, it seemed to come alive.

"Snaky," he said appreciatively. "Feels like horsehair."

"It's a mecate," Logan said. "It's a rein handmade from horsehair. Got my first one from an old vaquero I met down in New Mexico one time. He taught me how to make them. It's all I use. You want try it out?"

"Sure."

Logan took Ethan's hackamore and started untying the old reins from the bosal, the chunky noseband that substituted for a bit. "There's something about the life in this thing. You can feel it in your hands. You get a connection with the horse you don't have with leather or hemp."

"How come you never showed me this?" Ethan asked when he held the newly attached reins in his hands.

"I'm pretty sure I did. Maybe you weren't watching." Ethan looked up, and Logan smiled. "Hey, I probably didn't say, *see this, Ethan?* I always figured you'd learn when you were ready. You've always had your own need-to-know agenda."

"I didn't realize how much I'd learned from you until…"

"You needed to know?"

"Yeah. Until I needed to know."

Ethan exchanged the halter and lunge line for the hackamore and saddle, all the while thinking about how easy it had been to work alongside Logan and Bella earlier, painting a room that held good memories and an innocence he'd all but forgotten about. There was only one wall he'd hated to run up against in that house, only one wall he couldn't quite paint over, even though its color wasn't quite clear, and he wasn't sure how much of it had ever existed outside his head. An array of pictures hung on it, and he couldn't quite make *them* out, either. He'd been pretty young when he'd moved into the house, but not so young that a normal kid wouldn't remember.

So, fine, he hadn't been a normal kid. He'd come to this town, this house, this life, with a whacked-out mother, and he had a vaguely bad memory of her. He didn't know why it had to bother him now. But it did. And now that the bothering had started, it would continue until he faced it and dug down to the bottom of what was eating at him. But for now he forced those thoughts away. He had a job to do, a job he loved more every day. His four-legged partner was learning to trust and teaching Ethan a lot about adjusting to change. One day at a time was the key.

It felt good to show Logan the progress he'd made. He didn't have to do much to put Big Boy through his paces, and the mecate made it even easier. He'd decided to show the horse off in reining, and for that he would gradually switch to a bit. But it wouldn't be the bit that would coax Big Boy to stop and spin and back up as though he were making dramatic moves of his own accord. It would be the rider's body, the shifting of his weight.

Ethan dismounted on the far side of the pen and looked enquiringly over at Logan, who took the hint to cross the ring and check on the fit of his gear. He asked about the fabric of the cinch, then offered the use of a saddle he thought would be a better fit for a short-backed horse.

They both knew the conversation was superficial, but Logan played along until Ethan hit him with the question that had been bouncing in his mind for the past twenty minutes, using his father's own term.

"I guess you had your own need-to-know agenda, at least where my mother was concerned."

Logan looked at him curiously.

Ethan stared at the house. "She'd been on her way out the door five minutes after she first walked in." He shrugged. "That's what Trace says. Seems like you should've seen it coming."

Logan smiled wistfully. "Your mother was an on-the-job learning experience. By the time she left, I knew she was gone for good."

"And that it was good she was gone?"

Logan closed his eyes and shook his head, still with that sad little smile. "I never said that."

"Maybe you should have."

"It was my need-to-know moment. I didn't think it was yours."

"I remember feeling relief that she was gone, and I knew I wasn't supposed to feel that way." Ethan ran his hand along Big Boy's warm neck. "Hell, she was my mother. But *I* knew, too. She couldn't come back."

"Why?"

"Because I didn't want her to. And I put her out of my mind for good. Can't even re- member what she looks like." He looked to Logan for help with the shadowy pictures on the nonexistent wall. "It bothers me sometimes. Gives me a kind of a cold, sick feeling. Guilt, I guess."

"You have nothing to feel guilty about."

"I wanted you to…"

"Stop her? Get her back for you?" Logan laid his hand on Ethan's shoulder. "I'm sorry it went the way it did. If I could've—"

"No. That's not it." Frowning, Ethan shook his head. "I don't know what I wanted."

"Let's put it behind us." Logan gave Ethan's shoulder a parting pat. "How about we take a ride? I'll saddle up two more horses."

The suggestion was vaguely unsatisfying, but it was a relief at the same time. Ethan embraced the relief end of the spectrum.

"You got a kid horse?"

"I've got the mustang Mary and I decided not to enter in the competition because we didn't want to show you boys up." Logan nodded toward the side of the pen where Bella stood waiting. They started walking, Logan grinning broadly. "Just kidding. We're not putting Adobe up for auction. We adopted him."

Ethan smiled. "You're on a roll."

"And I've got that great little mare." Logan nodded toward the pasture.

"How about taking a ride with us?" Ethan

said as they approached Bella. "Logan's got a horse for you."

She shook her head. "You two go ahead."

"We can double up on the mare."

"No, you guys go ride your wild mustangs. I have my own gadgets to play with. I've got some good pictures." She took a small camera from her amazing bag and showed him a couple of pictures of him riding Big Boy. "Want to see the video?" He laughed and shook his head. "I want to make some notes while it's all still fresh."

"In other words, you don't ride?" Logan asked.

Bella gave a diffident smile. "It shows, huh?"

Ethan put his arm around her shoulders, a gesture that, to his surprise, felt as natural as breathing, as comfortable as the smile on his face. "She does fine with a backseat cowboy along."

"Thanks, but you two go on," Bella said. "Just let me get a picture with both horses."

"We don't have to take them out right now," Ethan told her. He turned to Logan. "You got some time this week to maybe work with me on the maneuvers we talked about?"

Logan let the buckskin snuffle him up

again before scratching the horse's neck. "He's got the deepest stop I've seen."

"Yeah, we've been working on that." And Logan's appreciation was sweet icing on the cake.

"His spin is coming along. A smooth roll-back would be impressive." He nodded. "When can you get back this way?"

"You call it. I'll work it out."

"Why don't you leave him here and let me get to know him a little bit? Come back as soon as you can."

Ethan grinned. "I'll see about leaving the trailer, too. Then I'll *have to* come back."

Bella felt a little guilty about spoiling the plan to go riding. She would have been fine with staying back while the two men took off on their horses, but she was just as happy to head back home.

And surprised when Ethan took the wrong turn. They were headed down a dirt road instead of the highway.

"Aren't we going back to Rapid City?"

"Taking a little detour." He nodded toward the flat-topped, cone-shaped hill up ahead. "Haven't seen Sinte from the top of Badger Butte since the last time I rode up there with Trace. How long has it been for you?"

"Forever. Literally."

He gave an incredulous glance. "You've never climbed Badger Butte?"

"Never." She was probably the only person in town over the age of ten who could say that, but that just made her special.

"I get to show you the view for the first time? You can see the whole valley from up there."

"Do you have to hang off the edge to see it?"

"Hang off...oh, yeah." He smiled. "No, that's just me. You can stand anywhere you want. It's a helluva sight. Can't wait to show it to you."

"I'm happy with an up-close-and-personal view from the valley floor."

But they were still bumping along the roller coaster of a South Dakota dirt road. Ethan didn't even slow down for washboards. He drove like every other male she'd ridden with on these country roads. She had done an accidental one-eighty on a washboard once, an experience that taught her to seek blacktop whenever possible.

"Did you tell Logan your news?"

"What news?"

"About going back to college."

"Oh, right." He shook his head. "Forgot."

"Oh. I thought when you were having that little huddle on the other side of the corral…" They hit a rut, and she quietly reached for the grab handle above the door. "Can't wait to hear what he has to say when you tell him."

"Why? So you can add that to your story?" He glanced at her. "I don't want to be part of any horse-turns-bad-boy-around fairy tale, okay?"

"I just meant…" She sighed. "Listen, I'm not climbing that hill, so why don't we just turn around?"

"It's gonna take five minutes."

"Never climbing to the top of Badger Butte for me is kind of like never going hunting for you. I can't deal with—"

"Look, Bella, I'm not afraid to hunt. I'm just not interested."

"I'm not afraid of heights. I'm just not a fan."

Ethan spared her a cold glare before slamming on the brake, spinning the pickup around and gunning the engine.

"Stop! If you don't stop, I'm jumping out." She pulled the handle just enough to make it click. He slowed the vehicle and pulled over, and she jumped out. And then he drove away.

She watched him disappear over a rise in the rutted road.

What the hell was wrong with that man? She didn't like heights, okay? There were things he didn't like. There was no call to push—that was all she was saying. She wasn't trying to get him to take down a deer so she could eat meat. Not every man was a hunter.

And not every woman was a damn climber.

It wasn't a steep grade, but she was puffing as she approached the top. Like it or not, she was going to get a view from the high ground. She didn't like hiking. She certainly didn't like admitting she needed to start getting more exercise. But she didn't care about Ethan driving off and leaving her on foot. She'd asked for it. She'd *demanded* it. He'd said it himself—told her to walk away if he started acting like he had a few screws loose. She was a wise woman, a warrior woman, and she was doing just that. Walking away.

It was too bad she'd left her bag in the pickup.

The view from the top of the rise gave her a thrill. She could see herself bursting into song. She could also see herself heading down the other side and marching right past the pickup parked at the bottom and the man leaning against the driver's side door.

And she almost did.

"I'm sorry, Bella."

She stopped.

"Please ride with me."

She turned and gave him the coldest look in her arsenal—and she had some icy ones stored up.

"I didn't mean to scare you." He pushed away from the pickup, shoved his hands in his pockets and scraped his boot heel across the hardpan as he approached. "All right, I did, but I won't do it again. Ever."

Was that sincerity in those hooded eyes?

Damn, she should just keep walking.

But she didn't. She'd walked far enough. "I'm afraid of heights." She grabbed a handful of soft T-shirt and pressed her fist against hard belly. "Understand?"

"Perfectly."

"No pressure. No ifs, ands or buts. I don't do heights." She pulled back and punched this time. His gut was rock hard. "And no teasing. Got that?"

"Yes, ma'am." He was doing pretty well on the straight-face score.

She narrowed her eyes. "Because you don't

want anybody trying to coax *your* monsters out from under your bed."

"You're right. That's why I don't own a bed."

"Wherever you sleep, then." She let go of his shirt. "You and Logan were having yourselves a real reunion, Ethan. You could've topped it off with your college news."

"It's no big deal." He lifted his gaze above her head and shrugged. "Because, it's not like I've graduated or anything. I'm just taking classes."

"And I read a script in front of a camera. Your father goes to meetings and listens to a rehash of the proposals that didn't get passed last month. Your brother hangs on to a bucking horse for ten seconds at a time."

"Eight seconds."

"Not *even* ten seconds at a time."

He looked her in the eyes again. The corners of his mouth started twitching, and he couldn't hold back. He had to laugh.

And she had to laugh with him.

He draped his arm around her shoulders, and she took his hand with hers, lacing their fingers together. He walked her around the front of the pickup.

"You wouldn't really have jumped out of the pickup if I hadn't stopped, would you?"

"I'll never tell." She glanced up, offering a smug smile. "I might need that one again."

"You wanna hang out tonight?"

"I don't hang out."

"I do." He opened the pickup door. "Your place?"

"Where else?"

Their lovemaking, breathtakingly hot and spicy, was filled with the taste of salt and the pungent scent of musk. He took her standing, and she rode him sitting. They held each other off one more moment and pushed each other one more fraction of a fraction, and called each other's names one more way and one more time.

Their lovemaking was sweet and slow, filled with whispers and warm breath, and the fine feel of smooth skin and long cool hair and short damp curls. He took her gently and she received him deeply, and they traded endearments neither had ever spoken before. And when they were sated with all the pleasure either had ever imagined, they wrapped each other in their arms and legs and moved languidly to touch and reassure.

"Ethan."

"Hmm?"

"I admire you."

He gave a self-satisfied chuckle. "You've got a crush on me."

"That's old news." She traced a circle around his flat nipple. "I've learned a lot about you since you came to my rescue at the Hitching Post."

"The itching Post. Didn't you notice the sign? The *H* is missing. That leaves you *itching.*"

"You, maybe." She offered a saucy smile. "What are you going to do about it?"

"Enjoy it. It's that kind of itch. The kind you don't wanna scratch off." He closed his eyes and smiled. There was much to be enjoyed. "What do you admire?"

She pressed her lips to his chest. "The way you handle yourself. You're your own man. I like being with you. I like being my own woman while I'm with you." She pressed her lips to his chest. "I'm glad you don't want to scratch me off, but if you have an itch, a little scratching might be in order."

He kissed her forehead. "I've made some big choices in my life that didn't work for me. I don't want you to find yourself thinking of me that way." He threaded his fingers through her hair. Here in the dark it was easy to talk.

There was no heaviness. It was all wrung out of them, and so he could say without hesitation, "I don't wanna be the first bad choice you've ever made."

"You're a big choice for me, I'll grant you that. And so far, so very good." She scooted up along his side and rested her chin on the kiss she'd imprinted on his skin as surely as the tattoo artist he'd visited long ago. "But you have a way of distracting me when I want to say something, especially when it's about you."

"The scratching thing? That's a pretty basic male instinct, Bella. Even if I do it better than anyone else you know, I'm still just another—"

"It's not a competition, Ethan. I admire *you*. You're not afraid to make more big choices just because you've run into some obstacles. You haven't let the detours break your stride." She slid her hand over his hip. "I love to watch you walk, by the way."

"Same here. You should've seen yourself marching down that hill."

She growled.

"Look, I know where you're goin' with this. I feel good about what I'm doing, but I'm building on a pretty fragile foundation.

Let me work on it awhile. Okay?" He twirled her hair around his finger. It had life, like the mecate. "Your mom never got to see you on TV, did she?"

"No."

"She knew where you were headed, though. She knew who you were." She laid her cheek against him. "You're beautiful, Bella. You know that, don't you?" Her response—a small sound—wasn't quite an agreement. "She knew that, too. Hey, Belladonna is one of those miracle drugs, like aspirin. I looked it up. It's powerful. It helps people, but you don't wanna abuse it. Ladonna gave you her strength, and you ran with it."

"Logan's done the same for you."

"I ran the other way. But I'm back. Still, you're way ahead of me, Bella. I need time to catch up."

"The story behind the Wild Horse Sanctuary is something we can run with together. And there's more. I think there's a lot more."

"More story?"

"More *to* the story. More history."

"Is that your specialty? Digging up the past?"

"Let's see…what courses did you say *you* chose to start with?"

He groaned. "Damn, you're good."

* * *

Ethan woke up in a cold sweat. A bright horror filled his head and popped his eyes open, peeled them wide against the dark. He didn't know where he was, whether he was awake or dreaming. Part of him was in a dark place, and the rest was still somewhere else.

Somebody was dead out there in the field. He'd heard an explosion, but what flew wasn't shrapnel or body parts. It was a cloud of birds. Screeching birds, wildly flapping, desperately churning the air. A man popped up from the tall grass. And then *pop! Pop!* Firecrackers made Ethan jump and cover his ears, and the man's face went all red. And then he vanished.

Ethan rubbed his hand over his own face, hoping it was dry. It wasn't, but it didn't feel red. He knew what red felt like. Warm and watery at first, but when it went cold it felt sticky.

God help him, he was dreaming again. He'd gone months without landing in whacked-out places in his head at night, seeing things that looked like they'd been slapped together by a madman wielding a paintbrush—eyeballs popping out of birds' nests, Indians slithering through the grass like alligators, handcuffed men dressed in orange and women washing their hair in blood.

He wasn't going back for any more medical treatment. No more medication—all that did was make him groggy. He was gonna tough this thing out. It had almost faded away, and he could make that happen again. Stay busy, stay healthy, wait the devil out.

He turned to the woman lying close to his side, and he kissed her hair. She hadn't stirred, so he must not have made any noise. He must not have thrashed around. He was taking a chance of exposing himself by staying the whole night. Exposing the nature of his…little disorder.

Hell, plenty of people had nightmares. They weren't all crazy, and neither was he. Hadn't Bella just pointed out to him all the progress he was making? And it wasn't like she didn't know where he'd been.

Sometimes he wondered if *he* knew where he'd been. There was something different about this night's dream, though. There was urgency to it, the sense of a presence just below the surface.

But the surface of what?

Chapter Eight

It had been almost a week since Bella had seen Ethan, and she wasn't expecting to run into him at the Double D. The sight of his pickup barreling down the gravel road gave her butterflies. Here she was, doing her job, and there *he* was, parking in front of the house, and she couldn't wait to stow away the tools of her trade and turn to trading wise-cracks and secret smiles with her cowboy.

Her cowboy. It sounded crazy, even within the private walls of her suddenly giddy head.

But she wasn't starry-eyed enough to start shirking her responsibilities. Final preparations were being made for the Wild Horse

Makeover Horse Show, and she was finishing up her background work. That was her pretext, anyway. She was covering the big finale, but she was also getting closer to pinning down Senator Perry Garth's involvement with the allocation of the land that belonged to her people.

She'd met with the treasurer of the Cheyenne people in Montana—one of the tribes that was fighting with the Interior Department over missing payments—and she was convinced that Senator Garth's fingerprints were all over those billion-dollar bills. She knew she was working both ends against the middle on this story—and the Double D was somewhere in the middle—but that was the way investigative reporting worked sometimes. You started with one small piece out of place—a small player, a local matter—and you searched for a hole left by that piece.

And if you cared about the piece, if you couldn't abide that hole, your passion for the search intensified. The competition finale was her KOZY assignment. She was working on the Garth connection independently, and there was something a little too cozy going on with the senator. Why would he interfere with a Bureau of Land Management recommendation, stand in opposition to a determination made by the Tribal Council and essentially expend valuable political clout for a relatively small-time rancher like Tutan? Just because Tutan offered a good place to go hunting?

Suddenly there was all manner of coziness.

And more than one stimulus for passion.

Ethan waited for her to reach him and kissed her when she did.

"You don't mind showing us off publicly?" she asked.

"I don't see any public around." He glanced left and right. "Do you?"

"Not at the moment."

"I keep forgetting, you really have a public."

"I'd like to forget it. Well, most days. But the closer I get to home, the less I have to worry about it."

"It's been a while since I made the news. I don't think anybody remembers."

"I'm not worried about that." She reached up and tugged on his hat brim. "Not at all. But when you win this contest, you'll be making the news again. Is that okay with you?"

"I ain't livin' in the past, darlin'." He took her hands in his. "The present suits me better every day."

"What are you up to today?"

He nodded toward the front door. "Checkin' in with Sally on the facilities for the horse show. Logan's been working with me on a routine that'll show Big Boy off to his best advantage. I want to make sure—"

"Well, I'll be damned."

They turned to find Sally Night Horse watching them through the screen door.

"No, you won't, Sally." The deep voice came from behind her. "I did two funeral solos last month. In my heart I was singing for your salvation." A tall handsome Indian appeared in the doorway behind Sally, who was pushing the door open. "If my wife's trying to make another match, you might wanna check the fine print. Make sure she's got you registered for heaven."

"Aren't they adorable, Hank? You've met Logan Wolf Track's boy, haven't you?"

Hank Night Horse met Ethan at the top of the porch steps with a handshake, and then he extended his hand to Bella. "You've been taking more pictures today?"

"Never enough pictures. Actually, I was hoping we could talk."

"You guys can talk," Hank said. "I'm just a quiet man trying to keep up with a force of nature." He put his arm around Sally's shoulders and leaned close to her ear. "This man is not a boy. And no man wants to be called *adorable*."

"I mean as a couple. I had nothing to do with this one, but I see no reason why the Double D can't take credit." Sally waved her visitors inside. "We've got our hands full right now with the sanctuary, but in my next life I'm running one of those online dating services. I think I could make a fortune."

She gestured toward the office door. "Come on in and have a seat. We're just discussing a little hiccup we might be holding our breath over while we get this horse show on the road here. Like we need another detail to worry about right now."

Hank sat back against a counter, arms folded, while Sally took a seat in the wheelchair that served as an office chair in good times and as legs when hers weren't getting her where she wanted to go.

Bella started for a folding chair, but Sally pointed to a daybed piled with pillows. "You two take the…we'll call it the love seat. Bella, remember how you offered to help us get some community support messages on TV?

You know, about donating prizes for the competition?"

Bella nodded, but her smile was for Ethan as she patted the space beside her on the daybed.

"We don't need any more donations right now. Annie—my sister—she has a generous brother-in-law who's ponying up for all that. Says he needs the tax write-off. What we need is public support. We need horse lovers."

"The news coverage should help."

"And we've got Skyler Quinn—" she glanced at Ethan "—your brother's Skyler, another Double D matchup. We've got Skyler working on a documentary.

"But here's the latest thing that worries me." She snatched a folded paper off her desk and snapped it open. "I got a letter today about the public land. Some glitch in the paperwork. I've already fired off a response. I told them to ask their assistant. She's the one who knows where the mother of all glitches is buried."

"I'm pretty sure the holdup is a few pay grades higher than assistant," Bella said. "I have some low-level friends in high-level places. Reliable sources, we call them. Your neighbor, Mr. Tutan, doesn't want to give up the land. He has one of our South Dakota senators doing his bidding." She glanced at Ethan. "I know this hits close to home in more ways than one, but—"

"I got no skin in this game," Ethan told her. He looked at Sally. "Horsehide, but no skin."

Bella felt a chill. If she wasn't mistaken, Ethan's beautiful black eyes had just gone stone-cold.

"But the decision's been made." Sally looked up at her husband and then turned to Bella. "Hasn't it? What exactly do your reliable sources say?"

"It's being reviewed. What does the letter say the holdup is?"

Sally lifted one shoulder. "That they're waiting on some signatures."

"There's a big investigation going on with the Bureau of Indian Affairs," Bella said. "Billions of dollars in lease payments on Indian trust land are missing. Completely unaccounted for. Apparently there's been a slow, steady leak that's been going on for years."

"Stolen?" Sally asked.

"They don't know," Hank put in. "Some stolen, some never paid, they can't figure it out. Probably never will. It's just gone, and who has time to track it down? You know how that goes." He glanced at Bella. "Some of us do, anyway. Most of our Indian trust land has been handed down many times over, and Tribal members don't designate heirs, so it gets chopped up among the direct descendants. Since this has been going on for generations, you maybe get a statement showing pages of parcels of land that you have pennies' worth of interest in. The Bureau's a mess, which makes it easy to rob. You don't even have to bother to cover up your tracks. The red tape does it for you."

"That's terrible," Sally said.

Hank smiled. "Oh, yeah. It's terrible."

Bella chimed in. "Senator Garth has been sitting on relevant committees for as long as he's been in the senate—which is longer than most of us have been alive—and, of course, he says he's outraged. But there isn't much of a paper trail. There's an abundance of paper, but no trail. So he's all for offering a settlement, and then we let bygones be bygones."

"I don't see how our little public land lease would be connected."

"It probably isn't," Bella assured Sally. "Not directly. But according to my source, Garth is being questioned pretty closely. And on another front, he's suddenly particularly interested in certain parcels of public land, including Tutan's leases."

Sally frowned. "Why?"

"They're friends," Bella said. "They have been for years. According to my sources, Garth loves to hunt. He used to bring his pals out to Tutan's place every fall to go hunting. Tutan hosted quite a party back in the day. And Garth made sure Tutan had all the grazing permits and leases he could possibly want."

Hank was studying the toes of his boots. "Do you have any idea how far back this annual tradition goes?"

"Twenty years," Bella said. "Maybe more."

"My father used to work for Tutan." Hank looked up, his eyes suddenly haunted. "Seasonal laborer, but during hunting season a lotta times he'd stay on to help out with some of those parties. He disappeared. By the time they found his body..." He was talking to Bella's reporter persona now. "Well, they said he'd been drinking and he'd probably shot himself. Could've been an accident. Maybe suicide. Hard to tell, since he'd been dead for weeks."

"Was he with one of those hunting parties when he went missing?"

"The last time we heard from my father, he called to let us know he'd be staying down here for a couple more weeks, working for Tutan. But after he disappeared, Tutan said he thought my father had gone home to North Dakota after they brought the hay in. Some coyote hunter actually stumbled over my dad's body. There was an investigation. Tutan said he'd had some hunters come through, but he couldn't be sure."

"Was there a gun?"

Bella turned to Ethan. His question surprised her. He'd been so quiet that the very sound of his voice surprised her. He was staring at his hands. "Did they find a gun with his body?"

"They found a shotgun that had been reported stolen and a decomposed body full of shot. My dad didn't own a gun. He didn't hunt. His job was bird-dogging. Flushing pheasants—"

"Out of the brush. They put the gun…" Ethan cleared his throat. Bella could feel him shaking. "They probably put the gun there."

"They?" Hank said.

Ethan shook his head blindly. "Whoever."

"How long ago did it happen?" Bella asked Hank.

"Twenty-one years."

Ethan turned to her. "Is this all part of your story?"

"It could be. Hank, how much—"

"I've gotta get going." Ethan patted Bella's knee and stood to leave. "This looks like another job for Warrior Woman."

"It's definitely…" Bella got to her feet. "Ethan, you wanted to ask about the final—"

"The show, yeah. Some of the details…" He didn't even spare her a glance. "I'm working out my routine," he told Sally. "I'll call you."

And then Ethan was gone. She hadn't imagined his reaction to Hank's story. He was trembling. She wanted to tear after him, but if she caught up, the questions would roll off her tongue, and he didn't need that right now. She was dying for answers. He was running from the questions. What a pair.

"Bella," Hank said, "what's this all about? What story?"

"I'm not sure." She turned away from watching one of her passions retreat and faced the question that could be at the heart of the other. "I'd like to know more about your father's death."

"So would I."

She needed a corner piece of the puzzle so

she could start framing the problem. "What was his name?"

"John Night Horse."

Ethan's dreams were built on pieces of memory. He knew that now. There was a trail of crumbs locked inside his brain, and if he ever got hungry enough for the truth, all he had to do was gather those crumbs. He was in love with a woman who made her bones gathering crumbs.

And he couldn't get away from her fast enough.

Trouble was, he didn't know where to go. Truth was, he was getting hungry. Hungrier by the minute. It wasn't like he wanted to tell a story or solve a mystery or save anybody but himself. He just wanted to move on. He wanted to take what Logan called the red road—the good way—and he wanted to walk toward a dream, a good dream. He was tired of nightmares, tired of running away.

And so he ended up on his father's doorstep again.

"Did you forget something?"

He'd left Big Boy in Logan's pasture. He'd left the trailer. He'd left all of his training gear. But none of that was forgotten, and his father knew it. Logan could always tell when something needed to be said, even if half the time it never was. But that was Ethan's doing. Logan was always ready to listen.

"Yeah," Ethan said as he took a seat at the kitchen counter. The requisite coffee was being poured. "But I'm afraid it's coming back to me."

"Afraid?" Logan set the steaming cup of black coffee in front of him. *Pejuta sapa.* Brush up on your traditions, Bella kept telling him. He had grown up with Logan's traditions. Maybe more had sunk in than he'd realized.

"I won't be. If I can put it together, I think the fear will go away." He put his hands around the cup, comforted by the heat. "But you might not like it."

"Don't worry about me, Ethan. I have strong shoulders."

"I know. You're a good father. You always were." He glanced up. "You were a mother, too. You were both."

"I don't know about that. I could say I did my best, but, hell, I could've done better."

Ethan wasn't going to protest. Not now. He had to get the real stuff out before he lost his nerve.

"Did you know my mother was steppin' out on you?"

"I suspected." Logan sipped his coffee. "I should've known, but for a long time I didn't want to."

"Yeah, I know how that goes."

"You were so young," Logan said. "Did you…see something?"

"Yeah, I did. I saw lots of things that didn't seem right." Details. More than he wanted to dwell on. He had to stay on track. "I had to go with her sometimes. Got so I didn't want to, but I didn't want to make a fuss, either. I didn't want to make any trouble." He cleared an unmanly sting from his throat. "I didn't want to lose you."

"You…" Logan was beginning to struggle, too. He didn't want to show it any more than Ethan did. "She'd say she was going to Rapid or Pierre for something, and she was taking you. I didn't like it that she favored you over Trace, but you were younger than he was, so…" Logan drew a deep, unsteady breath. "And I told myself if she had you along, it had to be on the up-and-up, you know?"

Ethan nodded. They were gonna help each other out with this. Try not to look at each other too much. That would be rude.

"Where did she take you?" Logan asked.

"Hotels, sometimes. Parties at big houses. I'd sit in a room and watch TV." Ethan looked up at the ceiling and shook his head. "I couldn't tell you, but, *God,* I wanted you to make it stop."

"I'm sorry."

Ethan nodded. He took a quick drink, let the hot coffee burn his tongue and clear his throat. "I think I saw a man get killed."

"Wh-what?"

It wasn't like Logan to trip over a surprise.

Ethan nodded. "I just came from the Double D. Bella's got this whole political conspiracy theory she's trying to make a story out of, and, uh…" He gave an openhanded gesture to help pull the words out, keep the report going. "They got to talking about the Tribal leases and your father-in-law, and how he's trying to hang on to land he's been taking for granted because he's got Senator Garth on his side." He glanced at his father. "And you know I don't wanna hear nuthin' about Garth."

Logan nodded.

"Anyway, Hank lets on that his dad used to work for Tutan, and that he got killed. And he starts talking about these hunting parties

Tutan used to put on for people like Garth. Political people. Powerful political people."

"What happened to Hank's father?"

"Well, Hank says his body was found on Tutan's property, all decayed and shot up. Tutan said he didn't know anything about it, so...case closed."

Logan grunted in disgust. "One of those federal murder investigations with an Indian corpse. No clues, no witnesses, no arrests."

"There *were* witnesses. And I wasn't the only one." He could feel the heat from Logan's shock, but he couldn't look up as he told him, "Mom was there, too."

He felt the familiar hand take hold of his shoulder. It gave him strength.

"I've been having dreams," he said. "I've had crazy dreams for years. Firecrackers scaring a flock of birds. A man standing up in the tall grass. Blood." He looked into his father's sympathetic eyes. "Lately the dreams have been showing me things I don't remember. But I know they happened. When Hank told us about his dad, I felt like I'd been there."

"Did you tell him?"

"No. It was just a feeling." He shook his head. "No, it's more than that, Dad. It's a fact."

A heavy moment passed.

"What do you want to do?" Logan asked quietly.

"I was just a kid. It was a long time ago. I don't think anyone'll believe me." Ethan sighed. He felt the pain of that day as keenly as he had twenty years ago.

"Where were you when all this happened?"

"I don't know exactly. She left me in the pickup. I think I got out."

"Damn. You could've been killed."

"She always told me that if I said anything about the parties, you'd send us away. She said we were just having fun." He rested his head in his hand, rubbed his forehead, trying to wipe some of the trouble away. "I was so glad when she left, I just put it out of my mind. All of it."

"I guess we all did."

"I gotta tell somebody." Ethan lifted his head. "Coming from me, it probably won't mean a hill of beans, but…"

"I'll be there."

"It ain't your story."

"But you're my son."

He wanted to tell Hank first. He figured that would be the hardest, even with Logan there to stand by him, but it wasn't. Hank didn't doubt him, and he didn't hold it against him for keeping it to himself all these years. Ethan wondered how the man could take it all in without going off on somebody—or just going off.

"You weren't keeping it a secret," Hank said. "Your mind was protecting you."

"I don't know about that. Had a pretty thick head for a while there. Nothing got through to me. But lately, the last, I don't know, ten years or so, things kept popping up. Something happens to get stuff going in my head at night."

"You've been through a lot in the past ten years," Logan said.

"The thing is, all that stuff makes me look like either a liar or a nutcase. Like I'm just trying to get back at Garth."

"That's for the law to figure out. We know what happened," Logan said.

"Yeah. The law," Ethan echoed.

"That's where the story goes next," Hank said.

"Before that, there's one more person." Ethan gave a dry chuckle. "And she's gonna want to run with the ball. I don't know how we'll prove it, but—"

"We don't have to prove anything," Hank said.

"He's right," Logan said. "We'll turn everything over to the FBI. They have to reopen the case. Get Tutan to talk. Track down everyone who was there."

"What if they find Mom?"

"One more mystery solved." Logan shrugged. "Hell, she deserted us, and we moved on. I divorced her. You grew up. We're on the Red Road." He smiled. "We've found women who know how to love us."

"You for sure. After this bombshell, I'm giving Bella some space."

"Do you want space?"

"I want…" Ethan looked his father in the eye. "I want Bella."

"My advice—and I know you haven't asked, but this is your need-to-know moment—is don't keep it to yourself. Tell her."

"So that's it," Ethan told Bella. She'd met him at Logan's place. He'd said he wanted to show her what they had done with Big Boy, and he did. There was something to be said for bringing the story full circle, bringing it home and showing her that he had done what she'd given him the confidence to do. He'd been truthful with his father. And then he'd been truthful with her. "Pretty far out there, isn't it?"

"It all fits together." She held out her cup to Logan for a refill. Kitchen, frybread, coffee. It was the traditional way. The family way. "You know I'm going to follow this thing as far as I can."

Ethan laughed. "You wouldn't be Warrior Woman if you didn't."

"And you know that if ever I was ahead of you, you just caught up."

No more laughter. Ethan saw the sincerity in her eyes, and he cherished it. He also knew it was true.

"Can I run the camera for you?" he asked. "Carry your water? Saddle your horse?"

"No horse," she said. "You're beautiful on horseback. I just want to watch you."

"Chauffeur you around, then."

"I have to be allowed to do something for *you*," she said sweetly.

"Translation," Ethan said, casting a glance his father's way. "Baby, you ain't gonna drive my car."

Chapter Nine

The man and the horse appeared to be having a little tête-à-tête. Bella could see the man's lips moving as he raked his fingers through the horse's lush mane. Ears standing at attention, the mustang bobbed his head once. After a few more words from the man, the regal buckskin gave his head a quick shake, and the man laughed softly.

She slowed her pace as she approached the corral, thinking this must be the way a woman felt when she happened upon her man patiently sharing a teachable moment with their child. She wanted to turn into a fly and light on the fence post.

But she also wanted to be herself and be welcomed with open arms.

"Are you two planning your strategy for tomorrow?" she asked as she let herself in through the corral gate.

Ethan turned quickly, his eyes betraying his surprise. He glanced down at her feet. "You walkin' on cat's paws, woman?"

Bella grinned as she planted her right heel in the dirt, toe pointed skyard to show off her blindingly white walking tennies. "You like my new sneak-up shoes?"

"New boots, new tennies—you got a thing for shoes?"

"The boots hurt."

"They're not made for walking, honey. That ain't the way to break 'em in." He turned his shoulder to the horse, who then followed him across the corral. "'Course, jumpin' out of my pickup on the fly was a damn good way to break me in. Learned my lesson on takin' *no* for Bella's answer." He rewarded Big Boy with his left hand as he took Bella under his arm on the right.

And she was right where she wanted to be.

"Then it was worth the blisters on my feet."

He glanced down again. "You got blisters?"

"Lessons all around." She slipped her arm

around his waist. "Logan just left to pick up his wife at the airport."

"We're alone." He gave her a come-on look.

She glanced up at Big Boy. "How's your strategy coming?"

"So far, so good, now that we've got the place all to ourselves."

"How does that help you win the training competition?"

"Oh, that." He scratched the horse's neck. "We're set, aren't we, Big Boy?"

Big Boy bobbed his head, and they both laughed as the horse snorted and walked away.

"Actually, he's all set. But I need a little encouragement." Ethan turned to her, smiling. The shade from his hat brim fell over her face. "Encourage me."

The back of his neck felt warm under her hand, his hair soft between her fingers. She drew his head down and embraced the surge of female power as she kissed him.

Its effect shone in his eyes. He looked dazed for an instant, but then he took charge and pulled up another alluring smile. "You wanna go inside? Just painted my old bedroom. We could break in the new carpet."

She drew back, answering with a saucy

smile of her own. "I don't want to do it in a room full of baby furniture."

"Do what?"

"Give you rug burn."

He chuckled. "No furniture yet. Mary gets to pick that out."

"Still," she said, glancing toward the barn, "I'd be imagining baby furniture. I'd prefer a nice haystack."

He groaned as he took her hand and walked her back to the gate. "Now you've got me thinking baby, nursery, 'Little Boy Blue.' Some encouragement."

"I do my best." She looked up at him. "Hank called me after he met with an FBI field agent at the Rapid City office. They're taking your story seriously."

"You call that your best?"

"They're reopening the case."

"No kidding? Actually digging up the whole thing?" He was genuinely surprised. Skeptical of the kind of reception he might get for his twenty-year-old recollection, he'd gone to the regional FBI office on his own. Sure enough, the agent he'd talked to hadn't seemed too impressed, but he'd taken down all the names Ethan could come up with, along with the dates he'd figured out since he'd put his memory together with Hank's story.

Names, dates and forensics were the facts the agent had said he could check out. A long-buried memory was a little dicey.

What about a long-buried Indian and an unsolved murder? Ethan wanted to know. But he hadn't asked. He wouldn't risk being taken for a smart-ass. Never again. Especially not by a cop.

The agent had said he would be in touch, so Ethan bit his tongue while he offered a handshake. And since that meeting, he sure hadn't been holding his breath. He figured he'd done what he could. But it wasn't until he'd called Bella and then Hank to let them know what he'd done that he felt relieved of a burden he didn't know he'd been carrying.

"I don't know what they'll dig up besides the evidence that's been in storage all these years, but they will search for your mother," Bella said. "And they'll question Dan Tutan and Senator Garth."

"You think it's too late?"

"It's never too late. Murder will out." She gave his hand a quick squeeze. "Eventually."

"Here's one for you." He squeezed back as he opened the gate with his free hand. "'Justice is the constant and perpetual will to allot every man his due.'"

"Oh, I like that." She slid past him and through the gate he held open for her. "Who said it?"

"Some old Roman. I memorized it during my trial. It was on the wall of the courtroom." He closed the gate behind them and turned to her, smiling. "I like it, too. Put it in Warrior Woman's pipe and let her smoke it."

"I hope John Night Horse gets his due. Even if nobody goes to jail, let the truth be told. Let's get it out there."

"That's your job." He glanced past her. Between Bella and the horse standing in the corral behind her he'd found new purpose for his hard-earned freedom. "My job is to show the truth about Big Boy. Let people see what his kind can do."

"I thought your job was to win the big prize."

"That, too," he said with a wink. Keep it light, he told himself. He didn't want her to think he was counting on the money. It was more about the recognition and how he could use it—along with his education—to neutralize at least one of the strikes he had against him.

Okay, the money would help, too.

He glanced toward their two vehicles, parked side by side. The Square One horse trailer was hitched to his pickup. The boys had painted his name on it, along with a big horseshoe and something that was supposed to be a wolf's paw print but looked more like a high five. Ethan had assured them that it worked either way.

"You wanna hang around and meet my new mom, or should we do the decent thing and get out of their way?"

"I forgot to tell you. They're staying in Rapid City tonight. Logan said to tell you he'll be back in time for the show tomorrow." Bella stepped out ahead of him and turned, smiling, her hand still in his. "And so will I."

"You're not goin' anywhere. I need you with me." With a firm tug he reeled her back and drew her into his arms. "Tonight." He gave her a quick kiss. "Tomorrow."

"If we rule out hay wisps and rug burns, that leaves your father's—"

"We're getting a room."

The hotel at the tribal casino had one vacancy left. The desk clerk told Ethan that this was going be his lucky night and asked what game he would be playing.

"I didn't get lucky 'til I quit gambling,"

Ethan told the young man. He thought he'd sounded pretty damn clever until Bella mentioned cowboy poker while they were waiting for the elevator. As soon the doors closed he planted a kiss on that smart mouth of hers that left her breathless. He could tell by the way she was looking at him when the doors opened. She didn't seem to notice the guy who gave him a thumbs-up as they stepped off the elevator.

"You won big, huh? Slots or tables?"

"Horses," Ethan quipped.

"Bet on the buckskin," Bella added, all dreamy-eyed.

"Are you nervous about the competition?" she asked gently.

They'd made love twice—once like hungry young lovers who couldn't get enough, once like deliberate, devoted admirers who took it slow and still couldn't quite get enough. They'd lain in each other's arms, stirring now and then to touch and be touched, until she tried to feign sleep in the hope that he could get some rest. It didn't work for either of them. "I'm pumped," he said after a while and pressed a kiss into her hair. "I don't mean to keep you awake."

She gave a soft, pleasured sound. "I'm pretty pumped myself."

"Win or lose, I feel good about Big Boy," he said quietly. "He's in peak condition—nothin' prettier than a lineback buckskin—and he handles like a precision-tuned race car. Better, even. A car's got no heart. Big Boy... size, color, speed, all that's a bonus. Big Boy has heart." He drew a deep breath and blew it out quickly. "Yep. I like our chances."

"You can't lose, Ethan. Even if someone else wins."

"I guess everyone who makes it to the show has the right to feel that way. Sally said a couple of them brought the horses back and dropped out." He chuckled. "And then there's my dad, who pulled his horse from the competition so he wouldn't have to give him up. Gave him to his wife."

"You won't mind giving up Big Boy?"

"Sure, I'll mind. But he's gonna sell high, bring in some serious money for the program."

He took her snuggling against him as his cue to slip his arm beneath her head so she could pillow it on his shoulder. She imagined his thoughts bouncing around wildly in his head, tumbling into the back of his throat and onto his tongue.

"And you can't just walk off with one of these mustangs without meeting Sally's requirements," he continued. "Actually, the BLM's requirements, but you gotta deal with Sally, and she's got her own smell test."

She smiled to herself, because it was dark and only she knew how deeply she was into him. "Could you pass it?"

"You kiddin'? Not even gonna try. I don't let just any woman get this close to my armpit, you know."

"It's your shoulder I want." An understatement.

"The armpit is like the shoulder's underbelly. Can't have one without the other. But you gotta admit, I clean up pretty good." He gave a deep chuckle. "I'm workin' on it, anyway."

"You don't have to convince me." She turned her head and kissed the closest part of him. Warm skin and hard muscle. "I have a crush on you."

"I'll see your crush and raise you..." He groaned. "Hell, I'm all in, Bella. I'm crazy about you."

"You're raising my crush with your crazy?"

"Yeah." He touched her temple, tucked her hair behind ear and whispered, "I'm crazy in love with you."

She felt light-headed, the rest of her body whooshing out from under her the way it did when she neared the edge of a high place. She didn't even have to look down. She could feel the fall coming.

Stay focused, she told herself. "Is the crazy part the underbelly?"

"Does that scare you?"

"No." She was no liar, but how could she say she wasn't scared? On the other hand, how could she say anything else?

Except maybe that she loved him right back.

"If it ever does, I want you to walk away. I mean that." He kissed the top of her head. "We need time to figure this out. I've never been in love before. Crazy, yes, but love? Uh-uh."

"I don't think I have, either. Unless it's the same as a crush that never went away."

"Maybe that's the underbelly for you, huh? The seed? Maybe we can make it grow."

She had only to lift her head, and he met her halfway for a kiss.

"I like our chances," she whispered.

* * *

Mustang Sally's Wild Horse Makeover Horse Show was held at the Sinte rodeo grounds. It was a beautiful, warm autumn day, and the grandstand was packed. Sally Night Horse and her sister, Ann, were in charge of the program. Sally insisted on being called *Master* of Ceremonies—never *mistress*. Ann didn't need a title. She was the detail person. Their husbands were busy moving the show along. When Hank spotted Ethan saddling Big Boy on the shady side of the horse trailer, he took a quick detour, his beautiful yellow Lab, Phoebe, in tow.

"Did you see your brother's horse perform?" Hank asked.

"He looked good, didn't he?"

"Not as good as the rider. Skyler's got a nice seat."

Ethan patted the dog's silky head and grinned. "I'll tell Trace you said so."

"Just don't tell my wife."

Bella stuck her head out the pickup window. "I don't think your wife has anything to worry about."

"No, but I do," Hank said. "Sally has a nice seat, too. Plus a bottomless sleeve full of tricks. Remind me to tell you how we met sometime."

"Can I put that tidbit in my story?" Bella brandished her camera.

"Oh, no. It's not for prime time."

"Sounds like just the kind of anecdote that could help me sell the story."

"Please don't tell Sally that." He glanced up at the crow's nest next to the ring and waved. Sally waved back. "I swear, that woman's ears are better than Phoebe's."

And then the atmosphere changed. Hank shifted, turned slowly and offered Ethan a solemn handshake. "I want to thank you."

Ethan looked down at their clasped hands. "It might not come to anything. You know, legally."

"It's already come to something for us, hasn't it?" Hank laid his hand on Ethan's shoulder. "Some people call it closure. I don't see it that way. The truth opened us up. That's the way I feel."

"So do I."

Hank lifted his chin in Big Boy's direction. "You've got a winner there."

Ethan nodded.

"Hey, Ethan!"

He turned toward the familiar voice. Big

Bongo and bigmouth Demsey. Trouble and more trouble, and damned if he wasn't glad to see them. "Who turned you two loose?"

"We're all here," Dempsey said. "Shelly brought us on the bus. She told us not to bother you before the show, but we just wanted to…"

Bongo stuck out a beefy hand. "…wish you luck."

Ethan shook Bongo's hand and ruffled Dempsey's spiky hair. Out of the corner of his eye he noticed that Bella had her camera going again, but he didn't flinch. He was getting used to having her lens pointed his way.

"He needs an oil change," Bongo said.

Ethan laughed. He was up next, and a good laugh was just what he needed.

He was magic. Bella didn't know much about horses, but Big Boy's rider was unrivaled. As long as the judges weren't deducting points for battered cowboy hats, Ethan had first place in the bag.

"I want that horse," the man standing beside her said.

Bella spared him a quick glance. "Trace. I didn't see you there."

"Hard to take your eyes off him, isn't it?"

"Yes, it is." Ethan was putting the horse through a series of reining patterns, seemingly effortlessly.

"We're talking about the buckskin, right?"

Bella had no more glances to spare, but she did smile.

"You think he'd mind if I got in on the bidding?" he asked.

"We're talking about Ethan, right?"

Trace laughed.

"I can't think of anything that would please him more."

After all the riders had shown, the trainers were asked to bring the horses back into the arena and chat up prospective buyers while the judges conferred. Bella covered the activity with her camera. She was charmed by Mark Banyon, the young son of a local teacher named Celia, who had no intention of letting the horse he'd named Flyboy go to just anyone. An interview with the horse's trainer, who introduced himself simply as Cougar, served to reassure her that a disabled veteran's group would be bidding on the horse, and God help anyone who tried to run up the bidding. He and Mark would have easy access to Flyboy, who was destined to become the centerpiece of the therapy program that had enabled Cougar to "rejoin the living" after recovering from his war injuries.

"And if you want a fairytale finale for your story," Cougar told Bella as he reached for Mark's mother's hand, "you can bring your camera to our wedding."

"As long as we get copies of all the pictures," Celia said.

"As long as I can bring a date." Bella nodded toward Ethan, who was chatting up his "new mom" on the other side of the arena.

"That guy?" Cougar smiled and shook his head. "Big showboater, that guy. I don't believe that horse was ever wild. Pretty sure that's a ringer you see there."

Bella returned the smile. "I'm pretty sure Ethan's the best there is."

Cougar laughed. "For a free wedding video I won't argue."

Bella made her way across the arena, pausing here and there for a still shot before sneaking up behind her man of the hour. One thing she'd learned by making the rounds to gather her story was that Big Boy was a big hit, even among Ethan's competitors.

Logan extended his hand. "Bella, come meet my wife."

Ethan turned quickly, smiling when their

eyes met. "I gotta get me some of those sneak-up shoes," he said.

"It's not the shoes," Bella assured him as she took her place in the circle. "It's the Lakota blood. Be prepared to jump out of your skin at least once a week, Mary." She offered Logan's wife a handshake, and then she automatically glanced at her emerging baby bump.

Mary's hand went to her stomach, completing the wordless acknowledgment between women.

Logan clapped a hand on Ethan's shoulder. "You were tired of being the baby, weren't you, son?"

"I'll gladly turn that role over," he agreed. "Is it too late to order up a sister?"

"I've decided to keep us all in suspense," Mary said. "I like the idea of letting the baby surprise us."

"Speaking of surprises…" Logan nodded toward the crow's nest. "Looks like our master of ceremonies has something to tell us."

Sally started out with an order.

"Everyone clear the arena except the trainers and their horses. I'm just as anxious as anybody else, so step lively, folks. I've got some introductions to make, and then we'll get the results from the judges."

Bella looked up at Ethan, smiled, and turned to follow everyone else who'd been excused.

"Oh, wait." Sally's voice boomed. "Everyone except the press."

Bella looked up. Sally nodded. "I don't care whose girlfriend you are, you're still the press."

It took all of about two minutes to empty out the arena. Bella took some footage of the lineup while Zach's brother, Sam, was introduced as the donor of the grand prize. He gave credit to his daughter, Star, who had inherited a winning lottery ticket after her mother's death. Sam didn't mention the source of the money, but Bella knew the story.

Next came the introduction of the judges, who were well-known in the horse world and included an Olympic champion, a man who'd trained horses for the movies, another who trained for the Royal Canadian Mounted Police and a stock show champion. The mustangs had been trained for various styles of riding and different kinds of work or sport. They would prove that mustangs made fine mounts. Their story would bring support for the Double D Wild Horse Sanctuary and for the preservation of the American wild horse.

And the auction would bring much-needed cash to the program. But the auction wouldn't start until the winner was announced, and the microphone was suddenly silent. Those in the arena pretended to ignore the crow's nest. They turned to each other, exchanged a few comments, laughed nervously.

Bella took more video, and then she sidled up to Ethan. He needed some distraction. "Have you met Cougar?" she asked. "The one with that gorgeous Paint."

"You like Paints?" He rubbed his buckskin's cheek. "Don't worry, boy. She's no judge."

"Cougar's an army vet, too. He trained Flyboy to be a service horse. You know, for therapy."

"I saw that. That's some fine work. I could get into that kind of work."

"Yes, you could."

He gave her a tight smile. "I've got a ways to go, though, haven't I?"

"Time or distance?" She slipped her hand into his and gave a quick squeeze. "Either way, I'm right beside you."

Ethan turned to her, and for a moment everything around them receded. He didn't care where he was or what else was going on. Wherever, whatever, Bella was with him. All was right with the world, and he told her so with a wink and a smile.

There was movement in the crow's nest. The Night Horses appeared first. Then the Zach Beaudrys. Then the Sam Beaudrys. And finally the judges.

"Here comes the announcement," Bella said.

"And the twenty-thousand dollar award for the best mustang trainer in the first annual Mustang Sally's Wild Horse Makeover Horse Show goes to…"

Ethan kept his cool when his name was called, but Bella did not. Her kiss would have shocked her public. The details of her whispered promise of a private celebration set his ear aflame. His sober, sensible, traditional Bella nearly knocked him off his feet.

For the second time.

And he was damn sure it wouldn't be the last.

* * * * *

MILLS & BOON

THE HEART OF ROMANCE

A ROMANCE FOR EVERY KIND OF READER

MODERN

Prepare to be swept off your feet by sophisticated, sexy and seductive heroes, in some of the world's most glamourous and romantic locations, where power and passion collide.
8 stories per month.

HISTORICAL

Escape with historical heroes from time gone by. Whether your passion is for wicked Regency Rakes, muscled Vikings or rugged Highlanders, awaken the romance of the past.
6 stories per month.

MEDICAL

Set your pulse racing with dedicated, delectable doctors in the high-pressure world of medicine, where emotions run high and passion, comfort and love are the best medicine.
6 stories per month.

True Love

Celebrate true love with tender stories of heartfelt romance, from the rush of falling in love to the joy a new baby can bring, and a focus on the emotional heart of a relationship.
8 stories per month.

Desire

Indulge in secrets and scandal, intense drama and plenty of sizzling hot action with powerful and passionate heroes who have it all: wealth, status, good looks…everything but the right woman.
6 stories per month.

HEROES

Experience all the excitement of a gripping thriller, with an intense romance at its heart. Resourceful, true-to-life women and strong, fearless men face danger and desire - a killer combination!
8 stories per month.

DARE

Sensual love stories featuring smart, sassy heroines you'd want as a best friend, and compelling intense heroes who are worthy of them.
4 stories per month.

To see which titles are coming soon, please visit

millsandboon.co.uk/nextmonth

JOIN US ON SOCIAL MEDIA!

Stay up to date with our latest releases, author
news and gossip, special offers and discounts, and
all the behind-the-scenes action
from Mills & Boon...

 millsandboon

 millsandboonuk

 millsandboon

It might just be true love...